A Woman at the End of Her Rope

Tyler Weaver

ISBN: 9798308582250

Dedication

This book is dedicated to author and educator Dr. Teri Pietso-Holbrook, who inspired me in 2014 as my professor at Georgia State University to "go forth, be a brilliant writer, composer, and educator," and for helping me to do so, at least in my eyes.

And also to my best friend, the incomparable Ashton Brasher, without whom I would have hundreds of pages of senseless ramblings, unformatted pages and graphics, and a pitiful cover. Thanks for everything, and for bringing me Brina.

Foreword

While this book is a work of fiction, I've tied in many of my own personal experiences and those of friends and family members (with permission, of course). Some of the best literary advice I've ever heard was simply to write about what you know about. There are a few things I really know about, three of those being the south, dysfunctional families, and growing up and living as a member of the LGBTQ+ community.

The south isn't just a geographical area; it's a way of life. It's slow drawls and barking backyard dogs. It's putting flowers on a grave every year for Decoration Day (or Homecoming, depending on what your church calls it). It's bringing your neighbor a pint of homemade jelly and them writing a thank you note for it. It's a casserole recipe that you'd better give credit to the creator for or risk entire excommunication.

Dysfunctional families come in a variety of sizes, shapes, and colors. You can find them on any street in Buckhead, any trailer park in Waycross, or any home in between. Dysfunction transcends wealth, political affiliation, religion, race, sex, sexual orientation or expression, and age. Families just don't get along sometimes, and that's okay. The truth is when you put a whole bunch of people together that are far more alike than any of them would care to admit, you can't act surprised when those big personalities clash. Families fight sometimes, and that's okay, too. People are wrong. No one is perfect. People do things that are wrong. If there's any wisdom I can impart, it's that it is okay to remove yourself from toxic relationships, situations, and environments. Whether that's with family, with the community you grew up in, with the community you moved to, or an organization you joined. Your parents may forsake you. Your grandparents may turn up their nose at you. Neighbors who you thought were friends may switch sides of the street when you're walking down the sidewalk. That's all okay because we are all imperfect individuals. Some of us try harder to correct that than others, but you can't work on improving anyone but yourself at the end of each day.

I came out as gay in 2009 at 16 years old. This was still six years before gay marriage was legalized in all 50 states. I look at other queer youngsters now and think, "They have no idea how good they have it." And I thank God that they don't know. That's not to say I don't want them to appreciate the struggle of the pioneers who got us here today, but I hope they will live and love in a world with less hate and discrimination than I grew up in. One of less prejudice and danger. When I came out, my mother worried about what people would think, but more than that, she worried about my safety. She didn't know what bigots in our small town might do to me. I think she worried less when I moved to the big city of Atlanta than she did when I would leave my car parked somewhere in our hometown. At least when I was in Atlanta, I was among some allies, of which there were significantly fewer in North Georgia. I didn't have to keep secrets anymore when I moved to Atlanta.

I say all of this to say that I write this novel from a place of both understanding and curiosity. If I can help another person, even just one, then the time I've spent writing this story will not have been in vain. You are not alone. You are in the same boat with your family as plenty of others. You live in a world vastly different from the one others only a few years older than you lived in, so know that it is always changing. You don't have to keep so many secrets. You can love who you want to love. Don't give a permanent solution to a temporary problem.

If one or more of these messages applies to you, know that we are crafted from the same cloth. If none of these messages mean anything to you, I hope reading this will encourage you to extend empathy to the rest of us.

1

Louvenia Virginia Jackson put out another cigarette in the ashtray on the breakfast table. It was her fourth cigarette this morning. She'd only been up for 20 minutes. She took one last glance at the Maysville Monitor, the newspaper for her little Kentucky town, and decided there was absolutely nothing going on this week. Not that there was anything noteworthy going on any week in a county of only 7,000 people, but occasionally there was an editorial worth reading or an engagement announcement worth analyzing. Some of the brides were so uninventive these days.

Lou got up from the table and went to the counter to warm up her coffee. She always drank it black with exactly a half packet of Sweet 'N Low. She'd drunk it that way since her grandfather allowed her to sip his coffee when she was eight years old. She may have been the only preteen who actually stayed for coffee and dessert in the living room after dinner and enjoyed it.

These early teenage years were when she knew she was different. She wasn't a kid. Sure, in age she was. But in soul she was much older and in body she was much more mature. By 14, men twice her age who didn't know her would ask her on a date or even make passes at her. Not that revealing her age bothered several of them. Dogs looking to hop on top of anything that would sit still long enough.

As she gazed out the dirty kitchen window at nothing in particular, she thought about the first person she actually felt something for--a basketball coach and driver's ed instructor at her alma mater, Lonely Pine Day School with strawberry blonde hair and fair skin that was always a little red from being kissed by the sun just a little too much. She didn't dare mention this puppy-love crush to anyone else. Lou had a reputation to uphold. She was raised to abstain until marriage, to be paired with a man of equal breeding as she, from an equally, but certainly not overly, affluent family in Clanton. At this point, Lou was just a physically mature teen who was in control, or who felt controlled by the expectations of her family. One who also felt confused by the attention of men and the messages she received from her family. Either way, she didn't like it.

Clanton, Georgia was where she was born and raised. She arrived at Mayflower County General exactly on her due date of January 12, a theme that would stick with her for the rest of her life. If she was early, she was on time. If she was on time, she was late. If she was late, she wouldn't bother going at all. Things always seemed to happen just at the right time, whether it was of her doing or not.

Lou's two Labrador retrievers, Lizzy and Lucy, whined for breakfast. Both were morbidly obese according to the vet, but at 12 years old, Lou didn't really see the point in starting them on a sudden health craze. In fact, she preferred them now in their sedentary lifestyle. She appreciated efficiency in all things, her pups included. They expected meals like clockwork (she swore they could tell time on the grandfather clock in her front hall), and they did their business discreetly in the backyard. They came right back to the kitchen door and sat, waiting to be welcomed back in. You never heard a peep from them. Except for when they were hungry. She filled two old serving bowls with their breakfast and put them on the floor. Of course, they ate like starving children.

Leaving the girls to their meals in peace, Lou went down the hall for a shower. Her mother always said ladies should take a bath. Something like their bodies shouldn't ever be seen uncovered in the light or some ridiculous old made-up reason. Louise was always trying to impart her unique wisdom to keep her children from going to hell. But baths were gross. You sit in a pool of your own hot soup. And wash yourself with it. And then you're supposed to be clean?

Lou was just stepping out of the shower when the house phone began to ring. She didn't believe in cell phones. She didn't want anyone calling her while she was out, never considering she might need to make a call herself.

She donned her nearly threadbare house coat and made her way to the phone extension in the hallway alcove. She half-hoped whoever was on the other end would hang up before she could get there. It was

8:47 in the morning. No one should be calling before 9:00, period. Even Lou held fast to that rule imparted by Louise all those years ago.

When she picked up the phone, it was a solicitor offering to consolidate her debt. She curtly explained that if he was willing to take on her debt through his company, he probably wouldn't be employed much longer. She placed the headset back on the receiver, not slamming it. She didn't want to add insult to injury, even though he had called before 9:00. He must not have been raised right, she thought in the back of her head.

The conversation the two just had laid on the front, top, and sides of her head. The debt. There was a lot of it. Statements, past due notices, even pink and red letters full of threats to seize her assets and accounts. What callous and obscene attitudes over a measly few thousand dollars of debt. Didn't some people owe hundreds of thousands of dollars?

She laughed inside wondering what they thought they could possibly seize. Grandmama Virginia's Fairfax sterling silver? Louise's sable coat hanging in her closet? Or maybe all $39.43 currently sitting in her checking account at Maysville Bank & Trust? Good luck with that, she dismissed flippantly. Lou had been so plagued by these troubles for so long now that she felt numb to them. It was just another day and another dollar of debt.

2

Charles Davis Jackson, IV, was better known in Clanton as Little Chuck. Despite being almost 60, he figured at this point he'd always be Little Chuck. A towering and charismatic figure, Little Chuck was just like his daddy, Charles, III, Big Chuck, in the earlier years.

Now a frail shell of a man at 87, it seemed almost laughable that he was still called Big Chuck. The family had decided it was best that he stay at home for his comfort. They set up a hospital bed in his old study on the main floor, close to a bathroom and close to his wet bar. Nursing homes were for poor people and assisted living homes were for well-off people whose family didn't care about them. Big Chuck fit neither of those categories. So right there he stayed, in his home of over fifty years, The Gables, being cared for by his son, his daughter-in-law, Judy, his younger sister, Joan, and his faithful housekeeper of 52 years, Ruby.

Little Chuck's mother, Louise, had died 30 years prior, leaving Big Chuck alone. She was a stern woman who held close to her convictions, and people liked her for that, Big Chuck included. He always said he fell in love with her smart mouth, and she claimed she fell in love with his smile well before she fell in love with Chuck himself.

Little Chuck recalled as a child when his mother had hired Ruby to work for his family when she was just 15 years old. Other than odd jobs of sewing or laundering, Ruby had never really worked anywhere else. Of course, when she was too old to work, there would be no pension, no Social Security, and she had no retirement account, but she seemed happy. Big Chuck and Louise had taken care of her almost her whole life. As a wedding gift when she married Joe, they gave her the down payment for a house. They held her job and still paid her while she recovered from the births of both her sons. They were there when her second son died as a toddler. When Joe died, the Jacksons paid for the funeral and moved Ruby in with them permanently. She was a staple in the home and a mother to a now motherless Little Chuck.

Nary a cross word had ever been exchanged between Little Chuck, Ruby, or any of the Jacksons. Except for that one night. It was just awful. The way Ruby found it all out when they did, and the reactions from the family. The screaming matches that ensued. And the tears that followed when Ruby packed the bags hastily as she was told. Her tears, Big Chuck's tears, Ms. Louise's tears, and Louvenia's tears. The gravity of what happened was not taken lightly.

Little Chuck was putting on his sport coat getting ready to head into town for work. After working in banking for several years, he continued the family's CPA business of many decades, Jackson Auditing and Planning. Big Chuck had only retired a few years ago, leaving the business entirely to Little Chuck. The truth was, Big Chuck should have retired many years before that, as evidenced by the mess and disarray inherited by Little Chuck.

Inch by inch, he had mostly straightened things out. He hired a middle-aged secretary with a banking background, and a promising young accountant fresh out of college at Georgia. Things were looking up, by the looks of it from the outside. But from the inside, the business was currently hemorrhaging money. Big Chuck's daddy's clients were all dead. Big Chuck's clients were also dead, or in an invalid state. Little Chuck's friends did their own taxes and handled financial planning with the big dogs like Edward Jones and Merrill Lynch. The truth of the matter was that small firms like his couldn't keep up these days.

These financial woes sat on his shoulders like the weight of the world, and he was beginning to show it. His hair was growing grayer and he had a deepening crease in his forehead. He was scrambling to keep his head above water. Unbeknownst to the family, or his wife Judy, Little Chuck had mortgaged their house to keep things afloat. It was embarrassing, really–a deep shot to his pride as a businessman and a member of his community. It was a small mortgage compared to its worth, but a couple hundred thousand dollars would hold things together while he worked out all the kinks. They were staying at The

Gables practically full time anyway. They ought to have sold their house after their daughter Josie married and moved out, but Judy wouldn't hear of it; she loved that house.

If Big Chuck found out about the mortgage to cover the firm, he would be furious. It might even push him over the edge. They couldn't have that. He was the patriarch of a fine old-line family, a well-respected man in Clanton. Little Chuck would die before he would let anybody know about what he struggled with every single day, which is why he kept business between him and his old pal Kirby Riffle at the bank.

On his way out the door, Little Chuck heard a hollow holler from the study, Big Chuck saying, "Come in here before you leave, boy."

"Daddy, I'll be 56 in a month. I'm hardly a boy anymore."

"Don't sass me, mister," Big Chuck replied with his signature grin. A grin that still sparkled at over eighty years old.

"I wanna talk to you about something. Something that's been on my mind real heavy since I ended up in this damn contraption of a hospital bed right here in my own office." Little Chuck was already a few minutes late for work, but Rosie would open, and Peter would be there if anything was urgent, which it never was these days. He pulled one of the Chippendale chairs that had sat in the study for as long as he could remember closer to his daddy's bedside, so he could have this serious conversation in earnest.

"It's about your sister," Big Chuck said quietly. Little Chuck's heart dropped, and his head started swirling. Flashbacks, fights, regrets, misunderstandings, resentment. For years, Little Chuck had just put Lou out of his mind. After all, out of sight, out of mind, right? He hadn't seen her since all those years ago, hadn't heard a word from her. As far as the rest of the family knew or considered, Chuck's big sister Lou was gone. Dead, disappeared, vanished, whatever you wanted to call it.

After a lengthy pause, Little Chuck replied hoarsely, "What about her?" Little Chuck's daughter, Josie, knew she had an aunt from other folks mentioning her in passing, but she, too, believed Lou was dead. No one ever talked about her, and Josie never really thought to ask. As a child, Judy quieted her any time she mentioned Lou's name, as if speaking it aloud might make her appear like an apparition. Eventually, as she grew up, Josie just never asked again.

Big Chuck looked out the window, pensively. Little Chuck, his emotions rising slightly, repeated more confidently, "What about her?"

"I think you oughta call her." Now it was Little Chuck's turn to look out the window. He didn't want Daddy to see his face and neck turning red. It always did that when he was uncomfortable, or his feathers were ruffled.

Still looking out the window, Little Chuck tried to dismiss the thought, "I wouldn't even know how to find her or get in touch with her. Why would I call her anyway?" He was mostly telling the truth. They had no phone number for her. Who knew if she still lived at the address they last had for her? Who knew if she was even still alive? Surely, they would have been contacted if she wasn't, but maybe not.

"Why are you coming up with this idea to get in touch with her now after all these years? What's the point in dragging all this up?" Little Chuck quipped with evident frustration, feeling more anger than surprise now.

Big Chuck looked Little Chuck straight in the eyes, and without missing a beat, said in a serious tone, "Because I'm dying. I know it. You know it. Hell, even the mailman knows it. He peeks through that window about every day to see if I'm still breathing in this bed. I don't know when, but I know I'm on borrowed time. And we are past due for sorting some things out. Find her. I'm not taking all of this to my grave."

3

Lou made her way back to the bathroom to finish drying her hair and perfectly coiffed it. The hairspray rained down like a fine spring mist, triggering a coughing fit. Screw chlorofluorocarbons. She put on her makeup, choosing a more dramatic palette today. Off to her closet, she searched for something, anything decent. Purposefully ignoring the right side of the closet that still sat full but untouched, even after all this time.

Lou chose a smart suit that she had worn to church, when she still went to church, back in Clanton. One thing about Lou was that her figure hadn't changed hardly any in all these years. Sure, some things sagged a little more, and there were a few wrinkles, but she looked good. Especially for 58.

But who the hell in Maysville was going to hire a 58-year-old with a degree in Latin, no work experience to speak of, and no real connections to this town? She knew some folks here and there–her doctor, the Indians that owned the gas station where she bought her cigarettes, and her neighbor on the farm across the road. But it was time to put on her big girl panties and go get a job. The $39.43 currently sitting in her checking account reminded her of this fact.

Growing up, she never anticipated having to work. Neither did her parents. Of course, they sent her to a distinguished private school, then a nice, small Christian college in North Georgia where she was a Phi Mu and graduated with honors. All these things were elements of a game meant to introduce her to suitable men, and she was simply the pawn. Her parents weren't exactly delighted when she brought home mediocre boys here and there. They feigned interest and tried to set the tone of their expectations for their daughter. This usually scared the boys away, not that Lou really cared. She hadn't loved any of them. At 20, she hadn't even had a crush since the basketball coach at Lonely Pine Day School.

By 21, she had finished college early. And she didn't really know what to do. Her parents insisted the only proper thing to do was to come home until she found a suitor. Lou was less than thrilled at this plan, but it was the only option she had. It wasn't like there was much of a job demand for Latin majors.

So, she moved home. She spent her days with Louise and Ruby. Ladies' luncheons, bridge games, garden parties. Looking back on it now, her parents weren't as smart as they thought, taking her to all these women's events but expecting her to somehow find a man.

Lou was mostly content with that life. Until she wasn't. Until that one night that everyone found out why. That one breach of affluent, southern, ladylike, Christian behavior.

4

Little Chuck drove to work with a headache, his mind filled with the harsh truth his father had laid upon him. Big Chuck was dying. He was wasting away. The Leukemia had eaten him up, as Dr. Biermann had said. He tried treatments for a while, but later refused to go. They left him pale, bruised, breathless, sick to his stomach for days, and with ulcers all over his body. He said he would rather live out his time in peace and without putting himself through the treatments than delay the inevitable. Watching the strongest man he'd ever known become a shadow of his former self was gut-wrenching for Little Chuck.

Now all this talk about Lou.

He should have known it would come back sooner or later. These sorts of things never stay gone for good. But Little Chuck had spent the better part of thirty years just trying to forget. Forget what he saw, forget what he heard, forget what happened afterward. Now he was facing it all again, head on, and there was nothing he could do about it.

When he pulled into the spots on the Clanton town square designated for Jackson Auditing and Planning, he saw Rosie's big as a boat Oldsmobile Cutlass in its usual place. But Peter's silver Volvo wasn't there. Odd, he thought. Peter hadn't mentioned being gone or taking the day off.

Little Chuck walked in the door to see Rosie, red eyed, staring down at her checkbook.

"What's wrong with you? You look like somebody just killed your best friend in the world."

Rosie looked up, eyes wet, with more tears on the brim, and said, "How could you let this happen?"

Utterly perplexed, Little Chuck looked around and turned back to Rosie. “Let what happen? What the hell are you talking about?”

“Like you don’t know. Our paychecks bounced. When you didn’t get here by 9:00, Peter said he wasn’t working somewhere that couldn’t give him a paycheck and threw his stuff in a box and left.”

Little Chuck sank down into the chair in front of Rosie’s desk, his headache growing. Rosie continued, “I can’t make my house payment. Ever since Earl got laid off down at the mill, he hasn’t had steady work. I’ve got a boy in college and bills to pay, Mr. Jackson. How am I supposed to keep food on the table and the lights on?”

“Hold on just a minute, Rosie. Don’t go off the deep end. There must be some mistake at the bank. You know what a shit show that place has become since it was bought out. We’ll get this all sorted out in a few minutes. I’ll call up there and figure it out and you’ll call Peter now and tell him to get back down here. I’ll give both of you an extra day’s pay to make up for it, promise.”

Chuck watched Rosie sniffle, still looking at her checkbook that was in the red, but she agreed to take a breather. Little Chuck had been good to her the past few years. She had no reason to not trust him. She should have known there would be a logical explanation for all of this. After all, she worked at Mayflower First National for fifteen years with him before they were bought out by one of the large banks and downsized, eliminating her position. Little Chuck worked with her there as an auditor, but when things were taking a turn, he had this place to fall back on. He joined his daddy in business, and all was well for him.

Chuck was glad to have her and treated her with much respect. He was paying her as much money here as she was making at the bank, when the paychecks were good anyway. She trusted him after all these years knowing each other, but, understandably, this was making it harder for her to do so.

5

"Miss Louvenia Jackson," she answered when the desk secretary at the board of education office asked her name.

"And you have an appointment?" the young lady asked.

"Well, no, not exactly. I was hoping to meet with the hiring manager to see if there were any openings at any of the schools."

The secretary had an annoyed look on her face. Lou could tell she wasn't thrilled with this surprise visit. To smooth it over, Lou changed the topic and commented on her outfit. "Your dress is just darling. Where did you buy it? I wish I could pull off something like that!"

The girl beamed with the compliment. "I got this down at Kessler's out towards the mall on Highway 41! It even has pockets!"

Lou continued to fake astonishment at the bargain basement dress with its pockets. After a few moments, the secretary warmed up and said, "Maybe Ms. Ward could fit you in for just a minute. Let me call her and ask."

Lou thanked the young lady profusely. She took this time to scan the walls of the small board of education office. She saw awards of excellence, certifications, and accolades from different central office employees. Finally, she spotted something that might work in her favor.

Moments later the secretary hung up the phone and said Ms. Ward could see her, but only for about ten minutes before her next meeting. Lou again slopped sugar and thanked the lady profusely for making time for her.

"Sure thing! Down this hall, the second door on the left!" she motioned.

Lou walked down the hall, smoothing her skirt, touching her hair, and giving an internal pep talk to make this happen. She needed this to happen.

Ms. Ward was a small but formidable woman. She looked a lot like Jane Wyman in the later years. Hurricane Katrina couldn't have moved her facial expression, but she was dressed quite well. Especially for a woman in middle-of-nowhere, Kentucky. Lou immediately spotted the tiny lion pin on Ms. Ward's lapel. This might be easier than she thought.

Lou extended her hand, introducing herself with a powerful but genteel handshake.

Ms. Ward answered with a curt "Hello," and asked how she could help Lou, reminding her she only had a few minutes.

"I'll keep it simple, Ms. Ward. I need a job. I've come into some financial difficulties, and it's time for me to work on turning that around."

Ms. Ward sized up the attractive, but aged woman, and said, "What exactly are you looking for? We're a small district. We don't have many openings. Everything is posted online. And frankly, they're not looking for old ladies like me and you, no offense."

Lou nodded her head in agreement, and then, suddenly, motioned towards Ms. Ward's lapel. "You're a Phi Mu, too? I should have guessed it by just talking to you. I was a chapter officer back in my Shorter College years! I was a Latin major."

Ms. Ward's expression changed from annoyed school marm to giddy college girl like someone had just asked her to a rush party on Friday night. "You're kidding? I was a Rho Iota at University of Kentucky! College of Ed, class of '74!"

"You don't say?" Lou replied, smiling slyly while reciting the first line of the Phi Mu creed, "To lend to those less fortunate a helping hand…"

Ms. Ward was picking up what Lou was putting down. "Alright, you've got my attention. But I really do have a meeting in a minute. Leave your resume on my desk, and I'll call you this afternoon. Deal?"

"Well, that's the thing, Ms. Ward, I don't really have one."

"Have one what?" Ms. Ward replied, confused.

"A resume. I mean, I could make one, but it wouldn't really have anything on it. I went to school, of course, but I've never really had a job."

"Pardon?"

"Well, I've never worked. Not at a real job," Lou replied, tones of both defensiveness and embarrassment creeping into her voice.

"So, you want me to just give you a job, teaching some of the brightest kids in Kentucky, without any experience, with a useless 35-year-old Latin degree? You're outta your mind." Ms. Ward stood to leave her office, shuffling some papers on her desk into a folder.

A dejected Lou Jackson sat motionless. She should have known this would be the case. She didn't have experience, she didn't have connections, she didn't have anything to offer.

Ms. Ward walked towards the door but turned back to Lou. "Look, the negativity coming off you right now is enough to kill the African violets on my windowsill over there. I'll see what I can do, but I can't promise anything. And whatever it is, you're not gonna like it. And you'll need to find something besides that pant suit from '82."

Hope sprung back into Lou's mind. It was something. Maybe nothing, but it could be something. There was a chance she could turn things around.

On her way out, she smiled politely at the young secretary as she passed towards the door, then turned back around. "Hey, sweetie, thank you so much for getting me that time with Ms. Ward. She's a peach! Now tell me again where you bought this lovely dress with the pockets?"

6

“Hey, Suzanne, this is Chuck Jackson downtown. You got a minute to get me over to Kirby Riffle? Thank you, you sweet thing.”

Little Chuck knew this wasn't good. He didn’t yet know what exactly had happened, but it couldn’t be good. God, this was all he needed right now with everything else on his mind. As he sat on hold, waiting for Kirby to pick up, his mind started running through all the things he had done, all the steps he had taken to make sure this business stayed afloat. He felt like a child being unexpectedly called to the principal’s office, trying to figure out what he had done to end up in this situation.

Moments later, Kirby Riffle answered his office extension with a sheepish hello. Little Chuck and Kirby had known each other practically since birth. Their mothers were pregnant at the same time, and they came into the world only weeks apart. They went all the way through school together, both returning to Clanton after college to settle down and set up homes of their own. Kirby was a groomsman in his wedding to Judy. Then they both started at the bank together, working there for years and deepening their friendship. That’s one of the reasons Kirby was the only banker he could trust to keep this project quiet; he could keep a secret for him. When Kirby answered the phone, Little Chuck knew something was up.

“Kirby, Chuck. Hey man, how are ya?”

“I’m alright, you know, just the same ol’ same ol’.” Kirby knew exactly why Chuck was calling and Chuck was getting pissed that he was skirting around the elephant in the room.

“Yeah, well I’ve been better, to tell you the truth. Something’s happened with my account up there and Rosie and Peter’s paychecks from last week bounced. What do you reckon is going on?” Little Chuck was playing it cool. No need to go right in with, “What have you fucked up for me?”

"Well, I was just getting ready to call you." Doubtful. "That HELOC we were going to put through for you isn't going to work out after all," Kirby said nonchalantly, as if he was talking about tomorrow's weather and not the ruin of a man and his family business.

"What do you mean it isn't going to work out? How the hell not? I've got a lot riding on this, buddy," Chuck's voice rising with each word.

"Well, you know how it is. This market just ain't what it was a couple years ago. Damn, it ain't even what it was six months ago. Democrats and all. Plus, they've got this young, new appraiser they sent from Atlanta doing all the work. You oughta see the legs on her," Kirby chuckled sleazily.

"I don't give a damn about the legs of some appraiser. Tell me what this means!" Little Chuck was practically screaming at this point.

"Now calm down, man. Don't go gettin' upset. It's just that your and Judy's house didn't quite appraise for as much as you wanted on that line of credit. That's why things are sort of stalled and the money didn't go through like we'd planned on." Kirby's slow drawl was getting more and more annoying to the already impatient Chuck Jackson.

"Get to the point, Riffle. How much can we get? I wanted $250,000. What can we swing now? $150, $125?" Chuck was getting desperate, and he was sounding like it.

"Best we can offer is $50k. That's what I was just about to call you about before we redid all the paperwork and such."

"$50,000? That's all the equity you say I've got in that 6,000 square foot house in Crystal Springs with a pool and garage apartment? You're out of your goddamn mind."

Unbothered, Kirby responded coyly, "Well you're welcome to try another bank. But they might not be as keen to keep your secrets, pal."

Little Chuck hung up the phone and leaned back in his office chair. Thinking about everything and nothing all at the same time. Peter stood in the doorway to his office, unnoticed. He cleared his throat, jarring Chuck from his daze and confusion.

“Oh, hey,” Chuck said.

“Hey? That’s all you have to say? Payroll checks around here bounce, and all you gotta say is ‘Hey’?” Peter replied, obviously still pissed off.

“Listen, you know I’ve got a lot going on right now with Daddy and trying to keep this place up and running. Not to mention still recovering from Josie’s wedding and all. Things just sort of got fouled up for a minute. I’m gonna work it out.”

“Yeah, well while you’re trying to ‘work it out,’ I’ve got student loan payments due. Rent. East Kentucky Power doesn’t leave the light on for you like Motel 6. More people depend on this than just you. Me and Rosie work like hell around here trying to keep it afloat just like you are and it's a slap in our faces to end up not even getting paid for it!”

“I know, I know. I get it. Really, I do. I’m low on cash right now, obviously. I had a plan, and it backfired. I’m trying to figure out what to do next, but I can’t do it without you, or Rosie.”

Peter looked Little Chuck square in the eye and replied, “Well I need a check. And until you’re ready to write one that won’t bounce, I’m not gonna waste my time sitting up here. We work our asses off,” he gestured to Rosie in the other room, “And we’re gonna get paid come hell or high water.” He walked back out, and looked at Rosie, expecting her to follow him. When she stayed put, he just shook his head and went out the door.

Rosie slowly got up and shuffled to Chuck’s office door.

"I didn't know things were that bad. I mean, you always handle the payroll since it's just the two of us. I keep the books for everybody on the client roster, but I guess I never really knew what was coming in and what was going out of here," Rosie said sheepishly.

"I know. I guess I should have been more honest with you. With the both of you. But I didn't want to worry anybody, not to mention my damn pride. I've screwed up, Rosie. And I don't know how I'm gonna get out of it this time. Fifty-six years of trial and error, failures, and successes, and I always came out on top. Or I was rescued by Momma and Daddy. Now I'm not so sure. Momma's gone, and Daddy's got one foot in the grave. There's nobody left to save me."

7

Lou walked in the front door with its familiar squeak and heard the girls shuffle their big, old bodies to get up and greet her. “Hey, you couple of freeloaders,” she said playfully as she put down her purse and took off her shoes. “Let’s go outside.”

She slipped on a pair of house shoes and walked out back with Lizzy and Lucy, for the first time in a while surveying the land behind the house. It was all hers. As far as she could see anyway. Nearly 50 acres in all, give or take; she couldn’t quite remember. Her old house, the rusty barn, the small pond, dying apple trees, and the fence all the way around, if you could call it that; it couldn’t keep a giraffe in or out.

So much had fallen apart in these years. When they’d first rented it from the last member of the Brooks family who couldn’t have cared less about the place, it was still a functioning, bustling farm. For over a hundred years, Brookses had farmed this land and raised thoroughbred racehorses. Six Derby winners came from this farm over the years. But when Helen Brooks Van Patterson inherited the place, she couldn’t be bothered to leave Florida to even come look at it one last time or to take any of the furniture or contents. She called a real estate agent in Maysville after the notification from the lawyer and told them to rent it, sell it as is, or burn it for insurance money. She didn’t care, as long as she didn’t have to deal with it.

The agent agreed to manage the property as a rental, taking a percentage of the rent and profits for his time and efforts, and to send the leftovers to Helen annually. Helen signed her Jane Hancock to the agreement and faxed it back from her condo the same day, glad to be done with the whole mess. She wouldn’t return to Kentucky ever again, for love or money.

When they had first come to Maysville, it was just in the nick of time. The sign was going up at the Brooks house, and Lou careened the car to the side of the road to get a glimpse of the place. It was gorgeous–

peeling paint, broken windowpanes, and all. It reminded her of The Gables, leaving her homesick momentarily. But only momentarily.

She hopped out of the car and asked the man banging in the post for details. He said he didn't know much about it, he just worked for the real estate agent, a Mr. Baker, and he was told to put this sign up this morning to rent the farm.

Lou, confident as ever, told the man to pull the sign up. She was moving in. He didn't seem so sure about this, but he did as she said and tossed it in the back of his truck to return to Mr. Baker.

Lou didn't know how much it cost, how many rooms it had, or if it even had indoor plumbing. But she knew that was where she was moving. Ironic, she thought, that they had just been driving town to town, and then landed in this place called Maysville–quite similar in name to Mayflower County. She guessed God still had some humor in him after all.

Now, looking out at this expanse of land, Lou felt nothing but alone and defeated. So much work had been put into this place, and so much had now been let go. There hadn't been horses in years. The barn was empty, save some farm equipment that most likely no longer worked. Heart and soul had been poured into this land and this home for generations, and here it was, dying, with her.

When old Helen was finalizing her will some several years after she'd been living there, she extended a contract to her tenant. There had been a clause in the lease that the tenant was to absolutely never, under any circumstances, contact Helen for anything. If the roof leaked, it was up to them. If the furnace gave out, which it did the next winter, Helen wasn't paying for a new one. The tradeoff was that the rent reflected these responsibilities of the tenant, so it was a mostly advantageous agreement for both parties. And Lou had faithfully honored it.

Because Helen had no heirs, except for a greedy nephew she never saw and the Palm Beach Animal Rescue, she apparently didn't see any point in hanging on to anything she didn't need. Her Kentucky tenant had stood by their word for almost 20 years. She didn't know anything more than a name and that the rent was always paid on time. A generous Helen Van Patterson sent a letter to her tenant, offering to sign over a quit-claim deed to sell the house, its furnishings, and the land for $1,000.

When Lou opened the letter, she thought it was a joke. A scam, perhaps, or just a crazy, confused old lady. She immediately called Mr. Baker, something of a crazy, confused old man himself, to get to the bottom of it. Obviously perturbed, he confirmed the legitimacy of the offer.

"I've handled this woman's business for all these years and don't even stand to make a sales commission. Old bitch. I'd advise you to take her up on it before her family catches wind."

Lou couldn't feel any sympathy for Mr. Baker, who she knew took a hefty skim off the rent and the farm profits before sending Mrs. Van Patterson her earnings. So, she jumped. With a few signatures and in a matter of days, the farm, the land, and everything on it belonged to Lou for less than the cost of an acre in those parts.

She needed to do something. She needed this job. She needed to work on this place. If for nothing else than to give her something to do again.

8

Just as Little Chuck was settling into his second wave of depression looking at the firm's finances, his cell phone rang. It was his Aunt Joan.

"Hey, Joan, what's..."

Before he could finish the sentence, an exasperated Joan hollered frantically, "You've gotta get home. Now!"

Little Chuck was out the door without saying a word to Rosie or grabbing his coat or bag. This couldn't be good. It had to be Big Chuck. Just this morning he was predicting his own demise. Had it already come so soon? God, please don't let my daddy go, Little Chuck prayed while driving twice the speed limit to the edge of town where The Gables sat on an expanse of green lawn and towering old trees. Looking up at the house from the car, it looked so scary. It was a dark and foreboding Victorian style home that was entirely out of place out here in the country. The house was blue gray with darker gray trim. The porch railings were black, as were the oversized, intricate gables on the roofline for which the house was nicknamed. The floor of the porch was a lighter gray, and the foundation was Stone Mountain granite, like practically every other house in the state built from this era up to the 1950s. Chuck peered all around as he drove up the driveway, but nothing looked out of place. What on earth could be going on that was so urgent?

Little Chuck slammed the car in park, threw open the door, and bounded up the steps to the front door. It wasn't locked. It was never locked. Did anyone even have a key? It's funny the things your mind switches to when you're in an adrenaline rush.

Ruby heard Chuck's car pulling in and came out of the kitchen with a towel in her hand when she heard him yelling for his Aunt Joan. "Little Chuck, what in the world's got a hold of you? What's wrong?"

"Joan!" he hollered back. "Where is she? She called and told me to come home!"

Ruby frowned. "Miss Joan went over to your house in Crystal Springs about a half hour ago. Miss Judy said she was going over there this morning to clean out some of the old stuff in the basement, then Miss Joan decided she would go help her since she didn't have nothing else to do."

Home. Chuck hadn't realized "home" meant his actual home. They had been staying at The Gables for so long, and it was his childhood home, so his mind immediately went there instead of his and Judy's house on the other end of town.

He ran back to his car and started driving, dialing Judy's number. "Pick up, pick up, pick up, dammit," he muttered. No answer. He tried Aunt Joan again. No answer. He picked up speed, now practically flying across Clanton as fast as his Lexus would take the curves, ignoring stop signs and rights of way.

He swung into the subdivided community, the gate was open, and his heart sank when he saw the fire trucks, ambulances, police, and first responders.

He put the car in park in the middle of the street, jumping out with it still running. He ran towards his home. In the movies, you always see police officers holding people back, keeping anyone from entering the crime scene. The chaos playing out here didn't allow the police to stop anyone.

The front door was half open, and he pushed it the rest of the way with a bang hitting the doorstop on the baseboard. There was an eerie quiet in the house that didn't match the frenzy outside. There was a lot of murmuring, but the only thing he could clearly make out was a woman sobbing.

He went from room to room, searching for whatever activity was playing out in his own house without his knowledge. As soon as he noticed the door to the basement open, he saw two first responders carrying the sobbing woman out. It was Aunt Joan.

She looked up at Little Chuck with the most bewildered, fear-stricken, puffy, red eyes he'd ever seen on another human being. She started wailing all over again, letting go of the medics and collapsing into his arms.

"Joan, for God's sake, what's going on? I've been trying to call you and Judy! Where is she?" Chuck was practically yelling now.

Joan's wailing was so overwhelming she couldn't speak. She was hyperventilating. The medics were trying to calm her down, ordering her to slow her breathing in conjunction with theirs. It was no use.

Chuck yelled to no one and everyone, "Will somebody tell me what the fuck's going on around here?"

Right about this time, the sheriff of Mayflower County, Klark Kitchens, was coming up the stairs. In reality, he was nearing 30, but he looked barely 12. Barely old enough to get behind the wheel of a car, much less be responsible for all law and order in the whole county. Josie had babysat him as a child. He was nicknamed KK back then, and through high school. He came from a good family. Not wealthy, but hard workers who were well-liked in town and who were very civic-minded. He joined the force right after high school. In a few short years he had worked his way up: sergeant, lieutenant, captain. When the previous sheriff, Billy Walker, announced his retirement, Klark saw his opportunity to go from KK to Sheriff Kitchens. He was the obvious choice. A few other folks talked about putting their names in the running, but it was all talk. Everybody knew KK would win, especially when Sheriff Walker announced his endorsement of Klark.

But this was the first time Klark Kitchens had dealt with this type of thing as sheriff of Mayflower County. His force was used to issuing speeding tickets, dealing with disorderly conduct, and busting kids with weed. Rarely did they ever have a death occur that wasn't just an old-timer whose turn it was to give up the ghost. A suicide was simply unheard of in a small, Bible-belt town like Clanton.

9

When Lou woke up the next morning to the dogs whining for breakfast, she groggily got up and put her bare feet on the cold hardwood floor. She'd slept better and longer that night than she had in years. Maybe it was the feeling of hope that things were potentially turning around. Maybe it was the two vodka tonics she'd had before bed. Maybe it was the OxyContin she'd taken. Probably a combination of all three, she guessed.

She filled the two bowls with kibble and put them down for Lizzy and Lucy. She sat at the breakfast table, lighting her first cigarette of the day, and eyeing a banana in the wooden dough bowl in the middle of the table. She had no appetite. She wasn't even sure if she ate at all the day before. Ever since her diagnosis, Lou had struggled with a reason to bother eating, try treatments, or even go to the doctor. What was she hanging on for anyway? She was alone. She was broke. Essentially, she had no family. All she had was the dogs. And the farm. But it was enough to keep her going for right now. She still had a little fight in her. She wasn't going to give up quite so easily this time.

That was what brought the idea of working for the school system into her mind. Steady pay, medical benefits. A decent schedule. She'd probably not live long enough to be vested in teacher retirement, but maybe it was something to work towards, something else to live for.

The sound of the phone ringing brought Lou back to the real world. She got up, cleared her throat, and answered the phone. "If you want money, I don't have it. If you've got something to sell, I'm not buying. And if you offer another extended warranty on my 18-year-old car, I swear I'll scream."

"Well, I've got something to sell you and something to get you a little money, if you're still looking," a faintly familiar voice answered, with a grin that made its way through the speaker.

God, it was Ms. Ward.

“Uh, sorry about that. That pretty much covers all the calls I ever get,” Lou apologized with morbid embarrassment.

“All I’ve got to say is you better not answer the phone like that as the receptionist at Little Creek Elementary.”

A brief pause took place with neither party saying anything until Lou broke the ice. “I was kind of hoping for a teaching job, ya know? Like more than $25,000 a year as a receptionist?” She laughed, nervously.

“Look, honey, I told you it was slim pickin’s around here right now. In case you aren’t aware, we aren’t teaching Latin here in East Jesus, No Where. All our teachers get hired, work 30 years, retire, and die. Not a lot of turnover. And I had to call in a favor to get you this offer. So, you can take it, or you can leave it. I’ve got a dozen other girls that’ve applied and can actually work Microsoft Publisher,” Ms. Ward laid out plainly.

“No, no. I’ll take it. It wasn’t what I planned on, but I need a job. And I really do appreciate this opportunity and what you’ve done for me. Faithful sisters, since 1852, right?”

“Please, I’m old, but I’m not that old.”

Lou laughed, perhaps the first genuine laugh in some time. “Us ol’ Phi Mus have to stick together. Where and when do I report?”

“Come to my office in the morning, 7 a.m. sharp. I’ll get your paperwork and background started and then we’ll go over to Little Creek to meet Janine. Lucky for you, she’s an ‘ol’ Phi Mu’ gal herself. She only agreed to this because you’re a sister, so act like it.”

“Deal,” Lou responded earnestly.

“And for the love of God, wear something decent. I don’t want to drag a bridesmaid from 1990 in there with me in front of God and everybody.” She hung up without giving Lou a chance to respond. As someone who was used to giving orders, she was surprisingly comfortable taking them from Liz Ward.

Lou lit another cigarette, let the dogs out to the back yard, and tried to remember if she knew how to get to that mall out on Highway 41. She wasn't going to screw this chance up. It might be her last.

10

Little Chuck fell to his knees, taking his Aunt Joan with him. Together, the two of them blubbering and screaming in a heap, were a sight that made everyone else in the room uncomfortable. Even more uncomfortable than the dead body hanging from the rafter in the basement.

Yes, Judy had taken her life by hanging herself. She used a thick nylon camping rope taken right off the shelf from the basement to tie a near perfect noose. She stood on the old piano bench that had originally matched the upright piano she learned to play as a child. She fixed the rope around her neck, and she stepped off.

After what seemed like hours but was really less than ten minutes, Chuck got up, steadied himself against an armchair, and picked up Joan. They stood there, sniffling, shaking, confused, angry, sad. So many emotions, so much to bear. So, so many questions.

Sheriff Kitchens asked Little Chuck to sit with him at the dining room table. Joan went to follow, but Sheriff Kitchens asked her to take a seat in the front living room while an officer got her some water–a polite way of telling her she wasn't invited to this meeting.

The sheriff pulled a chair out for Chuck at the head of the table, presumably Chuck's usual seat, and took one next to it for himself. He was unsure of how to even begin this conversation. He had dealt with a few unexpected deaths in his years with the force, but this was the first one while he was in charge. And this wasn't just a middle-aged man with a bum ticker, this was a woman. A popular woman from an affluent family. Gone in a heinous manner. Hell, this might even make it to the state news.

"Now, Mr. Jackson, I want to start off…"

Chuck cut him off, "Chuck. You can call me Chuck, KK. I've known you since you were in diapers. You ate three hot dogs on the Fourth of July and barfed on that rug over there when you were six," Chuck motioned towards an oriental rug in the living room with a chair strategically placed over a stain that never came out.

"Chuck," he began cautiously. "There are some standard questions we have to ask in these kinds of situations to see if there's any foul play or anything like that."

These "kinds of situations." How did Chuck keep finding himself in abnormal situations lately? Nodding his head and silently weeping, he said, "Sure. Whatever you need to know."

Despite everything in his world falling apart around him, Little Chuck seemed to be able to keep his composure. He was raised by a stolid, even-kiltered man. It wasn't that Big Chuck was incapable of emotions, it was just that he didn't show them. He kept a calm demeanor in most everyday situations. Well, except for that one time.

Going through the motions of answering these questions from KK, Chuck's mind was drifting to that moment so many years ago when he truly lost his temper. He'd never seen his father or mother so upset, so shocked, so enraged, so… surprised. Overall, it shouldn't have been entirely a surprise on some accounts, but it was unbelievable at the time. Now Judy's current stunt was just as unbelievable.

Chuck was brought back to reality when a sheriff's deputy brought in an embossed, ivory notecard. He handled it with gloves and laid it on the flawless antique rosewood table. The deputy addressed the sheriff, "Sir, we just found this and knew it should go to you." Chuck recognized it immediately–Judy's monogrammed stationery. It was the suicide note she'd left behind.

His mind going from stupor to rush in a flash, he lunged for the notecard to read the contents, only to be stopped by the young sheriff who instinctively knocked it right down the table.

"Chuck, ain't no way you can touch that. It's gotta go back to the lab for analysis and fingerprinting and all that. We have to follow

protocol and cover all our bases. Sometimes what looks apparent isn't always exactly what happened."
Was Klark alluding to something sinister after all? He had said these questions were to rule out any foul play. He wasn't sure, but Chuck knew he had to see what the note said.

"KK, hold it with gloves, cover it in plastic, do whatever you need to do, but I have to know what she wrote in that letter. I'm owed some kind of explanation, ain't I?"

Klark considered the request for a moment and agreed that it wouldn't be a breach of protocol for Chuck to at least read what was inside. Not to mention the sheriff was curious himself, this still being a novel case for him and all. He put on a glove handed to him by the deputy and gingerly pulled the note closer to them from where it was shoved at the end of the table in Chuck's thoughtless lunge moments earlier. He opened the note to show a message in beautiful cursive handwriting. Together, the two men read the note silently.

Chuck's eyes and face burned. Klark's cheeks reddened and he shifted in his seat. The information in this piece of paper painted a very dark picture that Judy had been living in. Chuck jumped from his chair at the table, making a move towards the still open basement door. His Aunt Joan sprang from the sofa in the living room, grabbing him, along with the sheriff and his deputies.

Clueless to what had just taken place in the dining room, Joan said, "Honey, you don't want to see that. Nobody oughta see that," she said, shuddering but somewhat composed by now.

Klark reiterated, "She's right, you don't need to go down there. They are still working on everything and trying to…"

Chuck cut the man off mid-sentence and shoved him away, "Trying to cover all your bases and go through your stupid protocols," he yelled. "Fuck your bases, this is my goddamned house and my goddamned wife. You don't get to decide anything!"

Despite Chuck's indignancy, the sheriff tightened his grip on Chuck and put on his game face that showed he meant business. "Chuck Jackson, you follow my word, or I'll arrest you right here in your own living room in front of God and everybody crowded outside for obstruction of a crime scene."

"Suicide is considered an unnatural death, and we are required by law to investigate. Suicide ain't against the law, but there's been plenty of homicides made to look like suicides. So, I suggest you do what I say and don't give us any reason to take you out in cuffs or give us any reason to think there's anything funny about this."

For the first time since this nightmare began, Chuck was truly considering the heft of this situation. He backed away and tried to steady himself, both figuratively and literally.

He sat on his front living room sofa and started to watch the troops receding. Aunt Joan had gone to The Gables but agreed to wait until Chuck was back to break the news to Big Chuck and Ruby. Then they would make the call to Josie to come home together.

There was no need for the fire department anymore. The ambulance was pointless. The police stayed, of course, but some of the officers that weren't needed left, too. By now, the coroner had arrived in the county van to conduct their examination.

She and her assistant gingerly rolled in the stretcher with the body bag folded on top. When they made it to the top of the stairs, they began folding the legs under it to make their way down the stairs to the unfinished basement, to where Judy's body met its demise, after their review of the situation.

The coroner went down first and assessed the situation after speaking with the deputies and confirming the positive identification of the body. She photographed the body and surroundings and pronounced the death. Although the body had been there for hours, nothing was really official until the coroner called it. That was when it was real.

Chuck stood. He walked across the front hall into the dining room where the sheriff still sat at the table, which had become a de facto office with forms and papers and statements strewn about. Chuck had one request.

“I want to see her,” he said calmly.

Klark shifted uneasily in the chair. “Chuck, I’m telling you, you really don’t want to see this. Don’t you wanna remember her the way she was? This sight isn’t something you’re gonna forget.”

“I need to see her. I need to see what she did.”

“Before we go down there, I want to explain some things to you about what you’re gonna see. The ligature goes around the neck, and a running knot, which tightens easily, is formed, and the other end of the rope is tied to a ligature point. In this case it was one of the beams down there. The body is then suspended, which tightens the ligature around the neck. Suspension hanging kills in one of three ways: compression of the carotid arteries, the jugular veins, or the airway. Now, like I said before, homicides may be disguised as a suicide. That’s why we aren’t touching anything.”

Chuck simply nodded solemnly, whether he understood all that terminology or not. The sheriff sighed, seeming defeated but also annoyed that his advice was being ignored. “Alright. I’m gonna walk down there with you. But like I said, don’t touch anything, don’t move anything, and don’t step any farther than the bottom of the stairs or where I lead you.” His voice was serious, but also gentle. He knew this was not going to be easy, for either of them.

They walked to the basement door, and Klark asked the coroner to step aside. She looked concerned, but the sheriff threw up his hands. He went down the stairs first with Chuck behind him. “Stand right here at the bottom. After the body is removed, the hazmat crew will clean up all of this,” he motioned towards the puddles in the floor. “As happens in this situation, the body has evacuated.” The clothes Judy had been wearing were coated in urine and feces. Her chest had mucus and vomit on it, indicating aspiration. She had struggled.

There she was. Chuck's wife of nearly 35 years. The mother of his child. His partner. His family. The keeper of their home. Part time nurse to Big Chuck. Despite everything, this was the woman he loved with all his heart. The heart that was now beating out of his chest.

Lividity was starting to occur. The lifeless blood was settling into the lowest point of Judy's body. Her legs and feet were turning a bluish purple showing the depletion of oxygen.

New tears began to burn Chuck's eyes all over again. He felt a mixture of sadness, pity, rage, and loneliness. Without thinking he instinctively made a step closer to the body, but Klark grabbed him firmly. "What did I say?"

"I know," Chuck muttered, backing up. By this time, the coroner and her assistant had made their way back down the stairs and politely asked the pair to move aside. They unfolded the legs of the stretcher and pushed it towards the side of the basement. The assistant began preparing the body bag, while the coroner began reviewing the notes and considering the best way to cut down the body. The coroner turned to Klark and Chuck.

"With Mrs. Jackson being over 55, we don't have to conduct a full autopsy unless you want it. If you do, we'll have to send her down to the medical examiner's office in Decatur. Could take a couple days depending on how backed up they are. But that's up to you. Looks pretty straightforward to me."

Klark nodded signaling his agreement that, while there could always be an element of foul play, after reading Judy's note, this was the real deal as far as suicides were concerned.

"No, no, just take her on to Chapman's so they can get her ready for the funeral," Little Chuck replied.

Judy Jackson had been a staple of Clanton. A revered and respected native. She came from a fine family who made their money in cattle farming. Her father had died when she was just a girl, and her mother

Eugenia raised her by herself. With an iron fist. She parented Judy much like she ran the farm. It was business. There were tasks, there were responsibilities, there were expectations, and everything had a purpose, if not an ulterior motive.

Judy had been raised right. She was at church with her mama every time the doors were open. She never had to work a job, which in Clanton was the equivalent of being a debutante. Judy was raised to be someone's wife and someone's mother. Now she was reduced to a body in mid-air, turning dark purple, covered in her own filth. A body that would no longer kiss her husband, would no longer hug her daughter, would no longer shop at the Blue Star supermarket wearing pearls. A body that would no longer keep secrets.

11

With most of the remaining $247 of credit she had left on a Capital One card, Lou bought herself a new wardrobe at the outlet mall. Growing up shopping with Louise at Rich's, Davison's (later Macy's), Saks, Neiman's, Lord & Taylor, this experience paled in comparison. She couldn't remember the last new clothes she bought. Probably underwear at Walmart. Boy had things changed for her over these last few decades.

A memory flashing back, at least in the beginning of her new life, she'd brought her trunk from home filled with some of her nice things. Poor Ruby had packed all she could as quickly as she was able. Lou brought her hope chest filled with linens, her grandmother's silver, and peignoir sets, even though there was no "hope" left at that point. Those items that could fit in her car were all the material things she had from Clanton. The title to her car had been put in her name, so she owned it outright. She had a little bit of savings squirreled away for a rainy day which she kept in an envelope stuffed into a sable coat pocket in her closet. She had put the coat into a garment bag. The coat would bring a pretty penny, too, if she needed some money in a pinch, she thought. Looking ahead was all she would do at this point. There would be no looking back after that.

When Lou returned home from the mall, the memory of her departure faded, and she was in a surprisingly chipper mood for a broke cancer patient who just had to buy discount clothes off wire racks. Then she noticed a folded piece of paper wedged between the front door and its frame. She pulled the paper out and read it as fast as her eyes could process. The final notification of the tax liens against the farm. In six weeks, after being advertised in the Maysville Monitor, the house and the land would go up for auction on the courthouse steps to recoup the back taxes she hadn't been able to pay in several years.

Just when things had started to look up, here was what could be the downfall of it all. She knew the county would catch up with her sooner or later, but she had hoped for later. Honestly, she had barely thought about it, what with everything else going on. She'd have to call the tax office and figure this out. Surely there was an extension or a waiver or something.

She scanned the papers for the phone number to the office. When she found it, she decided against calling. She would go down there herself. Speaking to someone in person would have to be more effective than a phone call, she thought. She put the papers in her purse and got back in the car, heading towards town.

She pulled into the parking lot, deciding her strategy for this venture would be less demanding and more groveling. She'd begged for a job, she could beg for this, too. Apparently, her pride was slowly dwindling with her age. She needed to look the part for this production.

Walking into the building, she searched the directory for the property tax department, then made her way to office 119. She opened the glass door to a small room with a few chairs and two empty desks on either side of a wooden door. The wooden door was propped open with a thick book. A classy operation here…

She peered around the door to see a young man sitting behind a computer and stacks of papers everywhere. Going unnoticed, she cleared her throat to grab his attention. This took the man by surprise, and he jumped around to see Miss Louvenia Jackson standing there in jeans, a ragged sweatshirt, mussed hair, and white Keds with holes in the sides.

"Can I help you, ma'am?"

She hated being called ma'am. Of course, it was a sign of respect in the south, if you could hardly count Kentucky as the real south, but it made her feel old. She could be this kid's mother, grandmother even, so it fit, but still.

"Uh, yes, darlin," two could play this patronizing game, she thought. "I received this little notice in my door, and I just cannot make heads or tails of it. It says I owe all these taxes and I didn't know a thing about it. Can you help me figure this out? I'm just worried to death." As Grandmama Virginia would say, she was being so sweet sugar couldn't melt in her mouth.

"Well, let's take a look at this paper and see what we can come up with. Don't worry, we'll get it all sorted out, ma'am!"

There was that damn word again. But Lou persevered. She handed him the document that had been at her door, playing the dumb damsel in distress act as if she worked on Broadway.

The nameplate on his desk read Brian Phillips. That name sounded familiar. Where had she seen it before? She just couldn't place it, but, again, she barely knew anybody in this town. Lou looked around the cluttered office while Brian examined the papers with a look of consternation.

There it was. A picture of Brian and a woman. Another face she remembered. Next to it, a framed engagement announcement. That's where she recognized them from–the social section of the Maysville Monitor!

Brian's voice jarred Lou from her thoughts. "Well, Ms. Jackson, it looks like you're behind on your taxes."

No shit, Sherlock, I can read. Switching to actress mode, she replied, dumbfoundedly, "I just don't know how this could happen. See, I had been renting the farm for years, and all that time the documents had been sent to Mr. Baker in town, he was the rental agent for the old owner. I didn't know a thing about any of this. Do you think the bills could still be going to him? Or even the old owner, Mrs. Van Patterson? You know, she lives in a big condo down in Florida, maybe things got mixed up!"

Brian's face held a look of uneasiness. Mistakes did happen in the office. He had one secretary, an ancient woman that still preferred to use a typewriter, who started working there before he was born. He gazed around his office at the stacks upon stacks of papers and documents, then glanced over at the open closet door to the side of the room which held more stacks of improperly organized tax files.

While Brian was wondering if he should admit to a potential mistake or stand his ground with the paper in his hand, Lou piped up, "Is that little Amy Watson in that picture?" She pointed to the photo and the engagement announcement. Brian's face beamed.

"Yes, ma'am! Just engaged two months ago, been together going on three years now. She wouldn't give me the time of day when we first started talking, but I won her over somehow. Now I'm a lucky groom-to-be! You know Amy?"

In a small town like Maysville, everybody knew everybody. Except her. Quick thinking would have to come into play here if the distraction was to work.

"Lord, yes! But I'm sure she doesn't remember me. Her mama and me used to be in the garden club together a hundred years ago, before I got too old for all that." Lou was getting better and better at this self-deprecating act of hers.

Brian looked confused, "Amy's mama can't grow grass so I don't know what she must have done in the garden club," he chuckled.

"Well, we were on the luncheon committee a lot. That was what it was." Quick correction she hoped he wouldn't notice.

"Now that makes sense! That woman can cook better than anybody I've ever seen. But don't you go telling my mom that! Lorene is saying she wants to cook for the whole wedding! We haven't even found a venue yet that Amy likes, but she's fixing and freezing biscuits and cheese straws already."

"Isn't that just like her? Always prepared! Loved that about her," Lou grinned like a Cheshire cat. "I didn't mean to take your mind off business, I know you're a terribly busy man. But I was just so flustered when I came down here, I didn't know what else to do. To be honest with you, honey, I don't have the money for those taxes if that's the case. I'm ashamed to say it. Barely have two dimes to rub together for heat these days. I'm divorced, you know." She whispered the word divorced like it was bad luck. In these parts, it was. And it wasn't entirely a lie, after all. She hadn't been married, but she had been left. Left to do this all on her own.

Brian gave a sympathetic look. "Since you're an old family friend and all this is going on, let me enter an extension into the system. I can manually override it since I'm the deputy tax commissioner. I can extend it six months without checking with the head of the department. That'll give us a minute to get this sorted out."

Feeling an exasperated reprieve from at least one situation hanging over her head, Lou headed back home, shifting her nervous energy regarding the next day–her first day of work. Ever.

12

Little Chuck decided not to watch the coroner cut down Judy's body, complete with ligature as was customary in these cases, and bag it up. They could just do their jobs and get her to the cooler down at the funeral home. He had seen enough. More than enough. Part of him wished he had taken the young sheriff's advice, but part of him also needed that closure of seeing it for himself. He left a key with the sheriff and told him to lock up when they were finished doing what they needed to do. He needed to get to The Gables. He had a lot more to take care of now.

Sheriff Klark agreed to handle things but advised Chuck not to return to his home without police presence until everything was processed and sorted out. He obliged. Klark quietly added, "And I hate to say this, but I gotta say it. Don't go leaving town. It wouldn't look good for the investigation. Nothing seems out of place, but it still wouldn't look good."

He replied with a curt, "Of course."

What the hell could he leave town for? He had a funeral to plan, a family to hold together, a failing business, a daughter he'd have to tell that she would never see her mother again. God, he had barely thought about Josie in all of this. How was he going to break this news? She was always a nervous and anxious person, even as a child. She would bite her nails 'til they bled, pull out pieces of her hair. Not much had improved with age, but at least now she was medicated. Her husband, R.J., would also be there to console her.

Little Chuck liked R.J. a lot. He had hoped he might consider getting his CPA license and joining the firm, but no such luck yet. He worked at a credit union closer to Atlanta where he and Josie lived after meeting at Georgia State University, and they seemed pretty happy with their life. They had talked about starting a family. Now the family had just shrunk by one.

Josephine Jackson had always been a daddy's girl, from day one. It wasn't that she didn't love Judy, she just had a more natural bond with her father. Whether Judy would have admitted it or not, she parented in many ways like her own mother, as parents are apt to do, whether they realize it or not. She was always stricter with rules, she was always harsher with punishments, and she was always pushing Josie. Just like Judy had been pushed by Eugenia.

Chuck was cognizant of these facts, which is why he often held the "good guy" role. Josie did get away with more where her father was concerned, but it was because he felt he could trust her. Josie was a good kid. She had good judgment and a good head on her shoulders. She knew right from wrong; they'd both taught her that. She had never given them a reason to not trust her. But he believed Judy never fully trusted Josie. Just like Judy never fully trusted herself.

Josie would lean on her father in this situation. Aunt Joan, Granddaddy, Ruby, R.J., it didn't matter. She would go to her dad, the one person she herself trusted most in this world.

Driving back to The Gables, much slower this time because he was dreading his task, Chuck's mind was again swirling with all that was going on. The company was practically bankrupt. Peter had quit. Big Chuck was dying. Finding Lou after all these years. And now Judy was dead.

For a second time that day, he thought, "There's nobody left to save me."

13

Walking in the door to the girls greeting her, she went to the kitchen to let them out and to have a cigarette. She even felt like eating lunch today. Lou rummaged around the fridge and cabinets until she settled on tomato soup and a grilled cheese sandwich.

Lizzy and Lucy were ready to come back in, just as Lou was plating up her meal. She sat down at the kitchen table to eat, the dogs by her side, ready for any crumbs or morsels that might come their way. While eating, Lou planned her first day of school outfit in her head like she was a teenager again. She decided on a button up shirt she'd purchased with a smart light sweater. She would wear a fitted pair of Ann Taylor pants she'd had for years with the new shirt and sweater. Luckily clothing styles always come back around, and Lou rarely got rid of anything.

When she put her dishes in the sink, Lou looked out the window and decided to take another walk on her property since it was a nice day, and she was feeling well. The two Labs hobbled out with her and joined for the walk. Today's walk was different, though.

On her previous stroll, Lou had only felt loneliness and defeat. Today, she felt a little hope, for the first time in a long time. Perhaps it was that the county tax was held off for a little longer, or maybe it was the new job she was to start tomorrow.

This place really wasn't so bad after all. The fence could definitely use some mending if ever there was to be horses or livestock again. The old barn was still holding up pretty well. She walked over to it, pulling back the heavy doors with a whining squeak. God only knows the last time they were opened. She looked around and it was mostly dark, save the few small holes in the tin roof and the thin slivers between the boards that made up the walls. There were stalls where the animals had lived. Pens for the pigs. A loft for extra hay, some still up there, undoubtedly disintegrating with time.

Lou had seen articles where people were turning historic farms and barns into rustic wedding venues. In Lou's mind, that sounded less than proper, but times had changed. She guessed there was something appealing about the rustic charm of old places like this.

There was the big house on the property with its stately federal style. Stone posts with gas lamps (no longer functioning) donned either side of the straight, narrow, gravel drive. The home was perfectly symmetrical, with a large, screened porch on one end and a porte cochère on the other, which still had the high steps for ladies and gentlemen to step out of their horse-drawn carriages. The front stoop had a solid oak door, original to the house, Lou assumed, long faded, and somewhat warped. Above the stoop was a widow's walk with the short railing missing on one side. The house could use a coat of paint, and the old, wavy windows needed replacing or at least a reglazing and some caulking. But overall, it was still an impressive house; it just needed some love.

Still petering around in the barn, Lou began to think about the inside of the house, which was a slightly different story. Okay, a vastly different story. Lou never considered herself a hoarder, but she certainly had hoarder tendencies. Leaving Clanton with basically nothing had taught Lou to be practical, frugal, and resourceful, especially considering the clause in her lease indicating she was responsible for any repairs and upkeep. As grand and glorious as The Gables had been, the inside of this house left much to be desired.

In its heyday, the Brooks house was nice, but lacked most modern conveniences due to its age. There was a lovely wide staircase to the second floor, a foyer of large marble tiles, and intricately carved woodwork in the moldings and in the library.

But at the end of the day, it had been a farmhouse. There were nice spaces for company, but it was also built to be lived in and to sustain a bustling farm, one with hired hands that needed to be fed and needed places to take breaks in hot Kentucky summers and frigid Kentucky winters. This meant a large eat-in kitchen with a fireplace and mudroom was necessary. There was plenty of storage and counter space to prepare hearty meals. The big, screened porch was right off the kitchen and dining room through thin French doors. It had comfortable seating and a door leading out to the back of the house where the original outhouse had been. Indoor plumbing had come around by the time the house was built in the 1850s, fed by underground wells, but it was improper for the help to use the bathroom, especially when they were dirty from their farm work. Getting rid of the outhouse was one of Lou's first projects when she moved to the home. It was falling apart and certainly hadn't been used in years, if not decades.

The house may have had plumbing, but it was built before electricity. Gas lamps and sconces were used in every room, and it even had a gas crystal chandelier in the dining room with a golden rope to lower it so it could be lit. When electricity finally made its way to these parts, the house was hooked up, quite literally. At the time, the elderly Brookses didn't see the point in ripping up their horsehair plaster walls and painted wallpapers, so wires were run into the rooms. One wire per room leading to one hanging single-bulb light socket. They didn't need anything fancy. Just not having to light gas lamps was a luxury for them. So, cords were run through the house and tacked around the trims and moldings. Electric outlets were plugged into the sockets with the bare bulbs to power other appliances that came along later. It wasn't long before the kitchen looked like a spiderweb to plug in a toaster, an electric ice box, and more from the lone bulb and socket in the big room. The wiring was updated with the next generation of Brookses, but not by much. Real outlets were actually added, and fixture boxes mounted. But, like their predecessors, they didn't want to tear into the walls, so everything was exterior mount, sticking out from the walls and ceilings, all leading back to the fuse box near the back door. At least it was a cleaner, albeit still unattractive, look that improved the home.

The non-company rooms upstairs–the bedrooms, family room, and the lone upstairs bathroom–were what you might call bare-bones. It looked like the money ran out by the time the builders made it to the top of the stairs. Four identical square rooms with two windows each made up the upper floor. They were separated into pairs with the bathroom on one end and the family room sitting area on the other. This end of the room had the same thin, French doors that would lead out to the widow's walk. There were no fancy window treatments, just tattered, yellowed lace sheers, no wallpapers, no lighting other than the gas sconces, no paint besides antique white (had it originally just been white and was only 'antique white' now because the house was antique?), and no trim work except for simple walnut-stained crown molding to echo the walnut banisters of the staircase.

Heating and cooling the old house with its drafty windows and high ceiling was near impossible. Lou had put up large old quilts she found in the attic to essentially close off the upstairs. After all, what guests would she have? She converted the old library to a bedroom as it was close to the main level bathroom. It's not as if she had any books to line the shelves. So, she lived in the four lower rooms: the parlor, the dining room, the library, and the kitchen. All mirroring the upstairs construction with a hall down the center. You could see the back door from the front door with the staircase to the left-hand side. The lower-level bathroom was under the staircase but was surprisingly good-sized. The back door led to the mudroom which made up the rear of the kitchen. Double corner fireplaces were in each room to feed the spaces with warmth and add only one chimney on the outside to ensure the symmetry for which the style of the home was known. The entire home was large, but practical, and Lou had loved it since the moment she saw it.

Getting this job would help her with saving it, keeping her home, her shelter. As she turned and looked around the farm from the back steps on her way into the house, she looked at the farm with fresh eyes, optimism, and a renewed sense of spirit.

14

Chuck pulled into the driveway for the second time that day. He parked, much more cautiously and much more purposefully than before. He turned off the engine. And he sat there. He leaned his head against the steering wheel, trying to mentally prepare for what was in front of him. He stayed like that for a few minutes, until Ruby tapped on his car window. Startled at first, but then comforted by the loving, familiar face, he opened the door and got out. Ruby spoke first.

"Now you need to tell me what's going on here, boy." She hadn't talked to him like that since he was a teenager. He had been Mr. Chuck or Lil Chuck since he was grown. She was his elder, but at that time in the south there was still a certain expectation. Ruby knew the expectation, but she also knew when she could cross the line, and when she should. "Your Aunt Joan is out on the back porch, hasn't said a dang word since she got back here. Wouldn't come inside the house. I took her some sweet tea and her cheese crackers she likes, and she hasn't touched a thing. She's just sittin' there, nearly shaking to death." Ruby had a serious, almost frightening, look on her face. She wasn't asking for what was going on–she was demanding to know.

"Ruby," he began, slowly, "Judy's gone."

A confused Ruby replied, "Where? Where'd she go? Did she run off?"

Wishing Ruby was right, Little Chuck said it again more slowly, "Judy is gone. She's dead."

The angry and confused looks faded from Ruby's face, only to be replaced with a look of horror. "Whatta you mean?" asking as if she didn't hear right or understand what he said.

"She hung herself, Ruby. In our basement. Joan was the one who found her. She called me at work."

"But why did you come here first?"

"Well Joan said come home. This is home. Daddy is home, you're home. My mind just went here. It didn't even click for me to go to Crystal Springs until you told me they'd gone over there." Chuck was speaking more calmly than he imagined he would in this situation. He thought it must be Ruby. Talking to her was like being wrapped in a mother's hug. "By the time I got there, everybody was there. Police, paramedics. It was like something out of a scary movie."

Ruby kept nodding her head, waiting for more, looking more and more terrified with every word out of Little Chuck's mouth.

"So, I went in, and Joan was coming out of the basement. She was a god-awful mess. She couldn't even tell me what was happening. KK told me what was going on."

"That Kitchens boy who won the sheriff?"

"Yeah, Klark Kitchens," he confirmed to Ruby. "He told me Judy hung herself from a rafter in our basement. He wouldn't let me go down there for a while, but I had to see it for myself."

Ruby looked disgusted. "That musta been awful! Why'd you do that?"

"I don't know. I just needed to see it. I needed to know it was real," Chuck replied, surprisingly emotionless. "I'd sent Joan home by then. I made her promise not to say a word, that I needed to be the one to tell y'all, and Josie."

Ruby broke again, "Miss Josie. Lord, poor Miss Josie, that girl's gonna lose her mind."

"I know, but I need to be the one to handle this. Because it has to be handled a certain way."

"Whatchu mean, Mr. Chuck?" Ruby replied suspiciously, "What you talking about a certain way?"

Little Chuck pulled the piece of embossed ivory stationery from his pocket. Ruby read it to much horror and dismay without saying a word.

After a few moments, the pair walked through the front door. Joan had heard him pull in the drive and had come in from the back porch. Her arms were crossed, she was holding them tightly like she was cold, despite the midsummer heat. She looked at Little Chuck, eyes brimming with tears again. He held up his hand to signal to Joan that she needed to hold off. He couldn't handle that again.

He spoke in a low, confident tone to Joan, "Ruby knows. I just told her. I'm gonna go talk to Daddy. Alone. Then we're gonna call R.J. and make sure he can get home to Josie. We are going to tell him why, but I don't want her to be alone. I'm not going to tell her everything. I'm going to tell her they need to come home now. She doesn't need all the details right now. It'll worry her to death."

Ruby and Joan nodded quietly in agreement. Once Big Chuck was gone, he would be the patriarch holding the family together. Grimly, he was starting to grow into those shoes already.

He walked to Big Chuck's study-turned-bedroom and closed the door behind him.

Big Chuck, in his bed as always, stirred and raised his head. "Still alive. Sorry to disappoint you." Big Chuck had no idea how dark his joke was at this moment, but it was lost on Little Chuck right now. Little Chuck pulled his usual chair closer to the hospital bed and collapsed into it. Big Chuck sat the bed up with its remote control, looking at his son with worry. "What's wrong, son?" He knew something was very very wrong.

"Oh, Daddy, where do I even start?" He really didn't know where to start. Failed family business? No money? Missing sister? Dying father? Dead wife? He'd decided not to hold anything back from Big Chuck. Could Big Chuck save him one last time?

"It's been a bad day, Daddy," Little Chuck said flatly. "I've got bad news. A lot of it. And I don't know what to do. I need you. I need you to help me."

Big Chuck was serious now, perhaps more lucid than he'd been in months. "What's happened?"

Business could wait. "Judy's killed herself, Daddy." Maybe if Chuck whispered it, it wouldn't be real."

"Oh no, oh God. What happened?"

"She hung herself. In the basement. Joan went over there and found her."

"Oh my God, Joan must be a mess. Where is she?" Big Chuck looked around the room, just now noticing the closed door, and turning back to his son with an unsure expression.

"Joan and Ruby are in the kitchen, I think. I told Ruby."

Growing angry, Big Chuck said, "Why am I the last goddamned person in this house to know? I'm still the one in charge here. For now, anyway." Big Chuck instantly regretted that last remark.

"You're technically not the last, Daddy. I haven't called Josie yet. I'm gonna get R.J. to go home and get her and bring her up here. I can't tell her on the phone. I need to be there when she finds out."

"Yeah, that's probably the best idea. That girl needs you like she needs air," Big Chuck smiled slightly at the bond between Little Chuck and Josie, sort of like the one he once had with Lou.

"Daddy, you weren't the first to find out everything, but you're the only one that's gonna *know* everything. This is where it gets sticky."

Little Chuck pulled out the piece of embossed stationery from his pocket again. He read the words again for the millionth time that day while Big Chuck read them for the first time. He finished reading the message. There was a big, pregnant pause. Finally, Big Chuck broke the silence with anger, "So it all goes back to her secret, doesn't it?"

Little Chuck didn't want to respond. He was embarrassed, ashamed even. Times had changed. Things weren't like they used to be. But in a small town, it's amazing how much things change and just how much they stay the same.

When he didn't respond, Big Chuck said firmly, "Now how the hell did you get this note?"

Little Chuck stood firm in the fact that he didn't want what was in that note to be broadcast across Clanton, but at the same time, it was evidence tampering. He was a CPA, not a lawyer, but he knew that much. "Daddy, I couldn't just leave it there for the whole world to see! KK read it when I did and didn't say anything. I don't think he'd go advertising what's in it, but I didn't know what else to do."

"So, they know there's a note?"

"Yeah, that's what I just said."

"Well evidence tampering is a crime, boy. Suicide isn't. And tampering with evidence is obstruction of the investigation. They should have logged it and signed off on it, didn't they?"

"I don't know. A deputy brought it right to Klark and he opened it with gloves and wouldn't let me touch it. Said it might have prints on it or something in case there was anything suspicious about everything, but there isn't."

Annoyed at his grown son's ignorance and shaking his head, Big Chuck replied, "Well there's something suspicious about it now. You just took a major piece of the investigation that would have cleared you from being any kind of suspect."

Little Chuck finally realized the gravity of what he had done. This wasn't just a selfish act to save face. This was a crime. A real one.

*****

"Where the fuck is it?" Klark demanded with a shout that scared everyone in the room. "How do you lose a goddamned suicide note at a suicide crime scene?" he bellowed. The voice came from somewhere deep inside of the young, green sheriff. But Klark Kitchens wasn't one for mistakes. He took a lot of pride in his work and the work of his department. They may be small, but they did things right. They followed protocol.

Klark scanned the evidence logs for the hundredth time, not seeing it logged anywhere. "Akers, you're the one that handed it to me, you sonofabitch. Why isn't it on the log?"

"I-I just wanted to get it right to you, sir. I thought it was real important that you see it. I-I-I didn't think to log it first," Deputy Akers replied, fearing for his job, if not his life, for how angry his boss was at this moment.

"You listen to me, I know good and well they taught you at academy to log every damn thing you see, every damn thing you pick up, and every damn thing that might be one iota of a part of an investigation. Were you out dicking around on that day? Huh?" The sheriff was growing angrier by the second. Akers was near tears.

"No, sir, I promise I wasn't. I just, well, I handed it to you, and then I thought you took it 'cause I didn't see it again. I wasn't going to question a superior, sir."

Klark's mood shifted in the blink of an eye. He remembered Akers handing him the note. He remembered holding it with gloves and knocking it away when Chuck Jackson went to grab it. He remembered reading it, along with Little Chuck. He remembered the things written in the note. He remembered Akers walking away. He remembered the note on the table. And that's where his memory became hazy.

This wasn't Akers' fault. This was his fault. Failing to log the evidence that was taken into custody could be laid at Akers' feet, but negligence of securing the evidence was at his doorstep. If this note wasn't found, and found quickly, this would launch an internal affairs investigation. That was protocol. Everyone on the scene knew there was a note. There was a photograph of the folded paper left next to the body. The husband saw the note. There was no denying it existed. The Office of Professional Standards could come after him, possibly everybody in the department, for screwing this up.

This was not good. Not one bit. He had to find this note, even if it meant him crawling his way from the sheriff's office in town to the Jackson's house in Crystal Springs on his hands and knees. Good thing he still had a key to Little Chuck Jackson's house.

15

Lou woke up at five o'clock that next morning. She jumped out of the bed the moment the alarm went off, not that she had ever really fallen asleep in the first place. The old dogs stirred, trying to figure out what they were doing being awakened in what they considered to be the middle of the night. Lou nudged the girls, "Come on, time for breakfast and to go potty." The mention of breakfast was enough for them to pull themselves off the old blankets on the rug that served as their beds. They ate and hobbled out to do their business.

Lou scrambled an egg and made a piece of toast. Whether she was hungry or not, she needed something on her stomach to keep her going today. She let the dogs in and sat down to her breakfast, lighting a cigarette. She washed her medicine down with her coffee and ate most of the breakfast.

She went to the bathroom to shower, do her hair, and put on her makeup. Lou was an attractive woman. She believed in personal appearances, which was instilled hard by Louise. Even with little money and the sometimes-dated clothing she wore, she always looked clean and presentable. Even when the farm was still running and making a little money, you wouldn't have known she was a farmer.

Satisfied with her hair and makeup, she went back to her room to dress in the outfit she had painstakingly planned the day before. She dressed and looked in the full-length mirror. She looked good. She looked like a professional, perhaps for the first time in thirty something years. She was ready to work and ready to make things work for her now.

Lou looked at the clock and frowned. It was only 6:05. She still had almost an hour before she was to meet Ms. Ward. But better to be early than late! She blew Lizzy and Lucy kisses goodbye, without disturbing their resumed slumber, then walked out to her car. She started the car and headed to town to the school district's county office. She would wait there until Ms. Ward got there. She wouldn't be late and risk blowing this.

She pulled into the parking lot, seeing only one other car, a small Subaru SUV. Lou parked her car next to it, giving herself a pep talk for the day. She looked at the building, seeing only one light on in the windows. It was Liz Ward in her office.

For the first time, Lou really noticed Ms. Ward. She was well-dressed, she was put together, she was an attractive, accomplished woman. Unbeknownst to Ms. Ward, Lou watched her shuffling around her office, filing papers, organizing her desk.

Lou decided to get out of her car and tap on the window she was looking through. Ms. Ward nearly jumped out of her skin, turning toward the window to look for the source of the noise. Lou laughed heartily, and Liz frowned. Uh oh. Maybe it wasn't as funny as Lou thought it would be.

Ms. Ward left her office and Lou walked toward the front door of the building. Ms. Ward unlocked and opened the door. "You shouldn't have done that. You scared the bejesus out of me."

Lou laughed again, but apologized, "I'm sorry, I just saw you and thought I'd come on in and get a little more coaching on my first day."

"Well, I told you seven o'clock sharp."

"I know, but I like to be early. And I see I'm not the only one," Lou gestured around to the empty building. For some reason, she felt like she could really talk to Liz Ward. They were both straight shooters. They were kind but firm southern (again, if you can call Kentucky the south) women.

"No, I like to get things done before everybody gets here and bothers me. I like to be ready for my day. I like efficiency."

“Understood and agreed,” Lou responded. “So, at seven we go to Little Creek and you feed me to the ten year old lions. I’ll answer phones, emails, take memos, get coffee. Then I come back here to report back to you or what?”

Ms. Ward chuckled. “You really don’t have a clue, do you?” Lou looked insulted. “I’m not trying to piss you off, but this isn’t 1985. You’re not getting coffee and standing next to a water cooler and pulling out your steno pad.”

“Well what AM I doing?”

“You buzz people into the office. You make sure people sign in and out. You handle student registration and withdrawals. Yes, you answer phones and emails. You forward calls. You make copies. You handle the mail. You keep the marquee updated in front of the school. You…”

“Okay, I get it. I have a lot to learn apparently.” Lou was growing more nervous by the minute.

“You seem like a smart woman. I wouldn’t have put myself out on a limb for you if I hadn’t been impressed. To be honest, the thing that impressed me the most was how you worked me over with the Phi Mu bit,” Liz smirked.

Lou blushed, like a child caught red handed. “You figured that out, huh?”

Liz laughed. “Give me some credit. I was born on a Tuesday, but not last Tuesday. You made a connection, and you used it to your advantage. That was clever. It was quick thinking. Quick acting. That impressed me.” Liz paused and continued, “And you’re old. And you need a job.”

Lou went from grinning to pissed off in a blink. “Yeah, I do. Yeah, I am. Just a couple years older than you, I might add. And what I’ve lacked in professional experience, I’ve made up for in learning how to take care of myself, learning how to stretch a dollar, learning how to build my life from absolutely nothing in a place where I know absolutely no one. I've been around the block, and yeah, I need a job. I need money and I need insurance." Lou laid it all out for Liz Ward, not holding back, whether she should have restrained or not. It just poured out because she felt like she was talking to someone she knew much better than an acquaintance of a few days.

Liz, unfazed by Lou's fiery outburst, replied, "Cancer?"

"What?"

"You said you needed insurance. I've smelled smoke on you every time you've been in my office. My guess is in the lungs. Maybe esophagus? I've heard the way you hack when you cough."

Lou wasn't the only observant person in the room. Lou hadn't said her diagnosis out loud with anyone except her doctor.

"My health is none of your damn business. Are you going to give me this job or not?"

Liz replied coolly, in contrast to Lou's emblazoned voice, "Of course I am. I said I was. I just want you to know that I don't like secrets. I don't like ulterior motives. I don't like being out of the loop. You stay honest with me, and I'll help you as best I can while you work for this district."

Lou softened and said a quiet, "Thank you," now regretting her defensive outburst.

Ms. Ward rose from her desk, grabbed the keys to her Subaru and her purse and spoke. "It's ten 'til now. Follow me over to Little Creek so I can feed you to the lions."

*****

Lou got into her car at three o'clock on the dot. Taking her shoes off. She might not have been fed to the lions, exactly, but she had been chewed up and spit out. Working for the school was no joke. The phone rang off the hook. Parents and kids wandered in and out of the office all day. The computer kept dinging with a new email to read and be answered every few minutes. She had to collect the lunch counts for the cafeteria staff, the attendance rosters from the teachers, deliver forgotten lunch boxes and book bags left by annoyed parents. She was pretty sure she hadn't sat down for longer than three minutes all day long.

And she hadn't had a cigarette since she drove to Liz Ward's office that morning. Forget the lunch she packed that she didn't have time to eat, she needed a smoke. She cranked the engine of the car and lit a Winston for her jangled nerves. Jesus Christ, she needed that.

As she made it home to the farm and let Lizzy and Lucy out of the door, the phone rang. God, if she had to talk to one more person on the phone she might scream. She grabbed the phone with a huffy hello to see who was bothering her again today.

"So how were the lions?" Lou could hear the smirk through the phone. Liz was calling to check on her after her first day. Sweet, but sort of unexpected after the events that unfolded this morning when Lou had her little tantrum in Liz's office before they went to Little Creek.

"Honestly, the little lions weren't that bad. It was the grown lions that were the worst. Needy parents, needy teachers, and needy coworkers," Lou reported.

"That's not too big of a surprise," Liz replied nonchalantly. "Learned helplessness if you ask me. I'm sure you're tired so I don't want to keep you, but I wanted to offer something I don't often offer–a little apology."

Hmm. This was a surprise for both.

"I'm sorry for making assumptions and calling you out this morning. It wasn't really anything to do with me, and I shouldn't have inserted myself into your business. I'm sorry. I hope it doesn't affect our relationship."

Relationship. Interesting choice of words, Lou thought. “I understand, I get it. You could see through me, and you could read me. It’s been a long time since I’ve been around anyone who could do that, which made me defensive. I apologize for my outburst and my abruptness. I misjudged your intelligence and your perceptiveness.”

“I can appreciate that. I saw a lot of it in myself if someone had grilled me like I had grilled you. The truth is, I don’t have a lot of friends in this town. I’ve lived here nearly ten years since I took this job with the schools, and I don’t know hardly anything about this place or any of the people. I could use a friend. You seem like the type of friend I could get along with.”

Lou considered these words, considered their relevance and similarity to her own life and situation. It was kind. It seemed genuine. It seemed like something she could use, too.

“Liz, I’m happy to be your friend. I think I could benefit from having someone to lean on besides my two senior mutts who see me as their meal tickets,” Lou laughed.

“Ugh, you’re a dog person? I like cats. Dogs are gross,” Liz retorted playfully.

“You’re not wrong, but this is a farm. It seemed like I needed to have dogs. But maybe a barn cat wouldn’t be so bad,” Lou considered.

“You live on a farm? I’d love to see it sometime. I live right in town and never spend time out in the rural areas, never had a reason to.”

“Well, Liz Ward, my new pal, why don’t you come out to the farm. You could bring us dinner from town as your peace offering and I’ll show you around and let the dogs maul you,” Lou offered, making the first move in solidifying this newfound friendship.

“I’ll leave here at about 5. Hope you like shitty Chinese. What’s your address?”

“Take Town Creek Road out of town about seven miles. Turn right at Bart’s store, first road on your right. Brooks Lane, only house on the road–the old Brooks family farm.”

“You’re speaking foreign language at this point since I don’t know who the Brookses are, but sure, I’ll find it.”

“By the way, sesame chicken with fried rice. And don’t forget wonton soup. Surely, they can accomplish that in this god-forsaken town.”

Liz chuckled, “I think they can handle that. See you after a while.”

Lou hung up the phone. As tired as she had been when she got in her car at three, she was now equally and inversely energized at the prospect of dinner with Liz. And the prospect of a new friend.

She looked around her shabby old house and realized that she wasn’t really prepared for company. She hadn’t been prepared for company in several years, as a matter of fact. She had roughly two hours to do something about the messy house. Of the four large downstairs rooms, she needed to hit three. Her bedroom could be the staging area and catch-all room.

Lou started at the bathroom in the back and worked her way forward. A good toilet and sink scrub would suffice. Then she moved to the front parlor. A quick dusting, rearranging some furniture to cover some stains and scuffed hardwoods, threadbare, mismatched chairs turned around. Grubby arm rests? An old blanket does wonders! She knocked the cobwebs from the corners and the light fixture, and toted stacks of junk into her bedroom.

Lou did much the same in the front hall. Tidying up the junk, throwing it into her room, Windexing the dog nose prints off the sidelights around the big oak door. Moving on to the dining room, which hadn’t been used since just after she moved in, she had probably the biggest to do list. The Duncan Phyfe table and Hepplewhite chairs were piled high with papers, notebooks, and mail (probably a few of those past due tax notices, if she was being honest). If she hadn’t looked at it in months, it was probably useless, so she just loaded it into big black trash bags to toss on the side porch. That room would also be conveniently left off the tour, she thought.

With the papers and such gone, the room needed a decent dusting and the drapes opened wide. The tarnished silver on the sideboard would just have to wait for another day. When Lou went to open the heavy drapes, they ripped and shredded like tissue paper. Dry rot. Lou groaned with annoyance. It was already 4:15. She didn't exactly have time to sew new window treatments. So instead of leaving the ratty old drapes, she ripped them down like the paper they had become. Big black trash bags to the rescue again. The rods and tie backs were still there, but it surprised Lou at just how nice the bright light made the room look. The wallpaper was old, but it was pretty much all intact, except for the two outlets that had been surface mounted and the line ran to the original gas chandelier that had been wired for electricity. The wallpaper was a beautiful blue toile that matched the now defunct heavy navy-blue velvet drapes. The sideboard, table, and china cabinet were polished. She hoped Liz wouldn't look inside the dusty cabinet that still displayed the Brooks family china. She pulled out two place settings of Grandmama Virginia's Fairfax to polish quickly and two place settings of the china to wash in the kitchen. She would set the dining table for a proper meal for Liz. For the first moment in a long time, Lou remembered the standards she had been raised to uphold.

The kitchen was the room that probably needed the least amount of work. Lou managed to keep it mostly in order as it was the room she spent the most of her time in these days, sitting at the breakfast table. When she vacuumed and mopped the rest of the rooms, she would give the kitchen the same treatment and she would be alright, she figured.

The front entrance looked rough and aged, the windows were dirty, but the house was in some sort of order, for the first time in forever. Lou was doubly exhausted now, but she also had a new spring in her step. Perhaps it was knowing she had a new job and impending income. Perhaps it was a clean and *less* cluttered house. Maybe it was Liz's visit, or the prospect of the first friend she might have in three decades. Probably a combination of it all.

Just as she was pouring out the eighth bucket of truly nasty mop water, she heard a car pulling into the driveway. The dogs stirred and gave half-hearted barks, whether because of the unusual instance of a visitor or the fact that it was dinner time was to be determined.

Lou looked in the mirror in the front hall. She was disheveled. She had spent all her time on the house and none of the time on herself. Oh well. Better a new friend see her how she normally looked at home than be embarrassed for them to see her home in utter disarray. She smoothed her hair, noticing for the first time just how much it had thinned since her diagnosis. It was really starting to show, she thought. She straightened her shirt and wiped her face with a dish towel in her back pocket just as Liz walked up the steps carrying the plastic shopping bags containing the stereotypical Chinese takeout boxes. Lou actually had an appetite now and was looking forward to the food.

She opened the door before Liz could knock, taking one of the bags from her hands and ushering her in through the door into the foyer.

"Welcome to the farm. Come in if you can get in," Lou stated, still embarrassed at the state of things around the place.

"I like it! It's rustic and has an old family charm!" Liz claimed with genuine enthusiasm. "Look at this woodwork and these floors!" She stood around the room examining every inch in awe.

Lou was mortified. She didn't expect Liz to look at things with such a discerning eye. She hoped most of the details and imperfections would go unnoticed by her guest. No such luck. "Well, it needs a lot of work. But I'm working on it," Lou lied. Today was the first time she worked on anything around the house in months since the roof leak upstairs last winter.

Liz walked towards the heavy quilt separating the upstairs and downstairs and pulled it back without hesitation. "Look at this magnificent staircase! Why would you cover such stunning architecture, you nut!"

Lou hadn't seen Liz this interested in anything, or this animated before. It was curious, but captivating.

"Well, to be honest, I don't really use the upstairs since it's just me and the dogs. It's easier to heat and cool the place with it just closed off," Lou admitted, again embarrassed at her shortcomings where the home was concerned.

Liz seemed entirely unable to sense Lou's uncomfortability and kept eyeing every door, every piece of furniture, every nook and cranny. When Liz made her way towards the library/Lou's bedroom doors, Lou lunged to jump in front of her. "This is just my room, nothing special to see in here!"

Liz jumped back, obviously surprised and a little confused. "Oh. Okay, well let's go have our dinner in that gorgeous dining room. I'm starving after today."

Saved by the Chinese, Lou thought, suddenly relieved. The pair walked across the hall to the dining room and Lou turned on the chandelier. Except it didn't come on. Lou couldn't remember the last time she'd actually turned it on. Earlier the bright light from the newly opened windows had been sufficient to clean by, but now it was almost 6:15 and the sun was close to setting. Lou frowned and tried to laugh off the mishap. "Oh, these things are always going out. You know, the Brookes were an 'old line' family!" she joked nervously.

"Thank goodness for these old oil lamps." She grabbed matches from the foyer bureau drawer and lit the old sconces around the dining room, creating an ambiance that Lou had never seen in the house before. The glow of the lamps warmed the room and restored a little bit of her pride.

16

In the dark of the evening, Sheriff Klark Kitchens drove back to Crystal Springs to Little Chuck Jackson's house. It was no longer Chuck and Judy's house, he thought. He pulled up the street as far up as he could go. He didn't exactly have anything to hide, but he also didn't exactly want to be seen or raise any questions among the neighbors who were already disturbed by what had gone on in their pristine neighborhood.

Klark got out of his car, looking around scanning the area like only someone in the military or law enforcement would do. He walked down the street to the Jackson house and put the key into the lock. He turned the deadbolt and made his way into the dark house, locking it behind him. It was sort of spooky. Little Chuck and Judy hadn't really been living here for months anyway since Big Chuck fell ill. The house was warm, quiet, and the air stale, despite the flurry of activity earlier.

He looked around the living room and dining room which had been the staging areas for the investigative team. Seeing nothing readily apparent, and before searching for his piece of evidence in more depth, he went down to the basement to ensure everything was properly taken care of by the coroner. Of course, it was. She was a very efficient and thorough worker, as was her deputy. She had a flawless reputation. You really couldn't even tell what had taken place in the basement except for one detail. After cutting down Judy's body, the part of the ligature tied to the rafter had been left. It was an eerie reminder of the day's activity; a sight he knew he would never forget. Suicides by hanging weren't as gruesome as gunshots to the head or terrible car accidents with mangled and gory bodies. But the effects of the body when all life was gone from it in these cases was something that would churn anyone's stomach. He didn't know how the coroner was able to handle it.

Making his way back upstairs, he heard a noise. His perceptive ears were like a canine. He could sense a noise or a movement from hundreds of yards away. He stopped in the stairs, listening. Trying to determine if it was the air conditioner, a water heater cutting on, the house settling slightly, or, more frighteningly, a threat. His hand rested on his department issued weapon, ready to pull it if his listening yielded something more dangerous than his benign initial thoughts.

Klark could clearly make out footsteps on the hardwood floors. Someone was in the house. Who, he didn't know, but he knew there shouldn't be anyone there under any circumstances. He readied himself to bust out of the basement door and confront the intruder. No matter how many times he did this, the rush of adrenaline never dissipated. There was always a chance that something could go awry, something that would change his life forever, or end it. The fact that no one knew where he was, and he had no back up magnified his concern. The department had put body cams on all their officers. But considering Klark rarely interacted in actual crimes or traffic stops himself, he opted not to wear one and save the funds for the department. Potentially a really poor choice in this moment.

His weapon drawn, Klark burst out the door hollering, "Police! Hands in the air! NOW! NOW!"

Little Chuck just about messed in his pants. He wasn't sure if it was the surprise of someone in the house, the surprise that it was the sheriff, or the surprise that he was caught red handed. When Klark saw it was Chuck, his heart dropped, along with his weapon.

"What the fuck are you doing here Jackson? I told you not to come back here without a police escort. I made that real damn clear," Kitchens hollered at the man, now that the potential for a heart attack had subsided.

"Listen, KK, this is still my house. Sheriff be damned. I can come here if I need to. I needed to get some clothes for the funeral home for Judy. I need them tonight so I can take them to Chapman's in the morning. I didn't have time to screw around and wait on you to return a call to let me in my own home."

Feeling a little inferior when still being called KK, but refusing to correct his elder, he said, "Fine, go pick out the clothes. I'll wait here for you." Klark figured he could use this time to discreetly look for the missing suicide note.

Chuck walked into the primary bedroom to Judy's closet. He switched on the light, thankful for the excuse he had planned if he needed one. Wait a minute, he thought. What was Klark Kitchens doing in his house at this hour alone? He turned to walk back to the front of the house where he saw Klark sitting coolly at the dining room table, his arms crossed, looking at the table at the folded note and then looking Little Chuck dead in the eyes.

"Where'd this come from?" Kitchens asked plainly.

"What do you mean? That's Judy's note, isn't it? Didn't y'all take it as evidence or something?" Chuck could play it cool, too.

"We should have. But we didn't. It was mistakenly not logged. Nobody had it. We all knew it was here, but it never made it into custody."

"Sounds to me like you and your buddies really screwed up," Chuck replied with a poker face.

"See, it would sound like that. And I thought we had. That's why I came back here–to look for the note in case we missed it. I got here a few minutes before you and looked around here and in the front living room. It wasn't here. Pretty sure I would have noticed it sitting in the middle of the friggin' dining room table, don't you think?"

Now it was Chuck's turn to feel inferior, but defensive. "I don't know, KK. Seems like a kid looking about 16 running around playing sheriff might not have all his bases covered, I really don't know, buddy."

"I think you do. I think you took this note. And I think you came back here to put it back. Once you probably Googled 'evidence tampering' and realized it was obstruction of an investigation and could potentially be a felony. Just my guess, though," Klark smirked. "Especially when one considers what was written in that note, huh?"

Little Chuck turned red and stepped toward the sheriff. Klark jumped up to meet Chuck face to face. "You listen here, and you listen good, that's my family's business. It doesn't mean nothing to you or your little investigation. My wife, the woman I loved, killed herself. She carried a lot of secrets for a long time, and that's how she decided to deal with it. And you go advertising that, I swear to God, I'll accuse you and your whole damn department of negligence in evidence handling, even if I have to go to jail myself. Then the governor can decide if you get to keep your job or not."

Chuck and Klark stood on even ground right now. Both were guilty of something. Both had dirt on the other. How they would handle it was still up in the air.

And Judy still needed a damn dress for her funeral.

17

“Is this Fairfax?” Liz asked out loud while Lou was unpackaging the Chinese food in the kitchen onto the china. She thought it was sort of funny to put cheap takeout on 19th century transferware, but again, Lou appreciated appearances.

“Ha! Yes, my grandmama’s wedding silver,” Lou hollered from the kitchen. She smiled, noticing again, how observant Liz was.

Lou brought out the food and laid it at their places, taking the head seat herself.

“I love blue transferware! I noticed it in the china cabinet. Are these all family heirlooms?” Liz sure did ask a lot of questions. Lou got the feeling that she was the first person Liz had any connection with in a very long time.

“Well, they’re family heirlooms, yes. But not really mine,” Lou frowned slightly.

“Then how did you get them?”

Another question she didn’t want to answer. “They belonged to the family who lived here. The Brookses. Practically everything in the house is theirs.”

Now thoroughly confused, Liz asked, “Why didn’t they want them anymore?”

“Look, I don’t know. When we moved into the house there was furniture and stuff, and the price was right, and I didn’t ask too many questions. Things were going great, and I wasn’t trying to foul anything up, okay?” Lou immediately regretted her second outburst of the day towards Liz who sat quietly munching on her eggroll.

Apparently, Liz didn't get the memo meant to be derived from the outburst. "Who was 'we' that moved into the house?"

"Huh?"

"You said 'When WE moved in.' Who else moved here with you?"

Lou needed a way out of this question. She couldn't answer this question. Not now. Not here. Not from Liz. Maybe not ever.

"My little mama, Louise. We were looking for a fresh start when we moved here from Georgia. There wasn't any family left besides us. We decided on this place and loved it right off the bat," Lou said confidently. Confident liars rarely get caught.

"Oh. Okay. Hey, is there any more of that soy sauce?"

Maybe Liz was a little more dense than Lou took her as. Or was this part of her game? She didn't know but she was ready to let sleeping dogs lie for one night.

The pair finished dinner, and Liz followed Lou into the kitchen with her plate and silverware. "Here, let me help you clean up."

"No way. You paid for and brought dinner. I've got the dishes."

Looking around for a dishwasher that never existed in the house, Liz commanded, "You wash, I'll dry."

Defeated, and tired, Lou gave in. There was a weird power balance between the two new friends. One was firmer than the other, but one was fierier than the other. One more calm, and one more contemptuous. Two trying to be in charge, but neither of them particularly winning. Neither had carried a real friendship in so long that they neither were quite sure what to make of it. Was this what friendships looked like? Had things changed in this day and age? Was it not just smiling at rush parties and then talking about each other behind their backs? The fact was that neither of them knew how to be a friend. They both were just being authentic, which had its own beauty and merit, but was still uncharted territory for both.

With the dishes finished and the food and boxes cleared away, the evening was coming to a natural close. Lou was utterly exhausted. She worked all day for the first time in years, then came home and cleaned half the house, then entertained one nosy dinner guest. However, the guest seemed quite content exploring more of the details of the house, even walking out the back door herself when Lou let the dogs out. Here we go again, Lou moaned internally.

"Is all this property really yours?"

"No, I'm a squatter," Lou retorted.

"Oh, hush, you know what I meant. There's that big barn and this great yard. You could grow vegetables right over there. Do you? I bet it gets plenty of sun."

"I don't care for growing vegetables, or gardening for that matter. You saw the place when you drove in. I'm doing well if I can keep the grass mowed."

"I'd just love to give this place a makeover. I did a double major in school. In addition to education, I'm certified in historic preservation. You could do tours or make it into an event venue even. This place has so much potential."

That explained Liz's eye for detail and all the questions about the big old house. Lou felt a little guilty now for shutting down all the questions when Liz was just trying to show her interest in Lou and her life.

"That's pretty neat. But I'm not sure this old place can be preserved or restored or any of that anymore. Not that I have the money for it even if it could," Lou replied, genuinely sad at the prospect that the home and farm were possibly too far gone to ever be saved because of her own neglect over all these years.

"Nonsense. There're loans that will help you restore the property and make it livable. You could get an FHA 203k rehab loan. It's backed by the government and bundles your primary mortgage and renovation expenses into just one loan," Liz said, matter-of-factly. It did sound like she really knew her historic stuff. Especially for a former school marm-turned district level coordinator.

"Ha, I don't think you're quite getting the picture here, hon," Lou was chuckling. "There is no mortgage. I own this place outright. I have little to no credit. What there is of it is in the tank. I'm praying that 4Runner out there holds out 'til I die 'cause I'll never be able to afford another one. I have no income from this farm anymore. And as a receptionist for Maysville City Schools, I will be making almost exactly enough to buy groccries, medicine, and keep the lights on. I'm out of options, Liz."

"You dumbass. Do you not know how any of this works? You own the place, right? Deed in hand?"

"Yeah, that's what I said, isn't it?" Lou could feel herself getting annoyed all over again with the questions.

"So, you take OUT a mortgage on the place. You use the whole farm as collateral. No, the house itself won't get you much, but the land alone will give you enough cash to float everything that needs to be done. You take that and pay the bills you need to, then spend the rest fixing this joint up."

A suspicious Lou replied, "What about my bad credit? You're forgetting that."

"What about it? The home is collateral. You default on the loan, they have the house to hold against you. You have a job now. You just have to prove that you can make the payment and you're set."

"Again, earth to Liz: I can barely keep the lights on with what I'll be making. That does not a loan payment leave room for." Lou wanted to slap the know-it-all.

Liz frowned. "I guess you do have a point there. What about a co-signer? Someone that could go in on it with you and front some cash and you pay them back somehow if you get the farm up and running again or rent out parts or something? A family member maybe?"

"Must be nice to have family like that. I wouldn't know," Lou said coldly.

"Oh. I'm sorry, I didn't know. I guess I should have realized that when you said it was just you and your mom who moved here."

Ignoring the lie that she doesn't have any family but appreciating that it substantiated her resistance, Lou simply replied, "See, no options. Nothing left to do around here but keep it livable as long as I'm living. End of story."

Lou turned to go back inside the house. When Liz didn't follow her lead, she turned back to see what Liz was doing. She was still eyeing the barn.

"It's late and I'm beat. You must be, too, plus you have to drive back to town. Gotta be up early tomorrow to tame the lions." Lou was telling her to leave without telling her to leave.

"I'll do it."

"Do what?" Lou said not understanding.

"I'll co-sign the loan and make the payment while everything is being fixed up. In exchange for the deed to the property when you die," Liz said confidently.

Lou looked at her in amazement. "You're out of your damn mind. You don't know me. And don't know where you get off trying to swoop in and inherit my home. You don't know what it will take to make anything out of this place. It's like putting lipstick on a hog. There's not enough paint in Sherwin Williams or Mop 'n Glo in Walmart to make this place something anybody else would wanna see, let alone rent for an event or take a tour of."

"I think you're wrong."

"I think you're a fucking moron. And a stranger. And obviously if you had as much money as you have common sense you wouldn't have enough to wipe your ass with. It's time for you to go home."

"Okay. Well, the offer stands," Liz said without hesitation and unfazed by Lou's insults. She walked back inside, ahead of Lou. "Thanks for a fun evening! I'll call you later this week and we'll catch up and maybe do something over the weekend."

It was really starting to grate on Lou's nerves that nothing she said could piss off Liz. She wanted a reaction. She needed a reaction. And Liz was refusing to give her one. Every single time she lost her temper, Liz simply refused to entertain it. It was absolutely, positively infuriating for Lou.

18

Klark Kitchens walked out of Little Chuck's house, not really addressing the crimes or the altercation that had just taken place. A lot could be at stake here, for both. At this point, Klark was pretty much convinced that Chuck didn't have anything to do with Judy's death but tampering with evidence was still a crime. Of course, so was negligence on the part of a law enforcement officer. Maybe they would both keep their mouths shut.

Mouth shut or not, Klark wouldn't forget what he read in Judy's note. It explained so much, really. Small towners talk, but they also sweep a lot under their rugs. He didn't know a whole lot about the Jackson family, truth be told. They were a pillar of the community. They had the accounting firm downtown for generations. They had more money than God. Josie Jackson had babysat him as a kid. He swam in their pool. He had been around Little Chuck and Judy his whole life, but they weren't quite "friends," they just co-existed in Clanton. He knew even less about the elder Jacksons. Big Chuck had been old since Klark had been a kid. Big Chuck's spinster sister Joan played bridge with Klark's Aunt Cookie. Louise died before he was born; massive heart attack at a young age, he'd always heard.

But Judy's note revealed other things. Unexpected things. Things that wouldn't sit right in Clanton. Klark wouldn't say anything, out of obligation to his duty as sheriff, out of respect for the deceased, and out of loyalty for Josie. She had always been good to him. He had been a little sweet on her as a kid, the attractive babysitter a couple years older. But she was just that, a babysitter. She never charged his parents much, knowing they couldn't afford much. She treated him like a little brother. They lost touch when she moved to Atlanta for school, but she always held a special place in his heart and his childhood memories.

Little Chuck looked around the house. So quiet. Maybe never this quiet before, except for when absolutely no one was there after Josie left and they had moved to The Gables. Not much was out of place, even after the slew of people who had been in and out of the house during the day.

Judy's Royal Doulton painted ladies figurines were still on the dining room buffet untouched. The green Wedgwood pieces were still on display in the living room. The chairs and tables were all still in their spots. It was as if everything was the same, yet absolutely nothing was the same. There was so much on his mind that he just sat down in the empty house on the sofa and kicked off his shoes. He put his feet on the coffee table. He was surprisingly comfortable in the house where his wife had just killed herself.

Chuck laid his head back and closed his eyes. Just for a moment.

Before he realized it, he had fallen asleep. He probably would have slept the whole night on the sofa if his phone hadn't rung. Who on earth would be calling at this hour?

"Hello?" he answered abruptly, wide awake now, suddenly realizing the last time he had talked to anybody on the phone was when he had answered Joan's plea for help upon finding Judy.

"Mr. Chuck, I'm sorry to call you so late, but the police are here. They said they need to talk to you. I told 'em I wasn't sure where you was but I'd call you. They said they'd wait. They're in the front parlor now. I think you need to get over here, quick."

"I'm on my way."

Chuck sped home to The Gables to see two police cars in the circular driveway. This wasn't good. Not at this time of night. Had Klark called his bluff and turned him in for evidence tampering? Chuck swore to God if he had that Klark would live to regret it. Busting through the front door, always unlocked, he turned to see three officers sitting on his mama's Queen Anne style sofa and East Lake chairs. It didn't exactly look like they were ready to arrest anyone.

"What's all this about?" Little Chuck demanded.

The officers all stood in unison as if they were operated with one set of marionette strings. One of them finally spoke up. "Mr. Jackson, it's about your building downtown."

What on God's green earth were they talking about? The last thing on his mind was the office.

"What about it?" Chuck asked, impatiently.

"There's been a fire, sir. By the time somebody noticed, it was pretty well lit. The fire department is still working on it, but we need you to go down there so we can start the investigation with the fire marshal."

Jesus Christ, another investigation. Another staple of his life falling apart around him. A building occupied by four generations of Jacksons gone up in smoke. Ruby had been standing in the hall behind Little Chuck, unable to believe what she was hearing. Something awful was afoot. She couldn't believe the misfortune surrounding them right now.

Before Little Chuck could even muster a response, an emotionless, hollow voice from the hallway said, "Well let's go see what happened."

"Daddy, what are you doing out of bed? Sit down!"

"Mr. Chuck, you can't be up out here like this without your walker!" Ruby wailed.

"Shut up, all of you," Big Chuck scowled. "This place is going to hell in a handbasket and I'm going to see what's going on since there's no damn body else competent enough around here to do it."

That stung Little Chuck's pride. Big Chuck meant for it to, but probably not as much as it did. He never could judge just how to talk to his son. Little Chuck's emotions were different. He was sensitive in a way neither Big Chuck, Louise, or Lou had been. But Big Chuck was right. Whatever black cat has crossed their road, whatever ladder they'd walked under, umbrella opened inside the house, or salt spilled on the ground, the Jacksons were having an unexplained bout of bad luck.

The family loaded up in Little Chuck's Lexus, led downtown by the patrol cars. When they turned onto the Clanton square, the smoke was all anyone could see. They stopped the cars in the middle of the blocked street. No one else would be traveling through at this point anyway. Joan and Ruby got Big Chuck out of the car while Little Chuck walked towards the site with the deputies.

He couldn't believe it. Over a hundred years of work, blood, sweat, tears, money poured into this building, this business. All reduced to a pile of rubble. Words escaped him. He just wandered around looking like a lost puppy. He looked to see if anything was salvageable, but it was hard to tell. The building was brick, so the general structure was still there, but everything inside and out was blackened beyond recognition. The front window of the narrow building had been smashed. The wide front door was broken off the hinges and hanging on by one or two screws into the frame. It was still too dangerous to walk into, so he just stood there, staring.

Big Chuck was leaning on his walker, talking business to the fire chief and the sheriff's deputies with a renewed sense of purpose, handling the matter at hand as if he was the Spruce Goose. "And as far as you can tell, there's no indication of foul play?" Big Chuck asked.

"Well, it's still too early to say really," the fire chief said. "The marshal will conduct his investigation once everything is cooled off. Could be tomorrow evening or even the next day."

There was that word again: investigation. It was making his stomach churn. Investigation had a negative connotation. A connotation he didn't like to think about. But could all this really be just a coincidence? Joan and Ruby hugged each other, not knowing what to do or say, just knowing this was bad. Things were bad.

After standing around and staring at the tragedy for long enough, Little Chuck decided the family should go home. Big Chuck was getting weaker by the minute, whether he would admit so or not, and there was nothing they could do anyway. They would think about it all tomorrow. Now, not only did they have to tell Josie her mama was dead, but they also had to tell her the family business had gone up in flames–literally.

No one in the house slept that night. Eventually Joan got up first around 5:30 and put on some coffee. Smelling the coffee and hearing the ramblings of a human in the kitchen underneath his bedroom, Little Chuck stirred from his dozing state and stumbled down the stairs in his robe to join his aunt. When he walked into the large room, he saw Joan standing looking out the doors to the screened in porch and the open meadow beyond. She sipped slowly from her coffee mug. "There's more in the pot," she nodded towards the counter without taking her eyes off the back yard. "Figured we'd all need it."

Chuck poured a mug and looked in the fridge for the cream. "We're out of cream," he said out loud, mostly just stating the fact.

"I wouldn't know. I take mine like your granddaddy, you know. Black with half a packet of Sweet 'N Low." She smiled a halfhearted smile remembering her father.

Chuck knew. He knew someone else who took their coffee like that, too.

He joined Joan at the back windows, assuming she was gazing at nothing in particular. "Same way Lou took hers."

Neither said a word. Then Chuck realized what Joan was really looking at. Louise's old garden shed. It hadn't been touched since she'd died. Before that, Louise only went in it if she absolutely had to, but she kept most of her gardening implements on the back porch in an old metal wash tub. She couldn't stand to go in there.

"Daddy wants me to call her, ya know," Chuck said, taking a swig of the bitter black coffee.

"I know, we have to call her and get her up here to tell her about her mama and the office and everything. I'm just dreading it," Joan replied, assuming Chuck had changed the subject.

"That's not who I'm talking about," he replied, looking at Joan eye to eye. "Daddy wants me to call Lou. Track her down. I don't know what to do."

"Well, I say he's an old sick man and he's out of his damn mind. That girl's good as gone and she needs to stay that way. All this family needs is one more embarrassment this week."

"I'm not so sure," Chuck said quietly. "I think he's right."

Joan looked at Chuck incredulously. "You've gotta be kidding me, right? After all this? After all that happened? Your daddy's a dying man trying to get into heaven. He doesn't know what he's talking about, and you'll forget about it if you've got a lick of sense, boy."

"I'm not so sure," Chuck repeated.

19

When the alarm went off on Wednesday morning, Lou gave a guttural groan. She wasn't nearly as enthused about day two at Little Creek as she was for day one. The appeal had certainly diminished. She laid in the bed for a few minutes until the dogs' whining eventually dragged her out.

She fed them and let them out, and then went to pick something out of the closet. She could barely get to anything with all the stacks of junk she had moved into her room to impress that weirdo, Liz Ward. What had she been thinking? Inviting her out here to her home, going to all that trouble. She truly barely knew the woman. For someone who had been so closed off and guarded for thirty years, she sure did let her guard down for Liz, which bothered her. And Liz's off-the-wall offer to restore her house bothered her even more. What kind of stranger offers to make a mortgage payment for someone and then demands to inherit the house when the person inevitably dies of cancer? A nutcase, that's what kind. And Lou had invited her in for supper!

Lou put together an outfit, taking the tags off one of her new outlet store tops. Letting the dogs back in, she jumped into the shower and readied herself for day two. With a travel mug of coffee and a Walmart muffin in a napkin, she headed out to the car.

She placed her tote in the passenger seat and her breakfast, if you could call it that, in the cup holders. She put the key in the ignition and turned it. No go. Lou began to panic. She turned the key again and again without an ounce of result. Son of a bitch. The car wouldn't even turn over. Must be the alternator, Lou thought. Shit, shit, shit. Here she was on her second day of work in her life, and she couldn't make it there. It wasn't like she could call a cab, either.

There was one person she could call, she figured. The nutcase.

Back inside she went, the dogs thoroughly confused. She dialed Liz Ward's cell phone.

"A bit early for an insult, isn't it?" Liz answered.

"Look, my car won't start, and I need a ride to work. Will you come get me?"

"Hmmm. Giving a ride to a perfect stranger? Wouldn't that make me, quote 'a fucking moron'?" Liz preened.

"I'm sorry, okay? Is that what you want? I'm sorry. You're a nice person. Too nice. And I'm not. And I don't have anybody else to ask for a ride so will you give me one or not?" Lou huffed.

"Be there in a few." Lou bristled as she made out a smirk in her voice. Her face felt hot.

Liz arrived in the Subaru and unlocked the doors. She didn't say anything, which, again, made Lou mad. "I'm sorry. I'm a bad person. I can't let my guard down. You've been nothing but kind to me and I've been a bitch. So, I'm sorry. I guess it's been so long since I've had a friend, I don't remember how to be one," Lou admitted, realizing she had apologized more this week than she had in decades prior. She really didn't mean to hurt Liz, but she knew she was, whether Liz was showing it or not.

"You don't have to apologize. I made assumptions. I made outlandish offers. We don't know each other, but I'd like to. I'd like to know more."

"More about what?" Lou wondered aloud.

"About this place," she said as they drove down the driveway. "About this town. About how you ended up in this hell hole."

"About you," she added, quietly.

What did that mean? Lou was willing to be a friend, but there was still a lot she wasn't willing to share. Things that were too painful to share, too embarrassing, even.

"Well, let's just take it a little slower is all I ask. And by a little slower I mean not reverse mortgaging my own house to me. Deal?"

"Deal," Liz replied, considering how her offer must have come off– not quite as well-intentioned as she had meant for it to.

The rest of the drive to Little Creek Elementary School was mostly quiet. Liz dropped Lou off and told her she would pick her up around 3:00. In the meantime, she would call her mechanic friend and have him drive out to the farm to check out the trouble with Lou's car.

Lou was surprised at the generosity but was in no position to decline it. She replied a simple thank you and went into work.

The women here weren't very nice, Lou decided about the rest of the office at Little Creek. Even Janine, the principal and fellow Phi Mu, was a bit cold. She decided it was only her second day of work after all, so the folks deserved more of a chance to prove themselves otherwise. But there was still something she just couldn't put her finger on. They walked around her and looked at her like she was stricken with the plague. She kept checking her makeup and hair in the mirror but found no surprises. She suddenly felt empathy for zoo animals getting ogled from afar.

Lou tried to make small talk with the other person in the office with her, the bookkeeper named Jill. Jill responded to Lou but didn't carry much of the conversations on her end. Lou thought everybody in the south was friendly, but this was yet another instance where it became clear Kentucky was not exactly the true south.

When Liz picked her up at 3:00, Lou was thoroughly perturbed. Liz could sense it.

"Who pissed in your Cheerios?" she asked.

"I haven't done anything to these people here and everybody looks at me like a bastard at a family reunion. I've done everything they've asked me to do. I'm learning all the systems. I feel like I'm doing a good job, especially for someone who hasn't ever worked before."

"Hmm. That seems odd," Liz frowned. "Maybe I'll check in with Janine tomorrow."

"No, absolutely not. I don't want to drag the boss into anything. I can hold my own."

"You're not holding it together all that well if you're this upset."

Instead of going on the defense, Lou agreed for a change. "I know, but I don't want to be the guy running to mom on the second day of school. Let me just work it out, please?"

"Talking it out proactively instead of reacting. Progress!" Liz smiled annoyingly.

"Hush. I'm working on it, okay. I'm having to re-learn how to be a friend," Lou confided. "It's been a long time," she added quietly.

"So I gathered." Changing the subject, Liz said, "Jake took a look at your car earlier. Shitty alternator just as you suspected. He had a refurb at the shop he took out of a junked 4Runner. Running right as rain now."

"You mean, you just like, handled all that? Without asking me?" Lou said, not defensively but also not exactly thrilled.

"It needed to be done. I'm not an Uber driver, sis."

"I know that, but I don't know how I'm gonna pay for it. I don't have hardly anything until my first paycheck hits."

"Oh, worry about it later, no biggie," Liz brushed off the situation.

"It's big to me. I don't want a handout. It's going to look like I'm taking advantage of you."

"To whom? Neither of us have a friend in the world except the other!" Liz laughed. Lou couldn't exactly disagree.

"Still. I'd prefer not to be in debt to you. I'll pay you back when I get my first check, I promise."

"Sure, Jan," Liz said, mocking the famous Brady Bunch line.

Lou decided to ask about her friend for a change. So far, she had been the only one fielding questions. If this were to genuinely work out, Lou ought to know more about Liz, too. That way she could just consider her a nutcase, not a nutcase stranger.

"So how was your day?" she opened.

"Meeting with the superintendent first thing this morning. Had to provide my staffing report and he was pleased I had filled the vacancy at Little Creek," she smiled, "So if you'd not screw that up, that would be great. Had to go visit one of the middle schools to work on a job description for the new academic coach position they want to create for next year. Ate a late lunch. Submitted your new hire packet, you're welcome. Then came to pick you up. That's about it."

"Sounds boring," Lou chuckled. "Not nearly as entertaining as when I had to hold a wad of tissues up a bloody nose for ten minutes this morning or when I had to explain to an irate parent that their child actually, in fact, does not even attend our school so I wasn't sure why he was upset with our after-school offerings."

"Ah, to be back in the schools again. I don't miss it for a minute," Liz mused.

"So, you taught before you went to the county office?"

"Yep, 18 years, high school AP psychology, then school counselor. That was back in Louisville. When this job as hiring manager came up, I applied and got it. Sounded like a good idea to sail towards retirement in a smaller system in a higher role."

"Sounds like it," Lou replied, not knowing what to add to that. Then it hit her. "Wait a minute. That's why you can read me like a book, isn't it? You keep that calm, cool, collected attitude all the time. You're using your teacher skills on me!"

Liz laughed, "You found me out! I throw up my hands. I was a public-school teacher, nothing bothers me."

"It all makes sense now!" Lou laughed, too.

By this time, Liz was pulling in front of Lou's house. "Go check that car out. I don't want another morning call tomorrow."

Lou hopped out, pulled the keys out of the console, stuck it in the ignition, and it turned over just fine. "Like brand new!" she hollered to Liz from the car with a thumbs up sign.

"You're welcome, buddy!" Liz replied, putting the car in reverse. "Better go let out those mangy beasts of yours. They look pissed," she motioned towards the front door where Lucy sat in one sidelight and Lizzy in the other like lawn ornaments.

20

Once nine o'clock rolled around, the family agreed to call R.J. first to see if he was either still home or could go home. Little Chuck made the call. R.J. was driving, but seeing his father-in-law's name on the screen, he picked up almost immediately. Chuck never called him. Ever.

"Hello?" R.J. answered, not knowing what he could possibly be walking into on this call.

"Hey, buddy. I need to talk to you."

These words were never good. Like being called into the principal's office when you weren't sure what you'd been caught doing.

"What's going on?"

"R.J., Judy's died. I need you to go and get Josie and bring her home."

"Oh my God. What happened?" He began to panic. "What am I supposed to tell Josie?"

Firmly, Chuck replied, "Nothing. You're gonna tell her y'all have to come up here and see me. That it's urgent. You're not gonna tell her why. She's still working from home, right?"

"Uh, yeah. She was just getting on a call when I left. Let me call my office and tell them I'll be late, and I'll go home and get her and bring her up there," R.J. replied, already feeling scattered.

"You're not gonna be in late." R.J. was confused, but before he could say so, Chuck replied, "You won't be in today. Or for the next several days. Go get Josie and get up here to The Gables." It was a command, not a question.

“Yes, sir.” The line clicked as he uttered the last syllable.

R.J. pulled over to call Josie. He was as nervous as a cat in a room full of rocking chairs. Josie could see right through him, always. How was he supposed to get her to Clanton without telling her why?

“Hey hon, I need you to cancel your meeting and take the rest of the day off.”

“Ooooh! Are we playing hooky together? Should I put on those new panties I bought last weekend?” she giggled, cluelessly.

Without time for small talk, R.J. responded flatly, “No. We’re going to Clanton.”

Not understanding, Josie said, “What the hell would we do that for? We were just there for Fathers’ Day. That was quite enough to tide me over for a while…”

“Your momma’s dead, Josie. Now pack a bag and get ready to go. I’m turning around on Peachtree now and I’ll be home to get you in about 10 minutes.” R.J. had the phone hung up on him for the second time in less than five minutes. Apparently, it was a hereditary trait.

Little Chuck knew when he saw Josie’s name on the screen of his phone that R.J. had failed to follow the simple instructions. Damn that boy. He turned on the phone and before he could utter a word, Josie said, breathlessly, “Is it true?”

“Yeah, it is.” Chuck knew there was nothing other that she may be asking about. He knew there was no point in beating around the bush, he had to shoot straight with her, like she always had with him. He could hear her breathing becoming more labored over the phone. After all these years he could predict and notice her panic attacks before they happened. “Just breathe, baby. It’s gonna be okay. Just breathe with me. One, two, three…”

“What happened?” she demanded to know.

“We’ll talk about everything when you get here, I promise. I love you, but y’all need to just get here and we’ll sort everything out.”

Josie hung up on him, too. Just as R.J. was walking through the apartment door. Without speaking, the two packed overnight bags, medicines, and toiletries. They locked the door behind them and made their way to the car. It wasn’t until they were on I-75 for several minutes that R.J. broke the silence. “Are you okay?” he asked quietly.

“My mother just died, goddammit. Do you think I’m okay?”

Treading lightly, “Well, you haven’t said anything. You aren’t crying. You don’t seem upset. I’m just concerned about you is all.”

“I took two Klonopin and a Xanax while I was on the phone with Daddy. I’m ready to take on the world,” she said sarcastically.

R.J. didn’t say anything else for the rest of the hour and a half drive. Neither did Josie.

They pulled off the interstate and headed towards Clanton on the two-lane road that connected the small town to I-75, or the last chance at civilization, as R.J. referred to it the first time Josie took him home to meet her family in this backwoods backwards town stuck in 1960. An Atlanta native, he didn’t know places like Clanton still existed in real life. Manicured lawns on every street, huge canopy trees, a historic downtown district, people biking and driving golf carts without a care in the world. In their world, there may not be any cares, he mused, driving through the downtown area to get to The Gables.

That’s when Josie saw her next surprise. The charred remains of Jackson Auditing and Planning. Her eyes caught it seconds before R.J.’s but it stopped them dead in their tracks. What on earth was going on up here and why were they the last people in all of creation to find out?

Again, neither could speak. R.J. kept driving towards The Gables. Wondering what had happened. Wondering if it had anything to do with Judy's death. Wondering what Josie was wondering, or if she was wondering the same things.

When the pair drove through the gates and up to The Gables, nothing seemed out of place. Unsure of what they expected to see, it was a relief for both to see something exactly as it should have been. When they walked up the front steps, the only thing different on the porch was the wicker side table pulled out next to the door with sticky notes and an ink pen and loaded down with food.

In the south, people don't know what to do when somebody dies other than bake and have their best dark-colored clothes sent to the dry cleaner. Deaths in Clanton, Georgia evoked the three Cs: cakes, casseroles, and cards.

Since the news broke yesterday, The Gables had been overrun with all three. Ruby was doing her best to keep up with all of them. Food sorted and stored properly, recording who brought what. Stacking the cards in the order they were received. She hadn't had to do this for the Jacksons in nearly thirty years since Ms. Louise had died. That was the last death in the family.

When Little Chuck and Judy got married, then when Josie was born, and again when Josie got married, Judy had insisted on handling it all herself. She took such pride in these moments for her family. She cranked out thank you notes on her signature embossed ivory stationery from Crane's the day after her wedding shower. Then she was writing them again, still in the bed, two days after she had given birth to Josie. It was the same stationery she used to write her very last note, the one of much mystery, confusion, and misunderstanding. The one that revealed more than Judy had ever said out loud to anyone in Clanton.

Josie opened the big front door (unlocked as always–did anyone in this town even lock doors?) with R.J. behind her, looking in every direction for her father, forgetting everyone else.

Hearing the door bust open, Joan, Ruby, and Little Chuck got up from the kitchen table. Before they could make their way out into the hallway, Josie was yelling, "Daddy, where are you?"

Coming from the back of the house, the three met Josie and R.J. in the middle. Little Chuck went in for a hug, only to be pushed back. He was caught off guard. "What happened? What happened to mama? What happened to the office?" Her breathing could barely keep up with her questions, despite her heavy medication.

"Let's sit down, baby." Chuck tried to soothe her, physically turning her body towards the front parlor where they could explain the events of the past 24 hours, and why Josie was the last to know about them. The family sat down in eerie silence, only to be interrupted by a shuffling noise coming down the hall. Ruby got up to see what it was.

"Now Mr. Chuck, you know you supposed to be in the bed!"

"Oh, hush up. My only granddaughter is here. Despite the circumstances, I'm going to get up and give her a hug." Josie rose from the sofa to embrace her grandfather, leaving Little Chuck curious as to why he had gotten the cold greeting and his daddy the warm one. "Honey, I'm so sorry. About all of this."

The pair broke down together. The room broke down. Everyone had had their individual episodes, but this was the first time the entire family was together. The first time everyone could grieve the events in unison. When the tears seemed to subside after a few moments, Josie sat back down, and Ruby eased Big Chuck into a chair.

Taking back over as patriarch, Big Chuck began to narrate the story of one of the worst days the Jackson family ever had.

"Your mama said she was going over to the house to clean some stuff out. That was all she mentioned to anybody. She came into my room and told me where she was going. She hugged me, which wasn't out of the ordinary, and she left. When Joan came in from the drug store, she asked Ruby where your mama was. Ruby told her, and Joan decided to go over and help her since she didn't really have anything else to do." He motioned towards Joan, and she nodded her head in agreement. He continued, "Joan got over there and couldn't find her. She looked upstairs, outside. Her car was there so she knew your mama had to be there somewhere. She went down into the basement, thinking maybe that's where Judy had decided to clean stuff out."

Josie was looking as confused as ever. "Joan walked down, and that's when she found her."

"What happened? Did she fall or something?"

"No," Joan spoke up, looking at Little Chuck to finish the story.

"Your mama had hanged herself, Josie. She tied a rope around a rafter and climbed up on that old piano bench down there. She stepped off it."

Josie had the most horrific look on her face that Little Chuck had ever seen. She began to sob again, R.J. comforting her this time, holding her in his arms.

After a minute or so when the worst of Josie's crying had subsided, Big Chuck continued the story. "So, Joan called everybody 911 could dispatch, and then she called your daddy. He didn't know what was going on."

"Joan couldn't even get the words out," Little Chuck recalled. "I got there, and you would have thought it was September 11th all over again. Police, fire, ambulances. I went in and found Joan, found everything out," Chuck said somberly.

Big Chuck picked up the story. "And that's when your daddy decided tampering with evidence was a good idea and brought your mama's suicide note here," he said matter of factly, shocking everyone in the room, Little Chuck included.

"Dammit, Daddy, what did you have to go and say that for?" he screamed, jumping out of his place on the end of the sofa.

"Because it's true!" Big Chuck said with fire in his voice. "You dumb sonofabitch. What do we have to hide anymore?"

Everyone in the room was growing more confused by the moment, and no one knew what to say or do. "Daddy, I was trying to keep that note and what it said private. That was my note, written for me to see!"

"Wait a minute," a confused Josie said. Her eyes were red from crying, but her face was wrinkled in misunderstanding. "What did the note say?"

Joan, Ruby, Josie, and R.J.'s eyes looked to Little Chuck for an answer. But Little Chuck's eyes were on Big Chuck. Eyes with a look that could kill.

"Does this have something to do with the fire at the office?" Josie asked. Now it was Little Chuck's turn to look confused.

"How did you know about that?" he asked.

"We saw it when we drove through town on the way out here."

It didn't occur to Chuck that they would see that before he had a chance to explain it, but best that it was all laid out now for Josie to see the disaster she was joining in on.

"The office caught fire last night. It was all ablaze before anybody could even get over there. I was at our house, putting the note back."

Big Chuck spoke up, "Looks like a total loss, according to Chief Hendrix."

"But we won't know for sure until the fire marshal does an investigation. Not sure how long that will take."

"I told the chief there was really no need for an investigation," Big Chuck replied with no qualms at all. "They'll probably still do one, seems it's protocol these days for any structure fire."

"You what?" Little Chuck couldn't believe what his father said. "They have to investigate the cause of the fire in order for us to get the insurance payout, Daddy!"

You could hear a pin drop in the room, despite there being six people occupying the space. No one had anything to add or anything to ask because it seemed like the main conversation at hand was between the two Chucks. You could cut the tension in the room with a knife.

Big Chuck said, confused, "The building was old. The wiring was older than me. Didn't you wonder why you couldn't run the microwave and your space heater at the same time?" he giggled. "It was a lost cause. There wasn't an agency that would insure that place for years. There is no payout. They might still do an investigation, but there's not a dime coming back to us."

Little Chuck fell back into his seat again. He was feeling nauseous. His head was spinning. More and more surprises kept emerging, and he wasn't sure he could take even one single more. Just when he thought Big Chuck might save him once again…

21

"Maysville Bank & Trust, how may I direct your call?"

"Loans, please. SBA loans," Liz answered.

"One moment."

Liz sat on hold, thinking about what she was about to do. She wasn't going to go through with anything without Lou's consent, of course, but she wanted to have her ducks in a row before she presented her plan. This was a million-dollar idea if ever there was one. It would get Lou out of debt, make her a pretty penny, and save that stunning old property from withering away.

"SBA office?" a well-spoken older man answered.

"Hey there! My name is Liz Ward, and I wanted to inquire about some of the loans you offer."

"Well, you're in the right place! Tell me about your needs and we can figure out what we can do for you," he replied cheerfully.

"I'm just shopping around right now." Liz didn't want to sound too eager. "But I'm looking to start a business that's going to need some capital to get off the ground. I want to know what my options are."

"Gotcha! Let's start with the kind of business. What are we looking at here? That will help me guide you to the right offer for you."

"Well, nothing is for sure yet," she replied vaguely. "There's still a lot in the air. But the gist of it is that I have a property. A large one. Fifty acres outside of town, and a big, grand old house." She might have been stretching that last part a bit. "The property needs an overhaul to reach its full potential. I need to renovate and restore."

Not understanding, the man said, "Well I think what you're looking for is a home renovation loan. If you'll hold on, I'll get you to the right…"

"No, sir. It's going to be a business. I just haven't decided exactly what yet." Liz replied, trying to sound surer of herself than she was feeling."

The loan officer chuckled. "If you don't even know what kind of business you're starting, how am I supposed to give you a business loan? You know how crazy that sounds, right?"

Liz knew. To get the best plan laid out to talk Lou into this, she had to take her original idea and run with it. If it didn't work out, she could try something else.

"It's going to be a wedding venue. A historic Maysville farm converted to a new wedding venue."

22

The prospect of absolutely no insurance money had Little Chuck reeling. He had no hope now that there wouldn't be any insurance money. Everyone in the room picked up on the change in Little Chuck's demeanor, but no one quite knew why.

Jarred from his thoughts, Josie asked him again, "So what was in this note you messed with? What was such a big deal that you needed to hide? Did Mama do something bad?"

Big Chuck, Ruby, and Joan all shifted in their seats uncomfortably, leaving Little Chuck to field this question. Everyone knew the answer. Joan never saw the note, but she knew about what was in it, most of it anyway. But no one felt compelled to reveal family secrets quite this deep at this moment in time.

"Your mama didn't do anything bad," Little Chuck replied slowly and flatly, emphasizing the word bad. "It just wasn't anything good," this time stressing the word good.

For the first time since this family conference began, R.J. spoke out. "Christ on a Cracker, Chuck, spit it out. This isn't some southern gothic novel where you keep us on the edge of our seats. Out with it!" No one in the room, Josie included, had ever seen R.J. so infuriated, so in-charge in a moment's notice. It surprised everyone.

Prompted by R.J. and responding with a stern look to remind him who was in charge of this family, Big Chuck spoke next. He didn't know if his son had it in him to say what needed to be said. He also wasn't sure he wanted Little Chuck to be the one to paint the narrative, either. This was a delicate matter for all of them. Especially in the south, especially here in Bible Central.

"Your mother had a lover, Josie."

It wasn't a lie, everyone in the room but the kids knew it wasn't a lie. But everyone was so interested in how Big Chuck was going to spin this that none of them added to the story.

"Okay, so she was sleeping with some random guy. People have affairs all the time, they don't kill themselves. Hell, I can't name any of my friends whose parents HAVEN'T had at least one extramarital encounter," Josie mused at a time that no one should be amused. "But none of them committed suicide. What was different about this?"

The eyes in the room were still on the narrator of this story. "The lover wasn't just some random guy, baby," Big Chuck said gently.

"Then who was it?" Josie looked around the room for someone somewhere to please enlighten her because she was losing her patience quickly.

"Judy was caught. She was doing something which, at the time, was considered a lot more wrong than it should have been, but it was." Big Chuck's liberal attitude surprised the elders in the room, but they didn't feel it appropriate to mention it at this point in time.

"What was my mother doing? On all things holy, what was so bad that y'all are shielding it from me like this? Was she worshiping Satan? Drowning kittens in a well? WHAT?" She hollered, demanding an answer.

Unexpectedly, Joan felt it was her turn to speak up, taking the reins of the story right out of her older brother's hands without asking. No one knew exactly what bomb Joan was about to drop, but they had a feeling. "Yesterday, hanging in that basement, wasn't the first time we found your mama doing something bad," Joan said darkly. She paused before continuing, taking a deep breath before saying, "The first time was about 35 years ago when we caught her out back in the garden shed having sex with your Aunt Lou."

23

Thursday morning came with Lou even less thrilled about going to work than the day before. Could she call out sick, she wondered. How many sick days do you accrue after two days on the job?

Remembering the overdue bill on the kitchen table from East Kentucky Power Cooperative, Lou dragged herself out of bed, yawning. It was getting harder and harder to stumble to the kitchen and pour herself a cup of ambition, as suggested by the words of the sainted Dolly Parton.

Morning routine complete, Lou walked out to the car, crossing her fingers that it would crank this time. Thankfully, it turned right over, and she was on her way out the drive. She noticed her beat up mailbox close to the road filled to the brim again with junk mail and, undoubtedly, more bills. She made a mental note to empty it on her way in from work.

Lou pulled in at Little Creek Elementary, noticing a few faculty and staff standing out in the parking lot next to a car talking. When they noticed her parking, they all turned and stared.

What the hell was this? Some kind of cult? Was she going to be initiated or burned at the stake? To be determined at this point, she figured.

She got out of her car, grabbed her leather bag, and locked the doors. She walked into the school, acting as if she didn't notice her co-workers or their stares. When she clocked in and sat down at her desk, she realized her computer was already on. Strange, she thought, but she brushed it off. Maybe she just forgot to sign out of it yesterday.

Teachers and students started filling the halls of Little Creek, another ordinary day. Friday Eve! Lou was looking forward to the weekend. She realized this was the first time she had a reason to look forward to an actual weekend in years and she considered it a novel concept, amusing herself at her desk as she opened emails and started her daily duties.

It was about ten when Lou fielded a phone call. According to the caller ID, it wasn't a usual external call; it was a direct dial from the county office. Suddenly she was nervous, wondering what this was about. She answered the phone as usual, "Good morning, Little Creek School, how may I help you?" Expecting someone scary on the other end.

It was Liz. Still scary enough, she supposed. "Hey sis, what brings you on the horn this early in the morning?" Lou was finally growing more and more comfortable with her new friend.

"I heard about something this morning, and I wanted to let you know first."

Lou began to panic. What had Liz heard? Was it something about work? Was it something about the farm? Lastly, was it something about her past? Even worse–it was all three.

"Apparently someone got the ear of the deputy superintendent."

"About what? I've been doing just fine here," Lou was growing defensive again.

"Someone suggested something, and the superintendent had someone from IT come out last night and get into your computer."

"Well, that explains why it was on when I got here, but what were they trying to find? They don't let me handle the money yet. The worst email I've sent was telling a parent that, no, they could not send an emotional support parrot to school with their first grader. What could I possibly have done improperly?"

"It isn't something they think you've done at school. It's what they think you do outside of school."

"I don't get it," Lou said, genuinely confused.

"Someone told the deputy super that they thought you were a lesbian and that you were a danger to children, Lou."

She sat silently for a moment. "Who told them that?"

"I really don't know. But this is still a small town with some small minds. People see something out of place, hear something, speculate, and then things run rampant. Just asking here, not accusing you of anything, but was there anything they might find that was untoward on your computer?"

"No! Of course not! Give me some credit here, I'm not an idiot."

"Okay, I know, I just wanted to make sure before we approached this."

For the first time in a very long time, Lou didn't feel alone. Liz wasn't attacking her. She wasn't accusing anything. She was in this with Lou. She was legitimately trying to help her. And it helped in more ways than Lou had ever realized it might.

Lou spent the rest of the morning not saying a word to a single person. She had no way of knowing who started this rumor, and she wasn't about to give anyone a shred of satisfaction in being able to determine its credibility. So, she kept to herself. She did her work. She followed instructions. And she went home.

She turned into the road to her house after a quiet day and remembered her overflowing mailbox. She put the car in park at the apron of her driveway and jumped out. She loaded her arms with all the junk and tossed it to the passenger side of her car and drove towards the house, driving into the porte cochere as usual. She grabbed the bundle of mail and headed inside to be greeted by her girls. She let them out and laid the mail on the kitchen counter.

Fixing herself a Diet Coke over ice, she pulled the garbage can closer so she could sort the mail, knowing the vast majority would be junk. Separating the junk from the bills, she came upon the first piece of personal mail she had received since she moved here, except for the documents from Helen and the real estate agent.

Lou's name was addressed in perfect cursive on an embossed ivory envelope. Even after 35 years, she recognized that stationery without reading the return address on the back. It stopped her dead in her tracks. Her heart began beating out of her chest, her hands shaking. She wasn't sure if she should open it right now, or if she even *could* open it right now.

Feelings she had packed away years ago came spilling back. A chapter in a book she had closed forever was reopening in her hands.

24

The room was speechless–quite a feat for a family of loud mouths and strong opinions like the Jacksons. No one knew quite how Josie would react. They were all waiting on edge to hear her response as the only member in the family, besides R.J., who was clueless as to the events 35 years prior.

Josie began, “This was Aunt Lou, Daddy’s sister?” she questioned.

“Yes, that’s the one,” Joan answered with a sarcastic tone.

“Where is she?” Josie asked.

For the first time, no one in the room had an answer whatsoever, real or fabricated.

“She left here,” Big Chuck stated. “We didn't know where she went.” He conveniently left out that he forced Lou out of their home, but no one really felt like bringing that up at this moment in time.

Josie sat back in her seat on the sofa, noticing for the first time just how uncomfortable all the furniture in this room really was. Everyone was looking around, unsure of what to say, waiting for more questions, wondering what else they were going to have to spill.

“So, what does this have to do with Mom’s… suicide?” Josie was treading a little more lightly with the words right now. She didn’t know if the feelings were intensifying, if they were surfacing more, or if her medications were wearing off. Probably a combination of all three.

“That’s what was all in the note,” Little Chuck said. “Your mama lived with a lot of regrets for a very long time. They took a toll on her. I knew they would, I knew they did,” he emphasized the word did. “But I never did anything about it.”

“Now you have to know I loved her. I still do. My feelings never, not even for a moment, changed for her.” Chuck breathed out, “And I wish I could say the same for her.”

“When you were a kid and you looked through old photo albums, you saw pictures of Lou. Her room was still upstairs, essentially untouched since the night she left,” Big Chuck said. “You were big enough to start asking.

“But Ms. Judy wasn’t havin’ it,” Ruby spoke up for the first time since this whole session began. “Her and Ms. Louise had me throw out every trace of Ms. Lou in this house.” She shook her head, mostly in regret. “I threw away every picture, every dress. I took everything that belonged to her outta her back bedroom upstairs. Ms. Louise told me to burn the sheets and quilts and turn it into another guest room. She didn’t want nobody sleeping in that bed, outta fear they might catch it, I guess.”

“And that’s why whenever I asked, Mom told me we don’t talk about her. I guess after all this time, I just put her out of my mind,” Josie said regretfully. “But nobody’s answered my question yet,” she continued. “How is all this connected?”

“We don’t really know, baby,” Little Chuck answered, truthfully. They all knew Judy lived with the regrets, the embarrassment of being caught by family. But why do something about it now? That was the biggest mystery in the family right now. Second only to the situation of the fire at the office.

“Okay, so let’s back up a little bit.” Josie was always the type to analyze and over analyze every event. All ears and eyes were on her during this time, so they waited for her next questions.

“Daddy, you started talking about the fire a minute ago. And you turned about 20 shades of gray when Granddaddy said there was no insurance. It was no secret the business wasn’t doing good. That, among other reasons, was why R.J. wouldn’t come work for you before you hired Peter.”

Instead of gray, Little Chuck was turning dark red. "Now where do you get off saying that? I've worked my ass off to keep that place going. You all know that!" he said with anger rising.

In a soothing voice, Josie said, "We know how hard you've worked, Daddy. But we also know how hard it is to make it in this economy, in a small town, with other big firms able to do so much more for so much less. But your pride, Daddy, you wouldn't let it go. We could all see it, but we didn't have the heart to say it."

Big Chuck had a disappointed look on his face, but he was nodding in agreement. "If I had it all to do over again, I would have closed the place down or sold it for scrap before letting you get tangled in that mess." He put his head in his hands. "Should have let you go to Atlanta when we got wind that the bank was about to sell out."

"Yeah, well that still wouldn't have worked out, Daddy. What clients I did manage to get or keep, eventually went to the bank. I owed Kirby Riffle out the ass after everything, you know that. He kept poaching folks, and I was helpless to do anything about it."

Here we go again, Josie thought. This was like peeling back onions layer by layer, uncovering more and more drama and backwoods bullshit. And they all wondered why she skated out of this town and never came back except for birthdays and holidays.

"Kirby was here that night, Josie," Chuck declared, knowing her next question before she asked it. "He saw everything like all the rest of us did. It was the night before I married your mama."

"Everybody in town knows about all this but ME?" Josie complained.

"Good work making this about you, honey," Aunt Joan quipped back with a dirty look.

"Listen, back to the previous topic. Why is the lack of insurance money such a big deal?" Josie was attempting to bring this discussion back full circle.

“Because now we don’t have anything to fall back on. With this economy, we don’t have a pot to piss in or a window to throw it out of.”

25

The phone rang, but Lou couldn't let go of the note. She let it go to the answering machine. Still holding the note, unable to move her body, she recognized the voice on the machine.

It was Liz. "Are you home yet? We have to talk. Call me." There was no warmth or friendliness in the tone of this message.

For the second time today, Lou was panicking with Liz on the other end of the line. She picked up the receiver just before the machine cut it off. "Hey, what's wrong?"

"I figured out the tip given to the superintendent. And who it came from. I was able to get the IT manager to give me the scoop. When he was going through my computer, too."

"Okay, so who was it? Who cooked this up? What are they trying to find? And why your computer, too?" she asked impatiently.

"Well, first of all, I don't want you to get mad. I was only checking out options. I hadn't done anything; I was only asking the guy at the bank some questions."

"So, some guy at the bank told the superintendent what?" Lou was not piecing this together.

"The guy at the bank told him a couple of lesbians who worked for him wanted a loan."

"A loan for what? I don't get any of this."

"It was my idea. Don't freak out. I haven't done anything, and I wouldn't do anything without talking it over with you, but I feel like I've come up with the perfect plan to save the farm and your house and make back some money–we turn it into a wedding venue!"

“What in God’s name are you talking about?” Lou was returning to her old habits. “Who the hell do you think you are, talking to somebody about loans on MY house and MY property? And what business do you have going around telling anybody I’m a lesbian. You’ve got some fucking nerve, you know that?” Lou spat out the words like used chewing gum.

Liz didn’t know what to say. She never planned for this to come out like this. She wanted a chance to present her plan to Lou, talk her through, ease her into the idea, and convince her it would work. Instead, they were working from the back end forward.

Trying to calm Lou, Liz said, “It was just an idea. I wanted to be able to share some options with you. The banker made it up based on how I was talking, I guess. Turns out, his rumor was right, unfortunately. But I was trying to help you.”

“Yeah, helping me out by telling people I’m an old queer. You oughta be ashamed of making accusations like that.”

“Accusations? Really?” It was Liz’s turn to lay down some law. “I sniffed you out the second or third time I saw you. The lesbian came off you worse than the smell of the Winston cigarettes. I’m no idiot, you know. I can identify another dyke when I see one.”

“A dyke, huh? Well now you know it. You know everything. Congratulations. You now know I’m a poor, old lesbian who never had a job that’s dying of cancer. Great work. Your detective skills are incomparable, fellow dyke!” With that, Lou hung up the phone.

For a moment, she was so upset that she had forgotten the note laying on the kitchen counter. She sat down in a chair and put her head on the table. She began to cry. For maybe the first time since she left Clanton. She was crying about her finances, she was crying about her job, she was crying about being outed again, she was crying about how she had just talked to Liz.

She wasn’t just crying now, she was sobbing. She was sobbing so hard she started hyperventilating. Her breaths couldn’t keep up with her cries. Her chest felt like it was caving in on her. The life was being smothered out of her. She fell out of the kitchen chair, hitting her head on the table on her way down to the ground.

Lou writhed in agony, still unable to breathe. At some point, she passed out on her kitchen floor. Alone. So very alone.

When Lou woke up, all she could see was bright light. Is this really what heaven looks like after all? She frowned. Only if heaven had IV poles…

She was lying in a hospital bed. Where, she didn't know. Why, she wasn't sure.

She was blinking her eyes and stretching her body when someone jumped up out of a chair and came to her bedside. A beautiful woman she couldn't make out at first. She was so groggy, in so much pain. It was Liz Ward.

"What do you want?" Lou barked. She may be ill, but she hadn't lost all her faculties.

"Is that really how you talk to someone who saved your damn life?" Liz chided.

"Saved me from what? I'm fine." Lou went to sit up, but she was stopped by wires, tubes, and cords. An alarm even went off, triggering a nurse's arrival. The nurse eased her back down.

"Ms. Jackson," the nurse talked to her very loudly and very slowly like she was a deaf 80-year-old. "You passed out and you're in the hospital."

"No shit, honey. I thought this was the Waldorf Astoria."

Liz laughed. "I think she's okay," she said to the nurse who had a disapproving look on her face. "I'm gonna keep an eye on her, but we'll buzz if we need you. Thank you for all your help, really," Liz smiled sincerely.

With the nurse out of the room, Lou turned to Liz and demanded to finally know what was going on.

"After you hung up on me, I knew you were mad. I left work and decided to drive out to your house to sort this mess out together."

Together.

"When I got there, the dogs were out, so I knew something was off. They never leave the backyard or the stoop at the kitchen door. So, I put my pistol in my waistband and…"

"Hold up, hold up, hold up." Lou acted her words out with her arms. "You carry a gun, but I'm the dyke?!"

"Oh, shut up." Liz was coming into her own, dealing with Lou's smart-ass remarks. "I was worried something might have happened, so I let myself in your front door."

"That's breaking and entering, by the way." Nothing could keep Lou down.

Continuing with a look that said, allow me to finish, please, Liz said "I made it through the front rooms, calling your name but there was no sign. I walked into the kitchen and found you on the floor. There was some blood, hence the bandage on your head, but you were breathing, albeit shakily."

"Then what, Wonder Woman?"

"Then I called 911. And now we are here."

"Oh Christ, do you know how much an ambulance ride costs? You really could have sent me to the Waldorf Astoria for less than this is gonna run." Liz just shook her head. "So, when can I go home? Obviously, I'm fine."

"Fine is a stretch. In more ways than one," Liz raised an eyebrow. "You passed out for some reason. You hit your head and might have a concussion, to be determined. You were dehydrated and malnourished according to your bloodwork hence the IV. And it seems there's a lot of blood in your chest and esophagus, which is likely from the cancer."

Lou just groaned.

"So, they're keeping you," Liz added quickly, turning back to her chair and her book.

"The hell you say!" Lou sprang up again, setting off yet another alarm. The same nurse came to the door, and Liz assured her all was fine. "I am not staying here. I've got stuff to do. I have the dogs. Work." Lou realized that was the extent of her to do list. She had been living for the dogs, and now she was also living to have a job. She got the job to keep living, to keep living for the dogs. What a miserable existence, she realized.

"The dogs are coming to my house. After a grooming and a good bath, which I scheduled for tomorrow morning. Work can wait. I already told them if they pressed this sexuality issue, I'd file a complaint with the Kentucky Commission for Human Rights and sue the district for every penny they have. They can't afford that, so we both got apologies. I told them we were taking tomorrow off for a three-day weekend. So there. Your to do list is done. Anything else I can take care of for you?"

Lou didn't have a response.

"This getting old shit is for the birds," Lou said aloud after too much quiet in the hospital room.

"I think it's less getting old and more the fact that you have untreated lung cancer," Liz reminded her.

"Oh yeah, maybe." Lou answered, obviously defeated.

Another long pause until Lou blurted out from the hospital bed, "So what are we?"

"What do you mean?' Liz replied, unsure of what Lou meant.

"Our secrets are out. Pun intended," Lou laughed until she realized it magnified the pain in her chest.

Pensively, Liz said, "I've never been the kind of woman who went out looking for someone else. I guess I just thought love passed me by. Especially in the day and age we were brought up in. Truth be told, I never thought I'd be anything but a lonely old woman with a cat. Until I met you."

Lou chose her words carefully. "Do you love me?"

"I don't know. Do you love me?"

"I don't know." Both laughed, despite Lou's pain.

"What I know," Lou began, "Is that I love being around you. I love how you've attached yourself to me, even if slightly against my will. I absolutely HATE the effect you have on me where I feel guilty after a tirade. I haven't had to apologize to anyone for a very long time."

"I think I understand where you're coming from. We're friends, which I think I pushed on you more than you were willing to commit to. And then it just sort of spiraled from there. I'd be lying if I said I didn't find that first night, in the glow of the gas lamps, having that terrible Chinese food on your dining room table, slightly romantic. I wasn't sure if it was the exhaust fumes or me just being so starved for the companionship of another human being."

"I get it. If it wasn't for the dogs, I'd have been stir-crazy years ago. At least when the farm was still going, I was around other people. Had a purpose. It's been a long time since I had a purpose, other than filling dog food bowls," Lou smiled thinking about Lizzy and Lucy.

Changing the subject without realizing it, Liz asked, "Why did you close the farm anyway? I looked in that barn. It's plenty usable. Sure, the fence needs mending, maybe some new equipment. But it still looks operational to me."

Lou sighed, "I didn't know what I was doing. I tried to figure it out for a long time, too long. I didn't know a thing about horses or hogs or markets or the Derby or green grass from blue. I let what clout the farm had in its day die, right along with those old apple trees. Did you know six Derby winners came out of my farm over the years? Second most of any farm in Kentucky." Lou wished she could be proud of that fact, but the reality was that she was the reason there weren't any more than those six.

"I didn't know," Liz replied sincerely. "But what caused you to hang up the reins?"

"I just couldn't get ahead. Seemed like nothing went my way. One step forward, two steps back. For years. I racked up debt. Then I'd be able to pay it off with a good sounder going to market. Next season I'd lose a horse and I was right back where I started. Everything just went to shit, and I couldn't take it anymore," Lou admitted.

Getting more personal, Liz asked, "So what have you done to stay afloat these years since you closed the farm?"

"The oldest profession in the world–I was a horse farm prostitute," Lou said with every ounce of solemnity she could muster, before bursting into laughter.

Liz didn't laugh until Lou laughed because she really didn't know where that comment was going! "For real, what did you do? How many years was the farm closed before you swindled your way into a job with me?"

"Ha. Ha," Lou mocked. "I sold or slaughtered the last animals fifteen years ago now. I tried selling produce after that, but I was organic before organic was cool," she mused. "I sold at farmers' markets but never made it to the big time. It kept me going for a minute."

“Then I worked on the farm next to mine as a farm hand. It was hard work, but it was something to get up for in the morning. Until it took its toll on me,” Lou closed her eyes.

“What do you mean?”

“They weren’t organic like me,” Lou replied. “The herbicides, the insecticides, the diesel fumes. I started getting sick.”

“That’s when you were diagnosed with cancer wasn’t it?” Liz asked, tears forming in the corners of her eyes.

Lou perked up, “Well, we can’t go throwing it all on the chemicals. I’ve smoked since I was 17 years old, ya know. But when they first told me, I blamed it all on the chemicals. Which didn’t earn me much friendship from the neighbors who had employed me.” She whispered, “Alone again.”

“So why the hell are you still smoking, Lou?” Liz couldn’t feign her irritancy.

“Well, I’ve already got the cancer, Liz,” emphasizing Liz’s name in the same fashion, “So how much more harm could really be done?” she laughed again.

Liz didn’t think it was so funny. “So, you still smoke, you’re not getting treatments–what’s going to happen to you?”

“Don’t go getting so self-righteous with me, sis. I haven’t had health insurance in, well, ever. I can’t afford those treatments–surgery, chemo, radiation, everything but a light probe up my ass crack,” Lou grimaced.

“I guess I didn’t think about that. Twenty-eight years with state insurance sort of lulls you into a sense of comfort,” Liz admitted. “I guess I’m pretty privileged; when I sniffle, I go to the doctor, I get an antibiotic, and a few dollars later I’m fine.”

"Yep, that's why I wanted a job working for the schools. A pretty cushy life if you ask me."

"And who asked you?" Liz retorted.

Lou looked surprised, "You're starting to dish it out instead of just taking it from me. I kind of like it!"

Liz grinned, "Don't go getting too attached. I may leave you in this room and never come back, you never know."

"You haven't left yet." That was more than Lou could say about anyone else she'd ever loved.

26

With most of the family laundry hung out to dry, the Jacksons actually sat down to an early lunch. All of them. For the first time in a while. There was quite a spread to behold from the women of Clanton.

Connie Bryans had sent her mother's squash casserole (the secret was pimientos), Peg Wyse had made (aptly named) funeral potatoes while Angie Maldonado sent twice baked potatoes, Anna Kenney brought her husband's award-winning brisket, Melitta Brandt dropped off a cheese platter. Lynn Boyd's idea of cooking was reheating a frozen dinner, so she had an assortment of staple groceries delivered to the house. Lynn Thompson dropped off a bottle of whiskey meant mainly for Little Chuck who loved to drink a good Old Fashioned. She figured he might need it. Christi Granger made a spinach quiche. Bruce Johnston left a coconut cake; Alice Guppy brought a caramel cake. Margaret Lunsford showed up with four pork tenderloins. Wanda Belline sent a platter of cheese straws, along with a gift certificate to her son's restaurant for when the family felt up to going out. Susan Barton left a lasagna, Susan Ragsdale, chocolate mousse (she knew it was Josie's favorite), Susan Stewart, a meatloaf, and Susan Merritt, pasta salad. Linda Coatsworth dropped off a green bean casserole. Ginna Evans had petit fours delivered from Rhodes Bakery. Nancy Martin sent deviled eggs on a platter with chickens on it. Kathy Delaney sent chicken piccata. Kathy Kingsbury baked mini loaves of cranberry orange bread. The third Kathy, Kathy Hatfield left a collection of pastries and cookies to munch on. Carol Reimer brought fried chicken because what's a funeral meal without it?

Every truly southern woman's pantry stays stocked with the basics: cake mix, cream of everything, Velveeta, mayonnaise, and canned vegetables. Now, summer funerals are a little different. It's always a blessing, well, sort of, when someone dies in the summer, because you just know there will be at least one basket of produce on the porch, still warm from the garden. That's when you've hit the funeral food jackpot.

The list going on, Camille Harvey sent a lovely peace lily from her and the Judge, Helen Dorroh sent a dish garden of various plants, Jane Darnell made a donation to the local elementary school PTA, and Beth Wielage sent a huge hydrangea in a woven basket. Alice Murray, a former Atlanta Journal-Constitution publicist, left a sweet note offering to write Judy's obituary for publication. The standard ones from Chapman's Funeral Home were fine for standard people, but Judy Jackson wasn't just anybody.

This community poured out love on this family. When someone dies in a small town, it's not just another day, another death. People mourn the loss; they mourn it together. Friends and neighbors come together to support the bereaved in ways they don't even realize they need sometimes.

When a black bow shows up on a lamp post or a white wreath on a front door, it's a bat signal to folks to stop what they're doing and start funeralizing. It's something that, in a way, transcends affluence, economic status, age, or gender. Like voting, it's just a civic duty.

Now what's usually not talked about in front of company is the behind the scenes work that goes into all of this. Ruby was already just about worn slap out. Not only was she in charge of receiving all these tokens and gestures, but she was also responsible for recording what they were, who they came from, and when they arrived. There was an unspoken competition to be the first to show up with a Pyrex in hand, which is why many women of Clanton kept casseroles in their deep freezers, marked especially for these occasions. These are recipes marked "Freezes Beautifully" with an asterisk in the Mayflower Garden Club cookbook.

This was why when the Jacksons sat down to indulge in this spread, Ruby pulled up a chair to the table herself. No one noticed; Ruby was family as far as anyone was concerned. But they did notice how tired she looked.

Joan was the first to mention it, between bites of macaroni and cheese. “Ruby, you look like you’ve been run over by an eighteen-wheeler.”

“Thank you, ma’am,” Ruby replied with an unappreciative look.

“I didn’t mean anything by it, don’t go getting your panties in a wad. We all know how hard you’ve worked getting all this taken care of,” Joan explained, gesturing towards the food and plants.

“We certainly do,” chimed in Big Chuck. “This may be more than what there was when Louise died,” he recalled. “I remember there being more flowers than food. And what the hell were we supposed to do with all those ugly ass carnations?”

The family laughed, enjoying a light-hearted moment amongst all the sadness and drama that had unfolded over the last two days. “Well, I, for one, am eternally grateful to the matrons of Clanton for offering food over flowers this time,” Josie stated, sucking every morsel of meat off one of Carol’s chicken bones.

“Well, I’ve got silver to polish before the rest of the family gets here.” Ruby said. Joan had been the appointed funeral handmaiden to deliver the news to the extended family. “I’ve got to get Ms. Louise’s wedding china and crystal out of the dining room sideboards. And the napkins all need a fresh press.” Ruby was not looking forward to all these additional behind the scenes funeral duties.

R.J. spoke up, “I’ll help.” The rest of the family turned to look at him. The sentiment was kind, but R.J. was not exactly known for his domestic capabilities. “What? It can’t be that hard. Ruby, I’ll pull out that heavy china and we can give it a wipe down. If you’ll show me what setting to put the iron on and how to fold them right, I can help with the napkins.” Ruby’s mood was lifting with every word. “The only thing I don’t know how to do is polish silver.”

“That’s alright, baby, that’s my job.” Ruby took pride in polishing Ms. Louise’s silver. She’d done so for fifty years now, leaving every piece sparkling like it was showroom new. Other people even brought their silver to Ruby to polish it. Nobody could get a shine or polish out years of tarnish quite like her. She swore by Wright's silver cream and elbow grease, none of those harsh chemicals.

When Louise had married Big Chuck, she had chosen her china, crystal, and silver at Rich's in Atlanta. It was the only place for anybody who was anybody to register at in those days. For her china she chose Lenox Ming Birds, a cheerful pattern of pastel blues and pinks. Her crystal was Waterford's Lismore, perhaps their oldest and best-known pattern. For her sterling pattern, Louise opted for something entirely different from her mother Virginia's Fairfax. She loved intricate designs, so she chose Burgundy by Reed and Barton, the less fussy cousin to Reed and Barton's Francis I. Burgundy was known among silver aficionados as Francis I without the fruit salad in the middle. The tablecloths and napkins were fine old white Irish linen with white embroidery, handed down from Louise's grandmother who had the same monogram (it had been planned this way).

R.J. continued, "Since y'all need to go down to Chapman's today to make the arrangements, I figured I could stay here and help out. Funeral homes give me the heebie jeebies," he said with a shudder.

Fair enough. This was a task for the family. Despite R.J. and Josie being together for five years and married for the past year and a half, they hadn't exactly included him in the expression "family" when they used it. Not for any reason in particular, just that he was still a newbie in their eyes. Not to mention an outsider from the big city. He didn't understand the ways and traditions (that's read as eccentricities) of small-town southern life.

Little Chuck finally piped up, "We've gotta get Judy's things ready before we go down there. Let me call KK and tell him we're going. Apparently, we have to make an appointment to go to our own home," he explained with annoyance.

Joan and Ruby had a perplexed look on their faces. "Didn't you go out to Crystal Springs last night to get all that together?"

Caught off guard, Chuck replied quickly, "Yeah, but I just couldn't decide on anything, so I decided to wait and leave it up to Josie to help me. She has better style than me," he chuckled off the awkward, almost accusatory tone from his aunt and Ruby.

"That's fine," Josie replied. "I haven't seen KK in years. He's the new sheriff, isn't he?"

"He sure is," Chuck answered with an animosity that went unnoticed at the table.

"Let me fix my face and hair and we'll go." Appearances still meant plenty to Josie, no matter how long she'd spent in Atlanta. "Daddy, you call KK and tell him we're going over there." Josie got up from the table, taking her plate to the sink, and grabbing her bag. She frowned. She hadn't been prepared for three or four days of funeralizing. R.J. could wear the same gray suit with a different shirt and tie and be fine, but people would really be looking at her. "Where in this town can I find some decent funeral clothes? There's no way I have enough, we rushed out of the house so quickly."

The family looked at each other, no one coming up readily with an answer. Joan said, "There's a consignment shop off the square next to the Bojangles?" she offered.

"Bojangles Bargains, Aunt Joan, really? Mama would die."

"Again?" Big Chuck quipped, morbidly.

"You hush," Joan chided him. "We'll see what we can find in my closet when y'all get back." Joan and Josie were about the same size. Judy was too petite for Josie to wear anything of hers, not to mention it might be more than a little weird to wear her dead mother's clothes to her own funeral.

"Great, I'll be decked out in the finest Alfred Dunner pants suit from Belk's in Kennesaw, Georgia," Josie teased her aunt.

"Well go in your slip and stocking feet for all I care." Joan dismissed her.

"A. The fact that you're suggesting I wear a slip proves my point, and B. It's the damn middle of summer and I'm 33 years old, I'm not putting on a pair of pantyhose for love or money."

Everyone at the table laughed at the accuracy, except Joan. Even Ruby knew better than Ms. Joan's suggestions. She just shook her head.

Soon after, the family, sans Ruby and R.J., loaded up into the Lexus and made their way across town to the house in Crystal Springs. Little Chuck had called the sheriff's office to ask for permission as he had been instructed previously to do, assuming they would send some deputy who would stand around watching them like fish in a glass bowl.

Imagine the surprise when they pulled up to the house to find the sheriff himself standing on the front porch. Josie got out first while Joan helped Big Chuck out of the backseat. She bounded up the steps and gave Klark Kitchens a big bear hug.

"Look at the goofy little kid I used to babysit, all grown up into a big fancy sheriff!" she teased, stepping away to size up the handsome young man in his perfectly creased uniform. His face turned red, and he couldn't make eye contact with her.

"Nothing too fancy here, same old kid who threw up three hot dogs on the Fourth of July," his eyes darted to Little Chuck, referencing the remark he'd made the day Judy hanged herself.

"Lord, I had forgotten about that!" She laughed. You would have never known her mama was dead, the way Josie was carrying on. "Now tell me, there has to be a Mrs. KK now, right?"

Klark turned red again, "No, ma'am!"

"Ma'am?? I am four years older than you, buddy! I'm not your mama!" She joked, unlocking the front door with her own house key.

The rest of the Jacksons were right behind her, making their way inside. They didn't find a single thing odd about the sheriff of the town being there to escort them into their home, all except Little Chuck, that is.

He hung back while Josie, Joan, and Big Chuck made their way inside. "Aren't you supposed to be watching us like hawks or something, Sheriff?" Chuck mocked the word sheriff with a sing-song voice.

"I'm watching alright, don't you worry. I'm watching the biggest threat in this whole operation." He looked Little Chuck square in the eyes.

Incredulously, Chuck replied, "Me? I don't have anything to hide. Not any more than you anyway," he smirked in the sheriff's face.

Klark stepped closer. Close enough for Chuck to smell the spearmint Skoal on Klark's breath. "You think you've got something on me. But it's nothing compared to arson, buddy."

Chuck turned gray again, just like he had when he heard there was no insurance money.

"Daddy, get in here and help me pick out which jewelry we should put on Mama! Is the good stuff at Granddaddy's?" Josie hollered from the primary bedroom.

"Just a minute, sweetheart," Chuck croaked out. Klark stepped aside, using his hand to lead the way for Chuck to enter his own home.

27

Lou slept hard in the hospital bed that afternoon. She sent Liz home, assuring her she would be fine, and they would continue their "Where is this relationship going?" talk when things had leveled out a bit. Lou joked that she shouldn't have that talk while she was high as a kite.

Laying there, in the darkness, sleeping so soundly, Lou had a dream. It could be blamed on the medications, one might suppose, but it was so real, so vivid. Lou felt like she could reach out and touch her. Judy was standing, just at arm's length. She was saying something Lou couldn't make out. Was she crying? What was she saying?

It looked like she was saying "I'm sorry," but Lou couldn't understand her, couldn't hear her. She reached for Judy, she ached to pull her closer to hear what she was saying. To understand why she was here now.

Shift change woke her from the deep slumber. Her eyes shot open, but her body was unmoving. A new nurse was writing her name on the dry erase board opposite Lou's bed. All she could do was scream at the poor, unassuming nurse to get out, go. She needed to see Judy. To hear her again. To feel her. It had been so long since she felt her. But in this moment, right now, she felt closer to her than she had in 35 years, so close she could almost smell her.

The nurse left the room terrified. She called in a nurse practitioner on duty for the evening, telling him how irate, loud, and rude Lou had been. She may have been exaggerating, but only by a tad. Lou had been so forceful it was almost impossible to not be frightened of her.

She laid there, closing her eyes tightly, willing Judy to come back to her. To visit her again. To tell Lou what she was trying to say. Tears began streaming from Lou's closed eyes, hitting the pillow beneath her head.

Lou knew pain. Thirty-five years of hard work farming took its toll on her body. Lung cancer, gone untreated, except for the pain pills she could sometimes afford. Being ostracized from her family, her whole life turned upside down in moments. Never letting her guard down enough again to try and make friends. But there was no pain worse than the day she lost Judy.

28

"Where did KK go?" Josie looked around, frowning, "I wanted to catch up with him a little more."

"I think he had to go, honey," Joan said, zipping up Judy's garment bag hanging on the hat rack. "He took off right after your daddy came in. Probably just had to be here to let us in for some protocol or something like that."

"He was always such a sweet kid. I wondered how he would turn out," she said to no one in particular.

"He's done just fine," Little Chuck replied dryly, his nerves still jangled by the word Klark had used less than one hour prior.

Changing the subject, Josie said, "Well, we better get down to Chapman's. Unless something's changed, they'll expect us right at 2:00 and not a minute later."

After the elderly and infirm were loaded up, the family made their way to Chapman's Funeral Home, a simple but classy older blonde brick building with white posts and a long front porch with rocking chairs. A Cadillac sedan was parked facing outward in the carport on the side for the funeral director to drive in the processions. A blue Cadillac hearse sat parked behind it for transporting the deceased.

Chapman's was one of three funeral homes in Clanton. It wasn't the oldest, but it was the nicest. There were three funeral homes to correspond with the unspoken Clanton caste system. The families with good life insurance, or plenty of money to pay out of pocket, had used Chapman's since 1951 when J.G. and Florence Chapman opened it.

Alternately, at the very bottom of the list, was Glory Abounds Funeral Home and Crematory. For the low low price of just $895 (without a service) you could put mama in a lovely plastic urn shaped like a peace dove. If you were a traditionalist on a tight budget, you could get “The Works” for $1,795 which included one hour of viewing before the service, the preacher on staff, a CD of funeral hits including "In the Garden,” and a solid woodgrain fiberglass casket. The vault was extra if you took that route, but with all the money you were saving, you could afford it.

The families that fell somewhere in the middle used Robinson’s. These were the folks that might have had a little life insurance, but otherwise were going to need a payment plan to put their folks to rest respectfully.

Old man Chapman had also been the Mayflower County Coroner for 42 years, only to be succeeded by his wife after his death. The town figured she must know a thing or two, after all that time, so she was appointed to fill his unexpired term. She held that role until ‘97 when she finally decided to retire. That was when the “new” coroner was elected. Twenty years into the job now, and the old-timers in Clanton still referred to the woman as “the new coroner.” In their minds no one could replace a Chapman, no matter how good they were.

When the Chapmans first moved to Clanton, J.G. worked for the old Lawson and Poole Funeral Home. During the big Whitestone Flood of 1938, a young J.G. was praised for working around the clock to make all thirteen of the bodies claimed by the flood, ten of them being Forrest and Martha Conner with their children, presentable for their funerals. The flood waters swept the Connor house from its foundation down Talona Creek, killing everyone inside. The tragedy made national news headlines and was also covered in Life Magazine. Mr. Chapman did everything in his power to ensure the dignity of each of the victims and followed suit in his career for many years later.

At this point, Florence Rabun Chapman was the oldest living licensed funeral director in the entire state of Georgia. She still kept her hand in every aspect of the funeral home, now handed down to her son, because her name carried real weight in Clanton. More weight, even, than Chuck Jackson’s.

When the deputy coroner notified Chapman's that they were bringing a body, Charles Chapman asked whose it was. It was a small town; chances were high that he knew the person it would be. When they told him it was Judy Jackson, he thanked the deputy and hung up the phone. Only to pick it right back up to call his mother. That was the perk of being in the funeral business, you always got the scoop first. Well, second to the responding officers. But close enough.

Florence had the Atlanta Braves on her television for background noise. She was cross stitching a set of eight napkins to give as a wedding gift when the phone rang. There wasn't a phone jack near her chair, but she'd strung a long line across the living room so she wouldn't have to get up when it rang, which it did often enough.

Charles was on the other end of the phone and relayed the news about Judy Jackson. Florence just shook her head. She had seen so much in seventy years of the funeral business, but suicides always seemed to be the worst. Even when they weren't gory. She had put back together bodies that had been severed and mangled in car wrecks without a second thought. But suicides were different. She couldn't help but feel sorry for the person, wishing they'd done something, anything, but this. She swore she didn't believe in ghosts or ghouls, but when she touched the body of a suicide victim, she could feel the pain and the hurt in their spirit. It was the kind of thing that stayed with a person.

Not too long after Charles called Florence with the news about Judy Jackson, her phone started ringing with others bearing the news or asking if she knew about this small-town rumor. While Florence always wanted the latest information, she always kept business separate from social life. She would never ever confirm or deny a death or the nature of death of a deceased in her care.

The phone rang again, and she assumed it was another independent reporter (that's read as *gossipy old bitty*) with unfolding information from the ground on the Judy Jackson tragedy. She wished people would just let the dead really rest in peace.

She answered the call, but it wasn't an unpaid investigator. It was Big Chuck Jackson, calling her to inform her about his daughter-in-law. Of course, she pretended to be utterly shocked as if this wasn't at least the twelfth time she'd heard about it today.

"I've got a favor to ask," big Chuck finally said. "I want you to take care of her."

Big Chuck loved Judy. He loved her as one of his children. She had given him his only grandchild, given his son the best 35 years any husband could ask for, up until this moment. He knew about her suffering. He knew the weight she carried. And he wanted her treated right.

"Chuck, I've been retired for years now. I can barely still see to get my blouse buttoned right! Charles and the boys will take real good care of Judy, I'll promise it," she claimed.

"It's nothing against Charles or Kevin or any of them, really. I want the absolute best for Judy, and as far as I'm concerned you are the absolute best in this town."

Florence was flattered. But these days were for baking her famous tea cakes and going to Clanton First Baptist. She wasn't fit to come in and handle a body anymore. But it was Big Chuck Jackson that was asking. He was a good man. He did a lot of good for Clanton. His accounting firm handled Chapman's books every year. He sponsored activities for her chapter of the Cystic Fibrosis Foundation that she had chaired for years.

She had handled his wife Louise's body when she died, but that was nearly 30 years ago now. Massive heart attack. Gone far too young, but she never was the same after that daughter of hers left town and disappeared. They said she moved away, which was probably true, but Florence was a discerning woman. She could sniff a lie like a lily, and she knew there was more to the story.

The rumor mill ran as rampant then as it does today, probably even more so back then when more women were bored housewives who didn't have anything better to do with their days. One person said Louvenia was pregnant, another person said she had a venereal disease. Someone else said she ran off with a traveling salesman who sold women's shoes and assorted greeting cards. Who knew the truth? Jesus and the Jacksons, that's who. But nobody ever pressed the issue, at least not in front of the Jacksons. You didn't call people out like that in those days. You still don't do it these days in small towns because everyone and everything is connected one way or another. Somebody's mother's cousin-in-law. You could piss off the wrong person and be left living in a world of trouble if you couldn't get out of town. It just wasn't worth it. Still, people couldn't be stopped from wondering.

29

Friday morning came, and a groggy Lou woke up to Liz absentmindedly tracing lines on her forearm. "What are you doing? Where's Judy?" she asked.

Liz frowned. Who was Judy? But instead of asking, she opted to explain the previous evening's events. "You were very restless last night after I left. Combative, they called it, even. When I got here, they said they had to sedate you because you were yelling at the nurses and crying. What was wrong?" She looked meaningfully at Lou searching for an answer that Lou had but didn't feel like sharing.

"I don't know," she lied. "Whatever they've got me on here has me seeing and feeling all kinds of crazy things." She turned her head away from Liz.

Sensing the unwillingness to talk about what happened, Liz changed the subject to current events. "Well, the dogs have been dropped off at the groomers. Baths and blow outs for both. Once they're finished, I'll take them back to my place and get them set up. I took some clothes from your closet to pack a bag. That bedroom of yours is a real mess, you know? Anyway, I think it's best if you stay with me when you get out of here."

"See, this is what I'm talking about," Lou spat back with anger. "You just start assuming and planning things. You went into my bedroom, my closet, my private space, without asking. You don't ask anybody how they feel or what they want to do or what might be right. Just like how you got us into this mess at work. Everybody in town knows my business now because of you!"

Liz sat silently, biting her lip and forcing back tears.

"I've never had anybody to care about. I guess I'm doing it all wrong," she sighed.

"I didn't say that! Don't put words in my mouth! I'm just saying it would be nice to be consulted every now and then. You barely know who I am. You aren't the expert on what I need or what I want. There are personal, private things in my life that I don't like to advertise."

A retaliatory Liz found her voice, "You know, if you'd let anybody through your Great Wall of China, maybe they could ask. Maybe they'd feel comfortable enough to consult you. Maybe they're just trying to do the best they can to help a stubborn, old bitch." Liz grabbed her bag to walk out but turned around at the door. "You know, I get that you've been burned somewhere along the way in your past, but you're an idiot for not accepting help from a person that's been nothing but nice to you." With that, she walked out.

Lou laid back in the hospital bed. Liz was right. She was always right. Lou couldn't let go. She had been so independent for so long; she didn't know how to accept help. How to accept kindness. How to accept affection. How to accept love, even. Lou also couldn't bring herself to admit this, not right now. But when would she? Would it be too late then? Would Liz, her first friend and first chance at happiness in years, be long gone by then?

She couldn't think about it. She didn't want to think about it. She closed her eyes, hoping to fall back asleep. Hoping Judy would come back to her again, but she was gone. Just as long gone as she was before.

Eyes still closed, she thought about Liz this time. She'd known the woman for less than a week. Lou was the sensible one here. Normal people don't attach themselves to each other's hips in five days' time. Whatever it was, it was moving too quickly for her tastes. Sure, she liked Liz. She felt something for her. But was the old joke about lesbians renting a U-Haul on their second date credible? The past three decades had moved so slowly that the speed of this was like being on the front row stands at the Daytona 500.

As quickly as everything was moving, Lou also had to recognize that she herself was running out of time. Facts were facts. Dr. Halpern had told her she wouldn't live more than a year unless she started treatments. What was the bigger risk? Moving too quickly with Liz or moving so slowly she might die first?

Her head was pounding. This was all too much to think about. But it was all she could think about. Again, she felt guilty for talking to Liz the way she did earlier. Lou was so unapologetic her entire life, even with Judy, that this level of sensitivity frightened even her. She needed to apologize to Liz. They needed to talk this out. They needed the "where is this relationship going?" talk. Lou needed it–she needed to know.

She dialed Liz's number, but there was no answer. Lou wasn't surprised. She wouldn't have answered her phone call, either. She left a voicemail. "It's me. Look, I'm sorry. I do wanna talk. I want to figure things out." With that, she hung up the hospital room phone and sat back in the bed. Now, without any other choice, things would be moving on Liz's schedule.

Several minutes later, the phone rang. Lou picked it up before the first ring was complete. Breathlessly, she answered the phone saying, "I'm sorry, really."

"Excuse me, ma'am? I'm trying to reach the room of a Louvenia Jackson?" Lou frowned.

"Sorry, that's me. How can I help you?"

"We need to update the information in our system for you."

Confused, Lou replied, "What information?"

"Your care partner information. We need a new emergency contact since Ms. Ward removed herself from the list and she was the only person on it."

Lou laid her head back, staring at the ceiling, forcing the tears to stay inside.

"Ma'am? Are you still there? Ma'am?"

Lou hung up the phone without replying. Her chance had passed. This was Liz's schedule–no schedule at all. Instead of Lou being in charge, the decision was made for her for a change. And the tears began to fall again. She realized she had cried more in the past week than she had her whole life. She was feeling so many emotions, more emotions than she had allowed herself in thirty years. She was learning to feel again. She was learning to value another person, to trust another person. Liz was the reason for all of it. Liz had changed her life in a week. Lou couldn't deny it. Since the moment she walked into Liz Ward's office and Liz Ward had marched into her life, things were never to be the same. After pushing her feelings for Judy away for all this time, Liz had cracked open Lou's feelings. She planted herself like a flower in a cracked pot. Beautiful. Careless. Oblivious, even. Authentic.

Lou was the cracked pot. Solid, but broken. Neglect had taken a toll on her in more ways than one: mentally, emotionally, and physically. Her stoic, private personality kept any seeds from being sewn anymore. But Liz wasn't a seed. She was a flower, showing up, and plopping herself down into the cracked pot.

Lou had fought her feelings for Judy for so long, and she swore to herself up and down that she would never let another person have that kind of control over her. She would never allow herself to be that vulnerable again. But Lou had been fighting a ghost for all that time, and, unbeknownst to her, she certainly was fighting one now.

30

Florence Chapman stood up from her chair, leaning on a cane, and walked to her bedroom. She put on her pantyhose, an ivory blouse with a fluffy bow at the collar, and a dark purple suit with jacket and skirt. She slipped on her black kitten heels. She went into the bathroom and teased out the back of her silvery white bouffant where it had been resting against her recliner so it would match the height on the rest of her head. She gave it a good spritz of hairspray and used her trusty pink pick to pull it out. When she was satisfied, she sprayed it down again with hairspray. It would be Tuesday before she had her next wash and set down at Mamie's Beauty Shop, so she had to take good care of this through the weekend, she thought, adding another waft of hairspray just for good measure. She looked in the mirror and applied some blush and her signature Revlon Paint the Town Pink lipstick. She filed her nails until they were perfectly rounded. Her ensemble was tasteful but understated. Florence firmly believed that funeral directors were to be presentable, not flashy. You were to add to the experience from the sidelines, not overtake the occasion with your own glitz and glam.

She went back into the living room, and she called her son. When he picked up his phone, she told him, matter of factly, "Come pick me up. I've got to go to work."

You don't question Florence Chapman. Her son knew this better than anybody. So, he simply said yes ma'am and came to the house on Nalley Drive to get her. When he pulled in the driveway, she was already waiting outside, black purse in hand to match her shoes. It was 90 degrees out, but she was unbothered. She was ready for work.

He put the car in park, but she was already getting in the passenger seat before he could get out to help her. What was this spring in her step? Where was he taking her? What work was she planning to do? All questions that she would answer soon enough.

"What's all this about?" Charles gestured to Florence as he drove out of the neighborhood.

"What's what about? I've worn this dress to work a hundred times," she replied, not even considering the root of the question.

"That's not what I mean, Mama. Where are we going? What work do you have to do?"

"Well, we're going to the funeral home, Charles. We still own it, don't we? Isn't that still where we work?" she asked, annoyed at the ridiculous questions her son was asking.

"No, Mama, that's where I work. You're retired." He paused, considering this could be either a mental break or beginning stages of dementia. Really slowly and loudly, he asked, "You remember retiring, don't you?"

Florence looked at him like he just cursed at her. "I remember going home. When I wanted. And now I need to go back to work. Last time I checked, I'm still licensed to work in this state."

Charles still wasn't understanding her, and Florence still wasn't understanding Charles. "I've got to handle Judy Jackson. A special request from Big Chuck, I couldn't say no after all he's done for us." She left out the high compliments he'd paid her, saving those for her own repertoire of praises.

"Mama, you can't handle the cat anymore, much less a body! How do you think you're gonna move her and embalm her and lift her into the casket?" he asked incredulously.

"Don't you sass me, Charles Linson Chapman," she hissed. "I'm gonna do this job, and you're gonna help me do it and that's the end of it." She looked out the window as he drove towards the funeral home, effectively ending the discussion.

When they pulled into the parking lot, she let herself out of the car and walked in the back door like she owned the place. Well, she did own the place, so who was to tell her to do anything differently? It definitely wasn't going to be Charles after the dressing down she'd just given him in the car ride.

She walked down the hallway to Charles's office, which had previously belonged to her late husband, J.G., and sat down at the desk. She would have gone to her office, but it had been handed out to one of the other funeral directors when she retired, so she figured this one would suit her fine for the time being. She put her purse under the desk and situated the chair to her liking. Charles sat down in the guest chair opposite her, waiting to be bossed. She looked around the cluttered desk and muttered, "I don't know how you find anything in this mess."

"Well, it makes sense to me," he offered quietly.

"And what about when someone else needs to step in in an emergency? Like right now. How can they make any sense of this?" she demanded back.

Charles didn't have an answer, which was in his best interest.

"Alright, get me a cup of coffee, you know how I take it. And I want it fresh. Then I want the coroner's report on Judy. Have they brought over the body yet?"

"No, ma'am."

"Fine. When it gets here, let me know. Until then, I'm going to call Big Chuck and tell the family to come in at 2:00 tomorrow." It was like Florence never retired. "After you get my coffee and bring me that report, you need to call down to Lynch Supply. They'll ship today if you order what I need before noon. I assume we still have an account with them?" She looked at Charles for an answer.

"Yes, ma'am, but what do you need first and I'll tell you if we have it?"

Annoyed, she replied, "She hung herself. I'll need bruise bleach. The skin will be rubbed raw from whatever ligature she used; I'll need Velva cream to rub into it before I start the makeup. Do you have those on hand?"

"We should have both of them," he replied.

"Of course, you SHOULD have them," she replied. "But that wasn't my question. I asked IF you had them. And you know I only use Esco bruise bleach, not the cheap stuff. It doesn't work the same."

"I'll place the order before noon. Is there anything else?"

"I'll let you know if there is," she said without looking up as she searched for the number to Big Chuck Jackson's house in the phone book.

31

Liz looked at her phone and recognized the hospital number. She ignored it. But then she thought it might be a nurse or doctor with news. She was angry, but she still cared, whether she would admit it or not. The call went to voicemail, and Liz pulled her car over so she could focus and listen to it.

"It's me. Look, I'm sorry. I do wanna talk. I want to figure things out."

Liz dialed the hospital back. "Nurse's station, third floor, please," she said to the attendant.

"Third floor?" someone answered.

"Yes, hi there, I just need to update some contact information for a patient on your floor."

"Sure, one second, let me grab a pen." Liz waited patiently. "Go ahead."

"I'm listed as the care partner for Louvenia Jackson in 312. I need to remove myself from that list, please."

"Okay…" the person said, "But that doesn't leave anyone else to call."

Those words seared through Liz's heart. That doesn't leave anyone else.

"Well, you'll just have to ask her yourself who she wants to be on that list. Thank you." Liz ended the call without waiting for a reply.

She threw the phone on her floorboard. Sitting on the side of Dogwood Drive, she screamed. She screamed at Lou. She screamed at the hospital. She screamed at God for making her this way and for laying this on her doorstep. She cried serious tears, beating the steering wheel and writhing in her seat. Liz didn't know another person could make her feel so much love and so much hate all at the same time.

After a few minutes of letting her emotions out physically for the first time in forever, she calmed down enough to shift the Subaru into drive and pull back onto the road. Getting her wits about her, she remembered she needed to pick up the dogs. As mad as she was at Lou, she wasn't going to let the pups suffer because of it.

She parked and went into the groomers' shop. The girls were laid out in front of the counter wearing matching bandanas. Liz couldn't help but laugh. Recognizing her from when she dropped the dogs off, the office manager laughed with Liz. "They refused to go into the crates when we finished. They came out here and laid out and wouldn't move. Stubborn as all get out!" she chuckled. Sounds familiar, Liz thought. "They've been out here for at least an hour. Everyone who's been in has just loved them. They're sweet old girls." Familiar again, Liz lamented, wincing a little.

The office manager gave Liz the leashes and into the back seat of the car they went. It took all of her strength to get their elderly rear ends up into her SUV. Out of breath, she opened her driver door and sat down. She looked in her rearview mirror at the two tired gray faces, panting as if they had just done all the heavy lifting. She hated dogs, but you couldn't help but love this pair of old girls.

Now to get them to her house and situated for the foreseeable future. She didn't know when Lou would get out of the hospital, and she wouldn't find out first now since she had removed herself from the situation. Either way, it was apparent Lou couldn't take care of the dogs in her current state, if there was to be any improvement from here.

She got home and got the girls inside, only to realize she had left their food bin at Lou's. She could drive fifteen minutes to the Walmart and get new food, or she could drive twenty minutes to Lou's and get their food. Weighing the options, she figured she would go back to Lou's. Not knowing how long Lou might be holed up in the hospital, Liz decided she would go back out to Lou's and make sure things were locked up and taken care of for the time being.

She drove across town to the farm, thinking about Lou the whole way there. She obviously still cared, at least a little, or she wouldn't be coming out here to check on the farm. If she was being honest, she was also still intrigued by the farm and its potential, so getting a few more looks around was nice, too.

She pulled into the driveway and grabbed the mail out of the box. She drove her car up to the house and went in the side door off the porte cochere that apparently didn't lock, despite her efforts to do so after yesterday's incident.

She walked into the time capsule and actually took her time looking around today. She wasn't in any hurry, and there was no one to stop her. Liz loved the classic architecture found in these old homes. Today's homes couldn't hold a candle to the type of craftsmanship of bygone days. No one took this kind of time or paid this much attention to details. Every home today was built as cheaply as possible with as many corners cut as allowable to pass muster. It was a shame really.

What was a bigger shame was this beautiful old house on the verge of falling in on itself. She had to save it. She had to preserve, if not restore, this place.

Lou hadn't let her go upstairs the other night, so she took this opportunity to check it out for herself. Pulling back the heavy quilt separating the staircase from the main floor, she set foot on the stairs, halfway expecting them to give in. When she deemed them stable enough, she began walking up, stopping at the landing midway up. She felt like Scarlett O'Hara standing in Tara. The landing had a large window with smaller windows on either side and a transom up top. The glass was broken in some of the panes, repaired only with cardboard and duct tape. Liz simply shook her head.

Through the wavy antique glass and the filth of many years of neglect, one could see what was probably the entirety of the farm. A look down to the left showed the barn with its thick wood plank walls and tin roof. The line of apple trees went down the opposite side. The pond was directly behind it all, practically perfectly centered in the view of the window. Liz speculated that it must have been built after the construction of the house because there was no way in hell that would have ever lined up so perfectly by happenstance.

Tracing the edges of the pond with her eyes, she was able to see where it was fed from a small creek and then emptied into another smaller creek, so it was at least a man-made water feature as Liz had thought. It wasn't big enough for more than a rowboat, but it was picturesque, even with the area all grown up around it, especially looking down on it from this view. It would be darling with a little gazebo next to it, a stone path leading towards it from the back of the house.

So many ideas, so much potential. She could see it clear as day. Realizing she still hadn't made it all the way to the upper story, Liz turned to continue up the stairs, only to be stopped dead in her tracks by the sight in front of her.

32

When Judy Jackson arrived at Chapman's, Charles placed her petite body on the table for his mother. Florence took a long inspection of her form, examining every mark, every wrinkle or line, the color of her hair, how her eyes looked. Like most suicide by hanging victims, the lividity in Judy's extremities had left her lower half purple-ish blue. Luckily the lower part of the body wouldn't be seen for the viewing. She had to "study on things" for a minute to ensure she had the correct plan of action. Big Chuck called her the best, and she was going to give her best on this. She didn't let subpar work leave her care.

She looked through every shade of makeup and cover up in the funeral home's vast collection, applying little swatches here and there like paint samples on a house to decide what was best. Of course, she had known Judy her entire life, since she was a kid. She knew what she looked like, how she did her hair, but she couldn't go off memory alone. Not at this age anyway. So, she asked the Jacksons to bring in their favorite most recent photos of Judy, and to pick one to be used in the obituary. They would arrive at 2:00 tomorrow, and Florence was going to have Judy as close to ready as possible before then, that way all she would have left to do would be the finished layer of makeup and the hair and get her dressed.

Florence set to work preparing the body. The coroner had done decent work in this removal and transport, she noticed. Maybe that girl wasn't such a novice coroner after all.

Washing and drying the body of the fluids and excrements still on it were first, then the embalming. She had to take breaks and sit down several times, so what was normally a two- or three-hour job took more than four hours. She was out of practice and tired much more quickly than she used to. Once the embalming was complete, Florence washed down the body again to make sure it was clean and in perfect condition. Well, as perfect condition as a dead body could look at this stage…

She would have to work pretty hard on the marks on Judy's neck. Florence could tell that it, sadly, was not an instant death. Judy was a small woman, in height and weight. Larger bodies put more weight on the ligature and caused a much quicker death. Smaller bodies could support their weights more, so it took longer to die, creating prolonged pain, as the individual struggled.

Charles had been checking on his mother throughout her work period, ensuring she had breaks and hot coffee, which she drank throughout the day. Finally, around 5:30 she declared she was finished for the day. She'd done all she could, and Judy looked good. Tomorrow's cosmetics and hair styling would help more, but Florence was satisfied with her work today. She called Charles in the room to help her out of her chair.

"I was beginning to think you were gonna close up for us," he teased his mother.

"If I didn't need a ride home, I would have," she laughed back.

"She looks fantastic, Mama, really," Charles complimented.

"She ought to. I'm beat. Run me by the Speedyburger and take me home. My dogs are barking."

Florence slept well that night after a hard day's work. Knowing she fulfilled the wishes of a good friend and had done her very best work on a decedent in her care. As her head was hitting one of her cross-stitched pillowcases, she felt the familiar pangs of sorrow she felt before when handling suicide victims. She said a prayer for Judy Jackson's soul and drifted off to sleep.

33

A big snake was slithering across the stairs as Liz screamed bloody murder! It was only a rat snake, practically helpful in an old house like this that probably had mice all over it, but as far as Liz was concerned it might as well have been a king cobra. A tour of the upstairs would have to wait as Liz bounded down the stairs and to the safety of the main living area. Shuddering, she decided her next trip to the second floor would be with a square shovel in hand, ready for slicing up or beating the hell out of whatever she might encounter.

Back in the center hall, Liz made her way to the dining room. The sunlight shining through the tall windows was much brighter than the sunset that she had seen the room in on her first visit. She was able to see the blue toile wallpaper much clearer now. With a more discerning eye this time (one that wasn't focused on Lou), Liz realized this wasn't run of the mill machine made wallpaper. This was hand painted. Liz wasn't certain, but it appeared to be French based on the design and color patterns. She snapped a few photos of it with her phone to check it out later.

Liz next turned her attention to the huge eight panel china cabinet. There must have been service for 24 or more in the stunning French Limoges flow blue china. It was hard to put an exact age on the china, but it was at least a hundred years old. The cobalt dye used in original blue transferware was primarily from Germany. The first World War cut off the supply and most china manufacturers altered their practices and methods to produce patterns of a wider variety of colors. Flow blue was different from typical blue transferware in that an additive was put in the kiln when firing the china. This allowed for a softer, more blurred feminine touch to otherwise crisp and vivid pieces.

Opposite of the china cabinet, between the two front windows, was the sideboard with a silver tea set on it. She picked up the creamer. It was stamped Dominick & Haff, sterling. Liz picked up all of the other pieces which had the same mark. This was a $10,000 tea set, just collecting dust! Throwing any caution of being called a snoop to the wind, she pulled the pieces of hollowware off the huge waiter tray it sat on. She picked it up, holding it to the light of the window and searching through the tarnish, she found another stamp for sterling. This was easily a $5,000 tray, if not more. She put everything back together, the hair raised on her arms and neck.

This type of stuff was like porn for Liz. Rarely did she get to nerd out over historical work like what was found in Lou's house. Stepping back and taking in the whole room, Liz was awed by the crystal chandelier and matching sconces. They were caked with dust, but still sparkled through it. God, if only she had some vinegar on hand, she'd mix some with water and take the thing apart right then and there and start cleaning those crystals.

She wondered if there was some vinegar in the kitchen. She could at least clean a sconce, just to see the refraction when the orange light of the sunset would hit it. She saw plenty of the kitchen earlier in the week and noticed the cleaning supplies in the mud room. The kitchen wasn't much to write home about except for the lovely, whitewashed cabinets with glass fronts and original butcherblock counters.

Liz grabbed the mail she brought in earlier and tossed it on a stack of junk mail she saw already sitting on the kitchen counter. Just as she was putting the mail down, the lights in the house went off.

Odd, she thought, looking hard out the windows to be sure it was still a fair-weather day. Not a cloud in the sky. It was starting to get darker, though, enough so that she could see a light on at the farm down the road. She went to the mudroom, looking for a fuse box. Nothing in there. She walked through the mudroom around to the center hallway and noticed the panel next to the back door. A mess of wires in and out that looked like a fire hazard. At some point along the way, the electrical had been upgraded to breakers at least. Likely in the 50s or 60s from the looks of things.

Too afraid to touch anything, Liz looked at every breaker and didn't see anything tripped. Even if there was a tripped breaker, it wouldn't have shut down the whole house, would it? She checked the outage map on the East Kentucky Power Cooperative website on her phone. Nothing. So strange.

She called the customer service line on the website. The automated system asked for the phone number associated with the account. She typed in Lou's home number. The system reported the account was three months past due to the tune of $574.19. There was Liz's explanation: the electricity had been disconnected for failure to pay.

"Dammit, Lou. Why did you let things get this bad?" she muttered, ending the call.

Realizing now she would have to get home before dark, Liz went back to the kitchen to get the dog food bin and be on her way. Pulling it out from under the counter, a note addressed to Lou caught her eye. Who was writing to a woman who claimed to have absolutely no family or friends? She picked up the envelope, immediately recognizing the feeling of fine Crane stationery, she noticed the perfect cursive writing. It was so flawless that it looked like a computer-generated font.

Liz turned the envelope over, thinking about opening it, only to read the embossed return address on the flap: Mrs. Judy Jackson, 84 Crystal Springs Close, Clanton, Georgia.

34

All the Jacksons filed into Chapman's at exactly 2:00 that Friday. Naturally, Florence was there to greet them, always a hostess at heart, and reminding the rest of the staff that this was her "to do." She shook the hands of Joan, Josie, and Little Chuck, but gave Big Chuck a heartfelt hug.
"I did my best on her," she sniffled with a mixture of some sympathy, some humble dignity, and some theatrics for effect.

"I know you did," Big Chuck replied, patting her arm.

Josie held Judy's jewelry, accessories, and pictures while Little Chuck had the garment bag with Judy's dress and underclothes in it.

"Y'all can just sit those down on the side table in here," she gestured toward the meeting room where the arrangements would be made. They did as they were told and all had a seat at the round, wooden table in comfortable office chairs.

"Well first off, I just want to say how sorry I am for your loss, especially in this situation," Florence began her usual speech.

Before she could get the whole thing out, Big Chuck spoke up, "We're not gonna spare any expense. I want the best of everything you have."

Little Chuck started sweating. He wasn't sure he could afford the inside of an outhouse right now, but he knew he definitely could not afford the best of everything that Chapman's had to offer. He knew that Big Chuck had begged Florence out of retirement for this gig and, as generous as she was, he seriously doubted she would be doing this free of charge. Little Chuck cleared his throat, attempting to remind his father that he had practically zero dollars and zero cents left to his name. "Let's not get too crazy now, Daddy. Let's see what all Mrs. Chapman has to offer."

Florence looked from Big Chuck to Little Chuck, unsure of who was calling the shots in this situation. Big Chuck had been the one to call her and get this ball rolling, but Little Chuck was the spouse and technically the next of kin. The real question was who would be writing the check. Speaking of... "Now will this be paid privately or with life insurance?" Florence asked delicately, trying to determine who was in charge here. Josie and Joan just looked at each other, neither knowing the answer

Big Chuck replied, "I'll be paying, Florence. Like I said, the best of everything. Whatever it costs." Florence simply nodded her head, making notes in her little steno pad.

Now Little Chuck was embarrassed. He couldn't even afford to put his wife in the ground. He shrank back and let his daddy answer the questions. He was the paying customer, after all.

Joan, always a talented writer, offered to author the obituary with Alice Murray, which Florence appreciated. She could crank one out in her sleep, but she thought it particularly nice when a family member chose to take that responsibility and put their loved one's spirit into words.

"Now we'll have Judy ready for viewing tonight after we've done her cosmetics and put her things on her, but I'd suggest starting the visitation tomorrow. We could do noon til eight tomorrow, if that suits you all?" Florence asked. Everyone nodded in agreement. "Then on Sunday we could have visitation here from eleven til the funeral hour. I assume you'll want the funeral at First Baptist?"

"Of course," Big Chuck confirmed.

"Sure. I'll call over there this afternoon and set everything up. We'll have to move quickly to get things over there on a Sunday between the end of church and the funeral, but we've done it before, and we'll do it again." Continuing to add to her notes and check all the boxes, Florence asked what the family would like the service to look like.

They all sort of looked at each other, no one having any answer in particular. Little Chuck said, "Just the usual, I guess?"

"Well of course, sweetheart," Florence soothed him. "I just want to know what songs to plan, if we need to organize the choir, stuff like that."

Josie spoke up. "I want to speak at the funeral. I want to give a eulogy," she said firmly. No one objected, naturally, and Florence added this to her notes.

"Let's touch base on the music real quick. Now my go-tos are always Amazing Grace, How Great Thou Art, It Is Well. Anything in particular y'all like?" she asked.

"Those sound good... Maybe throw in Abide with Me for good measure?" Big Chuck suggested.

He was out of practice at funeral planning way worse than Florence was, not that she showed it out here with the family. This was perhaps her strongest suit--working with the bereaved families in these difficult times.

"Now l'd like to see what you brought for us to dress Judy in," she proposed. "And I'll need to know what jewelry you'll want left on her when the casket is closed and what needs to come off.
It will be done very discreetly, of course."

Joan unzipped the monogrammed garment bag, revealing the navy floral dress Judy had worn to Josie's wedding less than two years ago. Josie was misty-eyed, seeing it again, even though she was the one who picked it out of the closet. "Just beautiful, really," Florence complimented.

Josie opened the jewelry roll. They'd had to go back to The Gables to get Judy's best pieces: the diamond drops Chuck had given her for their 25th wedding anniversary, her little gold Cartier watch, and her mother's amethyst and diamond brooch. They also brought Judy's wedding set.

She had taken the three rings, engagement ring, wedding ring, and tenth anniversary band, off the morning before she left The Gables for the last time. She apparently didn't want them on when she did what she was planning to do that day.

"These are all just stunning pieces," Florence gushed. "I assume you'll want all of them back," she started marking in her notepad.

"No," Little Chuck interjected. "Leave her wedding set on her." No one objected. Florence corrected her notes.

"Now let's go to the slumber chamber and pick out the perfect casket," she stood with her cane, ushering the family into the adjoining room.

35

Lou was asleep when Liz walked in. She had been sedated again by the hospital staff. Liz sat down. She had so many questions. She bet that envelope held so many answers to them. But if she had learned one thing about Lou, it was that she should never get into her business without permission. She wouldn't make that mistake again. Well, except for when she went through Lou's whole house earlier and sniffed out the sterling like a hound dog, but that didn't really count, did it?

Lou's eyes were still closed. "What are you doing back here? I thought you were gone."

"What?" Liz was caught off guard considering she thought she had been pretty inconspicuous coming in.

"It's your perfume. It gives you away every time. No damn body in this town even knows what Chanel No. 5 is, much less wears it."

"I'm surprised you recognize it," Liz responded dryly.

"I'm full of surprises, don't you know?" Lou smiled back.

"Yeah, I'm aware. But I've got one for you," she said, holding up the envelope from Judy. "What's this? Who is Judy Jackson?"

Lou grimaced. She was remembering it all now. She got a note in the mail. From Judy. That's what she was upset about when she was sobbing at the table.

No, no, it wasn't. She was sobbing because of Liz. Liz had called and told her how she had outed them to the man at the bank. Judy started it and Liz finished it. An exact replica of her love life thus far. Except this time the pain had landed her in the hospital.

Lou closed her eyes again in pain, but this wasn't from the pain in her body. This wasn't cancer pain, this was worse. This was the pain in her heart.

"How do you know about Judy?" Lou asked.

"I don't," Liz replied truthfully. "All I know is when I came in here yesterday, you asked for Judy, not me." Liz continued, "I went back to your house this afternoon to get the dogs' food. I forgot it earlier when I took them to the groomer. I left your mail on the kitchen counter when I saw this." Liz handed the envelope to Lou.

"You'll notice it isn't open," Liz added to make a point. "I didn't want to get into your business without your approval."

Lou held the envelope, tracing the cursive with her fingers. Truthfully, she was scared to open it. She was scared of confronting this ghost, the most painful part of her past. Liz was about to die if she didn't open it.

Stalling the opening of the note, Lou decided now was as good a time as any to explain everything and finally tell Liz the truth, the whole truth, and nothing else, so help her God. To Liz's dismay, Lou laid the envelope in her lap.

"You have to understand," Lou began, "That I never meant to lie to you about anything. I was just too guarded or too scared to tell you everything that happened. Maybe a little too embarrassed, too. I didn't move to Maysville alone, you know that. But it wasn't my mama Louise that came with me, it was Judy. She was my lover."

A confused Liz was trying to put pieces together. "But the return address said Mrs. Judy Jackson. Who did she marry with your last name? Was she your cousin or something?!?"

Looking away, Lou replied, "She wasn't my cousin. This isn't some V.C. Andrews novel." Continuing through the pain, "She is married to someone with my last name: my brother, Chuck."

Liz was so genuinely confused at this point that she had forgotten about the note. "I'm going to need more of an explanation here. You said there was no family left when you moved here. So that wasn't true either?"

"Another lie," Lou confirmed. "My mama Louise wasn't all there was. My daddy, Big Chuck. His baby sister, my Aunt Joan. Then my brother. I have, or had, distant cousins scattered all over the south, too, but none of us were ever really close. Since Mama was an only child and Daddy's sister never married, we didn't have any first cousins."

"When did Judy become your significant other and leave your brother?" Liz followed up.

"Well, that's where things get tricky," Lou stated.

Liz couldn't help but laugh. "THAT's where they get tricky? This whole thing is like a TV miniseries. How much trickier can it get?"

"You'll see," Lou promised, responding with a blank face. "Judy and I had gone to school together. She's one year younger than me and one year older than Chuck. We knew each other for years. And we just sort of always got along. She'd push my buttons and I'd push hers. We had this strange dynamic of fights and make ups, but we always worked it out and stayed friends. I could never explain it," Lou paused a long and thoughtful pause, "Until I met you." She looked Liz eye to eye.

"Then what?" Liz asked.

"One night, she was staying over, and, like girls do, we were talking. Talking about love and crushes and dreams and growing up. She asked me flat out why I'd never had a serious boyfriend. I'd brought boys home to meet Mama and Daddy here and there, but it never amounted to anything. So, I took a chance, and I told my oldest, closest friend the truth. I told her I didn't really like boys. That I had no interest in them. She didn't catch on right away," Lou smirked, "So I had to explain it to her real simple. I told her I was a homosexual. Nobody said gay or lesbian back then, you know. It was always homosexual, or queer.

"I couldn't tell if she was flabbergasted or fascinated. I told her I'd had a crush on the basketball coach at school for years. Judy went, 'But that's a man!' and I had to remind her of the girls' basketball coach. She just said 'Oh,' and laughed her head off. She wasn't bothered by it at all. I had been so scared to tell anyone, and she just took it at face value. She made me feel so comfortable that I just told her everything. How I had always felt different, even since I was a kid. How I found men mostly disgusting. How I appreciated the feminine form and mystique. She listened attentively like a student engaged with her teacher."

"Didn't you ever just bare your heart and soul coming out to someone like that?" Lou asked, searching for a connection Liz could make to this experience.

Liz thought for a moment, and answered, "Yeah, my gay guy best friend in college. But that didn't count 'cause we were both gay."

"Yeah, well, if that doesn't count then my story doesn't have much merit here…"

"Sorry," Liz quickly shot back. "Continue, please."

"Judy became interested. Interested in my life, who I found attractive, my thoughts, my dreams of running off with a beautiful woman one day and growing old together. I told her I'd leave Clanton, Georgia in my dust and never look back. I guess she found something appealing in that. Something appealing about me. Because one night, we were swimming in Higgins's Pond up the road from her mama's house. We didn't have bathing suits; we just stripped down to our underwear and jumped in. The water was cold, my nipples were showing in my bra. She teased me, poking at one of my breasts. I laughed and poked her in the stomach. At some point I popped underwater and came back up with some algae on my shoulder and she brushed it off, her hand lingering a little bit on my shoulder and making its way down the side of my arm underwater. It gave me goosebumps. It was the first time another woman had ever touched me like that. It was unexpected, but not unwelcome. I was forward, I'll admit. I leaned over and kissed her. It was also unexpected, but not unwelcome, according to Judy. That's when things started to escalate…"

Liz was surprised. She'd never had any encounters as romantic or as organic as what Lou and Judy had. It really did sound like love. Liz had bumped around with a few sorority sisters in college when they were all drunk. She went to a few discreet bars in the city and had some meaningless flings. But nothing like this. It was all making sense to her now why her feelings for Lou had been so different–why she attached herself to Lou so readily. It was organic chemistry, not fabricated or arranged. She had fallen for Lou, for another woman, for the first time in her life.

"Back up, though. Where does your brother come into this?" Liz asked, still confused about this aspect of the story.

"Well, remember how I said things got tricky. Judy and I started to spend a lot more time together, if you know what I mean. And it was getting harder and harder to come up with excuses or situations for grown women to be together so often or to share a bedroom. So, we hatched a plan."

Liz was reading into this, "Judy started dating Chuck to get closer to you."

Lou nodded her head. "And it worked. Nothing was ever called into question. She was a close family friend. It made sense that she and Chuck might go courting, as we called it in the day. Judy's mother was thrilled. Our family was a prestigious one in Clanton. It was a perfect match up, on the outside."

"Until?" Liz asked.

"Until Chuck started getting fresh with her. She didn't like it. Up to that point her only sexual interactions were with me. I don't think she minded the actual attention from Chuck. He was always kind and gentle, so she said. But she felt like she was betraying me in a way. No matter how many times I tried to reassure her that it was okay and that it was just the way things had to be to keep our ruse and our relationship going, she wasn't happy."

"But she was always happy with you?" Liz wondered out loud.

"I like to think so," Lou laughed.

"Well, I didn't just mean in THAT way, but your bond was growing stronger it sounds like."

"It was. It was getting stronger and getting harder to hide. We were being less careful, less watchful of our surroundings. Judy's mama got suspicious. One night I had called Judy at home. We didn't talk about anything graphic or really even anything having to do with a relationship, but at the end of the call, I said 'I just wanted to say good night, and I love you.' Eugenia was listening in on the extension." A grim look came across Lou's face, feeling the pain that ensued after that night all over again.

"What did Judy's mama do when she found out?" Liz asked, really invested in the story now.

"She beat her," Lou said, turning towards the window, away from Liz. "She beat the hell out of her. She used a cane, a fireplace poker, a coat hanger, everything she could get her hands on. And Judy just took it."

"Why didn't she fight back?!" Liz exclaimed.

"Because you don't fight your own mother. Not when you've been caught doing what we were doing. In those days in the south, it was unheard of. A worse sin than anything in the Ten Commandments. Eugenia beat her black and blue, blood coming out of her nose and mouth. She looked like she had been trampled by wild bulls when I saw her in the car."

"You saw Judy after that? For what? Wasn't she in enough trouble?" Liz asked, confused by Judy's motive.

"Her mother brought her. Eugenia called back to our house and told me she was gonna have Judy drive over to borrow six eggs for a cake for garden club the next day. Asked me if I'd just meet her at the end of the driveway so Judy could grab them and get right back home because it was already so late. She sounded sweet as pie."

"But when the car pulled up, and I saw Judy in the passenger seat, I dropped those eggs. Good thing, because Eugenia didn't need any eggs. She came bearing a message to take a good, long look at Judy and that if she ever caught the two of us in any improper activities again that I'd be left looking the same as Judy, or worse.

"Judy never said a word the whole time. She just stared at the floorboard of her mama's car. Defeated. Guilty. Scared, for herself and for me. Then they drove off, leaving me standing there in disbelief."

Liz sat back in the chair, needing some support after this tragic turn of events. "I can't believe this. No wonder you're as crazy as you are." Lou gave her a stern look. "Well, you are."

"So that's when y'all got caught then? And that's when y'all left town?" Liz continued, thinking the story couldn't possibly get any wilder.

"No. That's when we SHOULD have left town," Lou shook her head. "But we didn't. Nobody saw Judy for weeks. Her mama couldn't have anybody asking what happened to her with all those bruises and cuts. She told everybody, my family included, that Judy was very ill. So, people, my family included, brought layer cakes and wanted to visit. Eugenia always came up with a reason why Judy couldn't receive a visitor. But she sure took the damn layer cakes."

"I missed her like crazy. I worried so much. But I knew better than to try and call or see her. The only person who missed her as much as me was my brother, Chuck. Not being able to see or talk to his girlfriend was driving him mad. So, when she finally did make her miraculous recovery and re-enter polite society, it wasn't a week before my brother was asking Daddy for Grandmother Jackson's engagement ring."

"Oh no, they didn't get engaged, did they?" Liz couldn't believe what she was hearing.

"Oh, they did. And they got married, but that part comes in a minute."

Liz didn't know if she should pop some popcorn or take a sedative. This was a hell of a rollercoaster ride.

"They got engaged. Judy said yes. I tried to get her alone dozens of times to ask her what she was thinking, but she wouldn't end up anywhere alone with me. I think she was still scared of Eugenia, and I guess she should have been. So about six months later a wedding was planned. First Baptist Clanton was decked out in pink bunting on anything that would stand still long enough," Lou remembered. "And I was her maid of honor," she grimaced.

"No way! You had to stand next to the woman you loved and watch her say 'I do' to your brother?"

"I did. But again, you're getting ahead of yourself. My parents, as the parents of the groom, naturally hosted the rehearsal dinner. It was at our house, The Gables. Our maid, Ruby, spent weeks polishing every crystal, every baluster on the stairs." Lou smiled, remembering her beloved Ruby. She continued, "The house was beautiful, and it was filled with out-of-town family and guests. There were people in every square foot of the house, it seemed. Chuck and his buddies were all drunk as skunks. Even Mama'd been drinking. Everyone was having a great time except me."

"I needed to get away. It was all getting to me, the noise, the people, the heat. The dread of what was coming the next day. So, I went out back of the house, sat down on the stool in Mama's little old garden shed where she potted flowers and stored stuff she didn't have room for in the house, and I cried. I sobbed. Something I never did in front of anyone, ever."

"I must have been louder than I thought because Judy opened the door to see what was going on. I saw her face and started sobbing even more. She fell to my side, trying to console me. She hung her head and cried right along with me, both of us mourning the love that was dying between us on the very next day. I don't know what happened, but we ended up in an embrace. We ended up in a moment of passion. One last goodbye kiss, maybe? But it was more than a kiss…"

Liz was expecting more steamy details that she would never get to hear.

"That was when my brother, and his best man, Kirby Riffle, opened up the door to Mama's garden shed to steal some of Daddy's homemade peach moonshine."

"Oh, no. Lou, they didn't… Tell me they didn't," Liz begged.

"They did. It was all a blur, really. The screaming, the crying, the cussing. Me yelling, grabbing for clothes, Judy running inside, Chuck calling me everything but a child of God. Hearing the ruckus outside, Mama, Daddy, Ruby, and Joan came running. Chuck told them everything. They were appalled. Stunned. Shocked. Disappointed. Angry. Mama asked me how I could ruin everyone's lives like that. Daddy called me a sinner bound for hell. It was a nightmare come true," Lou sighed.

"Mama made Ruby pack everything I owned that night. They swore a drunk Kirby Riffle to secrecy. Daddy probably had to pay him off or something. Daddy and Mama said I was to be at First Baptist the next morning at ten o'clock with a smile on my face and my bridesmaid dress on. They weren't going to have *my* indiscretions ruin Judy's big day."

"You know, I think that's what bothered me more than anything," Lou said contemplating the circumstances.

"What?" Liz asked.

"That they never blamed Judy. It was all my fault. I was their daughter who never had a boyfriend. I was the miscreant, the black sheep, the predator that had taken advantage of poor, little, ole defenseless Judy. But I did as I was told," Lou continued. "I smiled for every picture, I drank champagne punch at the reception, I acted like everything was okay when absolutely nothing was okay."

Liz looked at Lou with sympathy, "So that's when you left?"

"Yes. Ruby had packed all my things that would fit in my trunk and suitcases that night before. Mama and Daddy made it clear that they didn't care where I went as long as I got the hell out of Clanton. Daddy gave me a little money and the title to my car and said that was all I'd ever get out of them. Mama just shook her head and walked out of my room. My brother never spoke to me again that night or the next day at the wedding."

"At the end of the reception, when it was time for the happy couple to drive off into the sunset, I pulled Judy to the side before she made her way out to the car where everyone would throw rice in her hair, and I told her I was leaving that night. I told her I didn't know where I was going, but I loved her, and I hoped she would be happy. She walked out the door on my brother's arm and I thought I'd never see her again."

"But I thought she came here to Maysville with you?" Liz asked, confused.

"Boy, you sure don't know how to build a story, do you, sis?"

36

Florence put the finishing touches on Judy's hair, using the photo from Josie's wedding as her guide. She looked just like the photo if Florence did say so herself. It took her longer than it used to, but she was more expeditious today than she had been yesterday. This part was much easier than the previous day's tasks, too.

Judy was ready in the casket, so they rolled her into the parlor where she and the family would receive visitors, viewers, and mourners for the next day and a half. The flowers had started pouring into the funeral home the day before, so they arranged them around the casket for a lush, inviting look. Finally, they placed the casket spray the family had ordered–a sweeping, lavish arrangement that had seemingly every color and kind of cut flower this side of the Mississippi stuck in it and draping down the sides.

Florence adjusted the placement and arrangement of flowers and plants as she saw fit. She made sure the tables and chairs were spotless, the tissue boxes full, and the lighting the perfect shade of mauve to accentuate the body. It was truly a sight to behold, as far as funeral viewings were concerned, anyway.

When the Jackson clan arrived back to The Gables from planning the funeral, it was sparkling. Ruby and R.J. had truly worked magic in the few hours they had been gone. When Josie opened the big front door, she heard the two laughing and cutting up in the dining room. She walked in there as the elder Jacksons headed towards the kitchen to indulge in some more funeral food.

"Look, I learned how to polish silver!" R.J. exclaimed, holding up a sterling fork for Josie to see.

She laughed, replying, "I'm impressed! Ruby, I'm gonna leave him with you more often so you can teach him some more things about keeping house, 'cause I'm tired as hell of picking up socks," she kissed the top of his head and Ruby smiled.

"Good to have some younguns in this house again," she remarked, her old heart full.

"Take a break, cleaning crew, and come eat supper with us," Big Chuck hollered from the kitchen.

They put down their silver polish and joined the rest of the family in the kitchen, washing the dark gray grime off their hands. They fixed plates, warmed them up in the microwave, and sat down at the big kitchen table with everyone else. They were all chowing down on the southern delicacies when there was a knock on the door. They weren't expecting any guests until the next day. Ruby looked around at the things that still needed to be put away and in order before the family came and she jumped up.

"Sit down, Ruby. It's probably a Jehovah's Witness. I'll get it," Little Chuck said, pushing away from the table. Everyone resumed their dinner and light conversation.

Chuck made his way down the hallway to the front door. He opened it to find Sheriff Klark Kitchens. He decided to step outside.

"Good evening, sir," Klark said coolly.

"Cut the pleasantries, what do you want? I'm getting ready to bury my wife."

"I just wanted to drop by myself to let you know that the investigation of Mrs. Jackson's death points to standard suicide."

"Thanks for that breaking news, KK."

"I also wanted to say the fire marshal is still investigating your office fire," the sheriff added. "They interviewed your secretary today. Nice lady. But more than a little perturbed that you didn't pay her last week, you haven't paid her this week, and now her place of employment is burned to the ground."

"I've been a little preoccupied lately, as you know," Chuck reminded him. "I'll call Rosie tonight."

"You ought to," Klark replied. "Would like to ask you a favor, though. If you hear from your understudy from the office, what's his name? Peter? Let me know. We need to talk to him, too, but can't seem to find him. Could use your help with that if you don't mind."

"I'll be sure to do that," Chuck confirmed.

"Appreciate it. Y'all have a good rest of your night. Give Josie my best," he smiled, stepping off the front porch.

Chuck just smiled. He did need to talk to Rosie and get her what he owed her. And he also needed to talk to Peter, too.

Standing on his porch still, Chuck called Peter. He picked up with, “Yes sir?”

“We need to talk, son. Come to The Gables tonight at about ten. I’ll be out on the porch.”

“Will do.” The call ended.

Little Chuck went back inside to finish his dinner.

“Who was that at the door?” Joan asked.

“It was just Klark Kitchens. He was updating me about the fire down at the office. Says they’re still investigating some things, but he hopes to have it all wrapped up in the next few days.” No one questioned him. They had no reason to, as far as they were concerned. It seemed straightforward to everyone. Big Chuck said the electrical was outdated. It was an old building. Things happen. It was just unfortunate that it happened at the same time as all the rest of this.

Josie put down her fork, chewing her last bite, when she asked the table, “So what was in Mom’s note anyway?” You’d have thought she just asked someone to pass the salt, she said it so nonchalantly. The family all shifted in their seats uncomfortably, looking at each other, trying to determine who was going to reveal Judy’s final words. Eyes settled on Little Chuck, who started sweating again.

“Why don’t we talk about this later?” Chuck offered, taking another bite of his dinner, attempting to shrug off this conversation as long as he could.

“Why don’t we not? I think I’m owed an explanation as to why my mother killed herself, and I’d like to have it tonight, please,” she said, not really asking but demanding.

“I just don’t want you getting all upset again, what with your nerves and anxiety the way they are,” Chuck responded patronizingly.

“My nerves are just fine,” Josie countered. “I’m well-medicated, no thanks to your and Mom’s allegedly superior mental health genes…”

Chuck narrowed his eyes at her, getting ready to deliver a smart-ass remark, when Big Chuck spoke up. "Not at the dinner table," he said firmly. "We'll talk it all out tonight. It's high time you learned everything. And we have some phone calls to make anyway," he said, looking right at Little Chuck.

The family finished their meal in near silence, the air thick with tension and the aroma of good southern cooking. When everyone was full and had put their plates in the sink, Big Chuck excused himself to his bedroom/study. He went through bookcases and document boxes, even the wall safe in the closet, to pull out everything he needed. When he was ready, he beckoned his family into the room.

They all looked uncertain entering the room. Their eyes began to roam over the collection of papers, photos, and scraps laid out on the hospital bed and coffee table. Big Chuck was sitting at his big, antique cherry desk where he'd worked far too many hours at home over the years. Hours he now realized, as he prepared to meet his maker, that he would never get back.

Perhaps the most notable thing among the collection was a stack of cash. Everyone looked to Big Chuck for an explanation. He told them to sit down, which they did, sitting on the pair of Chippendale chairs, the French settee, and the edge of his bed that sat in the window.

"In this room, is everything y'all need to know," he began, gesturing towards the things around the space, "Particularly you, Josie. To help you understand what happened back then, and what's happened since then."

"Since then?" Little Chuck blurted out.

"That's what I said, isn't it?" Big Chuck replied sarcastically. "Look around. Lou's pictures, everything she achieved. Her college diploma, which she received a year early. Her sorority things. Then you'll notice," he continued more quietly, "more recent things."

There were pictures of Lou at a grocery store. A copy of a deed to a property in Kentucky. Letters between Big Chuck and someone named Helen Brooks Van Patterson who lived in Florida about the sale of a horse farm. None of it made any sense to anyone.

"I don't get it," Josie uttered. "What does all this mean? You know where Aunt Lou is?" she asked.

"Do you really think I'd have my only daughter, my firstborn, leave without a trace and not know anything about her? You'd have to be crazy," Big Chuck commented. "I'll admit, I didn't know for the first several years. My heart was broken, I was angry, mad at her, myself, and Louise. It wasn't until Louise died that I felt comfortable seeking the assistance of a private investigator. Louise died with hate in her heart–probably what gave her the heart attack in the first place," he chuckled grimly. "And I wasn't going to let the same happen to me. I hoped Lou would come back, but after so many years it became apparent that she wouldn't. So, I decided to watch from afar. I helped her as much as I could without anything being traced back to me. Which leads me," he pointed to the stack of cash, "to the elephant in the room."

"I was wondering when we were going to get to that," R.J. spoke what everyone else was thinking.

"That belongs to you, son," Big Chuck said to Little Chuck. "That's your inheritance. I bought your sister the farm she's living on in Kentucky from the woman who owned it. Ruthless old woman who lives down in Florida. She wanted every penny she could get out of that place. So that's your equivalent in cash. Which we will use part of to pay for a decent funeral for Judy, I might add. The Gables goes into a trust immediately when I die, along with whatever money I have on hand. Joan and Ruby will continue to be able to live here for the rest of their lives, and the money in the trust will be there to help pay the property taxes and insurance. When they pass on, the trust passes to Josie and R.J."

"You can move here, sell it, or do whatever you want then," he said directly to Josie.

"You mean you actually have insurance here?" Little Chuck asked full of spite. "Glad to know at least something is covered. Glad to know you've been keeping tabs on my sister all this time and keeping it a secret."

"It wasn't a secret. You knew where she lived, too. You got the address in the mail a week after Lou left. That's how you knew how to find Judy." The conversation was taking a dark, twisted turn and Little Chuck was about to find out that there were not so many secrets among them after all.

"What do you mean 'find Judy'?" Josie and Joan asked at the same time.

“Judy left with Lou. The night of her and Chuck’s wedding.” Everyone in the room gasped, except for Ruby and Little Chuck, who knew the truth all too well.

Big Chuck went on, “He stayed here, barely left the bed. Ruby remembers.” She nodded her head solemnly.

“Then the note came, addressed to *me*, but my son opened it, threw it away, and took off for Kentucky. But he forgot who takes out the trash in this house.”

Everyone looked to Ruby for answers now. “I saw it in the trash can. It was before Mr. Chuck got home from work so I knowed he hadn’t been the one to open it. I picked it out and showed him when he got in that night.”

“We told everyone they took a long honeymoon in Mexico, which they were supposed to do, but never did. Nobody questioned it. I wasn’t so sure it was going to work, until he came home from Kentucky with Judy in tow.”

Little Chuck sat silently, staring at the oriental rug on the hardwood floor. Josie stood up and walked towards her father. He looked up at her, and she slapped him clear across the face. R.J. jumped up to restrain his wife, and Joan jumped up to come to Little Chuck’s aid. He still didn’t say a word, and Big Chuck just watched it happen.

R.J. calmed Josie a little bit, but in a low tone she said across the room, “You killed my mother. Might as well have shot her dead.” R.J. grabbed her arm and pulled her out of the study.

37

"I had my things packed and I was prepared to leave that night," Lou began again. "I was loading my car while Daddy and Mama watched from the window. Little Chuck and Judy were to stay the night at a hotel in Atlanta before leaving for their honeymoon. They came back to The Gables to get all their luggage. After my brother had brought all the bags outside, never saying a word to me, he went in to tell my parents goodbye. They were so happy that everything had worked out for him, despite my efforts to ruin his relationship and drag Judy to hell with me." She winced in pain.

"I can't believe your parents were so cruel. You were their child, their blood!" Liz exclaimed.

"Believe it," Lou countered. Her eyes growing wider, she continued the story, "But before I knew it, Judy had loaded all her bags into my car, along with all the money she and my brother had received as wedding gifts and told me to step on it. I drove out of that driveway, slinging gravel like I was being chased by the police." Lou laughed at herself.

Liz's mouth dropped open. For the first time in a long time, she was truly speechless.

"I drove about a hundred miles an hour all the way out of town like a bat out of hell," Lou recalled, smiling. "Nothing could stop us. I had the woman I loved, most of my important possessions, we had a little cash, and a full tank of gas. Screw anyone or anything left behind," she smiled. "I had no regrets."

"So how did y'all end up here from Georgia?" Liz asked.

"We just drove. We drove until we felt like we were far enough away that no one would bother us. We found my house, the farm, which had just gone up for rent. We rented it from a woman in Florida. Judy loved it. She had grown up on a cattle farm, so she was in her element. We became farmers!" Lou laughed for a moment, before her face became as sad as Liz had ever seen it. "We were a couple of lesbian farmers madly in love for exactly eleven days," Lou took a long pause with Liz on the edge of her seat, "until my brother showed up."

"No way!" Liz practically yelled. She received a stern look through the window from the nurse across from the hospital room. "Sorry," she mouthed to the disapproving nurse.

"Yes way," Lou said flatly. "I saw him pull up first, and I ran out the front door. I started yelling, he started yelling. He demanded to know where Judy was–he knew that I had kidnapped her and brought her up here. I grabbed him, pulled on him, doing anything I could to stop him. I think I even bit him," she added, her eyebrows raised. "By then Judy had heard the commotion and came outside. She just watched. She didn't move, didn't say anything. She just watched us fight. I remember looking over at her, begging her for help in fighting off my brother. And she just stood there."

"Just like when Eugenia beat the hell out of her," Liz stated.

"Yep. She had accepted her fate and thought there was nothing she could do to change it. She had already tried, running off with me like she did, and now she had failed. So, she walked inside, got her pocketbook, came back outside, and got into the passenger seat of Chuck's car."

"I think we were still fighting for at least a couple minutes before either of us realized what she had done, but I saw her first. I pushed my brother down and ran over to the car, begging her to stay. Chuck got up and jumped in the car and they took off."

"I never saw Judy again," Lou said finally. "After that, I just poured everything I had into the farm. Every ounce of money and energy and time I had. If nothing else in my life was going to go right, I had my beautiful farm. And it was stunning, for a long time," she beamed with pride.

"Why didn't you go back to Georgia, go after her?" Liz said, misty-eyed listening to this sad love story unfold.

"Go back for what? To convince a married woman to run off with me a second time? To apologize to my brother for kidnapping his wife? To beg my family to love me despite my being a queer? There was nothing to go back for, Liz. Just as Judy had accepted her fate, so had I."

"After a while, I grew tired. The farm wasn't doing great. The ebbs and flows of the economy took their tolls on it, and me. Things started falling apart around me, literally and figuratively. The house and the rest of the farm fell into disrepair, all I did was work and sleep. My work was always in vain. While I was fixing one thing, something else would fall apart. My attempts to sleep were in vain, too. Every time I closed my eyes, I saw her. I was a zombie; I had no emotions left anymore. I borrowed money and I lived off credit cards as long as I could after shutting down the farm completely. I worked odd jobs and such to make a little cash to survive on for several years. Then I started coughing up blood," Lou winced again.

"That's when you found out you had cancer?" Liz asked.

"Yes, ma'am. But in a weird way, cancer's sort of saved my life, ya know?"

"No, I can't say that I do know…"

"It gave me a deadline I could try to extend. Something to fight again. Something to fight for–life! I couldn't afford the treatments, but I could afford to try what I could. And that led me to you, and Maysville City Schools, and a job, and insurance, and here I am. I'm still fighting!" Lou proclaimed with excitement in her voice.

"I guess I do see your point," Liz replied, pensively. "But you're sitting in the hospital now. And I'm worried sick about you. We have to figure things out between us, but I think I have a plan that will keep things together if you'll listen to me."

"I'm open to all those things, Liz Ward. You have my word," Lou smiled, grabbing Liz's hand.

"But first," Liz replied, "you've gotta open this," pointing to the note from Judy still sitting in Lou's lap that had gone ignored and unopened this entire time.

"This can wait a minute. Judging by this post mark, it's waited all week. The past can wait a little bit longer. I want to hear your grand plan for the future!"

"Okay, fine. I'm going to preface this by saying I have done some snooping around your house…"

Lou gave her a stern look, "And?"

"And," Liz answered, "I now understand why your bedroom closet has one whole side filled with the outdated clothes of someone half your size."

"The plan, dear, the plan!" Lou reminded her.

"Okay, so you know how I suggested making the farm into a wedding venue?" Liz asked.

"Yes…" Lou replied reluctantly.

"Well, I've done some research. There's not a venue in a forty-mile radius that has to offer what your farm does. The pond, the historic home, the barn, the gardens, all of it. Nobody has that. We can also capitalize on the fact that six Derby winners came from the farm, doing a whole derby/polo vibe. People would love that, especially ones who can't afford to actually get into the races," Liz said, sounding like an expert in this field.

She went on, "Everything needs some love, and some places need a little more than love. But I also have a way to get there," Liz stated. "Your house has some treasures. Treasures I don't think you know about, or you would have pawned them a while ago."

"Like what?" Lou asked, confused at the suggestion that there was anything left in her house of any value.

"The silver, for one!"

"I'm not selling Grandmama's silver, you'll have to bury me with it," Lou said, cutting off that suggestion.

"Not your family silver, the Brooks family silver!"

"But I don't have the Brooks family silver! Have you lost your mind?"

"Oh, yes you do, my friend. It's sitting in your dining room. A sterling tea set worth over $20,000 according to my friend Trenton down at Beverly Bremer Silver Shop in Atlanta. Along with 24 place settings of antique flow blue, identical to a set that just sold at auction for over $4,000," Liz shared, smiling like a Cheshire cat.

"No way, there's no way they would have left anything that valuable there. The furniture was nice–several good antiques. But not anything worth near that much, I'm sure of it."

"Oh, we could sell a few of those antiques, too. That Georgian secretary in your bedroom is valued at nearly $5,000. Anyway, you said yourself Helen never even saw the house after she moved away, years before she inherited it. She probably didn't know any of it was even there," Liz reminded her.

"So, you're saying we sell this stuff to make improvements on the property and we just turn it over to being a wedding spot?" Lou asked, unsure of this whole scheme.

"That's exactly what I'm saying. We don't have to borrow money that way. If it was okay with you, I could even move in and pay you rent."

"Then where would I live?!" Lou asked, chuckling.

"Well, we would live together," Liz answered.

"Someone rent the U-Haul!" Lou hollered out the hospital room door. "Lesbians moving in together after a week!"

Liz laughed, "Shut up. It wouldn't be like that. It would be business partners, sharing the property."

"Right. Business partners. So, people would be traipsing through our bedroom, going through my clothes, like someone else I know, acting all nosey. I'm not sold."

"We would move upstairs. The upper floor would be closed in with a doorway at the top of the stairs, and it would be off limits to clients. The lower floor would be open for business. Oh, by the way, that wallpaper in the dining room and front hall? Hand painted French wallpaper. Valued today at $1,200 per piece, which is 16 inches by 26 inches. Based on my calculations you have about $360,000 in wallpaper alone. Huge selling point," expert Liz added.

"I don't know. This is a lot to take in, and a short time for me to take it in." Lou was nervous. She had to admit it was a decent proposal. Liz did know historic preservation. She knew people, being a hiring director. But what made Lou hesitate was the idea of doing this with Liz. Being business partners, and the prospect of being partners in the other way. After thirty-five years of no interaction to going to living with someone again, she wasn't sure she could do it. She shared that with Liz.

"I get it, I really do. So why don't we meet in the middle? We sell the things; we start work on your house. That's stuff that needs to be done with or without me." Lou agreed with that sentiment. "And over that time, we will get to know each other better, and then talk about moving in. Repairs and renovations will take a while. We won't rush anything."

"That sounds reasonable," Lou surmised.

"See how well we can get along when we talk things out?" Liz proved.

"Yeah, yeah, yeah," Lou feigned annoyance. She was really ecstatic at this idea, the whole concept now.

"Okay, NOW can we open the letter?" Liz asked impatiently.

38

"Daddy, how could you hide all this from me for all these years?" Little Chuck demanded with anger, slamming his fist down on his father's desk.

Big Chuck was unfazed. "I didn't keep it from you, I just didn't tell you," he quipped back. "Besides, Judy knew; I kept her in the loop because I know how much she cared for Lou. If you had cared about her that much, you would have tried to track her down or follow up, too," Big Chuck said.

"I cared about my wife. She was the love of my life. And Lou tried to take her away from me. I had no use for her. I'd softened over the years with my attitude towards her, but it's coming back to me now. Only this time it's directed towards you. You had no right to include Judy in your little investigation. Maybe if you hadn't, she'd still be alive now. YOU are the one who killed Judy, not me," Little Chuck declared as he stormed out of the room, leaving only Ruby and Joan behind with Big Chuck.

"Well, I for one, am stunned. Stunned is the only way to describe just how stunned I am!" Joan cried.

"Knock it off, for the love of God, Joan. I think you must have such a grudge against Lou because she went out and actually lived her life instead of being some sexually repressed, self-hating closet case like you," he shot back.

"Well, I never, Charles Jackson! You have some kind of nerve accusing me of that perverse filth! I am not like those people!"

"Those people are my child and my deceased daughter-in-law whom I loved like a child. So, you can shut your trap while you're ahead or Ruby will be the only one living in The Gables when I kick the bucket!" he ordered her.

Joan stormed out of the room next, leaving Big Chuck and Ruby alone. Ruby had barely said a word. She was the only other living person who had known about everything that had been revealed throughout this saga. She looked to Big Chuck for guidance. "I've done about all I can do," he said. "Except for making that phone call," he added, sighing. "We have to call her tonight. If she wants to come home for the funeral, we have to tell her, so she has time to get here from Kentucky."

"You reckon you'll call her or should Little Chuck do it?" Ruby asked.

"Good question," Big Chuck declared. "I don't know. I was sort of hoping that maybe you would do it?" he looked at Ruby with pleading eyes.

Ruby's eyes turned big as half dollars, "No, siree, Mr. Chuck. This isn't any of my business. I ain't got no right calling Ms. Lou after all this time, sitting myself down in the middle of family matters," she protested.

"Ruby, you are family. I consider you family, everyone does. But you're just detached enough that there's a better chance of Lou coming home if you're the one to ask. And I want you to explain everything to her. I want her to come home. I need her to come home. I've got one foot in the grave, and if I die without seeing my girl, I'll never rest in peace. I can't risk her not coming because she's mad that me or Chuck have called. She can't be mad at you. She'll do whatever you ask her. Please, Ruby."

Ruby thought about the request for a minute or two before following up with questions. "Now you say I'm supposed to tell her everything. You really mean everything? Your stomach cancer? The private investigator? Her house? The money? The fire" she asked, looking for guidance.

"Everything. If she's gonna walk in here after 35 years, she needs to know exactly what she's walking into," Chuck decided. "And if she chooses not to," his eyes closed, "then she needs to know everything that happened anyway. I'm not keeping any secrets anymore."

Ruby just shook her head. "I just don't know, Mr. Chuck. This is a lot to lay on a woman. Me and Ms. Lou both. You've always been good to me, but I don't know if I can do this."

"Please. You're the only one around here I can trust to tell the truth–the whole truth," Big Chuck begged.

"I guess so," Ruby finally capitulated. "Give me the phone number you got for her. I'll call in a little while once I get my head right about this," she sighed. "I can't tell her all this over the phone, but I'll figure it out somehow."

Big Chuck wrote down the phone number he had for Lou and handed it to Ruby. He couldn't explain the feeling of relief washing over him with this task delegated to someone else. And who better than to be the one to do it than an impartial party like Ruby? She would stick to the facts. Lou would undoubtedly trust her more than any of the rest of them. This was the best plan of action possible, given the circumstances.

Ruby walked out of the study to clean up the kitchen and pack away the slew of leftovers still sitting on the counters. Big Chuck leaned back in his chair, closing his eyes again. The pain pills were barely touching his ailments these days. He learned to just sit back and take it as it came. But he knew his days were numbered, likely in thc double digits range. He just needed to get all this sorted out before that time came.

39

Dear Lou,

I suppose I'm the last person you expected to hear from after all this time. There's so much I want to say to you and no words to say any of it. I've lived the last thirty plus years lying. Lying to my husband and child. Lying to friends and family. Living a lie. Lying to live, I guess. These lies and the secrets I've had to keep have been a heavy burden to bear all this time.

I want you to know that I have kept up with you all these years. I helped your father hire a private investigator not long after your mother passed, and we have been receiving updates for a long time. That's how I know you are still living at the farm. That's how I also know you've been diagnosed with late-stage cancer.

Knowing you were alive and watching you from afar all this time gave me much comfort. But now knowing that I would soon be living in a world where you don't, has led me to make a choice today, the day I'm writing this letter.

I've chosen to end my life today. I decided I couldn't bear to live in a world where you don't exist anymore. By the time you get this, I may be gone and buried. I don't know if killing yourself is an automatic ticket to hell, but I hope it's not. I hope we will be reunited again one day since I know it won't be in this lifetime.

I love you. I've always loved you. I will always love you. My dying will be better described as a broken heart than as suicide, if only they could list that on a death certificate. Not due to any actions on your part but solely those of my own.

-J

A deep, painful, guttural moan escaped Lou's lips as she read each sentence. She felt the pain washing over every inch of her body. A pain made up of regret, hatred, disgust, sorrow, sympathy, and more.

By now, Liz knew Lou well enough to know better than to ask what the note said or to interrupt Lou's emotional moment. She respected that. And she waited. She waited while Lou sobbed, while she balled up her fists in rage, and while she closed her eyes so tight it was like they had disappeared from her face completely.

Hearing the commotion, one of the hospital staff came into the room. "Out, out, everybody out!" Liz cried. "She's fine, just upset. Nothing to see here!" she shouted as she slammed the door behind them. She sat in the chair in the corner and just waited. She gave Lou the space she needed, and she waited for when Lou would feel like sharing what she read with her. After all the progress they'd made in the past couple days, particularly the past 24 hours, she wasn't willing to risk another scene like the ones before. In less than a week, Liz had learned Lou–learned how she operated, learned what to say and when to say it. She was more in tune with Lou than she had been with perhaps any other human being in her life.

After several minutes, the outburst seemed to diminish into just crying, then silent tears, and then just sniffling. Lou finally opened her eyes, looking around the room for Liz. Everything she just read, and the first thing she could think of with a somewhat clearer mind was Liz, the woman sitting in the corner with tears in her own eyes. Not because of what she knew, or rather didn't know, but for the pain she was witnessing from someone who meant so very much to her. This letter could be about the weather in Georgia, a dead relative, or losing the SEC championship, Liz didn't know. What she did know was that she would let Lou handle it in her way and she would be there in whatever capacity Lou needed her. That's what you do for a friend. That's what you do for someone you love.

When Lou had finally calmed down enough so that she could speak, she simply uttered out, "Judy," looking into Liz's eyes.

"What about Judy?" Liz asked cautiously.

"She's dead," Lou whispered.

Now it was Liz's turn for some mixed emotions, but even more so, some questions. For one thing, who was this letter from, if not Judy? How did a dead woman mail a note? That must have been a hell of a postage bill. How long had she been dead? How did they get Lou's address? What did they write? She knew she couldn't just blurt this barrage of inquiries to Lou, so she started slowly.

"Who wrote to tell you this?" Liz asked gingerly.

"Judy."

Hm. Okay. More delicately, "How did Judy write a letter to tell you Judy was dead?" She said it slowly and clearly, assuming Lou must be on the verge of a mental break.

"This wasn't just a letter, Liz," Lou retorted. "This was a suicide note."

Liz sat back in her chair, unprepared for that turn of events. Boy had this weekend been one hell of an event. Now this. Realizing that quenched the most pertinent of her questions, Liz turned her focus from being nosy (for now), to Lou. "How are you with this? What are you feeling?" she asked.

"I don't know," Lou lied, with Liz seeing right through it, but she didn't want to push it.

"Okay. I know you're really tired and we've talked about a lot today, so I'm going to give you some time with this, alright? I'm going to talk to the nurse for some updates and see when we can get you home."

Liz stepped out quietly while Lou sat in her hospital bed, her life replaying in her head. So many good times, then so, so many bad times. Dreams of Judy. Hatred for Judy. Aching for Judy. Cursing Judy for leaving her on that damn farm by herself.

She had been feeling better before this note. Things were slowly moving in the right direction with Liz, there was hope for her financial situation, she had a job, she could get the medical care she needed. Now Judy was back, taking the life out of her again. Lou balled up the note and threw it across the room, missing the trash can but refusing to care. Judy was gone–again. And Liz was here. She decided she was going to leave the ghosts of her past six feet under and focus on the beautiful flower growing in her broken pot.

When Liz returned, she opened the door slowly, unsure of what state she might find Lou in. Imagine her surprise when she found Lou sitting all the way up in the hospital bed with her hair brushed, putting on some makeup. Liz looked around the room for the fairy godmother, wondering briefly if she had concocted the whole experience less than 15 minutes ago in her head. She carefully approached Lou's bedside and slowly asked, "Is everything okay?" She was thinking this must be some psychotic episode, some delusion or hallucination that Lou was trapped in.

Cheerfully, Lou replied, "I'm fine! How are you?"

Liz was supremely freaked out now. Should she call the doctor or an exorcist? "I'm okay," she responded. "But I'm not sure you are," she frowned.

"You know, there for a minute, I wasn't. I was so sad, so mad, so filled with emotions that I couldn't even name. But then I realized that woman has been gone for a long time. Dead or alive, she was gone. I'm sad about it, but I've been sad about it for 35 years. It's really not a bit different now than it was all those years ago. I appreciate the sentiment, but it made me realize that I, and she, wasted our best years in hell, pining over a lost love. I'm not going to let that ruin what I have in front of me now. It ate her alive. So much so that the only solution she could muster was killing herself. I'm not going to let it eat me alive. The cancer's doing enough of that anyway," she joked darkly. "I'm going to live. I chose to live. I choose to live now."

Still with reservations, Liz had to agree with Lou's attitude. It made sense, actually. It was, perhaps, the healthiest outlook on this situation possible, to Lou's credit and Liz's surprise.

"Well, if you feel okay, the doctor doesn't see any reason for you to stay here any longer. He's consented to discharge you, as long as someone stays with you to ensure you're cared for. I would offer for it to be me, but I'm really your only option, so it's me or you stay in this plastic twin sized folding bed," Liz joked to match the new aura of the room.

"I guess that's agreeable. But no U-Hauls!"

Laughing, Liz replied, "Deal. I'll go get him to start the paperwork and sign off on it. Hopefully we can bust out of here in time to run through a drive thru on the way home. I'm starving."

"Same," Lou replied. "This hospital food tasted like shit," she grimaced.

In the blink of an eye, the day had turned around. Then it turned bad again. And now it was back to being okay. A true 360 degrees of emotions.

On her way out of the room, while Lou was gathering her things around her bed, Liz noticed the crumpled paper on the floor. She knew what it was immediately, so she knocked it out the door with the edge of her shoe until it was in the hallway. She closed the door and stuffed it into her pocket. As happy as she was for Lou's positive attitude, Liz wasn't sure if she was buying it. Regardless, she was going to get answers to all her questions, one way or another.

40

Ruby dialed the number Big Chuck had given to her, her hands shaking. Lord, what was she going to say to this girl after all this time? The phone rang, and with each ring Ruby's anxiety rose higher. She waited, but there was no answer, so she hung the phone up.

Ruby flopped down onto her bed, heavy with the weight of 30 plus years of lying and scandal. Part of her was glad it was all finally coming to light, coming to an end. But the other part of her was dreading it. Dreading what was still yet to come. Then there would be the death of Big Chuck to deal with. It wouldn't be too long now. So much for a woman to keep inside and so much for a woman to bear, especially for a family that wasn't even her kin.

Ruby had been brought up like everybody else. Being a homosexual was a sin, an abomination, according to Leviticus. But she read her Bible almost daily. And as much as people harped on that line of scripture, it seemed like they spent an equal amount of time forgetting the hundreds of other pages that talk about love. Loving thyself, loving thy neighbor. The whole commandment could be summed up with offering love to one another. That was the part she chose to focus on, unlike so many of the people around her in Clanton.

Kin or not, she loved the Jacksons, and she loved Lou. Every part of her. Lou was just a girl when Ruby started working for them, but she quickly became the apple of Ruby's eye. They spent more time together than Lou and Ms. Louise ever did. Ruby knew Lou was different, but she couldn't put her finger on it. She didn't know enough about it to describe it. But she loved Lou all the same.

Causing Ruby to almost jump out of her skin, there was an unexpected knock on her bedroom door. Nobody ever came into Ruby's bedroom. As close as they all were, it was understood that when Ruby was in there she was not working, and she was to have privacy and solace. For that to be broken, it must be something important. She rose from the bed and put on her house shoes. When she opened the door, she found a tearful Josie Jackson. Ruby immediately put her arms around her.

"What's wrong, baby? What you need?" she cooed and coddled Josie.

"I don't know," Josie whispered through the tears. "My whole world's been turned upside down in a few days and I don't know if I'm coming or going. I feel like my whole life has been a lie," her tears began falling freely.

"Shhh, shhh, baby. We're gonna get through it. You got ol' Ruby here to take care of you." She wrapped the girl in her arms as best she could. Josie was built like her Aunt Lou, tall, broad, and wide with child-bearing hips. Ruby was dwarfed next to her, but in this moment, Josie saw only the strength and fortitude Ruby had displayed her entire life.

The pair sat down on Ruby's bed covered in a beautiful patchwork quilt. Ruby's family had been some of the first quilters in Gee's Bend, Alabama. Now their work was featured all over the world. In Vogue, in museums, and just picked up by Target. Ruby had some incredible pieces that told the stories of her ancestors and their struggles. Josie ran her fingers over the quilt, distracting herself for a moment while she worked to regain her composure. "You know, Ruby, these things are probably worth a fortune. These are original Gee's Bend quilts, aren't they?" She studied them more closely.

"Yes, ma'am!" Ruby beamed. "My Maw was one of Mr. Gee's slaves, then she stayed on when Mr. Pettway bought the plantation and her along with it. That was my mama's mother. Everybody called her Maw. By the time my mama came along, the Big War was over, and they were sharecropping. When cotton prices fell after the crash in '29, they just about lost everything. But Mama and my aunts and cousins held on somehow. The Red Cross looked out for 'em because they didn't have nothing left. Then I came along a little later. Mama sent me to Atlanta to live with her cousin Arlethia when I was about eight or nine. Said there wasn't nothing left for me in Gee's Bend and the only way I'd make it was to get out and go to the city."

"Law, I hated her," Ruby shook her head. "I begged and cried and hollered. Daddy had to peel me off the porch when he took me out to the ferry to take me to the mainland and send me to Atlanta. He cried near as much as I did, I think. But he knew it was the right thing to do, too. So, I went to Atlanta and lived with Arlethia. She worked for a white family down off of Ponce de Leon Avenue. It ran all the way from downtown to Stone Mountain."

"Still does," Josie interjected, mindlessly adding her own parts to Ruby's story.

"They was on Oakdale Road if I remember right. I was just a kid, but they let me work with my aunt. She wore a black and white uniform every day. She worked every day but Monday, 7 in the morning til 7 at night. She put the fear of God in me 'fore she took me with her. I was to be seen and not heard. If I was spoken to, I did what I was told with a yes, ma'am or yes, sir. Lord, they was mean. Broke Arlethia's spirit in all those years, I'm sure of it. Only reason they let me come was 'cause it was another set of hands for free."

"How did you make it up here?" Josie asked, realizing Ruby knew everything in the world there was to know about her, but she knew surprisingly little about Ruby.

"Me and Arlethia worked for the Abrahams, and they finally hired me on, if you can call it that, when I turned about 13, I think. They paid me five dollars a week," Ruby chuckled. "But it was more money than I'd ever had. I told everybody in the apartments where we lived, I was gonna save up and go home to Gee's Bend and build us a house for me and my mama and daddy and my two brothers," she smiled.

"Then one day our little apartment down off of Forsyth Street got broken into," the smile drained from her face. "They took Arlethia's radio she'd saved up for. The gold wedding band that had been her daddy's. And my little stash of money I had hid under my bed. Couldn't have been more than $150, but that was big money back then. After we came home that night, Arlethia never felt safe again. I was pretty sure she never slept again, maybe just a nap here and there. So, she decided we needed to leave Atlanta. Mr. Abraham was surprisingly sympathetic, and he told us to come up to Clanton. He had an uncle who needed help. I went with her and when I showed up, they said they didn't need another mouth in the house, and they only wanted Arlethia. Since she moved in with them, there wouldn't be anywhere for me to live. She asked around and I was able to stay with a real nice older lady 'til I found work of my own. That's when I started working for your granddaddy and grandmama. I waited outside the Blue Star grocery store every day in the best maid's outfit I had, asking white ladies if they needed help. Your grandmama Louise was the first to actually ask about me, ask where I came from, what I was doing. When I told her my story, she said she had been needing some help around the house. She had two wild kids that needed to be wrangled–your Aunt Lou and your daddy," Ruby smiled. "She asked me if I knew how to take care of kids. I lied and said of course I did. She brought me home and had me on the payroll before Mr. Chuck ever came home from the office!" She laughed. "He just did whatever Ms. Louise said. So, I started working here. I stayed living with Ms. Brantley and paid her rent. Then I met Joe," her eyes gleamed.

By this point Josie was entirely enamored by Ruby's story and had completely forgotten about her own troubles. "Me and Joe moved into that little house on Locust Street and your grandparents gave us the down payment for it," she smiled. "They been good to me," she said firmly. "Your folks ain't perfect, ain't nobody's family perfect. But they did what they could. Did the best they knew how to at the time. Now I'm not excusing what they did to your Aunt Lou. But they were products of their time. Your granddaddy finally came around. Poor Ms. Louise, it ended up bein' too late for her."

"Now you got a choice. You can be mad as you want at all of 'em. Or you can look 'em in the eye, faults and all, and love 'em. You don't have to like 'em. But you can't go around with that hate in your heart, baby. You'll drop dead like your grandmama, God rest her soul," Ruby looked up like Louise was painted on her bedroom ceiling.

Josie wasn't crying anymore. She was just sad. "I just wish things had been different. I wish they had all been born in this day and age where they could be who they wanted to be and love who they wanted to love."

Ruby shook her head, "Not in this town, honey. Atlanta may be blue by now but this place still red as the rednecks that pack the carpet mill. They'd still turn out a woman like your Aunt Lou quick as you could toss old scraps to a yard dog. These towns steal young folks. Steal their spirits, steal who they are at their core. You can move to Atlanta and be yourself and get lost in the crowd and never be found. But not out here. I always wanted to go back home, but it would have been worse than Clanton," she remarked.

"You never went home after you moved to Atlanta?" Josie asked.

"No, ma'am," Ruby replied quietly. "Daddy died not long after they sent me off. By the time I could afford to get back, my brothers were gone, scattered across this land. Mama was out of her mind. They'd sent her to a nursing home in Selma. She wouldn't remember me no how, so I never went back. I decided to remember her the way she was."

"I'm sorry, Ruby. I didn't know all this."

Raising her voice in a positive manner, Ruby replied, "Well, now you do." She stood up and added, "And I hope you'll think about what I said about your kin. It's not their fault. It's these towns and the ignorance and the hate and the fear of the unknown. They're not bad people. Misguided, maybe. But your kin ain't bad. 'Least not that I know of," Ruby grinned.

Josie hugged her and held her tight. "I love you, Ruby. I mean it."

"I love you, too, baby. Ol' Ruby's always here for you, now you remember that, hear?"

"Yes, ma'am," she smiled.

Josie walked out of Ruby's bedroom towards one of the guest rooms, where she sat down at a writing desk, to draft the eulogy she needed to prepare for Judy's funeral in less than two days.

Ruby sat back down and dialed the number again. Maybe it was out of service. Maybe it didn't belong to Lou anymore. The phone rang and after a bit finally went to voicemail this time. Ruby inhaled as she began with what she needed to say.

41

Lou and Liz pulled things together and checked out of the hospital. Lou had an almost disturbingly positive demeanor, especially for someone who had just been informed of the death of the greatest love of her life. The truth was, however, that Lou had been set free. Judy's pseudo ghost had held an undue power over Lou for far too long. Now Judy's real ghost could float right on away into the clouds or the depths of hell or wherever she would end up. There was no longer anything Lou could do, which she accepted, and was content with.

Getting into Liz's Subaru, Liz remembered a fact that might bring the mood down just a tad. "So, one thing I didn't mention was that your power was cut off for non-payment. I called and paid the minimum to have it restored, but there was no estimate on when that would happen."

Surprisingly ignoring how Liz had inserted her help in the situation, Lou commented, "Aw, shit. Not that again. The reconnection fee is about as much as I owe. We don't get paid for two more weeks, what am I gonna do?" Lou asked aloud, mostly rhetorically.

"Well," Liz began, "You could stay with me." Lou flashed her eyes at Liz. "Just a friend staying with a friend until she can get back to her house. That's all!" Liz declared.

"Okay, you're right. Thank you. Can we go to my house so I can get some clothes and things and what I'll need for the dogs?"

"Ugh, the dogs. I forgot about them. Well, at least they've had a bath and were groomed. Shouldn't be *quite* so bad," Liz teased as she drove out to Lou's farm. It was only just past sunset, but with absolutely no electricity the big old house loomed with a shadow and was just plain spooky looking. Liz made a mental note of adding landscape lighting during the yard overhaul. Her restoration gears were grinding.

Liz helped Lou out and they stepped around cautiously to the stairs to the door. Liz turned on the flashlight on her cell phone and asked Lou where a candle or oil lamp might be to help guide them around.

"Mudroom, on the shelf above the dryer," Lou told her. "Should be some matches or a lighter in the kitchen, I'll go look," she added.

"How are you going to look in the dark?" Liz joked.

"Please, after 35 years in this house, I could navigate it blind as a bat. At least tonight there's a little moonlight creeping in."

Lou made her way to the kitchen to look for fire while Liz went in search of the oil lamp. Not seeing her cigarettes and lighter on the counter, she turned to the junk drawer. Now, in the south at least, everybody everywhere has a junk drawer. Said drawer could contain anything from Taco Bell sauce packets to Memaw's good pearls. There would be Sharpies, batteries, twine, stakes for last Christmas's lighted reindeer, gym clips, Gorilla Glue, a tape measure, and, surely, a box of matches or a lighter. Just as Lou grabbed the red and blue box of Diamond brand matches, the power flickered back on, and the gentle hum of the refrigerator cranked up.

"And God said, 'Let there be light!'" Lou declared loudly from the kitchen. Liz walked in, oil lamp in hand, just in case.

"Well, that happened sooner than I anticipated," she remarked. "We'll just add that payment to what you already owe me," Liz smirked.

"Ha ha ha," Lou retorted. Lou and Liz made their way to the library/makeshift bedroom. It was much easier now with light. "You know," Lou began, "Now that there's power back on here at my house, I don't really *need* to come stay with you…" her voice trailed off.

Liz tried not to look dejected, but she failed.

"But what I NEED is for you to stay with me," Lou said quietly, looking into Liz's eyes like it was the first time they'd ever seen each other. She waited for a response. She had played coy with Judy all those years ago and look where that got her. She wasn't going to let that happen with Liz.

Thinking about the proposal for a moment, Liz replied, "I wanna stay with you, Lou Jackson. I do. But I'm worried it's gonna be a little crowded with three of us in that bed," she said, inadvertently referencing Princess Diana's dig at Camilla Parker Bowles in an interview years ago.

"I told you, I don't know how to pinpoint it, but I'm over Judy. The ship has sailed in so many ways," Lou stated with confidence.

"What about all the rest of your family?" Liz blurted, realizing she just gave away the intel she was supposed to be hiding.

"How do you know about the rest of the family?" Lou asked coldly.

"Because I read Judy's note. I know that they know all about you. I know that they've kept up with you. I know that they think you're on death's door. That has to make you feel some type of way!" Liz's voice quickened and got louder as she spoke every word.

Lou was trying her damndest to stay calm. This was that thing that Liz did that drove her absolutely bonkers. She was trying not to overreact, but Liz knew this was a hot button action and she did it anyway.

"That note was for me, Liz. It was addressed to me," Lou said simply, attempting to retain her composure and not blow up on Liz yet again.

"I know, but you're acting so weird. It's like you flipped a switch. Nobody goes from utter despair and woe to the top of the world looking down on creation, Lou," Liz countered.

"You're correct," Lou said with an even-voiced agreement. "But that still doesn't give you a right to go through my personal things and extract information I wasn't exactly ready to share." Lou was surprising herself with her own calmness.

Realizing the gravity of yet another one of her missteps, Liz began to tear up.

"Now don't start that all over again, Liz. I can't take this 'kid getting caught' bit. I'm too tired. I just don't know how many times I have to ask the same thing over and over for you to respect my privacy. I will share things with you on my terms, in my time. If there's going to be any hope for this as a business venture, as a romantic future, even just as friends, you have to allow me that."

"I know you are just trying to help, just trying to understand me. But I need you to trust me. To understand that I know myself and I know what I need to do. I've been alone for so incredibly long that I am not used to anyone meddling into any of my affairs. I need some space and grace while I get used to going from nothing to hot and heavy in one week. Can we please, please, please agree to respect that?" Lou was being as mature in this argument as she had any argument ever.

The reason was because she wanted this to work— the business, the friendship, the romance, all of it. And if they didn't communicate these things now, there wouldn't be any chance for any kind of future.

The phone was ringing, but no one stopped to answer it. Liz looked at the floor, knowing her misstep and regretting it. She felt guilty because she *was* guilty. She knew what she had done would crawl all over Lou like a tick on a slow-moving hound dog, but she did it anyway.

Before Liz could say anything, the answering machine picked up the unanswered phone call. The faint southern drawl of an older woman began.

"Ms. Louvenia? This is Ruby. I wanted to call you because I have some bad news. There's some things we need to talk to you about, but I don't wanna leave that here on your answering machine. Call me back here at The Gables, 706-555-3288 as soon as you can, please. We have to talk."

Lou and Liz's eyes locked for the duration of the message, neither one moving, both forgetting the fight at hand. When the machine beeped indicating the caller had hung up, a split second of utter uncertainty passed, and Lou lunged towards the machine, pressing play. The pair listened to Ruby's words again and you could have heard a pin drop.

Lou searched the room, not knowing what she was looking for or looking at. She was dazed, confused, drowning in memories, anxiety, and fear. Liz held Lou's arms and steadied her, speaking directly to her to bring her back to the ground.

"Who was that?" Liz asked in a serious voice.

"It was Ruby, our maid," Lou answered with a hollow, unfeeling voice. "My mama and daddy's maid," Lou corrected herself.

"What do you think she meant when she said bad news?" Liz asked.

"I don't know. It has to be about my parents. Or Judy. I've gotta call back down there," Lou reached for the phone. Liz stopped her.

"Okay, let's just process this for one second before you call. Can we do that please?" Liz pleaded.

Too distraught to recall their arguments moments before, Lou agreed, wordlessly nodding her head. They sat down at the kitchen table. Lou was shaking. Liz wasn't sure exactly how to approach this, but she knew Lou, and she knew Lou didn't need to just call back right away.

"So, we know about Judy. You've had some time to think about that, and you're in a good place," Liz reminded her. Lou nodded again. "Now if it's about your daddy, how are you going to feel?"

"I don't know. I think I've thought about Judy so much over these years, I never thought about my parents' demise. There was so much left unsaid, so much anger. I'm still angry!" Lou declared.

"And that, my friend, is why we are taking just a moment before we call back," Liz gently reminded her.

"Yes, right. We need a plan," Lou concurred.

"First off, Ruby called you. Neither of your parents or your brother called. If it was something truly grave, wouldn't a family member call you?" Liz tried to reason.

"Ruby is family," Lou replied. "Ruby practically raised us. Especially Little Chuck. She was as much a mother to me, if not more than, my real mother. Daddy would have called me if he could have. We were always the closest. But he didn't call. Something's happened to Daddy, I just know it." Lou jumped up again to go to the phone. This time Liz didn't stop her, but she stood beside her, for both moral and physical support. And to figure out what the hell was going on for herself.

Lou's hands shook violently as she dialed the number to The Gables. She had to start over twice because she inadvertently pressed the wrong button, which made her even more frustrated. When the call finally did go through, it was the longest wait time in the history of the world.

An old familiar voice answered, "The Jacksons'?"

"Ruby?" Lou croaked out, "It's me." She said it as if she hadn't been gone for 35 years. Like they talked twice every week. Like Ruby would automatically know the voice without introduction.

She did, though. "Oh, my sweet, sweet girl." Ruby began to cry.

"What is it, Ruby? Is it Daddy? Or Mama?" Lou asked frantically.

"No, baby. I've gotta tell you something else. It's Judy. She's gone."

Lou was taken aback for a moment. The emotions and distress she had felt in the past few minutes suddenly slipped away. "Ruby, I know that already," Lou said, kind of annoyed.

Now it was Ruby's turn for the emotion, distress, and anxiety to slip away, only to leave more questions and confusion. "Well now how you know that, Ms. Lou?"

"She wrote me a suicide letter, Ruby. She told me everything."

"Everything? About the investigator and the fire and the money, all of it?"

Now it was Lou's turn to be confused. "Money? Fire? What the hell are you talking about, Ruby?" Remembering her manners, Lou retracted her statement, "Sorry, Ruby, I didn't mean to talk to you like that." Here she was almost 60 and she was still apologizing like a little girl where Ruby was concerned.

"That's what I thought," Ruby surmised. "Honey, you need to get down here. Judy's funeral is Sunday. There's a lot we need to talk about, all of us. Your daddy, Little Chuck, Joan, Josie."

"Josie? Who's that?" Lou asked.

"That's your niece, Ms. Louvenia."

"Oh. Well, what about Mama?" Lou inquired.

"I'm sorry to have to tell you this now, Ms. Louvenia, but Ms. Louise passed on close to 30 years ago now," Ruby answered.

Lou was somewhere between sad, unsurprised, overwhelmed, and even numb. Perhaps she was so overstimulated that she couldn't feel anything anymore in an appropriate manner.

"Okay," Lou replied. That was the best she could muster at this point in time. "Okay, so you want me to come down there?" Lou confirmed.

"Ms. Louvenia, I think you ought to. There's a lot going on, and you need to be here for it," Ruby told her.

"But the whole family hates me, or they did the last time I saw them. There's nothing for me to come home for anymore. There's no 'home' to come to," Lou said firmly.

"You have a home here. As long as I'm around, you have a home and a family. I took care of you since you was knee high to a grasshopper. You're as much mine as you are a Jackson. And I'm telling you I want you to come home. I need you to come home. Now tell me you will, please, baby," Ruby was pleading now.

How could Lou refuse this? Ruby was right. Ruby had always been there for her. If there was a lot going on, now was as good a time to face it as any. She began to consider her own mortality and decided what she needed to do.

"Okay, Ruby, I'll come. I can't make any promises of what I can do in all this, but I'll come down there. If you'll play referee," Lou said, partly defeated and partly afraid.

"Thank you, Ms. Louvenia," Ruby said graciously. "When you think you can be here?"

"I'll leave tomorrow morning. Should be there by early afternoon," Lou confirmed. "One thing," Lou added with embarrassment, "Where will I stay?"

That was a great question–one Ruby hadn't an answer for because she hadn't considered that. "Well, you can stay here at The Gables. Your old bedroom," Ruby stated with thrice the confidence she felt in making that decision.

"Are you sure about that? I don't think that's a good idea after all this time. Isn't there a motel or something?" Lou didn't have the money for a motel, but it sounded better than staying with all her family.

Ruby chuckled, "Ms. Louvenia, you've been gone a long time, but not that long! Ain't no motel closer than Kennesaw. The old Tarrer Inn closed down in '02. Nowhere to stay around here since then."

"Ugh," Lou groaned. "Okay. I'll be there, but I'm not making any promises to stay there, agreed?"

"Yes, ma'am," Ruby capitulated.

"Ruby, one more thing. You don't have to call me ma'am or Ms. Louvenia or anything like that anymore. It's Lou. Just Lou, okay?"

"Okay, yes, ma'am." Ruby and Lou both laughed at the same time. "Sorry, baby. Old habits die hard."

"Bye, Ruby. I'll see you tomorrow, okay?"

"I'll be here waiting for you–count on that, sweet girl."

Lou hung up the phone, purposefully not making eye contact with Liz. But Liz was ready for her. "So, we're going to Clanton?" she asked.

Lou looked at her blankly. "I'm going to Clanton." Then she walked to the counter to get a glass of water from the sink.

"Hold on there, missy. You just got out of the hospital. You're in absolutely no shape to drive six hours. Not to mention that car of yours may give out at any point along the way."

"You make a great point," Lou agreed. Liz stood a little straighter. "But you're still not going."

"Now Lou Jackson, you cannot go alone. I promised that doctor I'd keep an eye on you. I am begging you not to do this. Let me help," Liz was pleading so deeply she was on the verge of crying again.

"Fine. I'll let you help me. You can loan me your car. And you can watch the dogs," Lou said matter-of-factly.

"I am not doing that, Lou. Now I mean it." Liz was starting to get angrier than upset. "You need help, you'll need support through this."

"I won't argue with you on that point. But I have to do this myself, Liz. I just have to. I can't waltz in down there for the first time in 35 years with a woman on my arm, thinned hair, all skin and bones, face sunken in. I have to do this my way. Now, like our conversation earlier, which, no, I haven't forgotten about, I need you to give me some space for this and respect my wishes. Will you do that, please?"

Liz was tired–tired of arguing and fighting and trying to change Lou Jackson.

"Okay then. Take the Subaru. I'll stay here with the dogs, and I'll work on things to turn this house around."

"There's a good little business partner!" Lou patronized her. "I'm going to go pack a bag for Clanton," she said with a sureness in her voice that was coming from somewhere very deep inside her.

42

Josie sat at the desk for nearly an hour without any reasonable inspiration of exactly what to write about her mother other than basic stories and niceties. Truth be told, she was a distant figure for Josie's entire life. And after all that had come to light these past couple days, it was as if Judy was a stranger to her. She started to regret volunteering to write this eulogy, but if she knew old lady Chapman, the programs had already been printed, folded, boxed up, and delivered to the church. There was no way out of this.

Finding little inspiration in her brain, she made her way down to Big Chuck's study/bedroom, where he was dozing in his hospital bed in the big window. He never slept these days, only rested when he could. The opening of the heavy wooden door caused him to stir, his eyes turning towards the figure in the doorway. She was tall, broad, even muscular.

"Lou?" he called through his sleepy state. Without his glasses (or his right mind), he would have sworn it was his daughter standing there.

"No, Granddaddy, it's me, Josie."

"Oh, I'm sorry, peanut." He closed his eyes back. "What do you need?"

Big Chuck hadn't called her peanut since she was a kid. She hated it. She hated feeling like a nut. But now she considered the term endearing. Something about it comforted her in this moment when she wasn't sure of anything else around her.

"Can I look at the pictures and stuff?" she asked in a meek voice.

"What pictures? The family pictures? They're in all those albums on the bottom shelf, right of my desk."

"I do want to look at those, but also the others. The ones you showed us of Lou. Can I see them again?" she asked.

Not giving a solid yes or no, he told her, "There's a white cardboard bankers' box in the bottom of that closet next to the bar. That's where everything is." There was no use in hiding it anymore. Everyone knew about the contents, but Big Chuck was still shy about it, protective of the secret items, even slightly guilty at the secret he'd kept for so long from his family.

Josie went to the closet and pulled out the box. She began spreading out the photos on her grandfather's desk. She took the albums off the shelves and began flipping through the pages until she saw the emergence of her mother in the story told only in photographs. Josie noticed for the first time the clean cuts made on so many of the pictures, cuts she never questioned as a kid. Cuts that were far more symbolic than a simple snip of the scissors.

There was her mother and father leaving for their homecoming dance at Lonely Pine. One of Eugenia helping Louise tighten the corset on Judy's wedding dress. Little Chuck holding a newborn Josie in the hospital with a proud but tired Judy in the background. Here was Judy at the garden club's 50th anniversary tea with a big corsage on her shoulder. Another showed Judy, Little Chuck, Big Chuck, and Joan on a float for the Clanton Christmas parade.

Analyzing these photos for the first time in her adult life, Josie wondered, with the new knowledge imparted to her, if Judy had been happy in any single one of them. Was she ever truly happy as long as she lived?

Yes. The answer was yes. When she was with Josie's Aunt Lou. Fleeting moments of passion. A secret love. A deep bond. But, beyond that, Judy struggled for decades living a life she was "meant" to live. Living with a man that couldn't replace her lost love. Bearing his child. Raising a child in constant fear that she might end up like her mother, that she might make the fatal mistakes that she herself had made. Never fully trusting her child. Never trusting her husband. Never trusting anyone around her again. Weighted with secrets, with longing, pain, unquenched desire, and the regret of never doing anything about any of it. And the self-hatred she felt every morning when she opened her eyes and realized she was still caught in a dream she wanted no part of. Not a nightmare, but a weird dream. A dream in which she was so far removed from reality she felt like she was staring into a fishbowl of a life created by everyone but herself.

Touching these photographs of her mother, Josie felt the pain and the sorrow. Maybe it was the newfound knowledge she had. Maybe it was the spirit of her mother. Maybe it was the deep energy of regret that permeated the frail rectangles of paper.

Josie closed the albums and put them back on the shelf where they belonged and turned her attention to the box of photographs and items belonging to her estranged aunt. Looking through the pictures and papers, she could see why her grandfather might have mistaken her for Lou; their bodies and builds were almost exact. Josie assumed she got her height from her father but seeing her aunt the similarity was clear as day.

Lou was a beautiful woman in an understated way. She looked so put together and confident. Her senior portrait with her pearls, sorority photos, accepting her college diploma. And even one on Josie's parents' wedding day. The expression in this photo was different from all the others, though. The pain and sorrow Josie felt from the other pictures and papers was put into ink in this very photo–an unassuming photograph of a woman in love, losing her love right in front of her eyes. An unexpected tear dropped from Josie's eye onto the page, and she sniffled to suck up her feelings.

"You sound like I do every time I pull that box out," Big Chuck broke the silence, causing Josie to jump like a jack rabbit.

"I'm sorry, I thought you fell back to sleep, Granddaddy." Josie put the items back in the box and returned it to the bottom of the closet. She sat on the edge of Chuck's bed. She had so many questions but so few words to ask them in. "I'm just sad," she finally settled on.

"Well, that's to be expected, baby. Your mama just died. Nobody's expecting you to be brave in a time like this. It's okay to let it all out," he assured her.

"It's not that. I'm not even sad about that," she replied.

Big Chuck opened his eyes and raised an eyebrow at that statement. Reading his facial expression, Josie corrected her words. "What I mean is yes, I am sad about that, but I'm sadder about this life of secrets. For Mama and Lou. For you, for Daddy. Nobody could be themselves. Nobody could be honest, not even with each other," she said, eying her grandfather implying his secret with Judy about Lou's life and whereabouts.

"This town does a number on people. If you don't fit in, you might as well have never even existed. Does anyone even ask about what happened to Lou? My guess is no."

"They did for a little while," Big Chuck corrected her. "But we lied. And people took it, hook, line, and sinker. And after a little time, nobody ever asked again. They made up their own stories, their own versions of the truth. And that was that. She was as good as dead in the eyes of Clanton," he sighed regretfully.

"That's what I'm talking about. People matter. Lou mattered. My mama mattered. God only knows how many other people mattered to someone somewhere but just faded into the distance because this town killed them–figuratively or literally."

Josie rose from the edge of her grandfather's bed. "I'm sorry I woke you up, and I'm sorry for dragging all this up again today. I can't talk to Daddy. I don't want to talk to Joan. R.J. doesn't get it. I'm just at a loss for feelings."

"One thing I can promise you, little girl, is that you have never and will never disappoint me. I may not agree with all your newfangled liberal ideas, but you're my peanut and nothing will ever change that."

Josie smiled, kissed her grandfather on the forehead, and walked out of the room, shutting the door behind her. Under his breath, Big Chuck added to no one else in the room, "God, if you'll see fit, I won't make that mistake again."

43

Lou packed the Samsonite suitcase and train case engraved with her initials that her grandmother had given her as a high school graduation gift. She decided to put exactly two outfits in the suitcase: one for the funeral and one for the drive home. There would be no reason for anything more. But just what would she wear? This would be the first time in 35 years anyone in Clanton had seen her. She chuckled inside thinking everyone probably thought she was dead. "Not yet," she said darkly under her breath.

Appearances still mattered to Lou, and this would be no exception. She had to look good.

"Liz, come in here for a minute," she hollered from her room.

Liz made her way to Lou's bedroom. "Oh, you mean I'm allowed in this sacred, personal space? A lowly business partner like me? The dog sitter?" she said half serious, half joking.

"Shut up. I need fashion advice," Lou retorted.

"No shit. Half the time you dress like you just stepped out of the cornfield on Hee Haw, the other half you dress like Tammy Wynette in '88," Liz replied without missing a beat.

"Enough," Lou said firmly. "If you were going to be seen in your hometown for the first time in 35 years, what would you wear?"

"Well first off, I don't have a hometown, and nobody would remember me anyhow, but I'd pick something…" Lou cut her off.

"What do you mean you don't have a hometown? Everybody has a hometown."

"Not when you're shipped around the state in group homes and foster care you don't," Liz said coldly, flipping through the closet with disapproving looks at everything she passed.

"I didn't know," Lou said sheepishly.

"Well, if you'd taken more than two minutes to ask, you would have. But this whole week has been about you, hasn't it? Woe is Lou. Lou needs a job. Lou is sick. Lou needs a ride. Lou has nobody. Lou can't afford her power bill."

"I get it," Lou replied. "I'm sorry. I never asked. I've been too focused on myself to take a moment to learn anything about you." Lou's apology was sincere, and it left her feeling ashamed. This woman had done everything for her in a time of need. Had been there for her, had saved her countless times in one week. And she barely knew more than her name and where she went to college.

"I guess now you might understand why I've latched on to you in the way I have. I've never had anybody. I've never loved or been loved. Romantically, platonically, as a family member. I've had friends, but just that. I was too afraid to let anyone get too close because I was worried I'd be rejected again."

"I'm so sorry, Liz. Really, I am. I've not handled any of this the right way." She placed her hand on Liz's upper arm, and slowly slid it downward. This wasn't the first time a moment like this had occurred in her life, but this time it wasn't in Higgins' Pond. She moved in closer with a small step. Liz looked into Lou's eyes, a mixture of fear, uncertainty, and desire. Lou tilted her head to kiss Liz, gently holding the lower side of her jaw, pushing back a few strands of Liz's hair. Lou allowed Liz the chance to close the gap or step away. She needed to know that Liz wanted this as badly as she did. They stood in the tension of the moment, their breaths mixing in the few centimeters between their faces.

Liz moved closer, her lips just touching Lou's. She paused, still unsure. But Lou pressed forward, removing the last bit of tortured space between them. Fireworks is a cliche term and sparks are for gangly teenagers. This was warmth. Warmth from the heart and the soul, emanating from two sets of lips that had gone untouched, unkissed for far too long. The kiss deepened. The passion escalated. Each of their hands began to roam. They were frantic but gentle–a sureness between them both. A thirst was being quenched for both wilted flowers.

Liz was the first to break away, touching her heated lips, not believing what had just happened. Looking Lou dead in the eyes, breathless, she couldn't form any words to describe what she was feeling. Lou went in again, just holding her this time. Holding her in a way that a friend would. Tears began to stream down Lou's face. This human connection was so powerful that the excess emotion was spilling outside of her.

Liz began to cry, too. But for a different reason. She was afraid. She was still worried about the rejection, about being cast off. This was exactly what she needed and exactly what scared her more than anything in the world. She'd worked for scholarships, held three college degrees, had one of the most important positions in the school system, but none of that made her half as anxious as what was happening at this moment in time.

Liz was afraid if Lou went to Clanton she might never come back again. Her family was there, her past. What was keeping her here in Maysville? A crumbling farm, a pair of geriatric dogs, a job making pennies on the dollar. Liz worried that she would not be enough for Lou to come back to, and it scared her to death. It wasn't as scary when she thought Lou had no family, nowhere else to go. But the tide had turned. There was a family–one who apparently needed her. And if they needed her worse than Liz did, she was afraid of what Lou's choice might be.

Lou was the first one to speak. "I love you, Liz Ward," she declared.

Still crying, Liz whispered back, "I love you, too." She turned her head away, giving Lou the first inclination that these tears were not necessarily happy ones.

"What's wrong?" Lou asked in earnest, holding Liz's arms so she had to face her.

"You're going to go to Clanton and I'm afraid everything will change," Liz said through tears.

Confused, Lou replied, "What do you mean? What would possibly change? I'm going down there for a funeral and to straighten out whatever mess there is and I'm coming home. End of story."

"See, you say that, but what if you get wrapped up in the family? What if everybody apologizes and you have funeral fried chicken together and before you know it you've moved back in? Where does that leave me?" Liz asked, her voice rising.

Lou paused, clasping Liz's hand gently. "Liz, look at me. Do you really think I'm going to go down there and just pick up where everyone left off and pop into the garden club and join the Junior League? Think about this for a minute. What do I have to go back to? A family who wants nothing to do with me. What do I have to come home to? A woman I love, a farm I intend to save with that woman, the beginning of a career, and kicking cancer's ass!" Lou exclaimed. She knew Liz was far more sensitive than she was, but she was really having to reassure her that this was not the big deal Liz was making it out to be.

"Okay," Liz gave in. "Okay. Will you at least call me with updates? I'll stay here at the house with the dogs."

"Of course. I'll call the moment I get there, before I go to bed, when I wake up, when I go tinkle…" Lou smirked.

"I get it, I get it. Just promise me no surprises, please?"

"Cross my heart, scout's honor, pinky promise, whatever I need to do!" Liz shot back. "Now can we please find something for me to wear to this funeral? So I don't look like Tammy in '88," Lou said, rolling her eyes.

Liz went back to flipping through the closet, pausing on a dark blue and ivory patterned suit with ivory piping on the edges. It had a high collar, but the edge of the pencil skirt had a navy ruffle, creating some interest around the knees. Paired with the right shoes, this could kill them. Well, the ones that weren't already dead, she thought to herself. She pulled it out of the closest, brushing the dust off the shoulders.

"This. I think this is the one." Liz removed it from the hanger set to see it was vintage Chanel. "Oh yes, this is definitely the one," she decided.

Lou was packing her casual clothes when she looked up to see what Liz had dragged out of her closet. Her eyes bugged out when she saw Liz's suggestion. "Absolutely not! That thing is 40 years old if it's a day! I can't pull that off! I probably can't even pull it on, for Christ's sake!"

"This is vintage Chanel. This suit was probably a thousand dollars when it was new. I'll bet it's worth three times that now. They don't make this stuff anymore, Lou. This is the pinnacle of fashion now!"

"This," Lou said, taking it out of Liz's hands, "is the pinnacle of ratty old trash. I'm serious. I cannot wear this," she countered firmly.

"Try it on. Humor me," Liz directed. "If it looks hideous, we will find something else, deal? Although the only thing left to try is the bedspread," she added under her breath.

"I heard that," Lou replied, slipping off her clothes.

This was the first time Liz was seeing Lou undressed. The hospital gown with the slit down the back was one thing, but this was so much different. Lou had a great body, she had to admit, especially for her age. She was beautiful in Liz's eyes.

Lou put on the suit, asking Liz to zip up the skirt. "There. Now you see it, now you don't." She began to take it off.

"Hold up! That suit fits you perfectly. There's not a hole or blemish on it anywhere. I can hand wash it to get the musty smell out of it and hang it up to dry overnight. It will be ready to go with you in the morning." Liz wasn't entertaining any further discussion on the matter.

"Fine, Coco Chanel. What do I wear with it?" Lou said, annoyed but accepting Liz's superior fashion advice.

"It's a classic suit. Classic accessories. Nude heels. Nude handbag, or, preferably, a clutch. It has a high neckline, so either a scarf or a long strand of pearls. Which do you have?"

"The only thing I recognized in that whole explanation was 'nude'," Lou laughed.

"You're hilarious." Liz rolled her eyes and walked back to the closet. "Here are some shoes." She tossed them out of the closet to Lou. "See if they still fit. I'm not seeing a bag in here, though."

Lou was sort of enjoying playing dress up with Liz, but she certainly wouldn't have let on so.

"Oh yes! This scarf! This is to die for!" Liz declared as she stepped out of the closet.

Putting on the age-old shoes, she looked up to see the scarf Liz was holding. She immediately recognized that it was Judy's.

"Where did you get that?" Lou asked, her voice quivering slightly.

"It was in the closet, on the shelf. What's the big deal?" Liz asked cluelessly.

"It was Judy's. She was wearing it the night we left Clanton and never looked back," Lou said through misty eyes.

"Oh, Lou, I, I'm sorry, I didn't realize." She went to take it back to the closet.

"No," Lou stopped her. She took the scarf from Liz's hand and held it for a moment. She rubbed the silk against her face, almost certain she could still smell Judy on the fabric. "I'm going to wear it. It's my way of honoring her," Lou decided.

"If you're sure…" Liz's voice trailed off.

"I'm sure," Lou said with as much confidence as she had in the hospital when she decided she was over missing Judy, ironically.

"Now, I've packed casual clothes to wear back on Sunday after the funeral. Here's what I've laid out to wear tomorrow for the drive down. Do these meet your approval, Gianni Versace?"

Liz inspected the outfits. They were mediocre at best. "Let's swap out a couple little things, shall we?" She suggested.

"Oh, we shall!" Lou replied sarcastically.

"I think a cardigan with those black capri pants you laid out would be fine. A nice solid button up underneath it. You could accent it with a long necklace." Liz pulled out some items to choose from and laid them together, picking and taking away. Lou had to admit Liz had a knack for style. "This is perfect for a somber, but casual arrival. Now let's look at your departure outfit."

"My arrival and departure? I'm not a Boeing 737, Liz."

"This may be the last thing they ever see you in, Lou," Liz countered seriously. "I think it may be the most important thing you wear the whole weekend."

"That's fair. Here's what I have," Lou gestured towards the open suitcase.

"A sweatshirt and leggings?! Has the cancer made it to your brain?" Liz cried.

"Not funny." Lou reminded her, "I'll be driving home. I want to be comfortable. What do you suggest then?"

Liz took back to the closet to come up with something far better than what Lou had pulled out. She found a pair of pastel blue mom jeans and tossed them out to Lou.

"Great, I'll look like an Easter egg about to give birth…"

"You picked all this out at one point or another, didn't you? Why are you complaining so much?" Liz poked.

"Well, I was there when it was picked out, but Mama and Aunt Joan did most of the shopping. No one ever asked what I wanted; I just wore it. Sort of like now," Lou stuck her tongue out at Liz.

"They had good taste then, and, lucky for you, a lot of it has come back around, so this isn't as hard as it could be. Try this with the blue pants." Liz held an oversized button up with tiny blue polka dots.

"This is huge, I can't wear this!" Lou protested.

Rolling her eyes, Liz said, "That's the point. You wear it and tie it at the bottom. It flatters your waist, with the pants, without looking too tight and purposeful. You can wear the same loafers with that outfit that I put out for tomorrow."

Lou hadn't even noticed the broken-in Cole Haans with the tassels she liked. At least there would be one part of her that was normal and familiar. She tried on the "departure outfit," and it wasn't so bad.

Liz looked her up and down, impressed with her work. "You need a necklace–something simple. Do you have a small gold chain or pendant?" Liz asked, going back to the closet where the top dresser drawer held a tangle of costume jewelry.

Lou stepped over to the side table by her bed and opened the top drawer. There was a small dark green velvet box pushed to the back. Her hands trembled as she pulled it out of its hiding spot. She opened the box to reveal a small gold drop pendant with a solitaire diamond in it. "How about this?" She held up the chain and pendant for Liz to see as she came out of the closet.

"Oh Lord! Is that real? That diamond is flawless! That has to be at least two carats!"

"Two point four," Lou replied simply.

"Where did you get that?" Lou practically shouted.

"This was my college graduation gift from Daddy," Lou explained. "I never wore it. I was afraid something would happen to it, and I'd never forgive myself. Even after all these years, I couldn't bring myself to hock it, no matter how bad things were financially. It's sat in this box for as long as I can remember. I think now is as good a time as any to bring it out into the light," Lou declared. "There's no use in having it if you don't use it."

Liz helped her fasten the gold clasp around her neck and Lou turned around. "Well? How does it look?"

"Like a million dollars!" Liz beamed.

"It is a pretty nice piece to be put away all these years," Lou agreed.

"I wasn't talking about the necklace," Liz said smiling, causing Lou to smile back.

The pair finished packing what needed to go in the suitcase, and Lou packed the toiletries and accessories she would need in the train case. The rest would have to wait until she got ready in the morning. Lou was feeling hungry.

"What do you say we rustle up some grub? I've got a Stouffer's meatloaf in the freezer?" Lou offered. Liz scrunched up her face at the suggestion. "Okay, I have stuff to make sandwiches?" Liz offered as a second choice.

"How about we order a pizza? And eat it on that flow blue china in the dining room!" Liz said.

"Pizza on priceless china? Is that proper, Emily Post?"

"You served me Chinese on it, with your sterling, the first night we met, remember? No use in having the good stuff unless you're going to use it."

“Fair enough. I’ll order the pizza, you go pick it and the dogs up, deal?”

“Fine by me. I want ground beef and pepperoni with extra sauce. I prefer Papa John’s, but Domino’s will do”

“Of course, nothing but the best,” Lou replied playfully, picking up the phone to place the order. Liz went ahead to drive into town; the food would be ready by the time she got there. This gave Lou some time alone. She decided if Liz was to spend the night, she wanted to clean up the bedroom. She quickly changed the sheets and made the bed. She put away the extra clothes and laundry. She gave the shelves and furniture a cursory dusting and swept the floor. She even pulled out a few candles. Lou didn’t know much about romance, but she knew she wanted to make Liz feel special. This would be their first night together, and whatever happened happened. She didn’t want to count on anything, but she also knew the yearning that both felt for each other, a yearning that hadn’t been satisfied in a very long time.

44

Josie sat in the large kitchen alone at the countertop bar, pen in hand. Still unsure of what to write. Country Gold was playing softly on the radio. She was absentmindedly listening along and recognized the lyrics to Jeannie C. Riley's Harper Valley PTA right away. She started humming to the song and then was singing along before she knew it. When she got to the line that said, "This is just a little Peyton Place and you're all Harper Valley hypocrites," the proverbial lightbulb illuminated above Josie's head. She finally had the inspiration for her mother's eulogy.

Judy had been consumed by secrets. Secrets of love, secrets around town. She hadn't been the type to run and tell everyone else's business, perhaps because she didn't want her own secrets to make their way out to the general public. Josie herself knew a piece or two of gossip about mostly everyone in town. There are a few perks to having a busy body aunt like Joan. Suzanne Martin was sleeping with her golf instructor. Libby Sizemore, who was always wearing oversized dark sunglasses, had bought her way out of a DUI just last week. Raymond James was sleeping with the nanny of his twins. Blah, blah, blah. Josie could go on for hours. Practically all these people who were anybody in town were racked with scandal. Perhaps they were predispositioned to it. It's a well-known fact that small towns and a little money breed trouble.

Undoubtedly the rest of these folks struggled with their secrets that were not so secret. But none of them had been so heavily laden with fear and guilt that they'd offed themselves. These people, with their own faults, their own indiscretions, their own failures, were the people that a timid Judy Jackson had been afraid of. Josie found it almost laughable now. But then she realized she had been able to make it out. She didn't care what anybody in Clanton, Georgia thought about her not taking her husband's last name or what they thought about her work with Planned Parenthood or how she had been arrested in a Occupy Atlanta protest. Josie didn't have to live with the results of her small-town taboo actions. Judy did. Not only did Judy have to live with her own secrets and scandals, but she also had to endure what people thought of her daughter. Tongues wagged in towns like Clanton. Someone caught wind of one thing or another and before you knew it, Josie was declared a bra-burning communist.

The blame for Judy's death wasn't at the hands of her father or her grandfather, or even Judy herself. The blame laid squarely at the doorstep of nearly every house in Clanton, and for the first time in, well, maybe ever, Josie decided she needed to call them out on it.

But a funeral wasn't the place to do so. It would leave mouths gaping, blood boiling, and maybe even families ripped apart. Josie couldn't do this to her own family. Again, she would be leaving town soon enough, so she really didn't care what anyone in town thought of her. But her family would be the ones left behind to live in the shadow of the mess she created. It was a fun thought, though, while it lasted.

Instead, Josie penned a beautiful tribute to her mother. She spoke of Judy's civic activities, her charitable contributions, how she volunteered at the elementary school. She applauded Judy's work in the church, her cooking, and the memories they'd made in the summers on Saint Simons Island when Josie was growing up. It was a lovely, standard eulogy. One that Josie and the rest of the family could be proud of, despite the gruesome circumstances that had befallen the family over the past week, particularly the suicide.

When she crawled into the full-sized antique bed with a snoozing R.J. that she slept in as a child when she stayed with her grandfather, Josie laid there, staring at the ceiling. It still had those little glow in the dark stars of various sizes stuck on with putty that Big Chuck had put up there for her when she was afraid of the dark. She thought back to her childhood, remembering moments and instances of her father and her grandfather with the clarity of Baccarat crystal. What she didn't have memories of were her mother. They were hazy. She was there, of course. But Josie could barely imagine a single snapshot in her brain of just her mother. Judy had always been behind the scenes. She was never in the photos; she was the one taking them. She wasn't playing on the slip 'n slide at Josie's eighth birthday; she was inside decorating the cake. Was the distance between the two intentional or just the way it was?

Josie got up out of bed, causing R.J. to stir. "Where are you going? You just came to bed."

"I've gotta work on the eulogy a little bit more," she said simply as he faded back off to sleep.

Josie walked back down the stairs to look for her father. She hadn't seen him this evening since she blew up at him in her grandfather's study. She needed to ask him some things. Things that she needed answers to–now.

The front door was open, and she could see her father sitting on the porch through the old screen door. As she approached the door, she heard a voice that wasn't her father's. She peered through the sidelight and saw an attractive young man. She immediately recognized him as Peter Garrett, her father's employee at Jackson Planning & Auditing. She hadn't met the man before, but she had seen pictures from some of their ads and publicity.

"If you did it, I need to know. I can't protect you otherwise," she heard her father say.

"I'm telling you… I didn't do it. I was mad enough to, still am, I might add, but I didn't burn down your family's office," Peter stated.

"Klark Kitchens is calling it arson. I don't know if that's a scare tactic or if he has something, but I don't like him throwing that word around. Don't like it one bit," Little Chuck said plainly.

"What do I have to do to prove that I didn't do it?" Peter asked impatiently.

"I don't know, son. All I know is if it was arson, you're a suspect. I'm a suspect. And they're going to find out, one way or another. And I've gotta be honest, I noticed something that could be playing into their investigation, truth be told."

"What's that?" Peter asked.

"The front window, over by Rosie's desk. When I first saw it, I thought the fire department had busted it out fighting the blaze. But it didn't make sense after I thought about it," Little Chuck explained.

"What do you mean?" Peter asked, confused.

"If the fire department had busted it to get in or to pull some of the heat out, the glass would have gone inside. But it was outside, on the sidewalk in front of the office."

"So?" Peter questioned, still not understanding.

"So, the glass was busted from the inside out. Not the other way around. At some point, someone was inside the office, and they broke that window. The glass on the sidewalk wasn't blackened. It was broken before there was any fire. Know anything about that?" Chuck looked Peter square in the eyes.

"Chuck, I didn't bust anything. I wasn't there. I don't know how much clearer I can be. It sounds like something is fishy, but I swear to God it wasn't me," Peter protested.

"Okay, fair enough," Chuck gave in with his interrogation. "But I'd still advise you to lay low while this plays out. I care about you, and I don't want you to get wrapped up in anything."

"Yes, sir," Peter stepped down from the porch and towards his car. Little Chuck turned to come back inside, and Josie tiptoed quickly to the kitchen. If her father didn't come into the kitchen, she could make her way down the hall without it looking like she had been spying on him.

Obviously, what she had just witnessed raised more suspicion and questions regarding the fire, but that was not what she was most concerned about at this particular moment in time. She heard the screen door shut and the big door close. Just as she predicted, Little Chuck made his way to the kitchen, likely for a late-night snack. The two had that in common.

Josie was cutting a slice of Alice Guppy's caramel cake when Little Chuck walked in. She was the first to break the ice. "Want a piece?" she motioned toward the cake with the knife in her hand.

"Please," he replied simply, pulling a plate out of the cabinet. "Just a sliver," he added. After all these years, she knew what his idea of a "sliver" was and cut his piece accordingly. The irony wasn't lost on him, and he smiled down at his cake. "Need a fork?" he asked, pulling open the silverware drawer.

"Already got one," she said back. Little Chuck sat down at the counter next to his only child where they shared dessert in silence for a few moments.

"Daddy, I…" Josie began to plead for forgiveness, but she was cut off by Chuck.

"Don't apologize. I deserved everything you gave me, and more," he sighed.

"I didn't mean it. I don't really think you killed Mama."

"I know you don't. But I think I did," he said, a single tear streaming down his cheek. He finished the last bite of his cake and pushed the plate back on the counter. "I ripped your mama away from the one person she ever truly loved because I was jealous. I was selfish. I loved her and that was all that mattered to me. I tried and tried to convince her that we could be happy, and I think she even bought into it for a while. I bought her jewelry, that convertible. We bought that little place on Saint Simons. I did all I could think of to make her want to stay with me. Then we had you, and I thought that would for sure keep her here. Which it did, I will say that. She loved you, baby. You have to know that."

"I do, Daddy, I do know that. I don't think I ever thought that she didn't, but you and I were always closer. We went hunting together. You coached me in softball. I used to sneak downstairs after bedtime, and we would eat a piece of cake together late at night." She smiled looking at the empty plates and realizing how some things never change. "But I never felt close to Mama, you know what I mean?"

"Yep, darlin', I do." He paused. "Your mama was a very guarded person. Rightfully so. She didn't trust anybody as far as I know, not really. Your grandma Eugenia was a terrible woman. There were no two ways about it. When she found out about your mama and Lou, she beat Judy so bad she couldn't see straight. I never knew at the time, but your mama told me later. She figured I deserved to know everything after I brought her home from Kentucky."

"Some things I wish she had kept a secret," he added quietly.

"But Daddy, that's my whole point–all these damn secrets! It's murderous. It's enough to drive someone to kill themselves, and it did! Why does nobody see that in this God-forsaken town?" Josie was practically hollering.

"Calm down, honey. I get it. You're right. I'm not arguing with you. But the point I was trying to make was that she never trusted anybody, and I think that included you. I think she spent your whole teenage and college years worried that you'd turn out like her. Every time you posted a pride flag on Facebook or went to Midtown, she was a nervous wreck. She didn't trust herself after what happened, and she didn't trust that you wouldn't be influenced. I know now that nobody 'turns' gay, but, Lord, your mama was terrified for you."

Getting up from his barstool, Little Chuck declared solemnly, "If I had it all to do over again, I would still have gone to Kentucky."

With a disgusted look of resentment on her face, Josie asked why.

"Because I would have brought home my best friend and my big sister, and I would have left my hate and my prejudice and my selfish pride sitting on that farm." With that, he walked away, headed to his bedroom, leaving Josie sitting at the kitchen counter, her heart bigger and fuller than she had known it in some time.

45

Lou woke up first, unsure if the previous night had all been a dream or a reality. She looked to her right and saw a peaceful, almost angelic Liz Ward lying next to her wrapped up in the sheets. Lou studied her for a while. Her mussed hair, the slight crows' feet at her eyes, the perfect curvature of her chin, the soft lips with smeared lip gloss.

For the slightest moment, Judy's ghost crept in again, lying in the bed next to Lou instead of Liz. Lou wanted to reach out and touch her and wanted to caress her face. She wanted to tell Judy she was happy and that she was sorry for everything that Judy had to endure. She wanted so much for Judy to understand her heart now, to understand that while no one could ever take her place, Lou deserved another chance at happiness. She was sorry that Judy never got that chance, but she wasn't going to let hers pass because of a ghost, a memory, someone that only existed in her dreams now.

As if sensing Lou's intense stare, Liz woke up, also in a state of disbelief. "Did that really happen?" she asked Lou, pulling her back to the moment of next day, post-coital afterglow.

"I think it really did," Lou chuckled. Liz turned on her back and laughed, pulling the covers tighter around her.

"It's been a really really long time," Liz giggled. "Unless you count my personal massager!" she laughed, full of life, and living fully in the moment.

"I may be rusty, but I like to think I could provide a little more pleasure than a couple double A batteries!" Lou joked.

"Oh, please. You know what I meant." Liz thought about things for a moment and just decided to enjoy them as they were, to not over analyze the situation, to just appreciate what they had. "Breakfast?" she finally asked.

"Just coffee for me. I need to get ready and get on the road if I'm going to make it to Clanton before this evening," she said.

"I'll start a pot," Liz answered, hopping out of the bed in nothing but a bra and skimpy panties. God, she looked amazing, Lou thought to herself.

With Liz out of the room, Lou took a moment alone to reflect on the previous night and to mentally prepare for the two days ahead. She had conquered her feelings and emotions regarding Liz Ward, so she could conquer her family, for 36 hours at least. She was tired, even after a night of perhaps the best sleep she'd had in ages, sans medication, of course. But she chocked it up to a night of unbridled passion. She got out of the bed and slipped on her housecoat to walk to the kitchen, smelling the aroma of the dark roast coffee.

"I've never asked how you take your coffee," Liz said over her shoulder.

"Black, one-half packet of Sweet 'n Low," Lou replied.

"That's... oddly specific," Liz answered.

"It's how my Grandpa Jackson always drank it. My Aunt Joan, too. Just a habit, I guess."

Liz turned around holding the two mugs of coffee and nearly screamed.

"What in God's name are you wearing?!"

Alarmed, Lou looked all around herself. Seeing nothing out of the ordinary, she said, "This is my housecoat. I've worn it for years, why?"

"I haven't seen anything that hideous since Mrs. Roper's muumuus on Three's Company. Christ almighty," she sighed, trying to calm down.

"Well not all of us have little lacy lingerie from Victoria's Secret to parade around in, ma'am."

"No, but your birthday suit would be better than that thing," Liz replied.

"Well maybe that's all I'll wear when I get to Clanton then!"

"You are so very funny," Liz replied sarcastically.

"I'll pack some more suitable sleepwear and loungewear if that will calm your nerves."

Lou took her mug of coffee back to the bedroom to add the comfy clothes back to her bag and then got ready for her shower. She bathed and fixed her hair and makeup. She looked good, all things considered.

She packed the last of her toiletries in the train case and carried it back to her bedroom. Liz was getting dressed. "I don't recall telling you to put on clothes," Lou said seductively.

"What kind of woman do you take me for, Lou Jackson?" Liz feigned innocence.

"The kind that let out moans that would wake the neighbors last night," Lou quipped back. Liz just smirked.

Lou dressed in the outfit they'd agreed upon for her to wear for her travel and arrival to Clanton– the cardigan, a crisp button up, and some black capri pants. She put on the loafers and twirled around for Liz's inspection. "Do I meet the standards you've set to avoid embarrassing myself?" she asked.

"Not too bad. Not bad at all," Liz said proudly. "I've got your suit for the funeral hanging in the mudroom so it would dry quicker. Grab a garment bag for me to put over it. No chance in hell we are folding this up to be stuffed in a suitcase," she said walking out of the room.

"Don't forget it was stuffed in the back of a closet for 35 years, dear. I doubt six hours in a suitcase would do much more damage," she called after Liz.

With the suitcases packed and clasped shut, Lou carried them to the front hall. The dogs knew something was afoot when they saw the bags come out yesterday and had barely left Lou's side. She took a moment to give the girls some love. "I'll be back tomorrow, you big lugs. Promise. Auntie Liz will take good care of you til then." She kissed each of them on the tops of their heads.

Liz came out with the suit and took the garment back from Lou, zipping it up on the hanger. "Now you hang this in the back. Do not lay it down, you hear?"

"Yes, I hear," Lou said, annoyed that Liz was more concerned about the Chanel suit than her.

"Now here are the keys to my car. Set your mirrors and your seat. If there's an emergency, press the Starlink button on the upper part near the mirror and the sunroof. They'll call for help. God, I wish you had a cell phone…"

"I will be fine, Liz," Lou said sternly. "I will be gone for 36 hours and 12 of them will be driving. I will see my family, my father, say goodbye to Judy, and be home before you know it."

Liz helped Lou carry her things to the Subaru and load them up. She felt like a mother sending her teenager off to college for the first time. This was brutal.

"You're sure you have everything? Don't think you need any company?" Liz added.

"Liz," Lou began.

"Okay, okay, I get it. Just be careful is all."

Lou kissed Liz on the cheek, then pulled her in for a real kiss. "I'll be alright, and I'll be back in no time, okay?"

"Okay," Liz answered quietly, closing the driver door behind Lou as she climbed in. She stood in the driveway with the dogs watching Lou drive away. They stayed until they couldn't see the car anymore. Liz turned to make her way inside, but the dogs didn't budge. "I know, I already miss her, too. Come on in and we'll have a treat." The mention of the "T word" got their attention and they staggered up the porch steps back into the house.

46

The Jacksons woke up on Saturday morning to the smell of bacon, sausage, fried weenies, biscuits and gravy, eggs, and grits. Ruby was outdoing herself this morning. The family had been used to eating funeral food for so many days, it was a nice change to have something fresh and hot to line their bellies. Big Chuck and Joan were up first. She helped him to his seat at the breakfast table. Little Chuck came down the stairs still yawning and went straight to the coffee pot to pour a cup. He stood to the side of the stove and asked Ruby if she needed any help, stealing a strip of bacon off the platter.

"Not that kind of help, boy!" She teased him. He went to sit down next to his father, opposite his aunt. He was checking his phone for texts and emails when Josie and R.J. made their way down.

"Look who finally decided to join us!" Aunt Joan declared.

"Give her a break, Joan, she was up late last night," Little Chuck defended his daughter with a small, understanding smile. Joan raised her eyebrows but didn't acknowledge the wrist slap with a reply.

"Everything smells terrific, Ruby," R.J. shared.

"Thank you, baby," she smiled at the compliment from her new cleaning buddy. "Now y'all know this gonna be the last meal I cook today," she reminded them. "I've got to get started on the food for the company coming tomorrow." Everyone nodded in agreement. Ruby went on, "Mr. Chuck, I've decided on little ham biscuits, shrimp cocktail, mini quiche Lorraine, deviled eggs, chicken salad finger sandwiches, and pimiento cheese on mini croissants. That sound okay to you?"

"Sounds fine to me," Little Chuck said. "Anything sweet?"

"We've got a passel of cookies and cakes still in here, but I was gonna fix banana pudding in those little sherbet cups that match Ms. Louise's crystal."

"That sounds delicious," Big Chuck said. "Reckon how many we'll have here after the funeral?" he asked the room.

“No clue really,” Joan answered as the unofficial funeral handmaiden. “I know Patsy and Karla are coming. Karla’s girl, Alyssa and her two little hellions may come with them. Little Bo is bringing Aunt Betty, and it’s still unclear if Sharon and Debbie are coming with them. Jody and Chris are in Italy and won't be able to make it but send their condolences. Carl and Lisa will be here from Jasper. Marty and Diana are coming up from Edison. Teresa Jean and Kenny are on another cruise, so they won’t be here. I’m sure I’m forgetting somebody. Oh yes, Annie Ruth and Jeff, but Zachary and Sara are keeping Riley home. Not to mention whatever vultures who *think* they’re family that will show up.”

Ruby started sweating. “We’ve only got service for 16 in Ms. Louise’s china and crystal and silver. What will we do if more folks show up?”

“I’ll go to mom and dad’s and get theirs. Mom has service for 12,” Josie offered, still not used to referring to her mother in the past tense yet.

“All we really need is more dinner plates and dessert plates, cups and saucers, and dinner forks, salad forks, and teaspoons. Don’t go carting all of Ms. Judy’s stuff across town and break something,” Ruby warned.

“I’ll be careful, don’t worry. I’ll pack it all in those quilted zipper things she keeps in the bottom of the china cabinet. And R.J. will help me anyway,” Josie nodded towards her husband.

“Well, Ms. Josie, I was kindly hoping he might stay here and help me get things ready,” Ruby commented. R.J. blushed. “He was just such a big help getting all the other stuff out and cleaning. Why, he don’t even need that old step ladder to reach the light fixtures! We got through everything in half the time. I could really use him if it’s alright with you?”

“Well of course, Ruby. I’m glad he’s able to help you. Let’s just hope it sticks when we get home!”

“Hey, I’m not that bad!” R.J. came to his own defense. “I just didn’t know how to do all this stuff ‘til Ruby showed me. It’s kind of gratifying to see it all come together,” he decided.

“Well don’t let us stop your momentum!” the rest of the family conceded with a laugh.

“Just remember we all have to be over at Chapman’s at eleven to start receiving guests,” Big Chuck added, turning back to the solemn occasion at hand.

“Daddy, go over to the house with me to get the stuff for Ruby. I need to see if I have any extra clothes still there, and we need to pick out the right suit/tie/hanky combo for you anyway. We’ll get ready there if we run out of time, but we should be back. R.J., I’ll lay out your clothes for you before I go in case I’m not back.”

“And I’ll help Chuck,” Joan nodded towards her older brother.

“Sounds like everyone is accounted for then,” Big Chuck said. “Let the formal funeralizing begin,” he groaned.

As everyone picked up their breakfast dishes and began to go their separate ways, Ruby made a quiet announcement, “I’ve got something to say,” she said. “Everyone ain’t accounted for.” The family looked around at each other, utterly confused.

“Ms. Louvenia’s coming,” Ruby laid out. No sense in sugarcoating it or dancing around the truth. “She said she’d be here this afternoon. She’ll be staying for the funeral tomorrow, then she’s going back home tomorrow evening.”

Everyone in the room had questions, but no one had the words to ask them. They continued to look at each other, with looks somewhere between terror and disbelief. With no one else saying anything, Ruby continued, “Mr. Chuck asked me to call her. I got ahold of her and told her what had happened. Turns out she already knew.” Now everyone was supremely confused.

“How could she have known?!” Josie asked, bewildered.

“The note she left your daddy wasn’t the only note she wrote. She sent one to Ms. Louvenia that morning before she,” Ruby stammered, “Well, before she, you know.” She couldn’t bring herself to say exactly what had happened.

“Well, where on earth is she going to stay?” Joan questioned.

Ruby looked to Big Chuck for approval, “Mr. Chuck, I told her she could stay here. Ain’t nowhere else for her to stay except clear down to Kennesaw.”

"Of course, Ruby. She's my child. She'll stay here," Big Chuck confirmed.

"Well, that's just lovely, isn't it? Harboring a homosexual right under our roof. What will people say, Chuck?" Joan demanded of her brother.

"They'll say there's Chuck Jackson's daughter staying at Chuck Jackson's house, and I dare them to say anything else," he retorted with anger. "And, again, I'll remind you this is MY roof for as long as I've got left, and if you don't shut that giant trap of yours, I'll put her in your bedroom and have her rub her naked body all over everything you own, do you understand me, girl?" The horror lighting up Joan's face was all the answer anyone needed. She didn't say another word. "That's what I thought."

"Ruby, will you fix up Lou's old room? Fresh sheets. Put away Louise's old sewing notions and clutter, trash it if you need to. Call down to Clanton City Florist, tell them I want an arrangement of fresh tulips delivered this afternoon to go in there. Those are her favorites." Looking to the rest of the crew, Big Chuck said, "Well, what are you waiting for? We've got stuff to do before eleven."

Off everyone went on their separate journeys: Joan to her bedroom, R.J. and Ruby to the table to work on a grocery list before running to the Blue Star, and Josie up to her room to lay out R.J.'s clothes and grab some of her own if she couldn't find anything decent at her mama and daddy's. Only the two Chucks remained in the kitchen doorway heading to the hallway.

"Daddy, what's gonna happen here? What's this gonna look like? We haven't seen her in all these years. She probably hates all our guts."

"She ought to. We did her wrong. I take blame for that as much as you should. But she's coming down here. Whether it's to say goodbye to Judy, to see us, to tell us to fuck off, or all three, we're going to be here, and we are going to welcome her home. This is her home as much as it is anybody's, as long as I'm still living. Is that understood?" Big Chuck may have had to look up to Little Chuck physically now, but he was still very much in charge.

"Yes, sir," Little Chuck said, like a child with his hand caught in the cookie jar. "You're right. This is a second chance to make this right or die trying. I agree with you."

"Good boy," Big Chuck patted his arm. "Now later tonight, me and you have some other business to discuss." With that, Big Chuck made his way back to his bedroom on his walker.

What could he have meant with that?

"Daddy?" Josie called. "I'm ready to go. Let's get over to Crystal Springs before we run out of time."

Leaving Big Chuck, Joan, and R.J. prepared to dress themselves and get to Chapman's on their own, Josie and Little Chuck drove to the house in Crystal Springs in Chuck's Lexus. Josie saw this time alone to pick up the conversation they'd had the night before.

"So, how do you feel about Lou coming back after all this time?" she asked in earnest.

Remembering the conversation he'd had with his father the previous evening, he was honest with his daughter. "I'm worried about what this is gonna be like. I'm nervous as hell. We haven't seen each other in all these years, and now it's only because your mama's dead. She probably hates all our guts. Probably thinks we're all guilty." He looked out the window, adding quietly, "And maybe we are."

"Well, it's been a long time. I think you've obviously softened a bit, and I'm sure she has, too. Maybe this is a good thing," Josie offered. "Well, except for mom dying and all…"

"Now that's what I want to know about," Chuck changed the subject. "How are you feeling about all this? Not trying to be an ass, but a few years ago we'd have had to talk you off a ledge if something like this happened. What's changed?"

Josie took some time to think about the question, trying to formulate the right words to explain herself. "Daddy, I spent a lot of time in this town never understanding any of it. Never understanding how so many people didn't fit in and how so few people ran practically everything. If you said or did one thing that wasn't up to snuff, news about it made its way home to your family before you could. The anxiety and stress that this environment brought onto me for all those years took a toll on my mental state."

"I can understand that," he agreed.

"When I went to school, it wasn't so bad. Georgia State has five times as many people on the roster as this whole town has on the census. I was just a number, and that was what I needed to be. I didn't need to be Big Chuck's granddaughter or varsity cheerleader or the girl who huffed a can of computer duster in the locker room and had to go to the emergency room. I could just be a student. I could focus on academics, maintaining friendships of my choice–not the ones that I was expected to keep. But then every summer I'd come home and relive the nightmare all over again from May til the end of August, and it would screw with me again. I think that might have even been when I was at my worst, ya know? The drastic change in consistency."

"But you've been out of school ten years now and you still have your moments," Chuck reminded her.

"I do," Josie admitted. "But I see a therapist. I see a psychiatrist. I'm well-regulated on medicines that help me be the best, most authentic version of myself without giving a damn about what anyone else thinks. R.J. supports me. He wants the best for me. He still doesn't get what this town was like, what it's still like, but he's there for me. Instead of talking me off the ledge, he assures me that he won't let me fall off the ledge. There's a big difference."

A tear fell from Little Chuck's cheek. "I've never known how to handle these kinds of things. Not with you. Not with your mama. Not even with myself. I molded my personality into what was expected of me, and I never questioned it. I don't think I had the strength or fortitude to choose a path other than the one that was paved for me. Go to school, play ball, get a degree, come home, marry a girl, get a good job, have kids, and live happily ever after. That was the plan. But it turned out to be everything but that."

Sensing the tender moment, but not wanting to skirt the original question, Josie replied, "I say all this to say, that being here the past couple of days makes me realize that I, personally, am not the crazy one," she said firmly.

Chuck laughed. "Is that so?"

"Yep. It's everyone else and we are just caught living in their crazy world," she smiled. "I already miss Mama something awful, I really do. But I have this weird feeling that she is at peace. Does that make sense?"

Her father nodded. "I get what you mean. She wasn't happy here, there's no denying that. I hope she'll find that on the other side, whatever that looks like. I just wish I'd never pulled her back here," he said regretfully.

"Now Daddy, you can't keep blaming yourself for this. I think you know that it wasn't right, and I hope you've asked for forgiveness for that and thought critically about your actions in the future. But you're still living here. And you're still my father. You have a lot of living left to do, and you can't sit around wallowing in self-pity. What you have to do is acknowledge the mistakes and declare that you've learned from them. Agreed?"

"When did you get to be so smart?" he asked.

"I didn't. I went to therapy. Something you should consider for yourself."

"I'm too old to change," Chuck replied dryly.

"You damn sure are with that attitude," she shot back. "This has all been a lot. You need to consider talking to someone. The fire, the money, Mom, all this with Aunt Lou, Granddaddy going downhill. It's a lot for someone to bear, and I think you could benefit from someone looking in from the outside. And I don't mean all the old bitties around here coming up with their own explanations!"

"We'll see," he said, pulling into the driveway of their home.

They packed up Judy's wedding china and silver as requested by Ruby. She had chosen Rothschild by Noritake when she and Little Chuck had wed. Judy's silver pattern was Gorham's Strasbourg, which her mother Eugenia had chosen when she married and then Judy added to when she and Chuck married. Josie pulled the silver chest from under the guest room bed where it had lived as long as she'd remembered and brought it downstairs to take to the car.

She rummaged through her old closet and at least found a couple pieces she could use to spruce up her hastily packed funeral ensembles. Then she made her way to her parents' bedroom to help her father. When she walked in, the room was empty. She checked the closet–also empty.

Josie hollered for her father but there was no answer. She walked out and checked the kitchen, then dining room, and living room. Turning back towards the den, she noticed the door to the basement open. Oh God, she thought. Please don't be down there, please, please, please don't be down there. She walked towards the door where she heard the distinct sounds of crying.

Josie had sworn to herself up and down that she would never go in that basement again. She couldn't bear to be in that space where her mother had ended her life, but here she was creeping down the stairs. To her surprise, it looked entirely normal. She wasn't sure what she had imagined, but there was practically nothing out of place. No sign that anything untoward had occurred in this space just two days prior.

Little Chuck was sitting on the floor crying his eyes out. .This was more than Josie could take right now. She was getting ready to greet 6,000 people and shake as many hands as possible in less than an hour. She needed him to pull it together.

But she couldn't pull herself together, either. So, she sat down next to her father, and she held him, and they cried together. For what seemed like hours, they each let the tears flow in a cathartic manner. In all honesty, it was probably good for them both.

Finally, the tears began to subside, and Chuck stood up, helping his daughter to her feet. He hugged her again and told her he loved her.

"Please don't let anything I've done or anything anyone else has done drive you to do something like this." The "this" he was referring to was clear. "If something ever happened to you, I don't know what I would do." He kissed her forehead, then glanced up at the rafter which had claimed the last breaths of his partner, and closed his eyes, holding his daughter tighter.

Pulling herself together with a few sniffles, Josie asserted, "We have to get dressed. I've still got to pick out your tie, sock, hanky combo. And if we're late, Florence Chapman will start the whole show without us."

47

Lou made her way to I-64 outside of Louisville, and then headed south to hop on I-75. It would take her all the way to Clanton. It would take just over six hours according to the car's GPS, but she didn't need a map. She knew how to get back, she just never thought she would have to.

After about two and half hours of driving, Lou's body was stiff, and she was getting antsy. She pulled off the interstate into a QuikTrip to top off the fuel tank and get a Diet Coke. She still wasn't hungry. Her stomach was in knots at the prospect of coming face to face with family she hadn't seen in so long. She was probably more nervous about that than seeing Judy in a casket. At least Judy wouldn't be able to put up a fight.

After filling up the tank, Lou hopped back on the interstate for the remaining three plus hours on her journey. It didn't seem real until she crossed the Tennessee state line into Georgia. At that point, she wasn't just antsy–she was nervous, scared, even. She could turn back now and go home to Kentucky. The Jacksons wouldn't even miss her. Hell, they'd probably be as relieved as she would be. But Lou couldn't get the other words that Ruby had said when she called her. Investigator, fire, money? What had she meant by all that? Lord, what cluster was Lou walking into?

As she got closer and closer to the exit that would take her to Clanton, the tension was rising within her. She took a painkiller, which seemed appropriate. It was just kicking in as she drove across town. Almost nothing had changed in all these years. She looked at this time capsule of small-town America with its courthouse square, an independent drug store, Buster Callaway's filling station where you could still charge your gas on an account. There was Mamie's Beauty Shop where all the old bitties had their hair done. The only thing missing was her daddy's office.

Lou stopped the car in the middle of the street when she saw the blackened, soot-stained ruins of four generations of Jackson blood, sweat, and tears. A car behind her honked their horn, returning her to the moment. She turned right and parked the car. The family had waited 35 years to see her, they could wait another ten minutes, she figured.

Lou unfastened the seatbelt and opened the door, looking around, feeling the more intense, sticky humid heat of Georgia compared to the bluegrass of Kentucky. She walked down the sidewalk and crossed the street to the corner of where Jackson Auditing and Planning had stood for nearly a hundred years. It was reduced to little more than bricks and ashes now. She couldn't help but shed a few tears at the legacy that generations of Jacksons had left behind, now gone forever.

"A pity, isn't it?" someone said standing next to her. She didn't even realize someone had joined her. Lou turned to see a woman about her age also looking at the remnants of the building.

"Do you know what happened?" Lou asked the woman.

"Well, now this is just hearsay, but I heard that Little Chuck Jackson burned it down for insurance money. There were rumors that he was gonna have to close the place down. Somebody said Rosie Wilson's last paycheck bounced! Can you believe that?" the stranger said incredulously.

"Who's Rosie Wilson?" Lou asked.

"Well Rosie was Chuck's secretary. Used to work at the bank, you know, with Chuck," the woman said as if it was common knowledge.

Staring back at the scene of the fire, Lou replied, "No, I didn't know."

"You must not be from 'round here!" the woman declared!

"I am, just been gone a very long time," Lou corrected.

"Oh, really? Who are your people, honey?" the lady asked, suddenly intrigued.

"You probably wouldn't know them," Lou answered. "Have a great rest of your Saturday!" she said, smiling, as she walked back to her car, effectively ending the conversation. Lou just was not ready to make her official reappearance back in Clanton, at least not until she had done so with her family. The lady did look familiar, though. She probably did know her, at least in a former life. And the woman most certainly knew her family. But with how freely the lady was sharing the news, Lou wasn't keen on sharing too much with her.

Lou climbed back into the Subaru and pulled out of the parking spot. Then she promptly backed right into another car. Lou laid her head on the steering wheel for a moment. "Shit, shit, shit." she muttered. She unbuckled to get out of the car to assess the damage.

She stepped out and ran square into an attractive young policeman who had been approaching her. She looked at the car she'd backed into. God almighty, she had hit a police car. And not just any police car, the badge on the man's chest read "Sheriff, Mayflower County." Jesus Christ on a cracker, she'd hit the town sheriff.

He had a look of annoyance and disappointment on his face as he eyed Lou Jackson up and down. "License and registration, please," he said with absolutely zero emotion.

"Uh, yes, sir. Just one moment." She reached back in the car for her bag, fumbling around for her wallet. "I, I, well, I just had something on my mind and..."

"I don't really care. License and registration," he repeated. Lou handed him her license.

"I don't exactly know where the registration is. See, I borrowed this car from my friend and I'm just here for the weekend," she explained.

"Kentucky plates?" he motioned towards the back of the car.

"Yes, that's where I'm from. Well, that's where I've lived for a long time," she stammered.

Looking over her driver's license, Sheriff Klark Kitchens recognized the name. Louvenia Jackson. Could she be one of THE Jacksons? Then another click. He remembered the name Lou in Judy Jackson's suicide note. The puzzle pieces were starting to fit together, but the picture was hazy. Who was this woman? He'd known the Jackson's for all of his 30 years, and he'd never seen or heard of this woman.

Ignoring the lack of registration and diverting his attention from the fender bender that Lou was terrified about, he began to ask some questions. "Louvenia Jackson, huh?"

"Uh, yeah, but everybody calls me Lou," she told him. Another puzzle piece clicking in.

"You must be in town for the funeral?" he asked.

"Yes, of course, here for Judy's funeral. It's a shame, isn't it?" If he could forget about the accident, so could she…

"How are you kin to the Jacksons? Did you marry into the family?" Klark pried, trying to narrow down who she was exactly.

"No, I'm a Jackson, born and raised!" she shared with a smile and without oversharing.

"I see," Klark replied. "A cousin or something like that?"

"Something like that," Lou countered. Changing the subject, she turned to the impending matter at hand. A potentially costly matter, but one far less uncomfortable than the one they were currently discussing. "So, what's the protocol here? Do I get a ticket? Do I give you my insurance? I don't really know how all this works, I haven't been in a wreck since I hit old man McAllister's Ford pick up on Lakeshore Road in high school!" she chuckled, remembering how stricken with fear she'd been when she had to tell her parents.

"Well, this old Crown Vic has seen better days. Looks like it did more damage to your friend's car than mine anyway. Since you're here for a funeral and all, let's just forget it happened. Out of respect for the deceased," he smiled at Lou.

"Really? I'm off the hook? Just like that?" she asked.

"Well, if you really want a ticket, I can give you one, hon," he laughed.

"Oh no! I'm good!" Lou replied quickly.

"But I would tell your friend about her car. Don't want her as mad at you as old man McAllister probably was."

"Of course, sure thing. Thank you, Mr. uh, Sheriff, uh," she squinted at his brass name tag, "Sheriff Kitchens. You're very kind."

Lou got back in the car, laid her head on the headrest, and closed her eyes for a moment while the sheriff drove away. Her nerves were shot. She needed a drink or a pill or some combination therein. Not to mention, she still had her entire family to address after 35 years.

It was already two o'clock. She needed to get on to The Gables. Very cautiously, she backed out onto the square and drove toward her family's home. Even after all this time, she knew exactly where she was going. That was one perk of things never changing in a small town. She pulled into the driveway and parked at the edge of the circular drive. It was where she used to park her car so many years ago. She looked up at the massive oak door with the sidelights and transom which held a wreath made of magnolia greens tied with a large black bow.

Lou stepped out of the car and suddenly realized she was entirely alone. She looked all around the sides of the house, but there weren't any cars. Forgetting her bags in the cargo area of the Subaru, she took the steps slowly to the big front door. She peeked in the sidelights and didn't see anything. Did she knock on her own family's front door with the big, aged brass knocker like she was selling Girl Scout Cookies? Nonsense. She'd just go in.

Except she didn't have a key. "Did I ever have a key? Does anyone have a key?" she racked her brain. She touched the knob lightly as if it were a heating element on a stove. She turned the knob and pushed slightly. The door was, of course, unlocked. Just as it always had been. This brought some sense of nostalgia, and, subsequently, comfort.

Lou stepped inside and said, "Hello?" a little above a whisper, again feeling like a stranger. No one answered, but she heard commotion in the kitchen. Lou recognized the tune to Aretha Franklin's "I Say a Little Prayer" and walked closer to the kitchen, practically tiptoeing. From around the corner, she could see an old familiar face peeling hard boiled eggs in the sink, singing along to Aretha and bobbing her head. Lou watched her for a moment, simply taking in the flood of memories brought back by seeing this woman again. A woman she loved and admired so very much.

When the next line began, Lou stepped out from the corner and sang along with Ruby, "To live without you would only mean heartbreak for me…" Ruby jumped like she'd just been caught naked as a jaybird! Lou doubled over laughing while Ruby grabbed a towel to dry her hands.

"Come over here, girl, you give me a hug!" Ruby squeezed her so tightly she could barely breathe. "You 'bout scared me to death, you know!" she playfully chastised Lou, smacking the back of her hand against Lou's forehead.

"I couldn't resist! I always loved it when you played Aretha when I was home. I think I knew every single song she ever sang because of you!"

"I love me some Aretha, ain't no doubt about it," Ruby shook her head. She finished drying her hands, leaving the hardboiled eggs in the sink. "Let me get a good look at you now," she commanded Lou.

"Ruby, it's just me. Same old me," Lou protested.

"No, ma'am. I think you might have got prettier. But you skinny as a rail. They don't have food worth stomaching up there in Kentucky?" Ruby asked, almost serious.

"Nothing like yours," Lou replied, hugging Ruby again. This time she took it in. Ruby never drank, never smoked, never overate. Her one and only vice was dipping snuff occasionally which you might see on the edge of her lip. She still smelled of the same perfume she'd worn when Lou was a child–Estée Lauder's Youth Dew in the brown bottle with the gold bow. Lou and Little Chuck presented a bottle of it to her on her birthday every single year. Back in the day, Louise had Ruby in a uniform. Gray shirt and skirt, white pantyhose, and white leather oxfords. Louise was very traditional. But after she died, Ruby took things a little more casually, which didn't ever seem to bother anyone else. Today Ruby was in a jewel-bedazzled sweatsuit, and she was absolutely adorable. Lou loved this woman, every ounce of her. Probably more than she ever loved her own mother.

"I love you, Ruby. I want you to know that. I've never been an affectionate person. But I love you more than you could ever imagine. For all that you've done for me, for our family. And now for calling me back like this. That took a lot. I know they probably put you up to it, but you didn't have to do it. You did it for me. And I will always owe a debt of gratitude to you." Ruby brushed a tear from Lou's cheek.

"Oh, baby girl. Ever since I laid eyes on you, you were mine. I wasn't but a kid myself when I started working here. Me and you grew up together in a lot of ways," she laughed. "I learned so much from you, from Little Chuck, all of you. And I'll always take care of you and look out for you, long as the good Lord sees fit to keep me on this earth!" she smiled.

But then her face became more serious. "We gotta talk through some things first, though," she said. Changing the subject abruptly, "Where's your things? We need to get your bags in here so I can press your clothes and get things hung up in your closet," Ruby was already walking towards the front door.

Following her, Lou said, "I'm still not sure about this, Ruby. I can't stay here, not after all this time. I'm a stranger to my own family. I've got a niece I've never even met for crying out loud!"

"Well unless you gonna sleep in your car out there or drive all the way down to Kennesaw, you gonna stay right here. I'll sleep outside your door if you want me to, so nobody'll get you!" she laughed.

"It's not that, Ruby, you know that. I'm just nervous. I'm scared."

"Honey, that's why you're here. It's time to face the demons and the ghosts and all that scary stuff head on. It's been festering for too long. They say it all comes to light one way or another. Our light switch's just been cut on."

They went out to the car to bring in Lou's bags and take them upstairs. The first thing Lou noticed in her room was the big bouquet of tulips. "My favorite! Did you pick them up for me?" Lou smiled with affection.

"Nope, your daddy ordered those to be delivered here. Had me get this room in order, especially for you," she replied.

Avoiding talking about the accommodation arrangements anymore, Lou changed the subject. "Where is everybody anyway? I wasn't expecting the red carpet and the high school drumline, but I figured the family would at least be in the same house when I got here…" Lou wondered.

"They're all down at Chapman's. The visitation's started today and then tomorrow morning 'til the funeral hour. They won't be home 'til after eight this evening. So that gives me and you some time to get caught up on a few things. And for you to help me with some of this cooking before the masses make their way here tomorrow," Ruby sighed.

"Ugh. I didn't think about tomorrow after the funeral. Everybody and their brother's gonna be here, aren't they?" Lou was dreading it already.

"Yes, ma'am. According to your Aunt Joan, it'll be a full house, not counting who else will wander in off the streets. I had to send Jover to Ms. Judy's house to bring me more silver and china in case we run out of your mama's. At least I'll know Ms. Judy's silver won't need polishing. She always kept everything spotless, you know."

"I know," Lou agreed, remembering how set Judy had been on cleaning up and saving Brooks Farm. The irony that now Liz was trying to do the same thing was not lost on her. "What are we making?" Lou decided to change the subject. "What can I help with?"

"Ham biscuits, shrimp cocktail, quiche, deviled eggs," Ruby pointed to the eggs in the kitchen sink, "chicken salad sandwiches, and pimiento cheese croissants."

"I haven't eaten like that since I left home!" Lou declared.

"Ain't none of your friends up there know how to cook? Baby showers? Wedding showers? Receptions? No wonder you look like a swift wind would blow you away!" Ruby joked.

"Well, I don't really have many friends," Lou replied. Correcting herself, "I don't have any friends. Except for Liz. We work together." Lou decided to leave it at that for now.

"That ain't like you, girl. You were always social. Garden club, college sorority. What happened to you?" Ruby queried.

"After Judy left, my world just sort of fell apart. I never put it back together again."

Sensing the conversation going deeper than it ought to in the first thirty minutes of Lou's arrival, Ruby returned to the culinary tasks at hand. "Now I've baked the ham. All we'll have to do is warm it up tomorrow. Biscuits are done. We'll warm those up and split 'em for the ham as quick as I can get back here from the funeral. The shrimp is on ice. I'm using the good crystal punch bowl with the shrimp on the edges with lemon wedges. We need to fix the quiche and get it ready to bake tomorrow. Won't do for it to be reheated. We'll finish these eggs and put them in the refrigerator on the back porch. Won't have enough room in here in the one in the kitchen. Cut up those chicken breasts to boil. Put them in that stock pot on the shelf. Needs to be a low boil else the chicken'll be too tough. Then we'll make the pimiento cheese. I may serve it with crackers instead of croissants; I haven't decided yet."

Ruby was in charge and Lou was happy to oblige. Cutting up the chicken, Lou asked, "Why don't you use a whole chicken? You could pull all the meat off and use the carcass to make stock. That's what I do!"

Ruby looked at Lou with a serious expression. "You don't put dark meat in chicken salad. It's the rules."

"Who's rules, Ruby?" Lou laughed.

"Well. I don't know, but I know you don't do it. And that's that." Lou just shook her head and smiled. "You salt that water real good?" Ruby asked, looking over Lou's shoulder.

"Yes, Ruby! Lord have mercy. You act like I've never cooked a day in my life!"

"Okay, okay! I give up, I trust you. Now that the chicken's on, start grating those blocks of sharp cheddar that's in the refrigerator. There's about four pounds."

"Four pounds?! Can't we just use the shredded cheese in the bags?" Lou pleaded.

Ruby gave another stern look. "Now, see, you making me wanna not trust you again. That's Mrs. Mary Lovings's pimiento cheese recipe and it don't call for no bag of cheese."

"Fine, I shall grate you four whole pounds of cheddar cheese for the sanctity of the southern funeral handbook," Lou curtsied.

"Oh, hush up, girl."

Lou set to grating her cheese without any more smart remarks. Ruby broke the silence. "Now, before everybody gets back tonight, we need to go over some things like I told you about on the phone last night," she said seriously.

"Okay, what about the fire at the office first?" Lou suggested.

Putting down the hardboiled eggs she was peeling yet again, Ruby turned and asked, "Now how do you know about THAT?"

"I had to pass through town to get here. Did you think I wouldn't give at least a cursory look around my hometown after three decades? I saw it and pulled in to look closer. It's just awful. What happened?" Lou asked.

Ruby studied on it for a minute. "Well, we aren't real sure. Not yet anyway. Your daddy said the electrical was no good. But they seem to be taking a real long time investigating to me if it was something simple as bad wires."

"You're saying it could have been something more intentional?" Lou was trying to figure out what Ruby was alluding to in this conversation.

"I ain't saying nothing. All I'm saying is we don't know yet. But like everything else lately, I'm sure it's gonna come to light, one way or another."

"Mmhhmm," Lou agreed reluctantly, wanting to know more but not pressing her luck. "So now what's this talk about money and a private investigator?"

"You mean you don't already know?" Ruby replied with uncharacteristic sarcasm.

"Well, I know mostly everything, except that," Lou quipped back.

"Alright, to understand the money, you've gotta understand the investigator," Ruby prefaced the next conversation. "And before that, you've gotta turn down that chicken. Heat's too high."

"How do you know? You're standing clear over there at the sink!"

"I can smell it. You cook as long as I've been cooking, you learn a thing or two," Ruby reminded her.

Lou turned down the boiling chicken and returned to her cheese grating. "Now about this private eye?" she prodded Ruby.

Ruby sighed. "Lou, your mama had a mean streak a mile wide. I don't think I have to tell you that. After everything that happened, you and Judy running off, I don't think she ever found peace again. Even after Little Chuck brought Ms. Judy back down here, Ms. Louise never forgave her. Treated her like a red-headed stepchild. She softened up a little bit when they got pregnant with Josie, I'll give her that. But she had a heart full of so much hate I swear you could see it in her eyes." Ruby shook her head.

"I'll never forget how she talked to me that night they found me and Judy. We never got along; you know that I never lived up to her expectations. I was always closer to Daddy. But I was never afraid of Mama. Not until that night. She scared me worse than I had ever been scared in my life. Probably worse than I ever have since then," Lou confirmed.

"I know. Now her and your daddy were good to me, don't you ever forget that. I'm thankful for everything they've ever done for me and my family. But we all walked on eggshells around Ms. Louise, especially after you left.

"Little Chuck and Ms. Judy had Josie, and, like I said, she softened up a little bit. But she was too far gone by then. Congestive heart failure they said. Heart full of hate if you ask me. She died when Josie was about two or three if I remember. It was five years after you left. I swear, I heard Ms. Judy breathe a sigh of relief when Ms. Louise took her last breath. Can't say I blamed her."

Lou nodded her head in agreement, still grating that damn cheese. "But how does all that lead to this private investigator?"

"You sure don't know how to build a story, do you?" Lou had to laugh, remembering that she said those same words to Liz just the day before.

"Sorry, go on, I'm listening," Lou replied seriously.

"Well after your mama died, it was like Big Chuck was a different person. He had a whole new lease on life. Out of respect for your mama, I don't wanna say he was a happier man, but he was in a better mood, a better place, for sure. I think Josie coming also made him think," she stopped short.

"Think about what?" Lou asked.

"Think about you. Think about the years he'd lost. Thinking about his little girl that he sent away and might never see again. So that's when he hired a private investigator."

"How did he know where to find me?" Lou asked, confused.

"Your address. He had it from when you and Judy mailed it after you left," Ruby confirmed.

"So, he's the one who told Little Chuck where to find us." Lou's face was turning red. "That sonofabitch." She had been grating the cheese so hard without realizing it she skinned her fingers, blood oozing out the tips. She pulled her hand away and Ruby wrapped it with her damp kitchen towel. "I can't believe he sent Chuck up there to pull her away from me," she practically yelled with the rag around her fingers.

"Don't you be mad at your daddy, now, you hear me, girl?" Ruby was almost frightening with the tone she had taken so quickly. Softening, she explained further, "Little Chuck took that letter before your daddy could open it. He took off for Kentucky that minute. Your daddy didn't know 'til it was too late."

"Little Chuck brought Ms. Judy back down here by the next morning. She didn't say a word to any of us. She took to her bed for more than a week. I don't think Ms. Louise ever even looked at her. But when they came back, your daddy tore into your brother like a yard dog to a possum. He told him he had no right to, one, read mail meant for him, and two, to go marching up there to kidnap a woman who left of her own accord. Then he cussed him six ways from Sunday for leaving you up there by yourself–asked him how he could leave his own sister like that."

Lou's mouth just about dragged the kitchen counter.

"Anyway, didn't nobody speak to nobody in this house for weeks it felt like. I cooked and everybody ate separate. I made four beds because everybody slept separate. Your Aunt Joan was still working in Washington for Congressman Jenkins, you know. She didn't move in here until she took that early retirement in '93 when he retired. Your daddy never did like her working for a Democrat, but Mr. Jenkins was a good man. He worked hard to keep the mills in all these towns running, not to mention the capital gains cuts, which worked in favor of your daddy's business big time." Lou looked surprised at Ruby's political prowess, to which she addressed by saying, "I know more than you think I do."

"Okay then. So…wait. Aunt Joan lives here now, too? Christ almighty," Lou hung her head.

"She didn't have nowhere else to go, Lou, she never had a family of her own," Ruby raised her eyebrow, implying something without words. Lou got Ruby's message but didn't belabor the suggestion. That was Joan's business.

"So, everybody was just coexisting here in misery for how long?" Lou asked.

"It was nigh a couple months at least," Ruby concluded. After that, Little Chuck got that job down at the bank and not too long later he started building that house out in Crystal Springs and then moved him and Ms. Judy out there."

"What is Crystal Springs?"

"It's a fancy gated neighborhood out across town, all hoity toity where the young folks with money live," Ruby scrunched up her face.

"I see. Was any of this ever really resolved between any of them?"

"Your daddy grew closer to Judy. I wasn't sure if he was trying to replace you, the daughter he lost, or if he was trying to comfort her. Maybe some of both, I guess. They forgave each other, but it was just between them. Ms. Louise still wasn't playing. And neither was Little Chuck. Just like his mama," Ruby shook her head.

"Then," Ruby continued, "Josie was born, your mama passed on, and things really seemed to calm down quite a bit. Little Chuck was wrapped around Josie's finger," Ruby smiled, remembering. "And I think Judy just sort of faded into the background for a long time as far as he was concerned. Josie got older and I feel like Little Chuck tried to put more into their marriage. They went on trips together, he bought her nice things, sent her flowers. I don't think it was ever enough. She never seemed happy. She just hid in the background; you know what I mean?" Ruby asked rhetorically.

"And I think she was never happy because she was pining for you, honey. See, after Ms. Louise died, that's when your daddy hired that private investigator up there out of Louisville. He kept tabs on everything you ever did. And Judy did, too. I told him it wasn't smart, but he said he figured Judy had a right to know what was going on with you as much as she loved you. So, whenever he got an update, Judy got an update. Your brother never knew anything about it, not 'til just this week. Again, just more that's coming to light."

48

All the Jacksons plus R.J. were accounted for by 10:58. It was cutting it a little too close for comfort for Florence, but at least they were here by the time it was to start. Straightening the ruffles on her blouse and smoothing her black jacket and skirt, she prepared to open the double front doors of the funeral home to the throng of Clanton mourners already waiting outside. One last look in the mirror hanging beside the doors, she pulled a single strand of silvery hair back into her perfect bouffant and welcomed the guests inside.

More than a few people were surprised to see the retired Florence Chapman working again after all this time, but people were genuinely gracious in seeing her and offered sincere compliments for her going out of her way to take care of the Jacksons like this under such trying circumstances. "When the Lord calls, we are but to answer," she always replied, the perfect portrait of what a funeral home director and hostess should be.

After a few moments, her son brought her a chair to sit in at the door, knowing that there was no way she could stand the entire time. Giving into the short heels on her feet, she took the chair but didn't depart from her post of directing the visitors to the parlor where the decedent and the family were located. She also reminded everyone to sign the guest book–the most official social register in the south that substantiates your appearance for the occasion. If you don't sign the guest book, you might as well have never gone at all.

In a large wave, the guests poured in at the beginning of the visitation–easily a few hundred people within the first hour. It being a Saturday, you could expect more visitors than on a weekday when many people would be working, and the same applied to a funeral. A Saturday or Sunday funeral was always significantly more well-attended than a weekday funeral. It has been said that anyone who was practical would die in the middle of the week so more people would be able to partake in the funeralizing festivities that would occur on the weekend days.

As folks filed in to berate the bereaved, the parlor was packed with standing room only. The place was abuzz with low voices greeting and hugging each other, remarking how they never saw each other except for at these sorts of things, making hollow promises to get together more often.

In Appalachia particularly, the commercialization of the funeral industry had changed things a lot. Florence remembered a time when her husband traveled with Gleason Boards in the back of their family car. They were folded out to be used as embalming tables when J.G. was called out for a death. In those days, people did everything at home. They washed the body themselves, dressed it, and laid it out. Families who couldn't afford a casket would ask J.G.to loan them the Gleason Board, which they'd drape with a sheet, while the body laid out in their home. If they couldn't afford a casket, the men of the communities would build a coffin, often of roughhewn hardwood cut from the property of the deceased. The younger men would dig the grave for the family.

The more affluent families didn't do it much differently. They might have the decedent taken to the funeral home for the embalming and preparing, but the funeral home was a small place back then. Their family homes were often much larger, allowing more space for mourners to move about, food to be offered and displayed. Providing food lifts the burden off the families of having to entertain everyone for every minute of their visit. Formal living room furniture would be moved to the sides of the room and the body would be placed in a casket on pedestals in the middle of the room.

Families would then do what they called "sitting up with the body," staying awake all night long in the room with their loved one that had entered the gates. In years past, this served multiple purposes. Eyes of the deceased may be weighted with coins to ensure they stayed closed, appearing asleep. Mouths might need to be adjusted if they opened as rigor mortis continued to set in. In the summer months, family members were needed to fan the body to keep it cool, keeping as much decomposition and stench away as possible. Lastly, the watchers were there to keep the bugs, mice, and other varmints away from the body. This took a lot of work on the part of a grieving family.

Sitting in her comfortable chair by the doors to the beautiful building she and J.G. had built, Florence couldn't help but reflect on how modernized things had become from when she and her husband first started to today, where every aspect was now handled in their office. But she also noted that, in a way, things had become quite a bit less personal. Deaths were mostly shielded in hospitals and behind closed doors. Families no longer had these connections to the final care of their loved ones. She considered this could be part of the reason Big Chuck Jackson had asked for her specifically to handle his daughter-in-law. He knew that Florence would treat her with respect and the job would be done in a personal way. He trusted her, as had countless other families over the years, and she had a lot to be proud of.

People continued to mill about the funeral home, some coming with others leaving. It was a steady stream for the full nine hours of visitation the family had booked. Florence only left her unofficially official spot to use the restroom, Charles keeping her coffee refilled when she asked. He didn't even bother to ask her to come eat some supper; he knew she was at work, and she wouldn't stop.

As the sky dimmed and the crowd subsided, Josie made her way out to the front porch. She needed fresh air. Her nostrils stung with the smell of all the flowers placed around the parlor. Medication be damned, her nerves were jangled. Today had been a lot. She pulled a Klonopin from her purse and dry swallowed it, tilting her head back. She put the cap back on the bottle, placing it back into her bag, and turned to see a disapproving Florence Chapman sitting next to the open front door.

"Don't worry, Mrs. Chapman. You don't have to give me that look, it's not anything illegal, cross my heart," she promised.

"That's not what I was wondering, but it's good to know," she said with a raised eyebrow as she got up. "I was wondering something else." She came closer to Josie slowly with her cane. "I was wondering how you're doing with all this," she nodded her head back towards the inside of the building.

"I'm alright, really," Josie claimed.

"Horse pocky," Florence shot back. "Nobody's alright after their mama hangs themselves, I don't care who you are." Florence wasn't one to hold back when there were facts at hand.

Giving in, Josie turned to face the aged funeral director, a woman beloved by the community, respected throughout the state, and wiser than most. "I'm sad for her. I'm sad for us. But I'm sadder for the people in this town," Josie said, finally able to put into words what she really felt regarding her mother's death. Florence's face indicated she expected more of an explanation, so Josie gave her one.

"Mrs. Chapman, everybody in this town is in everybody else's business. That's no surprise, it's a small town, there's nothing better to do." She chuckled, "I tell all our friends in Atlanta this place is best described as one store, two whores, and a carpet mill." Florence gave another disapproving look, which prompted a quick apology from Josie.

"But you know what I mean. I told daddy, this town steals peoples' lives, their futures. If you don't conform to what their expectations are, you might as well be dead," Josie said with finality in her voice.

"Those are some mighty big assumptions, my dear," Florence replied, looking out across the emptying parking lot at the orange-pink sunset. "I don't think this place is hardly quite as bad as you make it out to be, but I do see your point. What do you think made your mama do what she did?"

"The secrets. Her secrets, Daddy's secrets, Granddaddy's. The lies about her, ones she never fought. I think those were her reasons," Josie said matter-of-factly.

"So, you think if everything came out, that every secret, every lie was exposed, everything would be hunky dory around here? 'Cause I'm not so sure. It might lead to more trouble if you ask me."

"Maybe we'll just see," Josie said walking back into the funeral home to join her family for the last few minutes of the visitation.

The family was gathered around Judy's casket, looking down at her, not saying much. "You know, she looks just like she's sleeping," Joan offered.

"That's what everybody always says," Big Chuck replied, "but she looks dead to me." Joan's mouth dropped open.

"Grandaddy!" Josie chastised her grandfather but started laughing. Soon enough they were all laughing around the body. After a day of being on their best solemn behavior, crying with friends, neighbors, strangers, and everyone in between, they needed a moment of cheering up.

While everyone was laughing, Josie got behind the casket and crawled under the cloth apron surrounding the rollers.

"I'm sure you're wondering why I've gathered y'all here," she said from under the casket, mimicking her mother's voice. "I guess this is as good a time as any to tell y'all that I'm dead," Josie declared through giggles. Everyone was busting out laughing, but it was making R.J. a little nervous. He never quite understood the penchant for dark humor all the Jacksons seemed to possess. "Somebody shut that lid or get me a quilt. Old lady Chapman's got the air conditioning in this place set on 'morgue'!"

Josie fell out from under Judy's casket. She was laughing so hard her stomach hurt. R.J. got her up out of the floor and she dusted off her dress. Charles Chapman cleared his throat from the doorway to indicate their time was coming to an end and he was ready to close, so they all began to gather their belongings and make their way to their cars. Josie was the last to leave the room. She looked at her beautiful mother lying there for a second, and whispered, "Don't worry Mom, I'm gonna set the record straight for once." She kissed her fingers and laid them on Judy's cold cheek. She walked outside to join her family to head home to The Gables.

49

“So, Daddy hired this private investigator to find out what about me? Where I live? They already knew that.” Lou was supremely perplexed.

“He hired the man, well, the man’s company, to keep tabs on you. Which they’ve done now for thirty years. He knew where you lived, where you worked, how you made money. And that’s when he bought your house. When he found out how broke you were. He couldn’t have you tossed out on the streets, ‘cause he knew you sure wouldn’t come home.”

“That’s a lie, Ruby. I don’t know what he told you, but I bought that house outright myself. I used part of what little money I had socked away, and the landlady sold it to me,” Lou said, sure that Ruby was mistaken.

Looking at her with a mixture of pity and affection, Ruby replied, “You think that rich old woman in Florida sold you a whole house and farm for a thousand dollars? For real?”

“How did you know how much I…” It all started to click. Big Chuck had, in fact, bought the house from Helen. “That old bitch. She acted like she was doing me a favor,” Lou said, shaking her head, unwilling, or unable, to accept that she had been duped.

“Once your daddy figured out who owned the house, he got in touch with her. Told her what he wanted to do. She drove up the price of that place like you ain’t never seen before. Your daddy paid it in cash money, on the condition that she put it straight into your name and would make it look like he had absolutely nothing to do with it. And apparently,” Ruby added with a superior tone, “the plan worked.”

“How much did he pay for it?” Lou wanted to know.

“Now that I do not know,” Ruby replied truthfully. “They had to show it in the record books as a sale for $1,000 so that lady could hide the profit money and so it could legally pass into your name and your name only. What I do know is that that place is your inheritance.”

"My inheritance?" Lou scoffed. "I never figured I'd get a dime," she said, resuming her mixing of the pimiento cheese.

"Well, that house you got is your inheritance. He set aside the same amount he spent on it for your brother, which he's giving to him now, since your brother's broke as a joke." Ruby shook her head.

Alarmed, Lou asked Ruby, "Why on earth is he broke? I assumed Daddy gave him the business. He apparently has this fancy house. What am I missing?"

"The business hasn't made money in a long time, honey. 'Bout bled your daddy dry. That's when he retired and handed it over to Little Chuck, thinking he might could turn it around with some of his connections and younger friends. And he did try. But of course, Little Chuck always lived high on the hog. Champagne tastes on a beer budget if you ask me. I 'spose he's got a mighty bit of debt. Couldn't even afford a nice funeral for Ms. Judy–your daddy's paying for it. But you didn't hear that from me," Ruby warned.

"Hmm. More secrets. Color me surprised," Lou said aloud to the room.

"Well, here's another one for you, little girl. We all know you've got cancer, so what gives?"

Lou turned red as a beet. "I don't want to talk about it. That's not what I'm here for. I'm here to honor Judy and that's it, nothing else really matters," she lied to Ruby and herself.

"Mmhhmm," Ruby simply replied. "Well, that's the last report they got on you, and that you couldn't pay for treatments. But judging by how thin your hair is, how those clothes hang on you, and how weak your eyes look, it's pretty far along, I'd say. If you're still smoking like a freight train, I'd bet it's lung cancer. I don't smell it on you much, though."

"I quit recently," Lou shot back. "But Ruby, I said I didn't want to talk about it," she said firmly. Going back to the rest of the repertoire of Jackson Family Drama, she asked in a smart tone, "Now is there any more shit I need to know about that's hit the fan around here?"

"One last thing," Ruby said, still offended by the way Lou was keeping secrets from her after her big diatribe about covering things up. "Your daddy," Ruby continued, "He's eat up with Leukemia. He took treatments for a while, but they made him so sick he gave up on 'em. Doctors said the only chance for him would be a bone marrow transplant. Your brother isn't a match, neither is Josie. Joan would be a match, but she can't donate on account of her rheumatoid arthritis. It's a whole lot harder to find any kind of match outside the family. I even got myself tested," she said, hanging her head. "No match."

Summing the conversation up, "So all that to say, Mr. Chuck's days are numbered. Coming here this weekend isn't just about you saying your goodbye to Ms. Judy. You're gonna need to say goodbye to your daddy, too," Ruby stated with sadness in her voice.

The pair continued prepping their funeral reception food without much more talk. Enough had been said to last for quite a while, they both decided.

Lou excused herself to go to the bathroom, but she really went upstairs to call Liz. She had promised that she would call her as soon as she got to Clanton, but she didn't.

Lou dialed Liz's cell phone number, which she picked up before the first ring could finish. "You've had me worried sick," Liz complained.

"How did you know it was me? You don't have this number," Lou replied, surprised at the automatic chastising.

"The hell I don't. Your maid left it on the answering machine. I saved it so I could call if I didn't hear from you, which I was going to do in about another hour."

Lou wanted to be annoyed, but instead her heart felt a little fuzzy. "You're a stalker."

"Cut it, sis. You said you'd call regularly, and I expect it, got it?" Liz was acting like she did the day they'd first met when she was laying down the law about getting a job with the school system. Lou didn't want to admit it, but she admired the way Liz would stand her ground regarding her convictions.

"Yes, ma'am. I promise. I'm here now, and things are even more twisted than you, or I, knew about, if you can believe it."

"Sweetie, from what I've learned about this family in the past five days alone, absolutely nothing surprises me. You could tell me they're having your dead lesbian lover's funeral on the roof of the nearest Longhorn Steakhouse while Nancy Reagan played the ukulele and I'm sure I wouldn't bat an eye at this point," Liz stated with the seriousness of a heart attack.

Lou couldn't help but laugh, picturing the scene Liz had just painted in her mind, which eventually made Liz giggle a little, too. "Well, nothing quite like that, yet, but there's some doozies. I've got to go now, they're all gonna be back from the funeral home any minute. I've been helping Ruby get ready for tomorrow. That's how I know I've gotten all the right information, not the Ted Turner colorized version. I'll call you before I go to bed, but I have no idea when that will be," Lou promised.

"Don't worry. I doubt I'll sleep much anyway. First thing I'm buying for this house is a new mattress," Liz declared.

"Fair enough. Just don't go spending all our silver money just yet. Give the guard dogs a kiss for me, and I'll talk to you later."

"Sounds good," Liz yawned. "I'll be waiting."

As Lou hung up the phone, she heard vehicles pulling in on the gravel driveway. The knot in her stomach from earlier swelled to three times its previous size. This was it. The moment 35 years had been building up to when she would again see her estranged family.

She made her way down the stairs, stopping at the landing. She couldn't will her feet to go any farther, not just yet. And hers weren't the only feet stalling out. The family was all gathered in the driveway; no one was even moving towards the door. She creeped down to where she could see a little better from the round window on the staircase facing out of the front of the house. This was where she always peeked out as a little girl when company had come calling on the Jacksons. Now, however, the folks she was checking out were her kin.

Of course, she could identify them all. Three decades had aged them, but she knew them well enough. She sized up the young couple, surmising this must be her niece and nephew-in-law. Should she have brought a baby shower gift or a wedding present, she mused to herself, considering she never knew the girl was born or that she'd married.

The group appeared to be having a serious discussion, the topic or details of which could not be heard from Lou's vantage point, but there was a nod to the car with the Kentucky plates, so she assumed it had to do with her.

It was her father doing the talking with everyone else listening and nodding. Some things never change, she thought, fondly remembering her powerful father who was always listened to whenever he spoke anywhere.

Here he was giving orders as usual but looking pitiful. Lou knew to expect this given Ruby's information regarding his Leukemia diagnosis, but this was not how she had imagined her father after all these years. When you're a child, you believe your parents to be invincible. When you grow a little older, you see the wrinkles and gray hairs creeping in. But when your own gray hairs begin to make their appearances, your mind tricks you into believing time should stand still for your parents. You long for the youth they had when you first thought they were old. Now, seeing this decrepit man on a walker, wearing a suit that no longer fit his withering body, a tear escaped Lou's eye, triggering again the inevitable thought of her father's mortality and the effect it would have on her family.

With Lou caught in her feelings, the family began to make their way up the steps slowly. So slow that it seemed like a time warp. Lou's feet were glued to the stair steps again. Big Chuck's walker entered the foyer first, then Joan held it steady while Big Chuck stepped inside the door to regain hold of it. The rest of them followed suit.

No one noticed her on the stairs that were to the left of the door just yet. Lou's heart was about to beat out of her chest. Did she say hello? Did she run and hide? Did she sing the Star-Spangled Banner? Her mind was scattered three sheets to the wind.

Josie was the first to notice her aunt on the steps. It took her breath away for a split second. R.J. caught the surprise in his wife's eyes and followed her gaze to the staircase, seeing Lou for the first time. Sensing the extra presence in the room, the rest of the family's eyes landed on their daughter, niece, and sister, Louvenia Virginia Jackson.

50

"You're absolutely sure of this?" Klark Kitchens said slowly on his department-issued phone to the Mayflower County Fire Marshal. "So where did it start?" He continued to listen to the explanations, his mind running ninety miles an hour. "And you'll have all this written up tonight? Good. Send it over the minute you finish typing." He ended the call.

Klark sat back in his chair, crossing his arms behind his head, and staring at the ceiling of his office. It was late, but he never paid attention to time. Maybe that's why he was deemed such a good sheriff–he never really stopped working. He didn't have any family left except his mother and sister. His sister had moved off to work in Mississippi where she met and married a real nice guy and had two kids. He loved when they would come home to Clanton to visit because it was pretty lonely with just him and his mom.

When he started rising in the ranks of the sheriff department, he didn't think it appropriate that he should still be living at home with his mama, so he bought a house: the house next door to his mama. This allowed him to bypass the stigma a little but kept it easy enough to still have supper with her most nights and be there if she needed him or he needed her. Tonight, he needed her.

He rose from his desk, straightened his papers and such, and headed out. He told his evening staff good night and made it to his patrol car, eyeing the dent in the front bumper caused by one Lou Jackson.

He pulled into his driveway and parked his patrol car. The kitchen light was still on at his mama's, so he walked across the yard to her house and opened the back door. She was sitting in the den working a crossword puzzle when he came in.

"How many times do I have to tell you about keeping that door latched, old lady?" he growled.

"My son's the sheriff," she hollered back, "Ain't nothing to be afraid of in this town," she smiled to herself.

He made a plate of room temperature spaghetti and got a beer out of the fridge. He popped the top and sat next to Lois Kitchens in her den to eat his supper. He sat in the same recliner his daddy had sat in.

Watching whatever she had switched the TV to for a second and taking a deep swig of his beverage, he opened the conversation. "You ever know of a Louvenia Jackson? Might be kin to Chuck Jackson and them?"

"'Course I do. That was Big Chuck's daughter," she said, not removing her gaze from the crossword puzzle, "She's dead."

"No, Mother, you're thinking of his daughter-in-law. That was Judy. She's the one that just died," he replied, shaking his head.

"Well, I think I know that. I saw her at Chapmans myself just today."

"You went up there?" he asked.

"Well yes, Klark. We've known them longer than I've been alive. My daddy used to bushhog fields for Big Chuck's daddy. And Josie used to babysit you, for heaven's sakes."

Klark's gears were turning in his head, but they were moving awfully slow.

"I'll never forget," Lois began, "that fourth of July you ate four hot dogs and tossed your cookies all over Judy Jackson's rug. That thing probably cost more than this house did when me and your daddy bought it. I was scared to death we'd never be able to replace it without taking out a loan."

"It was only three hot dogs," Klark said grumpily.

"Anyway, Judy was as sweet as she could be about it. Said she'd have it cleaned and nobody would ever know, and that I wasn't to worry about it at all. Next time I was there, I noticed they'd bought a new club chair to sit in that spot. I thought I'd never be able to show my face in town again, but she never said a word about it, far as I know."

"Back to Louvenia, Mama, enough of memory lane," Klark was embarrassed at this point.

"Oh, well, yes, as far as I know she died. Well, she disappeared. Somebody said she ran off with some old man twice her age to live in New Orleans and work at a casino. Somebody else said she was killed in a car accident and there wasn't nothing left of her but tiny little pieces, so they never had a funeral. I really don't know what happened to her, I guess," Lois considered the sordid explanations she was recalling.

"What did she look like?"

"Lord, I don't remember, son. That's been thirty years or more. I've slept since then."

"Just an idea, please?"

"Well, she was tall, like all of them Jacksons. Wide shoulders and hips. That was how you knew Judy married in; she was such a cute, tiny little thing. Looked like a little fairy when she was around all of them big, strapping Jacksons," Lois laughed for a second, then got her wits about her. "Why are you asking all these questions about her anyway? She was gone before you were born. You wouldn't have known anything about her."

"Part of a case, Mama. You know I can't discuss that with you. Confidential matters," he said gulping the last of his beer and getting up out of the recliner. He placed his plate in the sink and tossed the beer can in the trash.

"Oh, bull. What's the point in having a sheriff for a son if he won't tell you all the good secrets?" she asked.

"Already too many secrets out there, Mama. I'm not adding anymore," he said on his way to the door. "I'm locking this behind me," he hollered. "Love you."

"Love you more," she called after him.

51

"Hey, y'all," Lou said awkwardly from the steps. After all, how does one greet estranged family and strangers who are family?

"Baby," Big Chuck uttered, looking at his daughter for the first time in so long. She stepped down the stairs and he reached to hug her over his walker. Yikes. She was not ready for a hug, but here they were. She leaned in and hugged her father back.

Little Chuck gave her a forced side hug, saying "Welcome home. This is our daughter, Josie, and her husband R.J."

"Josie, it's so nice to meet you. You, too, R.J.," she said warmly. It was a lot easier to be nice to people you don't know than to people you know a little too well.

Joan was the only family member to not rush in for some affection. "We're glad to have you here this weekend," Joan said coolly. The emphasis on "this weekend" was not lost on Lou. But Joan must be playing nice according to Big Chuck's rules.

"Aunt Joan," Lou just smiled.

Ruby had been standing around the corner, watching this whole saga play out like a soap opera. She decided this was the perfect time to interject.

"I know y'all must be starving!" she declared. "Come on into the kitchen. I've laid out some food and got some stuff to make sandwiches. Ms. Lou been helping me all afternoon!" she added warmly.

"You've been here all afternoon?" Big Chuck asked Lou, surprised. "You should have come to the funeral home."

"I'm sure she was busy getting in and was tired from the drive and all, Daddy," Little Chuck rushed to his sister's defense, glad that she had not, in fact, come to the funeral home.

"Yes," Lou agreed with her younger brother. "That drive is a killer. When I got here there was just enough time for me to unpack my things for tomorrow and help Ruby with some of the preparations."

"And just enough time for me to get Ms. Lou caught up on all the dirty little secrets around here," Ruby added from the kitchen counter.

Lou froze. Little Chuck turned red. Joan's mouth dropped open. And Big Chuck hung his head. Josie spoke up, asking Ruby for confirmation, "You told her *all* the secrets?"

"Every last one of 'em," Ruby replied. "Less you got another one since y'all left here this morning," she said without looking up from piping the pastel yellow filling for her deviled eggs.

Big Chuck cleared his throat to say something, but, maybe for the first time ever, words escaped him. He had planned for this to go this way, but now that it was here, it was still a bit overwhelming. No one else dared utter a word until he found his.

"So, Ruby told you everything?" he asked Lou.

"I think so," she replied quietly.

"The investigator?"

"Yes."

"The purchase of the farm?"

"Mmhhmm."

"My Leukemia?"

"Yeah," she said quieter, like that was still a secret.

"The failed business?" Little Chuck intervened.

"Yes, I'm very sorry."

"The money he's giving me?"

"It's only fair," she confirmed.

"The fire at my office?"

"That, I found out about on my own," Lou stated. Seeing the confused faces around the table, she explained the story as she told Ruby, "I saw it when I drove through town. I had to stop to look at it. It was really sad for me, so I know it must have been, or is, harder for y'all."

"It's been a whirlwind week around here," Little Chuck told her.

"Do they have any information on it yet?" Lou asked innocently.

Everyone turned to Little Chuck for an update, realizing they hadn't heard much about any recent developments. "Well," he cleared his throat to gather his thoughts, "There are some suspicions of arson, according to Klark Kitchens."

Lou's ears perked up, not adding what she had heard from the stranger in town, but simply listening to what she would hear.

"Oh, that's impossible," Joan scoffed. "Who would want to burn down your office?"

"We don't have any enemies in this town… do we, Dad?" Josie asked.

"No, of course not," he dismissed the question.

"Could it have been someone who expected an insurance payout?" Big Chuck laid it out on the table heavily, looking his son in the eyes.

"The hell you say!" Little Chuck's eyes blazed with contempt.

"You're broke. And you were awful upset when you found out there wasn't any insurance money. I was gonna ask you about it tonight in private, but since we're all talking about it, I figured I'd just ask now. Again, there's been enough secrets around here. So out with it," Big Chuck looked at his son, expecting an answer promptly.

Shaking his head and rising from the table, Little Chuck said calmly, "You know, I've done a lot of things in my life I'm not proud of. I kidnapped a woman and forced her into marriage which practically forced her hand at suicide. I left my own sister stranded hundreds of miles away from home without a second thought. I tried to secretly mortgage my house to keep your legacy alive." Big Chuck's eyes shot daggers into his son.

"You did what?"

"I tried to mortgage our house in Crystal Springs so I could keep the firm afloat. I wasn't going to let it die before you. I respected you too much to lose it. But the bank wouldn't loan me enough. The market's turned and I couldn't get enough. The last paychecks I wrote Rosie and Peter bounced. My next plan was to sell the house and move in here under the guise of us being your full-time caretakers to save face, even though you, of course, have Joan and Ruby."

"You're dumber than you look, you know that?" Big Chuck spat out. "There is no business worth sacrificing everything for. You should have come to me. And now you've committed arson, haven't you?" He said in a disgusted tone.

Still calm, Little Chuck continued his previous explanation, "As I said, there are a lot of things I have done that I am not proud of. But none of them are arson. If you don't believe me, ask Klark Kitchens. He caught me putting Judy's suicide note back in our house the night after she died. I agreed not to sue for negligence on the part of the department for not properly accounting for and logging the note as a crucial piece of evidence, not to mention his entering our home alone using the spare key for his personal cover up, if he agreed to keep his mouth shut about me taking the note."

"I was at the house when the fire broke out at the office. I have an airtight alibi, courtesy of the Sheriff of Mayflower County who will bend over backwards to make sure I'm not questioned. He's still poking his head around to get it figured out, but it was not me. For you to accuse me of that is nothing short of insulting." He pushed his untouched plate back on the table and left the kitchen, going up to his bedroom.

Well. The question lingering on the minds of both Big Chuck and Lou was at least finally answered. But it left a new question–if Little Chuck didn't do it, who did?

52

This wasn't exactly the welcome home anyone had planned, but, then again, did anyone have any idea of how this was going to play out? The rest of the family finished their meal with polite conversation. Lou asked her niece and nephew a lot of questions about their life in Atlanta, giving her best attempt to get to know them in earnest. Lou found Josie to be as sensitive as Judy but as short-fused as Big Chuck. She was quite an interesting amalgamation of her family members, but she seemed to have more sense than any of the rest of them combined, Lou concluded.

Lou communicated as much. "You seem like a brilliant young woman," she told Josie. "I know we've just met, but I want you to know that I'm really proud of you and the strong woman you are." Josie was touched by the sentiment.

Lou turned to R.J. and sized him up, "Can you go along with an independent woman like this?" she gestured to Josie.

He looked at his wife with so much love and replied, "I've never once questioned my commitment to this girl. What I'm not so sure about is the rest of y'all."

Everyone at the table laughed, even Joan with a strained "Ha. Ha."

"Among other reasons why do you think I got the hell out of here?" Lou quipped back at R.J. "Josie's a smart girl, but Atlanta may not be far enough away."

"Alright, now, enough complaining about Clanton," Ruby admonished. Josie saw this as an opportunity to ask a question she really needed the answer to.

"So, Aunt Lou, I have to know, and forgive me for being so forward considering we've just met, but when did you know you were gay?"

Lou's eyes widened. Big Chuck put down his fork. Joan got up from the table, saying, "My God, right here where we eat."

Wanting to answer her niece's question, Lou looked to her father for permission. "Might as well enlighten us all," he threw up his hands.

"I'm enlightened enough, I'm going to bed," Joan declared.

"Better shower before bed so you don't catch it!" Big Chuck hollered after her, making the rest of the uncomfortable table laugh.

"Well," Lou began delicately, "I always knew I was different even when I was a kid. Different from everybody else. I didn't know what it was. I couldn't name it. But I knew I felt something."

"You felt something for other girls?" Josie prodded.

Smiling slightly, Lou replied, "I had... urges. Urges that any young person has when their hormones start to rage."

"So...you were looking for some nookie?" Ruby asked. Josie put her head down on the table, R.J.'s cheeks turned red, and Big Chuck just laughed.

"No, Ruby!" Lou replied, embarrassed. "Mama told me I was saving that for marriage. I didn't even consider sex an option, with a male or a female. But I was drawn to the female form. I was mostly just curious more than anything. The men I had come in contact with were sleazy. They would make passes or comments. And in those days, you didn't say anything back or tell anyone. Women just took it. I decided I didn't want to 'just take it' like some proper girl. I didn't want anything to do with these guys that really only wanted two things out of me: breeding and feeding."

"Honestly, that makes perfect sense," Josie replied. "If I hadn't found the absolute perfect man, I might have been a lesbian myself," she declared.

"Oh Lord," Big Chuck cried, "Not another one!" The whole table laughed. "It's getting late. I need to get to bed. We've got a big day ahead of us tomorrow," he concluded.

"We're having a funeral, not plowing the lower forty, Granddaddy," Josie rolled her eyes. She was really enjoying this time with her aunt.

Ruby replied, "No, but I might as well be. I've got to wrassle all of you up, feed you, send you to Chapman's, get this house ready for after the funeral, then get myself ready, and get up to First Baptist all before 2:00. Then rush back here to start receiving the family. We all better get on to bed," Ruby commanded.

She helped Big Chuck to his room while the others cleared the kitchen and breakfast table and recovered the mourning meals to return to the refrigerator and munch on the next day. R.J. went upstairs, deciding he would shower tonight instead of in the morning.

Josie and Lou were left in the kitchen alone. "How are you holding up?" Josie asked Lou.

She was a bit surprised at the question. "Shouldn't I be the one asking you that?

"It's all anybody's asked me for days. I'm tired of answering, so, tag, you're it," Josie replied with Lou's sense of sarcasm.

"I'm okay. I was not okay for a very long time," Lou sighed. "But I mourned your mom for 35 years before she ever died. When she left, she might as well have died, and me right along with her."

"But now you have cancer. Does it bother you that there's all this drama that you've come back to?" Josie asked. "Assuming you are in fact coming back?"

"Well, I've decided to not die." Lou said emphatically.

"Is that how it works nowadays?" Josie mused.

"Heaven don't want me and hell's afraid I'll take over. So, I'm not going anywhere." This triggered a hearty laugh from Josie who had to admire the tenacious spirit and quick wit of her aunt. "There is also someone else to live for now," she added quietly.

"I. Need. Details." Josie begged, causing Lou to laugh this time.

"Her name is Liz. We work together, well, sort of. We've become close," Lou explained.

"Really? Close? That's all you're going to tell me?"

"Some things are better left unsaid, especially between two people who just met," Lou replied with a motherly look.

"I feel like I've known you my whole life," Josie said, glancing absentmindedly at a family photograph taken at Olan Mills in Kennesaw hanging on the wall next to the back door. She was about eight years old in that picture. Judy and Little Chuck were standing in the back, their arms around each other but opposite hands resting on either side of Big Chuck who was holding Josie on one knee. The photo always seemed like it was missing something. Josie didn't remember her grandmother Louise much at all, but Josie always wished she had been in that photo. Now Josie wished her Aunt Lou had also been in that picture. She belonged there.

With everything put away, Lou announced that she, too, was heading to bed. She told her niece good night and climbed the stairs to her bedroom. Josie sat at the kitchen table for a while, caught somewhere between feelings and reality, stuck in the comfort and complacency of the world she'd always known, but doing what she dared. She took a pencil and notepad and started writing again.

Josie looked through all the phone books and directories in the house. None of them had a phone number for Klark Kitchens. She'd have to call in backup.

Her best friend from high school had reached out on Facebook to express her condolences upon the news of Judy's passing. Like Josie, Melanie had been smart enough to get out of Clanton, too, but not until a few years later. She still had some closer connections to Clanton than Josie.

She sent Melanie a message and saw that she read it. Soon a reply came in with exactly what she needed, no questions asked, just like a good friend would do!

Josie dialed the number and waited for Klark to pick up. Not recognizing the number, he ignored it, but a voicemail was left. It was Josie Jackson asking him to call her as soon as he could. His heart fluttered a little. He had crushed on her for years, but she was even more beautiful now.

This was hardly the time for him to be thinking these lascivious thoughts, but he couldn't deny them. He stopped his work from his desk and called her back.

Josie answered immediately. "I'm so glad you got my message, I've gotta see you."

"Whoa there, partner, what about your husband? Is this really the right time?" he laughed.

"KK, for God's sake, what are you talking about?" Being called KK shifted the mood drastically and he realized this wasn't a social call.

"Uh, nothing, it's just late, what do you need?" he asked.

"I need to see my mom's suicide note," she told him.

"I can't give that out, Josie, you know better than that." He was serious now.

"You don't have to give it to me, I just need to read it, or know what it said. Nobody will tell me."

"There's a lot of personal stuff in there. I don't think you'll be comfortable reading it."

"Can't I be the one to decide that?" she asked. "Please, it's really important to me."

"Ugh, fine. I've got a copy of it in my files. I'm not sending a photo of it, but I will text you what it says, okay?"

"That's all I need. Thank you, really. You don't know how much this means to me."

"Sure, no problem," he replied, hanging up the phone, his ego crushed and bruised.

53

Ruby had turned down the covers in Lou's room, which made her smile. She also had unpacked Lou's bag and hung up the Chanel suit Liz had picked for her to wear the next day. Lou moved the tulips from the dresser to the nightstand, so they'd be the first thing she saw when she woke up the next morning.

Climbing into bed, she picked up the phone extension in the bedroom to call Liz to check in for the night, but there wasn't a dial tone. Instead, there were voices on the line. One she knew, the other she found familiar but couldn't identify. She didn't want to listen in, but they were making it so easy, how could she not?

The unfamiliar voice said, "I don't like being the bearer of this kind of news, but I thought you'd wanna know as soon as possible."

"No, I'm sorry that it's happened, but I'm glad to know the truth." This voice belonged to Lou's younger brother. But what news? What were they talking about?

Little Chuck continued, "When will you arrest her?"

Arrest who?

"She's not a flight risk. I probably won't do it 'til tomorrow, after the funeral. I don't want this to overshadow your time of grief." Lou was certain she could identify the strange voice now–the sheriff she'd hit earlier in the day when she got into town.

Good Lord, could he really be planning to arrest her? Was it a hit and run if the sheriff told you to go on your way? What else could she have possibly done wrong? This was all she needed now. If she got arrested in Clanton, Georgia, this would surely be the end of her, the pinnacle of shame and embarrassment for the family. And her brother already knew about it. What a mess.

Lou slowly and as quietly as possible put the phone back on the receiver, lying in bed, staring at the ceiling, ready to cry at any moment. She was trying to keep herself together. She had to keep it together. She promised herself that she wouldn't let her emotions run her over this weekend. But the prospect of being arrested in her hometown 24 hours after her return from 35 years away was not part of her plan.

She had to go talk to her brother. If he knew about this, he oughta tell her. Whatever bad blood was between them, if her arrest was being orchestrated, he could at least give her a heads up. She got out of the bed and opened the door, looking down the hallways. The door was cracked, and the light was still on in Little Chuck's bedroom. Lou tiptoed down the hall and lightly rapped on the door. She didn't want to disturb any of the others.

"Chuck? Can I come in?"

"Uh, sure," he said, evidently flustered.

"I, um, just wanted to say I'm sorry for earlier. About the talk about the fire and accusations. I know it must have been hard." This conversation was so supremely awkward. There was so much to say. So much had come between them. But at this very moment, something else more pressing was on Lou's mind. "Look, I don't know what was relayed to you, but it was entirely an accident. I just wasn't paying attention and I was thinking about coming back here and I was overwhelmed, and I'd just seen the burned down office. Can they really charge me for this?" Words just kept flowing out of her mouth; she couldn't stop them. And with each word, Little Chuck was growing more and more confused.

"I know I shouldn't have listened, but that was also an accident. I was going to call Liz and I heard y'all when I picked up. Now, Chuck, you've got to believe me when I say that he told me to just go. There's got to be some kind of dash camera footage or something, right? Do you think I need a lawyer?"

"What in God's name are you talking about, Lou?" Little Chuck asked, absolutely stunned with the deluge of gibberish coming out of his sister's mouth.

"They're going to arrest me! Tomorrow, right after Judy's funeral! I can't take this. I'm sick and I'm a wreck as it is. Please don't let them arrest me, Chuck. I can skip the funeral altogether and go home if you think they won't catch me. But then I'll be on the run from the law! A fugitive!" Lou cried.

Little Chuck took his sister by the arms and shook her lightly, "Slow your roll. I need you to calm the hell down and talk to me like a normal person, otherwise I can't help you. What have you done?"

"As if you don't know! I backed into that sheriff's patrol car, and he called you to tell me they're gonna arrest me for it!"

Little Chuck started to laugh.

"I'm glad you're enjoying this, you bastard. I guess if I'm locked up, I'm not a threat anymore, is that it?" she said, disgusted.

With a more serious look on his face, Chuck replied, "Nobody is arresting you, Lou."

"You're lying, I just heard it. Tomorrow after Judy's funeral. To save you all from being even more ashamed of me," she said, full of spite.

Chuck was beginning to get angry, "You know, if just for once in your life you'd listen to somebody else and get some facts before you flew off the handle, you might learn a thing or two."

"Yeah, my temper is the one that always runs amuck, isn't it? My temper was the one that drove up to Kentucky and took the love of my life, right?" she spat out.

"Your temper, or your contempt, rather, was the one that kidnapped my wife on our wedding night, you piece of shit."

"It all comes out now, doesn't it? All the niceties at the door. The pleasantries. Another one of your pretend acts, just like when you went through with that wedding, knowing good and damn well that Judy was in love with me." Lou was finally saying what she needed to say to her brother for a long time.

"I guess I deserve that," Chuck admitted to Lou's surprise. "But if you wanna talk about acts let's talk about how you and Judy teamed up to fool me. How you two were carrying on for years, and even still while we were dating, sucking, and scissoring and God only knows what else. Under this very roof! Disrespecting our parents, our whole family!"

Lou didn't know what else to say. She just looked at her brother, tears streaming down her cheeks silently. "I'm sorry I'm such a disappointment to you," she said in an even tone. "I'm sorry that I fell in love with someone that I never should have loved. And I'm sorry I ever came back here." She turned to go back to her room.

"You know, common sense has chased you your whole life, but, by God, you are faster, you know that?" he hollered after her.

She sat on the edge of the bed, collecting herself enough to make the call to Liz. She dialed the number, and it rang several times before the machine picked up. Lou broke down. The only voice she needed to hear right now wasn't there. At the beep, she said, "Things have taken a turn, if you can imagine. I'm going to try to sleep tonight, and I'll be back tomorrow by lunch. I need you to talk to an attorney about charges regarding hit and run accidents. I'll try to call in the morning before I leave, but it'll be early." She went to hang up the phone, but followed up the message with, "I love you."

Lou took one large sleeping pill and drifted off to a fitful sleep. Indiscernible dreams invaded her slumber. Dreams with Louise in them, some with Judy. The night Eugenia drove Judy up to show her how she'd beaten her. Dreams about Liz. Lou running and running and running without ever stopping. What she was running from or to, she didn't know.

She woke up around 6:30 as the sunlight began to seep into the bedroom through the drapes. She laid there, trying to remember the dreams, trying to figure out what had been fake and what had really happened the night before. She was slowly achieving coherence when the phone rang next to her head. She picked it up instinctively, even though this was not her house to answer the phone in anymore.

"Hello?" Lou croaked out.

"Oh God, it's you, I didn't know who might pick up." It was Liz. Lou began to cry. Liz could hardly understand her through the sobs and the tinny landline.

"Lou, I need you to calm down so we can talk. I got your message from last night. I'm sorry I fell asleep early, but I need to understand what's happening so I can help you, okay?" She was using her best counselor voice.

Lou tried to control her breathing so she could speak. "I hit a police car. And he told me to just go, that it was okay. But he found out who I was and then he called my brother and said he was going to arrest me, and I heard it on the phone. Now I have to get out of here and we have to find a lawyer, okay?"

"Okay, let's break this down. You hit a police car? Was it bad?"

"No, I was just distracted, and I backed into him. There wasn't much damage, I swear. But it was the sheriff in this Godforsaken town."

"But you're okay? And he was okay?" she asked slowly.

"Yes, I'm fine. But apparently, he was not fine. He called my brother last night and I picked up the phone to call you and I heard them. He told Chuck he was going to arrest me after the funeral today. 35 years later and I'm still a disappointment." She began to tear up again.

"Calm down, we'll get through this. I just need to understand a little bit more, okay?"

"Okay," Lou replied, sniffling.

"Why would the sheriff call your brother about arresting you?"

Annoyed, Lou barked, "This is classic small town, Liz. Don't you get it? Everybody knows your business before you do!"

"Lou," Liz said calmly, but firmly, "They do not arrest people for hitting cars. If it was just an accident, you get a citation and a fine at most. If you do it on purpose, it can be a felony, but that really doesn't sound like the case here."

"And just how do you know? Are you an expert in criminal law now? God, almighty," Lou was shaking her head.

"No, dipshit!" Liz's voice was rising. "I'm literally just Googling what happens when you hit a police car! Now will you shut the hell up and listen to me?"

Now that she had been dressed down really good, Lou sheepishly agreed.

"You need to ask your brother what was said specifically, and then you need to contact the sheriff's department. If you approach them, it looks much better than if they come looking for you. Do you understand?"

"Well, yes, but that's the other thing," Lou said.

"What other thing?" Liz groaned.

"I did call Chuck out on it last night. I wanted him to help me, but we just ended up fighting. It was like the day he left with Judy all over again. It was awful. I'm a wreck."

"Fine. Bypass your brother then. Get ready and go straight to the sheriff's office. I'll get ready and I'll drive down there. We can figure this out together."

"Oh no, I can't let you do that. I don't want to drag you into this," Lou pleaded with her.

"It's a little late for that, hon. I'm coming down there and I'll meet you. I should be there by 12:30 if I can get out of here now. I'll call my friend Scott and get him to watch the dogs. Call my cell number if something happens." With that, Liz hung up the phone. Lou held it in her hand until the busy signal started. She returned it to the receiver.

Lou dressed quickly and made her way downstairs. With any luck, no one else would be up yet. But there was no such luck. Ruby was already downstairs preparing for the day. She caught Lou coming down the stairs.

With an unsure look, Ruby asked, "Where are you going so early?"

"Ruby, I'm sorry, I've gotta go. I can't stay." Lou grabbed her purse hanging by the door. Ruby had dropped her freshly pressed linens and was coming after her.

"Ms. Lou, what you mean?" she whispered loudly, trying not to alert anyone else to what was conspiring right there in the foyer.

"Ruby, I have to go before I bring any more shame to this family. I love you, okay?" She hugged Ruby and fled down the steps to her car.

"Lou, wait! Whatever it is, we can talk it out!" Ruby shouted, no longer caring if anyone heard her.

Her words fell on deaf ears. The Subaru was already peeling out of the driveway. Ruby began to cry, just like she had when Lou left the last time. Like she was losing one of her children all over again. She sat on the steps, her head in her hands, and cried like a baby.

54

Liz was in Lou's car heading towards the interstate before she even had a chance to fully process what was happening. Scott had agreed to come check on the dogs through tomorrow if needed. Liz said a silent prayer that Lou's car would get her to Clanton, unsure of what she would be walking into.

Jesus, Lou, she thought. What have you done? Liz's mind jumped a million places on the drive, but it kept returning to the fact that she had quite literally dropped everything to drive six hours to save a woman she had known for exactly six days. It was more than a little odd, all truth be told. But this entire experience had been odd.

The draw Liz felt for Lou was unexplainable. Truly. There weren't words to describe how she felt about this woman–this ill-tempered, stubborn, frantic, basket case of a woman. If it were another person relaying this story to Liz, she would have declared the person mentally unfit to be left alone. But here she was, driving to Middle of Nowhere, Georgia to be there for Lou, without even considering what it would mean.

This would be a turning point in their short, but passion-filled relationship. Could it even be called a relationship at this point? Liz had only just successfully defeated the ghost of Judy Jackson, now she would potentially be facing all the other Jacksons. She would see the place of which Lou was a product. There was some beauty in that, she considered. She would finally get a taste of the sheer madness Lou had told her about in this town.

Liz also felt sorry for Lou. She had been the one to encourage Lou to return, to pay her final respects to Judy, to see her family. Now here Lou was, probably sitting at the Mayflower County Sheriff's Department as she drove ninety from nothing.

The GPS continued to guide Liz southward, she was making good time due to the little traffic on this bright, sunny Sunday morning. She was on track to make it to Clanton fifteen minutes earlier than she had even anticipated. Until she heard an unfamiliar rumbling under the hood of the Toyota. How did she know this was going to happen? She knew it so well that she sent Lou in her own car. Now she was the one pulling off to the side of I-75 in Tennessee with gray-white smoke barreling out the front of the car.

This was all she, or Lou, needed at this point.

55

Lou pulled into the parking lot at Mayflower County Sheriff's Office and Jail. She was accepting her fate, but she was still being very ginger in her parking around the police vehicles. All she needed to do was add insult to injury.

She parked and grabbed her pocketbook, her hands shaking like an addict in withdrawals. Lou walked in the front door of the facility and approached the receptionist.

"I'm here to turn myself in," she declared quietly, trying to hold it together as best as she could.

The receptionist looked at the bailiff sitting next to her reclined in the office chair. This was a first, they said to each other with silent exchanges of the eye.

"This is all you," the receptionist deferred to the peace officer, returning to her computer to appear busy whether she really was or not.

"Good morning, ma'am. Uh, just what is it you're turning yourself in for?" Lou couldn't help but notice his hand poised near the gun in the holster in his belt.

"Hit and run," she admitted with confidence. "I hit the sheriff yesterday, and it's my understanding that I'm to be arrested this afternoon. I'd like to go ahead and get that process underway if you don't mind."

This was perhaps the most pleasant surrender in Mayflower County jail history. Everyone in the room was surprised, well, except for Lou, who was prepared for cuffs and a jumpsuit.

"Hmm. Okay, well, let me call the sheriff just to verify a few things, okay? He ain't in, it being a Sunday and all." The gentleman was perfectly lovely, which put Lou somewhat at ease. "What did you say your name was?" he asked. Thirty-five years ago, she would have known all the people in this whole place, but she'd been gone a lifetime. She didn't know any of them and nobody knew who she was.

"It's Lou, uh, Louvenia Jackson," she said.

"Sure thing. You just sit tight, ma'am, and we'll get this sorted out. Lurlene, will you look through the records and see what we have pertaining to Miss Jackson?" he asked the receptionist.

"Mmhhmm," she replied simply.

Lou sat down in the uncomfortable chairs of the sterile room. Being taken into police custody wasn't nearly as terrible as she had anticipated. She wasn't exactly sure what to expect, but she didn't have to fall to the floor or raise her hands above her head or anything. Hell, they'd probably offer her a cup of coffee next, she thought.

As if reading her mind, Lurlene offered Lou water from the water cooler across the room and restrooms in the far corner. Lou kindly thanked the woman but explained she wasn't exactly in the mood, with a guilty smile.

"You wouldn't happen to be kin to the Chuck Jacksons, would you?" Lurlene asked without looking up from her computer.

"That's me. I'm Big Chuck's daughter," Lou answered, "Unfortunately still causing disappointment wherever I go," she added, mostly to herself.

"We went to school together," she said. "I was Lurlene Tipton then."

"You're *that* Lurlene? You look so... different." The words escaped Lou's mouth before she could catch herself.

"You mean old and fat," Lurlene laughed.

"I didn't say that!" Lou quickly answered. "It's just, well, dammit it's no fun being so old we don't recognize people we once knew quite well."

"You've been gone from here a long time, haven't you? Seems like nobody's seen hide nor hair of you in thirty years or more. Where'd you move off to?"

"Kentucky. I have a small horse farm up there"

"Oh, that sounds real nice," Lurlene cooed. Then, more solemnly, she asked, "I guess you're here for the funeral, huh?"

"Uh, yes. Just here for that," Lou answered, although now she doubted she was here for more than anything but an arraignment. Seeming to have answered all of Lurlene's questions, Lou sank back in the uncomfortable chair awaiting the news.

The officer re-entered the room from behind the counter and looked at Lurlene's computer, whispering. This is it, Lou thought. She was ready to be booked and printed and locked up with the key thrown away.

"Miss Jackson?" Lou stood, preparing herself. "Sheriff Kitchens will be in in just a few minutes. He asked for you to hold tight if you don't mind?"

"Well, I don't have much of a choice, now do I?" she said smartly, instantly regretting mouthing off to the man who would decide which cell she would occupy. Lou sat back down, the anticipation restarting. She felt like she was going to throw up.

56

Liz considered her options. She knew nothing about cars, so she had no idea what could be wrong with Lou's 4Runner. She would have to call a tow truck and try to rent a car, but that could take hours–hours she didn't have to spare. Another option was to call the Mayflower County Sheriff's Department and hope they would relay the message to Lou, then try to get there as quickly as possible. And the final option would be to call Lou's family and explain what was going on.

Weighing her options quickly, knowing that time was not on her side, Liz settled on a combination of all three. She would call roadside assistance and figure out that piece when she was presented with the diagnosis of the trouble. Then she would call the sheriff's office and plead for them to tell Lou she was okay and, on her way, but just delayed. And finally, she would call the Jacksons and see if they would be willing to go to the sheriff's office to sit with Lou and try to help sort this out.

The conversations fell naturally in order of simplest to most complicated. She called the roadside assistance provided through her insurance. They promised a mechanic and tow within the next 45 minutes, which wasn't so bad. Check. She called Mayflower County Sheriff's Office and a receptionist answered. Liz explained that she was on her way to help her friend Lou Jackson who should be there, and very politely asked if she would relay the message that Liz was running a little behind but was on her way. The lovely woman obliged, leaving Liz a little less in a tizzy worrying about this situation.

Now, for the big one. Liz dialed the number to the Jackson residence for the second time that morning. The phone rang twice before it was picked up by what sounded like a young lady. "Hello?" the voice said, sounding somewhat dejected and depressed.

"Hi, um, you don't know me," Liz began, nervously, "But my name is Liz Ward, and I'm a friend of Lou Jackson's. Is she by any chance there?"

Josie's ears immediately picked up at Liz's name. She quickly began to explain, "No, she left this morning without telling anybody anything. We have no idea where she went. Do you know where she is?" Josie asked frantically.

Who is it? Big Chuck mouthed to Josie. She held her hand up to be left alone during this important conversation.

"She's at the jail, I think. She didn't say anything to anybody?"

"At the jail? What the hell for?" If Josie wasn't frantic before, she surely was now. This was serious. The whole breakfast table was not-so-patiently waiting for answers. Little Chuck ripped the phone out of Josie's hand.

"Who is this?" he demanded.

"I'm a friend of Lou's," she replied with her own harsh voice. "Who are you?"

"I'm her brother," he replied. "Now what's this about her at the jail?"

"You oughta know, you asshole." Liz was fuming. "She heard you last night on the phone. You're in cahoots with whatever Hooterville Green Acres police department is down there and you're gonna try to get her in trouble so she doesn't show her face and ruin your precious image!"

"Look, lady. I don't know who you are or what you're talking about, but you're as batshit crazy as she was last night. Now if you could leave us alone as we get ready to bury my wife today, that'd be great," he seethed.

"Yeah and now Lou won't even be there to say goodbye to the woman she loved, just like you probably planned. Makes sense why she left now. I called to see if someone there could help her, but I guess I'm shit out of luck. I'll be down there as soon as I can." With that, Liz hung up the phone on Little Chuck.

"What in God's name was that all about?" Big Chuck demanded to know.

"Some woman says I'm trying to get Lou arrested so she won't be here today. Lou came in my room last night spouting off something to that effect. Now I don't know where they're getting this made-up shit, but I've had enough, Daddy. I promised I'd be nice. I promised I would try to do the right thing, but by God I'm not putting up with this," he swatted his plate of toast and eggs across the table. It clattered to the floor in a hundred pieces.

Angrily, Josie spoke up, "That woman was Liz. She's Aunt Lou's partner. She's worried about her and so am I. If she's down at that jail, I'm going to find her." Josie stood to leave and grab her things.

The others followed behind her. "Now just how do you know all that, missy?" Joan chided.

"Because I asked, Joan," Josie hollered, inches from the woman's face. "Did anyone here bother to take one minute out of their day yesterday to talk to the woman? Did anyone ask her anything about her life or what she had done for thirty years without a single family member by her side?" The room fell silent. "That's what I thought."

Josie walked out the front door to her car. R.J. followed her. She gave him a look and he gave one back, overriding her contempt. Little Chuck bounded down the steps to go, too.

"You've got a hell of a lot of nerve trying to go down there now!" Josie yelled at her father.

"Dammit, I think I know what this is all about. I'm going, and I'm going to set the record straight. Now drive," he commanded, fastening the seat belt. For a second time that day, a car peeled out of the driveway of The Gables, headed towards town and the sheriff's office.

The drive was eerily quiet. You couldn't even hear any of the three of them breathe. Little Chuck was on his phone, sifting through his emails.

"Really?" Josie said with strong indignation. "Reading your emails at a time like this?"

"I am looking for an email from Klark Kitchens, Josephine," Little Chuck stated through gritted teeth.

"About what?" her tone improving slightly.

"He called last night to tell me they had identified the suspect accused of setting fire to the office. They planned to arrest her today. That's what Lou thinks is happening to her, I'm sure of it." Josie was quiet now. "KK said he was emailing me the fire marshal's report. I'm pulling it up to show you and Lou and everybody else who doesn't believe me the truth of the matter. Got it?"

“Yes, sir,” Josie replied weakly, her driving slowing just a tad as she made it to the final stretch of the road to the sheriff’s office.

57

Thomas Hodge, Chief Fire Inspector, Mayflower County Fire Department

425 Burton St, Clanton, GA

Case Number: #42293

Summary of Incident

Investigators Harper and Samuel responded to 4 N Main St, location of incident in question, at the request of Mayflower County Fire Chief Jones and Mayflower County Sheriff Kitchens for routine fire inspection. The dispatch time was roughly 2100 hours, arrival at the scene was approximately 2115 hours. Investigators observed a brick construction, single-story commercial business space. The investigation revealed that the fire had originated in the back right office. The indicators observed, the evidence taken, and analysis revealed the fire was started by the distribution of flammable items (paper, books, boxes) and ignited by an open flame such as a match (no fire-causing items were recovered). No one was in the building at the time of first responder arrival. No suspect was immediately identified as there were no eyewitnesses.

During the investigation, it was noted by the investigators that the front window was broken outwardly, indicating forced breakage from inside the structure. This is inconsistent with firefighting procedure. In situations where a structure is fully engulfed, responders will bust windows in to improve visibility and lower heat conditions for the firefighters inside, allowing them to extinguish the fire quickly and safely. Considering this inconsistency, the initially responding fire fighters (W-1, W-2, & W-3) were questioned and no one admitted to breaking the window from the inside, but none had any recollection as to whether the window was broken before or during their response either. Surveillance footage from the business directly across the street from the structure was requested by and freely offered to the investigative team. Footage indicated the suspect (S-1) was seen entering the building by unlocking the front door, remaining inside for roughly 0015 hours, then leaving through the same door quickly. Footage revealed the breakage of the front window during this time. The owner of the structure identified the suspect (S-1) by name and identified her in the video footage. The motive for the fire was spite/revenge. The suspect (S-1) had not been compensated for work performed prior to the occurrence of the incident. It is believed the intent was to make the incident appear as a result of vandalism.

Laboratory Analysis

Taken into evidence were stacks of record books strewn around the scene and shards of glass from the front window containing trace amounts of blood. Blood analysis identified the suspect (S-1) as the person who broke the glass. Furthermore, a nurse at Mayflower General Hospital (W-4) identified the suspect (S-1) as coming into the emergency room the same evening of the incident.

Suspects

S-1 Roseanne D. Wilson, 51 Gordon Rd, Clanton, GA, 706/555-3670. DOB 4-2-68, Occupation - financial assistant/receptionist.

Witnesses

W-1 Karl Dobson, 1368 Hobson Rd, Clanton, GA, 678/555-5244. DOB 2-24-85, Occupation - firefighter.

W-2 Robert Mullins, 225 Old Cove Rd, Clanton, GA, 770/555-0801. DOB 6-2-87, Occupation - firefighter

W-3 Andrew Walker, 84 Dartmouth Ave, Clanton, GA, 770/555-0886, DOB 10-10-86, Occupation - firefighter.

W-4 Caroline Morgan, 1 Lakeshore Dr, Clanton GA, 706/555-7785, DOB 1-12-83, Occupation - registered nurse.

Statements Made by Witnesses

Witnesses 1, 2, & 3 all claimed to have not broken the window to the structure. They said they would have done so to alleviate the heat of the fire, per procedure, but that it was already broken before they needed to do so. None of the witnesses knew at the time who had broken the window but assumed it had been a fellow responder.

Witness 4 can identify the suspect coming into the hospital on the same evening as the incident requiring 4 stitches on the top of the suspect's (S-1) fist. The stitches were done in triage by the witness (W-4) and the suspect (S-1) was released shortly thereafter. The suspect (S-1) claimed to the nurse that she had broken a drinking glass while washing dishes.

Statutes Violated

GA Code 16-7-60:	Arson in the 1st degree - deliberately setting fire to a structure of another. Fine up to $50,000
GA Code 16-7-21:	Unlawful entry - criminal trespassing. Fine up to $1,000.
	Total Bail/Fine $51,000

The Mayflower County Fire Department doesn't recommend the suspect be detained without bond or bail. She is not believed to pose a flight risk.

Enclosed Documentation

D-1: photographs, numbered sequentially in chronological order during the investigation process

D-2: surveillance footage from Clanton City Florist with date/time stamp

Just as Josie, R.J., and Little Chuck were being escorted to Klark Kitchens's office, he had laid out this report for Lou to read. She was scanning it over without seeing a trace of her name.

"But this is a fire marshal's report?" she said, confused.

"That's because," Little Chuck spoke up entering the room, "the conversation you overheard was about the results of the fire investigation at the office. It had nothing to do with you, Lou."

Josie looked from her father to Lou to the sheriff. "KK, what's this all about?"

"We called in the fire marshal, and it was revealed that we were dealing with a case of arson at your dad's office. They investigated the blaze, which is standard procedure with any structure fire, and we knew something was up. I'll admit I thought it was your dad for a bit," Klark said, looking at Little Chuck. "But it was determined there was no way he could have been involved," he said, looking away.

"They know everything, Klark," Little Chuck revealed. "Nobody's saying anything." Klark looked pissed off, but it was what it was. No sense in losing his temper over what was now a moot point.

"So, who did it then?" Josie asked. "Was it someone we know?" Lou stood up, handing the report to Josie, and pointing at the line marked "Suspect" containing only one name. "Rosie?! No way. I don't believe it, not in a million years!"

"Believe it," Klark spoke to the room. "Got her on camera."

"But why would she do this, Daddy?" Josie asked her father.

"Well, as you know, I was out of money. I let her and Peter's last paychecks bounce because I thought I would be covered with that mortgage I was taking out on my and your mama's house. When it didn't go through, there were insufficient funds."

"All this because you missed one paycheck. Doesn't that seem a little extreme?"

"Money drives people to do some crazy things. Especially when you really need the money, which none of us have ever really had to worry about. We don't know about the shoes she was wearing. But I wouldn't have guessed it would be her."

"My bet, and Klark's, too, for a bit, was on Peter. He was really mad when it happened, sulked off and wouldn't talk to anybody. I promised him I'd get the money to him. I called him to try to talk to him and feel him out. I guess he thought he was getting paid because he showed up to talk to me. Klark and his guys were listening out for a confession that never came. They even told me how they determined it was arson because of the window so I might get him to admit it all, but he didn't."

"We sent the broken glass shards to the lab for analysis, but it came back no match. Whoever broke it didn't have a record. Now we can still use blood to identify an individual. You know, all that ancestry DNA stuff they got out there nowadays. But that takes a while. So, we started pulling video camera footage of every store around your dad's office. Big surprise in a small town, most stores don't have video cameras," Klark rolled his eyes. "But one did. Clanton City Florist. I guess flowers are a hot commodity. Naturally it took the old ladies hours to figure out how to get the footage to us, but we got it. It was, of course, very hazy because it was from clear across the square. But we were able to figure out it was a woman at least."

"So, we called the hospital. Asked if anybody had come in bloodied up on their hands or arms or anything. There wasn't a ton of blood on the glass, but we were grasping. They looked through their intake files and three people came in that evening through the next morning that required stitches. Only one of them was a woman."

"Fast forward," Little Chuck picked up, "They had the record of Rosie coming in and they had the footage. They sent it to me, and I was able to positively identify her. So that was that. Due to the nature of the funeral and everything happening, we agreed that they wouldn't arrest Rosie until tomorrow afternoon, so the news didn't overshadow everything, at least not right away anyway," Chuck sighed.

"So… this means I'm free to go?" Lou asked tentatively.

"Ms. Jackson, you were never detained!" Klark laughed. "You put one ding in my car, we don't arrest people for that."

"Well, I didn't know. I'm a little out of sorts this weekend," she defended herself.

"I get it. Your sister-in-law gone and all. I'm really sorry for all of y'alls loss," Klark said sympathetically to the whole family.

"Thank you, KK, but my mama wasn't just Aunt Lou's sister-in-law. They were also lovers for years." Mouths dropped, heads turned, and absolutely no one knew what to do. Josie took the lead, "Now come on, Aunt Lou. We've all got to get ready so we can get to Chapman's by 11. Florence Chapman will have us on the table next if we make one of her services run late."

Not another word was spoken, by anybody. As they were pulling back in at The Gables, Ruby rushed outside to get the news. She hollered when she saw Lou.

"Oh, baby, come here, I thought I might never see you again," she hugged Lou through tears.

Still shaken and still uncomfortable from Josie's brazen declaration in Klark Kitchens's office, Lou hugged her back and said she needed to get inside. She asked Ruby to relay the news to her father and aunt, and that she would be getting ready as quickly as she could with the rest of the crew.

Lou ran up the stairs, but before doing anything else she dialed Liz's cell phone. She picked up immediately. "Hello?" she scowled, expecting it to be another hateful Jackson.

"It's me," Lou said, nearly out of breath.

"What? Where are you? How are you calling from home?" Liz demanded.

"It was all a big mistake. A misunderstanding."

"That's it? That's all you have to say? I've been worried sick to death, Lou."

"Liz, I've been wrapped up in so many secrets for so long and have been on the defense for so many years, I didn't believe I could trust anybody. Hell, it's taken me this long to trust you and you've been nothing but wonderful to me."

Liz softened. "Well, I had to rent a car. It put me behind, but I'll be there about 1:30, unless you want me to just go back where I broke down and wait on your car to get fixed if you really don't need me?"

"No. I want you to come on down," Lou said with sureness in her voice. "I need you to come here."

"Are you sure about this?"

"As sure as I've ever been about anything in my life," Lou replied.

"Well, where do I go? Your family's house? I can wait there until y'all get back. Or I can go somewhere else? A Starbucks or something?"

Lou couldn't help but laugh. "City girl, there ain't a Starbucks for thirty miles. Come to the house. I'll have my niece lay out something perfect for you to wear before we go. Then you can meet us at First Baptist for the funeral."

"Absolutely not. Are you off your rocker? What will people say?"

"Liz, I don't really care," Lou replied bluntly. "This is a time of mourning, and I'd like you by my side for support. I'm asking for you to please join me."

"I don't know about this."

"I'm not asking you to know about it. I'm asking you to learn about it. And I'm asking you to do this for me."

"Alright, I'll do the best I can, but I look a mess, Lou."

"Ruby will help you get ready. You can come to the church with her. Now I've gotta go," Lou said, realizing the time.

"Okay, I'll see you soon." Liz ended the call.

Now before she could get ready, Lou had three to-dos to check off her list: ask Josie to find something for Liz to wear to the funeral, ask Ruby to help Liz get ready and to drive her to the church with her, and the last was to ask Big Chuck for forgiveness. She was past permission.

58

"Daddy?" Lou knocked lightly on her father's study door.

"Lou! Why did you run out of here like that? You scared Ruby to death, scared us all to high heavens," he admonished her.

"Daddy, I got caught up in something else that wasn't really my business, and I did what I do best–I ran." She sat down on her father's bed, opposite of the chair he was sitting in trying to adjust his tie.

"Why did you run again?" he asked.

"Because what else do I do? How else to avoid disappointing this family? How else can I protect your good name?" she asked, sniffling, and wiping her nose on her arm.

She got up from the edge of the bed and knelt to help her feeble father fumbling with his tie. "You recognize this tie?" he asked her.

"No, I can't say that I do," she replied mindlessly.

"You bought it for me for my birthday. It came from Rich's, I think. Your mama and Ruby had taken you down there shopping with them, and you came back with this, wrapped up for me. You were so proud of it. You wanted to make me so proud. I opened it and I oohed and ahhed over it."

Chuckling, Lou said, "I'm sorry, Daddy, I don't remember any of this."

"I hate this tie," he said seriously. Lou looked up at him, confused by the statement.

"Then why the hell are you wearing it, Daddy? Just throw it away," she said, exasperated.

"I'm wearing it for the same reason I've worn it for nearly fifty years. Because you gave it to me. Because you were proud of it, and I was so damn proud of you. You thought about me. Y'all went shopping that day, you, and your mama, and whoever else tagged along to Atlanta, and you came home with something for me."

Lou pulled the diamond solitaire necklace out of her shirt. "You remember this?" she asked.

"I sure do. Your college graduation gift. You earned it," he replied.

"This weekend is the first time I've ever worn it. I was worried something would happen to it. I came close a time or two, but I never hocked it. It meant so much to me."

"It's a lot prettier than this tie you bought me," he grinned.

"Daddy, I hate to ruin this sentimental moment, but I'm pretty positive I charged that tie to your account!" They both laughed hearty laughs, Lou falling back on her rear. She sat there, staring up at her father. "I never wanted to embarrass you. I never wanted to break your heart or hurt anybody, but I know I did. Can you ever forgive me?"

"No, baby. The question is can you ever forgive me?" he said, tears flowing through the deep wrinkles of his weary, aged face.

Lou got up and hugged her father, crying into his starched white shirt. "I'm sorry, Daddy. I'm sorry for everything I've ever done."

"Shhh, shhh, shhh. You don't have anything to apologize for. I'm as proud of you now as I was the little girl who gave me this tie."

"Well," Lou said, wiping the tears from her face. She'd cried more this week than she had in the thirty years prior. "I do have one more thing to ask for forgiveness for..." her voice trailed off.

"What's that?" Big Chuck asked.

"I've met someone. Someone who is very important to me. And I want you to meet her."

"I'd be delighted to meet anyone who makes you happy," he assured her. "Maybe y'all could come down for a weekend later this month?"

"Okay, I wasn't exactly clear in what I was asking forgiveness for," she countered. "I sort of, well, she's coming here. Today. And she's going to the funeral with me. It was sort of a last-minute kind of thing," Lou spat it all out quickly in one breath, ripping the band aid off completely.

Big Chuck's eyes widened as he considered this new development.

"Daddy, if you want me to, I can tell her to stay here. I understand," Lou said, meaning what she stated. It was a big ask.

"I'm not telling you no, Lou, it's not that. But I think you need to tell the others. Don't ask them. You don't need permission for a God dang thing from them," he added firmly. "But tell them, so they don't act like fools. Agreed?"

"Okay. I will," she said as she went to walk out of the room. "Daddy?"

"Yeah, baby?"

"I love you." With that she pulled her father's door closed a bit and went upstairs.

She only had 15 minutes before they needed to leave for the funeral home. Thank God for dry hairspray, she thought. Lou deodorized and perfumed and hit the high spots in the bathroom, taking what her grandmother used to refer to as a whore bath.

She put on her base makeup, deciding the rest could be done in the car, and put on the suit she and Liz had packed together. Looking back in the looking glass stood a woman with a new lease on life. A woman who had come from one place, grown in another, and returned to conquer her demons. The nude heels she had put on weren't the only thing that raised her step. She tied Judy's scarf around her neck loosely and dropped the essentials in the nude handbag Liz had tracked down for her to carry.

Making her way down the steps, the rest of the family was already in the foyer and ready to go. They all turned to Lou, taken aback by the radiance descending the stairs. "Aunt Lou," Josie gasped, "You look amazing! Is that Chanel?!" she asked, her voice rising as she went to feel the fabric. Lou laughed and confirmed the question.

Still standing on the bottom step, a head above everyone else there, Lou made her announcement. "I will have a guest today at the funeral," she explained to everyone, as if Big Chuck, Josie, and Ruby weren't already in on the plan.

"And just who might that be?" Joan asked shrewdly.

Looking her right in the eye, Lou responded, "Liz Ward. The woman I've been seeing. She'll be here in time to meet us at the church."

Joan turned to the two Chucks, "Are you going to allow this disgrace?"

Big Chuck answered first, "I'm not allowing anything. I am supporting my daughter who is a grown woman and who is plenty old enough to make her own decisions and do what is right for her," he declared. Then he and Joan looked to Little Chuck for his commentary.

"I, uh, I think that's fine, Lou. I'm glad you'll have someone there to support you."

"And that's all you have to say, Chuck?" Joan practically hollered.

"Give it up, Aunt Joan, please. I am begging you. We are ALL begging you. We're all just trying to live our lives the best way we know how. We've had shame, we've had disgrace, we've had people talk about us, but guess what? We're all still here. We're all together, for the first time in 35 years, and I'm not going to let that be ruined by anything."

The entire family was surprised, but none quite as surprised as Lou.

Lighting in again, Joan said, "Well you know who isn't here? Judy. So, I hope you're all happy just living however you want and saying whatever you want when the talking and the secrets and the backstabbing is what killed her."

For the very first time, the family was seeing a vulnerable side of Joan. She was tearing up. "I've spent all these years trying to uphold some dignity around here. Never letting the digs and rumors run me down, but they do. If you don't believe me, you go on down to Chapman's and look in that casket. That's what these people do." Joan was crying fully now.

Again, no one knew how to respond. This wasn't Joan the shrewd prude they all knew and loved to hate and hated to love. This was raw emotion.

Little Chuck stepped towards his aunt, placing his hands on her shoulders, and looking down at her. "Joan, I love you, we all love you. Isn't that enough? Does everyone everywhere have to love you or approve of you or get along with you for you to be happy? Can we not just be thankful for each other, thankful that we're getting this out without holding on to regrets like Judy did? I loved that woman with every part of me, but she let the opinions of others, the actions of others affect her more than they should have. She allowed that over herself. If I had it to do over again, I would have sought counseling for her. For both of us. She dealt with her demons in a way no one ever should. I don't want that to ever happen again to anyone in this family or anyone I love or anyone I even know, okay?"

Joan was wiping her eyes, but she nodded her head silently. Quietly and somberly, the Jacksons made their way outside to their vehicles and drove the path to town to Chapman Funeral Home.

They pulled their cars into the processional line that would take the family and attendees to the church. The Cadillac sedan was first which would be driven by Charles, undoubtedly with Florence in the passenger seat. The hearse would be driven by Mark, the next most trustworthy funeral home employee. Then Little Chuck's Lexus would be next in line holding the next of kin: Little Chuck, Josie, and R.J. Behind that would be the closest extended family in Big Chuck's Lincoln Town Car: Joan would be driving, Big Chuck, then Lou. Beyond that, the rest of the extended family, the cousins, aunts, uncles, nieces, and nephews, etc. would follow next. Friends and others would pull up the rear. Police vehicles would anchor the beginning and end of the procession for safety along the route.

The family made their way inside to find a few of the extended members had already arrived and stationed themselves around the parlor. Most of the flower arrangements and plants had already been transported to the church to be arranged prior to the arrival of the funeral guests. All that was left was the spray on the casket, the two wreaths from the family, and the large oil painting of Judy from her wedding day which Eugenia had given to the happy couple as a gift, after Judy's return from Kentucky, of course. Judy always considered it a gift of spite and never cared for it, but she never said as much. She just stood back and took it.

The couple of hours of visitation prior to the funeral were typically pretty slow, but this was the time any of the out of towners who couldn't come the day before would arrive and remain with the family until time to go to the church for the actual funeral.

Josie remembered that when her grandmother died, a distant cousin who hadn't seen Eugenia in years made her way up to the casket to view the body. Josie was the only one with the body at that particular time, and she didn't have a clue who this woman was. The old lady took a look at Eugenia in the casket and commented to Josie, "She was a big 'un, wasn't she?" Josie was rendered speechless, which was not an easy effect to achieve on someone like Josie who always had something to say.

Anyhow, the out of towners milled about the parlor, making small talk, and catching up with other family members, and passing right by Lou. At first, she felt slighted, but then she realized that probably none of these people knew her either because she had left before their birth or because she had been gone so long, they had forgotten what she looked like.

Lou decided to go stand with her daddy who was seated in an armchair next to the casket so she didn't feel quite so alone. Her daddy took this as his cue. Whenever someone would come up to speak to him or see the body, he would make it a point to say, "And don't you remember my daughter, Louvenia?" Eyes would either dart back and forth or show utter confusion, neither of which Big Chuck would allow to bother him. Lou would just put on that old pageant smile and slop sugar with them like she'd seen them the week prior. Everyone was confused, but of course, no one would actually say anything. That didn't stop the whispers among each other, either.

As time for the funeral drew closer, Lou started feeling more and more uneasy. Maybe Liz coming wasn't such a good idea. She was second guessing herself, and her father could sense it.

"I'm looking forward to meeting this Liz person," he offered. "Tell me about her."

Lou started telling him how they met, what they had in common, Liz's background. He was genuinely interested. By the time Florence Chapman was ready to usher the others out and offer the family a moment of privacy and prayer before going to the church, he had made Lou feel much better.

The family had their last moments alone with Judy, and Lou said a quiet prayer.

"God, I know you haven't heard from me in a long time. But I'm here, asking you to take care of Judy on your side. And I have a favor to ask, but you're probably not surprised by that. Take care of me on this side, too, will you? I have a lot of living left to do if you'll see me through. I pray for safety, security, and your will be done. Amen"

When she opened her eyes, her father was there leaning on his walker, ready to lead her to their car. They walked out of the front doors of the funeral home together as the staff rolled the casket out behind them. The pallbearers--the nephews, and other young men in the distant family--lifted the casket from the pedestal and placed it into the hearse, rolling it up into the vehicle on the metal spinners and locking it in place with the heels at the back. The big blue hearse door closed for the ride.

Lou looked up at the police escort in the front. It was none other than Klark Kitchens, the sheriff himself, with his hat placed over his heart.

59

The procession made its way to the church at a snail's pace. It was only seven tenths of a mile from one place to the other, but it took forever to get there. Or maybe it just felt like forever because Lou was so anxious about seeing Liz.

They finally pulled into the driveway of the church and pulled in behind the hearse. Lou's heart was beating out of her chest. Her eyes were searching frantically for Liz and Ruby. She was twisting every which way and craning her neck to find them.

She finally spotted them standing near the doors to the church. Lou was somewhere between thrilled and scared to death. She was eager to get to them, but she needed to follow suit with the rest of the family. The casket would go in first, then the family. Ruby and Liz would join her, Big Chuck, and Joan to sit in the second row. The first row was reserved for the closest of kin, the second row was saved for the next closest. Then the rest would fill in the remaining designated rows. Everyone else would already be gathered in the unmarked pews.

When she reached Liz, Lou grabbed her hand and squeezed it. She whispered in Liz's ear, "I am so glad you are here. I don't think I'd be able to do this without you." Liz didn't reply but squeezed Lou's hand back.

Everyone walked in and Florence Chapman was passing out hand fans with the funeral home logo on them. It was a scorcher, and everyone was sweating already, including Lou, but for a different reason. Deep breaths, she kept telling herself.

Once everyone was seated, the service began with Joan reading the obituary she and Alice Murray had written for Judy that would be published in the newspaper.

All of Clanton's society was contained in First Baptist's sanctuary. A microcosm of everyone who was anyone was in that room now, clad in suits and ties, dark dresses, a few hats. As one southerner, Mildred Cagle Mullinax, once remarked, "You won't find more food, more diamonds, or more girdles in one place than at a southern funeral!" The major component of southern funeralizing, paying your respects at the actual funeral was the highest level of commitment.

The summer air was thick, and the church's three air conditioning units could barely keep up. Thick with heat and humidity, thick with sympathy, thick with tension, thick with angst. While there were several genuine people scattered throughout, Josie knew with one look that most of these people were nothing but onlookers gawking to see if the rumors were true. Trying to get the scoop firsthand about what had been going on between the Jacksons for the past few days.

How does it happen? She wondered. How can people who were supposed paragons of Clanton be wrought with so much nosiness, stuck in everyone else's business instead of their own? These people were educated in some of the best private academies Atlanta could offer, shipped to the best colleges (if their parents' donations were big enough), and yet still so unequivocally scandalous, pernicious, filled with prejudice, and soaked in sin.

How could she have ever been one of them?

Josie Jackson had come quite a long way from this tiny town with big heads. Yet here she was, sitting in First Baptist Clanton filled with oh-so-familiar strangers.

While Joan was still carrying on about Judy's accomplishments and accolades, Josie noticed her cousin Burma Jackson Day entering the church fashionably late with her boys so everyone would notice her. She felt the need to always steal the spotlight, being a former Miss Georgia. Ever since her failed attempt to be Miss America, she took it upon herself to steal everyone's thunder and take everyone's glory. Judy's funeral would be no exception. She stood there draped in a gown from Saks or Nordstrom she probably paid a thousand dollars for. She looked stunning. As stunning as a patchwork quilt. Burma had been ripped, nipped, tucked, filled, and sewn more than last Thanksgiving's twenty-five-pound turkey. Only she didn't weigh near that much or look near that delicious.

The hymns were sung by the church choir with the congregation invited to join in. As How Great Thou Art was coming to a close, Josie knew she was up next. Reverend Fields motioned for her to come up to the pulpit from the front row pew. She rose with her notebook and carefully took the steps upward to the lectern to place her things.

With a very deep breath in and out, Josie began.

"Good morning, everyone. On behalf of the entire Jackson family, I want to begin by thanking each of you for your presence, cards, calls, food, flowers, and prayers for our family." Looking down at her notes, she picked up the first few pieces of paper and held them up. "This was the eulogy I wrote Friday night, reflecting on my 33 years with my mother. Things we did together, things she did for our family, ways she helped our community. A lot of those things that my Aunt Joan just recalled in the obituary she so lovingly wrote as a tribute to my mother." Still holding the papers up, she continued, "But this is not what I'm reading today." She crumpled up the papers and dropped them to her side.

The folks in the sanctuary shifted in their seats. They knew that Little Chuck and Judy's girl could be a loose cannon, but they weren't prepared for what was coming.

"Instead, today I will be reading the eulogy I wrote after that one." She flipped to the next pages in her notebook. "Friends, family, neighbors. I'm here to call each and every one of you out."

"Oh God," Little Chuck muttered under his breath. He knew there was no use in trying to stop what was coming. He wasn't sure he wanted to, because Josie was probably about to say a lot of things that needed to be said.

People started looking around at each other not knowing what was about to happen.

"I'm here to call you out for killing my mother." The church gasped. "Now most all of you know, my mother committed suicide. But she did not, in fact, kill herself. The people in this town killed her, like you've killed the spirits of young and old alike across these hills. Now before you all go huffing and guffawing, I want you to think about what I have to say today. I'm here to tell some secrets and some truths. My mother was consumed by secrets. Secrets of love, secrets around town. She hadn't been the type to run and tell everyone else's business, perhaps because she didn't want her own secrets to make their way out to the general public."

"Here we go," Big Chuck poked Joan's shoulder.

"If you take a look at the second pew behind my father and my husband, you'll notice the rest of my family. You'll all recognize my Aunt Joan, of course. She's the well-known political mind of our area who worked for late Congressman Ed Jenkins. She never married. We don't have an explanation for that, but I will say she is available to whatever *person* might be interested." Josie winked at her aunt with the dropped jaw. "Next to her is my grandfather, Charles Jackson, III, who is a pillar of this community. He continued his father's financial firm downtown, which my father then took over. You know, it burned to the ground earlier this week. Would you believe it was arson?" People started whispering. "Now before y'all go cranking the rumor mill, let me set y'all straight–it was Rosie Wilson who set fire to the place. She'll be arrested today, just so you know. Keeping with the theme of transparency, she set the fire because her last paycheck from my daddy bounced. Kirby Riffle can vouch for that. Where are you, Kirby?" Josie looked until she pointed him out and waved.

"Like I was saying, Daddy's out of money. He didn't have enough to bury Mom, so Granddaddy had to pay for it, but don't worry–it comes out of his inheritance. Now missing from the pew next to Granddaddy would have been Grandmother. A woman who had a mean streak a mile wide, to quote our beloved maid, Ruby. Ruby's been with us for more than 50 years and she knows every single secret there is to know about us, and most of you. Ruby was there the night my grandparents threw out my Aunt Louvenia, who you will notice is sitting next to Ruby. She's wearing a stunning Chanel suit today that I hope I'll one day inherit," she laughed, seemingly alone in the room.

"Now some of y'all thought she was dead, some of y'all never knew she existed, some of you thought she just ran off." If Lou wasn't sweating before, she was dripping now. "Truth is, Lou did run off. She ran off with my mother, way before meeting the lovely Liz Ward seated next to her, because they were lesbian lovers."

Gasps and hollers filled the room, along with some giggles. "That's right, you heard it here first. My mother and my aunt were in love and partnered for more than two years in secret. Until my grandparents and my father found out about it, which led to my aunt being thrown out. Where's Kirby again?" She looked around. "He was there that night. He knew everything and extorted business from my father over it for years in exchange for his silence about the scandal." Kirby's wife and son just stared at him while he refused to make eye contact with anyone.

"The next day, my parents married, and that night my Aunt Lou prepared to leave town. My mother ran off with her. They moved to a farm in Kentucky, but you all were told Mom and Dad went on an extended honeymoon. Some of y'all are just so gullible," she shook her head emphatically. "But my dad ran up to Kentucky and found them and forced my mother to come home, which she did without a fight. He left my Aunt Lou up there with nothing, just as my grandparents had done. Oh, I almost forgot how my grandmother

Eugenia beat the tar out of my mother with a fireplace poker when she first found out about her and Lou."

At this point, the preacher was stepping up to take control of the room, but Josie took the microphone and stepped away to avoid an awkward confrontation with a man of the cloth.

"As I was saying," she looked at the preacher with a look that said try me, "My aunt is here for the first time in 35 years. She has cancer, but you wouldn't know it to look at her. Funny thing is, my mom wrote to Aunt Lou the morning she killed herself and told her that she couldn't bear to live any longer with all of her secrets in a world where my Aunt Lou would not be living. That's because she knew Aunt Lou had cancer. Mama and Granddaddy had a private investigator tailing Aunt Lou for years. Now Granddaddy also has Leukemia, but that's not been too big of a secret. Again, just for the sake of transparency here. But Aunt Lou has met the lovely Liz Ward, who I have just had the opportunity to get to know. She was coming down here originally because my aunt hit KK Kitchens' patrol car and she went to the jail to surrender herself, but it really wasn't that serious. So, we are lucky to have her here joining us for this special occasion. To spell that out for some of you that are a little slower," she intentionally whispered loudly, "that means that she's a lesbian, too, for those of you whose idea of a brainstorm is a light drizzle."

"Now I don't mean to only share our secrets, but that just about sums it up for us as a family. So, think about all of that that my mother was carrying around with her. Now it's time to talk about y'all."

"Over here on the fourth row sits Tricia McMilan, illustrious president of Clanton Garden Club," Josie said. "But behind her lush garden sits a lonely, bitter, controlling dictator of a woman. Her husband won't retire because he's too afraid to be stuck at home with her! Mama left the garden club because of sweet Trish. Then to get back at her, Trish blackballed her from every event in town. Mama was the bigger person, though. She let Trish win. And she came home more days than I can count upset because she'd lost another 'friend' thanks to a woman who had nothing better to do than sit at home and nit-pick, micromanage, and find new ways to plot and scheme her way to get what she wanted." Tricia's face turned ashen behind her rimmed glasses, matching her short dirty gray-blonde hair. At least six people in the sanctuary were snickering because this may very well have been the first time anybody had stood up to Tricia McMilan in her life and they were absolutely living for it.

"Next, let's not forget Richard Wilkins, I saw him and his wife here earlier, but he may have skedaddled out when he found out I was telling secrets. Mom worked for him for several years at the furniture store part time. She never worked there unless someone else was on the schedule because he tried to force himself on her several times. But she wasn't the type to run and tell that, either. Finally, she just quit because she couldn't take it anymore. She didn't work again after that because Richard Wilkins told his buddies that she'd perform acts of a sexual nature for him in his office, and the job offers started pouring in, from some of the gentlemen still seated here. I won't share your names because those were another secret my mom kept that I never found out about until her suicide note."

"That note also mentioned Kristie Magno with the Clanton Community Club. Kristie is all about her numbers and calendars and websites, but she couldn't effectively manage any of them. You know this for a fact if you received the last member newsletter! Mama made some suggestions of how they could improve things at the club, offering to help out as best she could. After all, it is a community organization. Instead, passive-aggressive old Kristie made sure she did everything to get mom and dad to quit the club, including scheming with our dear old Trish," Josie said, nodding back to Tricia McMilan. "But nobody stood up to Kristie. Nobody was willing to defend my mother, just because Kristie had been in the club and doing the calendars since they were still chiseled into stone. Again, my mom carried that with her."

"Now I could go on and on, and maybe someday I will. Maybe I'll write a book about all of you. About Susan Hanson's prescription pill problem or Lynette Barron's gambling addiction. But the point I'm trying to make here today is that these secrets you all keep, or try to keep, are toxic. The way you treat each other is toxic. If you don't get anything out of what I've said today other than fodder for your next gossip sessions, I hope you'll at least think about the impact of your words and your actions. I'm not perfect myself. Far from it. I fail every single day to live up to my potential and my purpose for which God put me on this earth. But when I am wrong, I reflect on it. I try to learn my lesson. I try to evaluate both sides of the story. I try to imagine how I make others feel and how passionate they must have felt to be comfortable enough to call me out for my shortcomings."

"Am I expecting any of you to change? Not really. But I hope you'll think about it. I hope that you'll stand up for each other instead of tearing each other down with your secret meetings and keyboard tirades. Because one day you might just be the one at the end of her rope." Josie looked down at her mother, lying in the casket in front of the crowd, noticing the very faint marks just under her neck that the cosmetics had not been able to cover, and she added, "Literally. And there are no second chances then."

"Now I didn't say all of this to overshadow the generous and genuine acts of gratitude, remembrance, and comfort shown to my family. We feel the love from so many of you, and I hope you feel our love towards you. And if you've listened to everything I've spat out today, I hope that you will sympathize with my family, with my mother, and I hope you won't turn a blind eye to bad behaviors and you'll call them out when you see them, too. We're all too old to be acting like this, but here we are–through complacency, through 'going with the flow,' through not wanting to 'overturn the apple cart,' whatever you call it. Sometimes the apple cart needs to be turned over. Because a few bad applcs will spoil the bunch."

She put the microphone back on the stand and returned to her seat. Maybe it was the adrenaline, maybe it was her nerves, but she felt alive. She didn't feel an ounce of regret in what she said. She was tired of secrets.

The preacher tried to regain control of what was left of the congregation. It was an exercise in futility. At least a third of the visitors had left, even some of the family members. He said a few words about salvation and being liberated from our earthly bodies, but nobody really listened or even remembered what he said.

Florence Chapman had been sitting in the back. She couldn't believe what she'd just witnessed. She never thought when she questioned Josie the day before if telling the truth would really change anything that Josie might actually try to do just that. But here they were.

Breaking herself out of the stupor she was in, she kicked it back in professional mode and directed the pallbearers to return the casket to the blue hearse and for the family to follow behind.

The hearse would take Judy to Clanton City Cemetery where generations of Clanton families had been interred. A short graveside prayer would be said, and the body would be lowered into the ground, encapsulated in a bronze vault.

The families returned to their cars for the short procession to the cemetery from the church. Both the Lexus and the Lincoln were entirely silent. No one knew what to say. No one had anything left to say that Josie hadn't already laid out for all of town to hear.

The procession parked with all who chose to attend this last part of the service. They gathered around the grave, the red Georgia clay freshly unearthed under a tarp of fake turf left to make the site a bit more presentable. The flowers had begun being unloaded from the van that had transported them from the funeral home to the church and now to the cemetery. As was custom, the pallbearers each laid their carnations that designated them as such on the top of the casket. The preacher said his quick prayer, returning Judy to the earth from whence she had come. The funeral was over. Until Lou stepped up from her seat next to her father.

Here we go again, Joan thought, holding her head in her hands.

"I'd like to take just a moment, if it's alright with my brother, to say something." She looked at Little Chuck who threw up his hands, "By all means at this point," he said quietly.

Lou returned her eyes to the small crowd that had remained. "I loved the woman in this box," she said, tapping the top of the casket. "I loved her in a way that some people never get to experience. I loved her despite her flaws, despite my own. Ours was a love that a lot of people, some of you included, wouldn't approve of. I've been called every name in the book over the years. I've feared for my job, for my life, all because of who I chose to love. Galatians chapter five, verse 14 says, 'For the entire law is fulfilled in keeping this one command: Love your neighbor as yourself.' Yes, I read the Bible, too, believe it or not. Now my fiery, feisty, brilliant, passionate niece had a lot to say today. But let me paraphrase it for you: keep this one command–love your neighbor as yourself. It really is that simple. Your gay neighbor, your neighbor you disagree with, your neighbor of another race, your neighbor of another nationality. We are all fighting our own battles–don't be the one to add to anyone else's battle."

With that, Lou returned to her seat. Her father patted the top of her leg. Ruby cried again, knowing she was the first one to teach Lou that piece of scripture. The gravediggers lowered the casket and placed the vault lid on top. They began shoveling and the crowd dissipated. The few that stayed to speak to Lou or any of the rest of them had kind words to say, words of love and support, which was a refreshing reminder that not everyone in this town was guilty.

Little Chuck remained at the grave. While the rest of the family was making small talk, Lou walked back to stand next to her brother. Silent tears dripped from his face. She reached for his hand, and he held it tightly. "We both loved her so much," he said. "But neither of us could save her."

"We were too busy fighting each other to save anybody," Lou remarked. "Can we work on that?" she asked, turning to face her little brother.

"I'll try my best," he promised, hugging her tightly.

60

The family returned to The Gables to the feast that Ruby had rushed home to spread immediately after the church service. As the family members roamed from room to room with their plates in hand, no one had much to say about the service. Instead, they told stories about Judy and laughed about family memories, which Josie and the others decided was for the best anyway. After all, they were supposed to honor Judy today.

Lou introduced Liz to family members, proud to do so for the first time in her life. She told folks about her life in Kentucky, the job she had started, and her plans to refuse to die. People admired her strength and tenacity. Liz told the family about Lou's historic farm and their grand plans for restoring it and turning it into an event venue. The guests were impressed with their plan, and Big Chuck was glad to hear that his purchase for Lou had been a smart investment that would potentially pay off well for her.

Josie made Ruby sit down while she and R.J. refilled cups and replenished the silver trays and china platters of finger foods. Ruby resisted at first but was grateful for the respite after a hell of a week. As far as funeral receptions go, you could say this one was a humdinger.

Little Chuck sat in an oversized armchair in the corner just watching everything happening around him, enjoying the camaraderie being shared by his family members. He was just sad that it was under these circumstances.

That night, as the out of towners left and the whole family pitched in to clean up the mess left behind, they continued to share stories, more personal ones, embarrassing ones, ones that made each other double over in laughter. For the first time in, well, ever, they were all under one roof and having a good time.

With most everything put away, Ruby announced she was heading to bed. Joan claimed she was right behind her after she helped Big Chuck to bed. Lou and Liz vowed to finish the cleanup, straighten the refrigerator, and take out the garbage. Josie and R.J. started to climb the stairs, but Little Chuck, back in the armchair in the corner, stopped his daughter.

"Josie, would you stay down here for a minute? I wanna talk to you about something."

"Sure, Daddy. R.J., go on up and start packing for us to go home tomorrow. I'll be up in a bit," she told her husband.

Josie sat down on the sofa opposite her father. "I guess I'm about to finally get my punishment, huh?" she said, her eyes looking at the floor.

"I've been thinking about what I'd have to say about that stunt," he began. Josie's stomach was turning flips. "And I think what I have to say is thank you," he declared with confidence.

Josie lifted her head in surprise. "You're thanking me?" she asked, unbelieving of this turn of events.

"Yep, I'm proud of you. That took guts. Now, of course, you don't have to live here and ever see these folks again if you don't want to, but I still think it was brave."

"I know, you have to stay here and face the backlash," she hung her head again.

"That's something else I wanted to talk to you about," Little Chuck began. "The house in Crystal Springs. I can't bear to go back there, Josie. Not after what happened there. It's too painful and there are too many memories, good and bad. If it's alright with you, I'm gonna sell it."

"I think that's fine, Dad. I can't say I blame you. Plus, it will give you some cash to do what you need to with the business and all," she said, considering the pros of this proposal.

"Well, I'm retiring from accounting, actually."

"Just how many surprises do you have up your sleeve here, Daddy?" Josie laughed.

"I'm not retiring altogether now. I'm gonna use that money, and what your granddaddy gave me, and I'm going to invest it."

"Invest it in what? This market is terrible. You buy stocks now and you'll be back in the poor house next week!" she exclaimed.

"I'm investing in real estate, again, with your blessing."

"I mean, I guess," she scrunched up her face, "But what? Rental houses? Daddy, that's such a headache."

"No, a wedding and event venue, actually."

Josie's eyes widened, "You don't mean…?"

"Yes, ma'am, I do," Little Chuck said with confidence. I haven't asked them yet, so this is preliminary. But I heard them talking about saving money to flip this place. They put a lot of research into it. I think it could be the real deal."

"I, well, I think that's awesome, Dad," Josie said, surprised but also excited at the sound of this. "So if you sell the house, I guess you'll move in here with Joan and Ruby and Granddaddy full time?"

"That's my plan, as long as the old man doesn't kick me out. But Josie," Chuck continued, "Grandaddy doesn't have a lot of time. He knows it, I know it. I want to make his last days as nice as possible, so I'd appreciate it if y'all could make time to visit more."

With a sad voice, Josie replied, "I will. It's just so hard. Watching someone who's been so strong, so invincible your whole life grow so weak."

"I know, believe me, I know." He patted Josie's leg. "Now, go on up to bed. I'm gonna talk to Lou and Liz."

"Good night, Daddy," she said, hugging her father. "I love you."

61

Liz and Lou wrapped up in the kitchen and threw in the towel, quite literally, starting a load of laundry to finish off tomorrow before they returned to Kentucky. They were laughing and joking about the events of the day, particularly Josie's big scene at the funeral.

"You know, I just met the girl yesterday, but she didn't surprise me one bit," Lou laughed.

"Yeah, a strong Jackson woman calling people out. Who would have thought?" Liz replied with sarcasm and a laugh.

"Good night, brother," Lou said as they passed the front room to head up the stairs.

"Need to talk to you for a minute, if you don't mind?" he said.

Liz continued up the stairs as Lou came back down to join her brother. "No, both of you," he motioned for Liz to join them.

She wasn't sure what this was going to be about, but it had to be something personal, and family related. She and Lou may be what the kids called "an item," but what could Chuck possibly have to say to her?

"I heard about your farm wedding venue idea when you were telling Annie Ruth and Jeff. It sounds like a real neat idea."

"Oh," Lou replied, surprised. "Well, uh, that's mostly been Liz's project so far. She's the brains of this operation," Lou joked.

"Lou provided the place and I'm providing the expertise. I did a double major in historic preservation in college. It's a huge passion of mine. And this farm is just an amazing piece of Kentucky history. We have the place and the know-how, now all we need is the cash," the two looked at each other laughing and sighing.

"I think I can help there," Little Chuck replied.

"What do you mean? I thought you were broke?" Liz blurted out, referencing Josie's announcement earlier at the funeral. Lou gave her a look to shut up.

"Well, I am. Or I was. You know Daddy bought your house. He's giving me the same amount in cash money as my inheritance. Josie and I have decided to sell the house in Crystal Springs. We both agree it's full of too much emotion for us to keep hanging on to. I don't owe much on it since I never was able to get that second mortgage. So, I'll have that extra money on hand once I sell it."

"But where will you live?" Lou asked, just as Josie had.

"I'll stay on here with Daddy. His days are numbered. In case you haven't been told, this house goes to Joan and Ruby when he dies. So, I'll need somewhere to move to after that happens…." his voice trailed off.

Seeing right through her little brother, even after all these years, Lou said, "So in exchange for your investment, you also want a place to live when the time comes?" she asked.

"Sis, I think after today's sermon, and I don't mean the one from the preacher, I don't have a friend left in this town... But I'm okay with that. The business is toast, literally. And once Daddy's gone, there won't be anything keeping me here. Josie's in Atlanta and I ain't about to move to that big, awful, traffic-filled joint. So, I think spending some lost time with my sister sounds like a better option. What do you think?"

Lou looked at Liz for a moment, asking for approval with her eyes. Liz said, "It's your house, it's your call."

Looking her brother in the eye, Lou said, "Deal." The two shook hands, sealing the transaction with their words.

"Now you know I'm sick, but I'm getting help. And I'm working, so I won't be able to trek back and forth down here as much, but I'm gonna start coming back to see Daddy, Joan, and Ruby. And, of course, you. I'll try to help as much as I can."

"I'd appreciate that," he said. "No, actually, I'd love that." He hugged his sister and then he hugged Liz.

Turning to Liz, Little Chuck said, "Do I say welcome to the family? Or do I call you a business partner, or what?" They all laughed.

"Just as long as you call, we don't care what you say," she smiled.

“Alright, all that business out of the way, I’m finally heading to bed, too,” Little Chuck announced. The three made their way up the stairs to their rooms to rest up. The next day would be a busy one of packing, traveling, and putting things in order.

62

Laying in his hospital bed, in his makeshift bedroom, Big Chuck looked out the window. With his hearing aid on high, he could hear a canary break wind in Savannah. He'd heard every conversation that had happened this evening, and particularly everything transpiring in the formal living room just diagonally across from his room.

He felt at peace with everything that had happened that day. Like his son, he was proud of how brave Josie had been. Like his daughter, he wished love upon them all and wished they would love each other. Like his faithful Ruby, he kept too many secrets for too long that made his burden heavy. Like his sister, he wasn't exactly thrilled with how everything came out, but he knew it was the right thing to do in the end.

But unlike his wife, Louise, Big Chuck wasn't going to go to the grave with a broken heart. A heart filled with hate, longing, regret, or anger. He was meeting his maker with a clear conscience. Clear for maybe the first time in 35 years, but clear, nonetheless.

He took one last look at the half moon hanging outside the big picture window in the starry night sky. He breathed in the smell of confederate jasmine that climbed the trellis on the side of the house and the row of evening-blooming four o'clock flowers planted under his window. And he closed his eyes for the very last time.

Somewhere in his slumber, he found Judy, and Louise, and his parents, and other people from throughout his life that had gone before him. No one was tired, no one was ill, no one was decrepit. Everyone was renewed, their burdens lifted, their secrets left behind. None of that mattered up here.

Appendix

While the town of Clanton and its people are all fictional, I took great care to include personal and historical elements throughout the pages of this novel.

This Appendix will give you a peek into many of those elements—from landmarks in my hometown of Jasper, GA, to the people who breathed life and inspiration into the story. If you're from the south, you may recognize some of these people, places, and traditions—but only the lucky few of you will have tried Mrs. Mary Lovings's pimento cheese.

There is a smattering of other names which are nods to family, friends, and neighbors of mine. If you made it into this little story, you truly mean something to me. Or my imagination was just out of fake names.

Thank you for taking the time to learn more about these precious bits of history.

Wyndell "Wendy" Clanton Johnson

Wyndell “Wendy” Clanton Johnson

Clanton, Georgia is a fictional town, though it is inspired by many small hamlets found across the south. While this locale does not exist anywhere other than in my imagination, the surrounding areas are real places, as are some of the other points of interest. The town name of Clanton was inspired by my best friend Ashton Brasher’s Mema, Wendy Clanton Johnson.

Wendy was born in Valdosta, Georgia on May 4, 1939. A wild child and a rule-breaker to boot, she preferred climbing trees and rough-housing with her older brother to playing with dolls. She loved her dogs and riding horses. She looked up to her daddy and spent her early years watching him work and wanting to be like him, picking up a collection of skills and odd knowledge along the way.

After graduating from Valdosta High School in 1957, she took those skills and all that odd knowledge and became a certifiable “jack of all trades.” She spent her years working as a bartender, a salesperson, a receptionist, and even an EKG technician for a time. Whatever she did, she was good at it. She could sell hair care products to a bald man. Her customers adored her and became her friends. While she had a dozen stories to tell about every job she ever worked, the highlight of her life was managing Grego’s restaurant in Valdosta. The only job she ever loved more was being a mother and a grandmother.

Wendy had three children and three grandchildren of her own, and she was uniquely proud of each of them. She bragged about little else in her life, but for them she made an exception. Wendy was a dancer (specifically, a jitterbugger), a storyteller, a jokester, a smart aleck, and a firecracker. She loved to reminisce on her days spent living in Chicago and Nashville, but Valdosta always had her heart. Even in her final days, she still missed tending bar. She still argued about her real age. She still came ready with a wisecrack and a quick-witted joke. And even when her memories began to betray her, she never forgot where she came from or the people that mattered to her most.

-Ashton Brasher

Silver Polishing Day

Silver Polishing Day

Whether a wedding, a funeral, a baby shower, a ladies' tea, or just a Tuesday, the silver is out in the south. Silverware, particularly silver serving sets and tea sets, remains an integral part of Southern hospitality and entertaining. The tradition of presenting silver as wedding gifts or passing down silverware as an inheritance is deeply ingrained in Southern culture.

The first photo was after I polished three generations of the silver belonging to my friend Sara Henderson. We were preparing for the wedding reception for her son, Edward and his betrothed, Jessica. Sara's son is the fourth generation of her family to live in her home in Atlanta's Buckhead neighborhood.

The second photo is when I was polishing silver at my home before my wedding shower. I've always found it hard to stick to one pattern, personally. I have my kitchen sterling that we use every day, which is a mish-mash of patterns, my husband's grandmother's French Provincial by Towle, Reed & Barton's Francis I that I collected, our wedding silver which is Queen Elizabeth I by Towle, then 160-some odd pieces of Fairfax, made by Durgin, which was before Gorham purchased the company in the '20s and continued the manufacture of Fairfax. It has my great grandmother's three-initial monogram.

Beyond that, I have serving pieces in dozens of patterns just because I think they're all beautiful!

Weekly Wash & Set

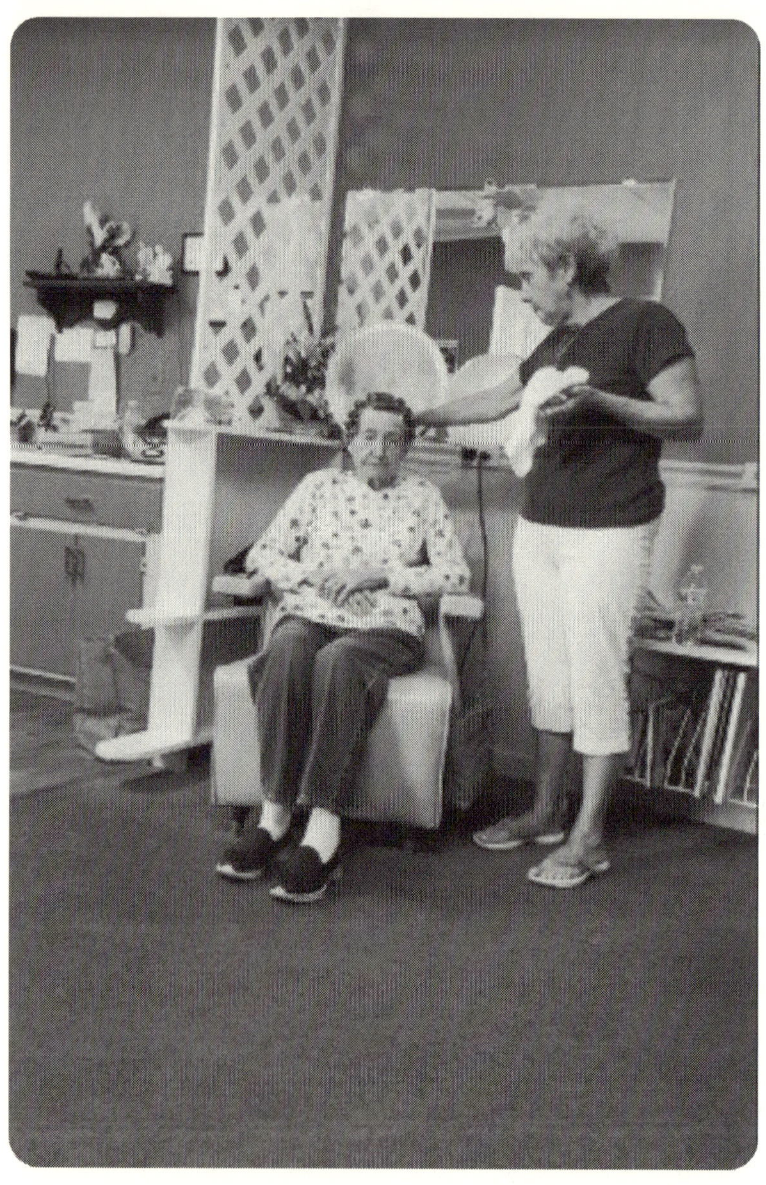

Weekly Wash & Set

Mamie Forrester knows a thing or two about a wash and set. She ought to be an expert since she's been giving them for decades.

A novel concept to ladies of today, women used to only have their hair washed once a week, at the beauty shop. The stylist would then set the hair with rollers or curlers. When the hair was set, you would go under the dryer to dry things in place. Once dry, the hairdresser would style the hair and spray it down good.

If you ever wondered who bought hairspray by the case, it's a hairdresser in the south. Let me tell you, these helmets are solid.

This process was popular among women who preferred classic, well-groomed hairstyles. It was not just about aesthetics; it was also a social and communal activity. Most women would visit the salon weekly for their wash and set, and it became a part of their routine for self-care and maintaining a polished appearance.

While trends in hairstyling have changed over time, the "wash and set" process remains a nostalgic symbol of a bygone era in the beauty industry.

Mamie did my great-grandmother ("Nanny") Pauline Mullins's hair for years. Nanny swore nobody could give a perm quite like Mamie.

Here she is taking care of her longtime client Billie Joe Roach at Mamie's Beauty Shop which stills stands on Solomon Avenue in Jasper.

Photo use courtesy of Mamie Forrester

Rich's Department Store

Rich's Department Store

I was helping a dear friend clean out some things and came across the family silver wrapped in a Rich's bag. When we "clean out" in the south, we often don't find Walmart sacks. You might catch a Belk shirt box here and there, or even a bag from Penney's. It's always fun to see if the things inside were wrapped in the Atlanta Journal, the Atlanta Constitution, or the Atlanta Journal-Constitution depending on how long those boxes have been down in that basement or up in that attic. More often than not, you'll find a bag from Rich's.

The store was a cultural hub, hosting events, fashion shows, and community gatherings. It was a place to connect, celebrate, and create memories. Rich's played a pivotal role in the lives of Atlantans, shaping the city's identity and fostering a sense of belonging.

Most of my memories were of Rich's at Town Center Mall where my mother took us to shop regularly. Her first credit card at age 16 was from Rich's, and I remember her still using that green and gold card when we were kids and the bill still going to my grandfather's house to be paid!

Before marrying my great grandfather, my great grandmother was what you would have called a spinster. She and Papa didn't marry until she was in her thirties. Naturally, at the time Grandma still lived with her father. She worked a job in our hometown, but she had no bills to speak of. So, on Saturdays she would ride the bus from Jasper to Atlanta (she never learned to drive) and shop the downtown store all day long, blowing her weekly paycheck! Then she would hop on the last bus bound for Jasper loaded down with packages from Rich's.

Though the physical store is no more, the spirit of Rich's lives on in the memories of countless Atlantans. The tales of holiday shopping sprees, special family outings, and the lighting of the iconic Great Tree are stories passed down from one generation to the next. The store may have closed, but its impact on Atlanta's cultural tapestry endured, reminding everyone of a time when a trip to Rich's was not just a shopping trip but a cherished tradition.

The Blue Star Supermarket

The Blue Star supermarket was owned and operated by Dub and Jeanette Lawson first in 1957, starting out on Main Street in town, and was then purchased by the Thomas Wilkie family who moved to its final location on Highway 53 East.

It closed at the end of 2010 after serving Jasper residents for 53 years.

Photo use courtesy of Will Lawson.

Congressman Ed Jenkins

Congressman Ed Jenkins worked for the 9th district of the state of Georgia from 1976 to 1993.

Mr. Jenkins was a lawyer, conservative Democrat, and tax-code expert who led efforts to protect the textile industry. During the Iran-contra hearings of '87, he drew national attention when he confronted National Security Council aides involved in organizing secret arms sales to Iran.

After his retirement from Congress, Jenkins worked as a lobbyist and continued to be involved in political and community activities. He passed away on January 1, 2012.

My Aunt, Ann Dobson, worked for Congressman Jenkins, but I would like to dispel any rumor that the character of Aunt Joan was based on my beloved aunt. They just happened to have had the same job.

Chapman Funeral Home

Chapman Funeral Home was a real funeral home for nearly 50 years in Jasper, Georgia—owned by J.G. and Florence, who really were the coroners—until it was purchased by Kevin Roper in 2001 and became Roper Funeral Home.

Photos courtesy of Leslie Chapman Miller.

The Chapmans

Florence Chapman really was the oldest living licensed funeral director in the state of Georgia. She was the grandmother of my elementary school music teacher and lifelong friend, Leslie Chapman Miller. Leslie's father, Charles Chapman, worked at the funeral home and was a faithful caretaker of his mother.

Photos courtesy of Leslie Chapman Miller.

Olan Mills Photography

Olan Mills Photography

Olan Mills was a prominent photography studio known for its portrait and family photography services. The company was founded by Olan Mills Sr. in 1932 in Nashville, Tennessee. Over the years, Olan Mills Studios became one of the largest and most well-known photography chains in the United States, providing a range of photography services.

Olan Mills was where everybody in North Georgia went for their annual family photos. The signature corner mark held their moniker. It was the quintessential 1960s-2000s photo studio with the photos that have double exposures and multiple faces in different angles with weird shadows.

This Olan Mills photo is of my maternal grandmother, Patsy Young Duckett.

The Quilters of Gee's Bend

The residents of Gee's Bend, Alabama are direct descendants of the enslaved people who worked the cotton plantation established by Joseph Gee.

After the Civil War, former slaves remained on the plantation working as sharecroppers. In the 1930s, the price of cotton fell. The Federal Government purchased ten thousand acres of the former plantation and provided loans enabling residents to acquire and farm the land formerly worked by their ancestors.

In the 1960s, spurred on by Martin Luther King Jr., community members became active in the Civil Rights Movement, ferrying to the county seat at Camden to register to vote.

Authorities reacted by eliminating ferry service altogether, isolating the community and cutting it off from basic services.

During this period, local women came together to found the Freedom Quilting Bee. A quilting tradition that began in the 19th century has endured. Hailed by the New York Times as "some of the most miraculous works of modern art America has produced," Gee's Bend quilts constitute a crucial chapter in the history of American art and today are in the permanent collections of over 30 leading art museums.

One of those quilters was Caster Pettway (pictured on the top), the mother of my friend Nicola Moore. I have a piece of her work framed in my home (pictured at the bottom).

Southern Spreads to Feed the Masses

Feasts of days gone by in Tennessee and North Carolina, with family photos courtesy of Hans Craig and Donald Beeding. It can be a little hard to tell, but not much has changed in 50+ years.

Southern Spreads to Feed the Masses

A modern-day Baker County, Georgia spread with photos courtesy of Diana Collins. If the dinner offerings don't include at least one platter of halved pears with a dollop of mayonnaise, a sprinkling of cheddar cheese, and a cherry for decoration, the meal "just won't be no count", as my Nanny would say.

The Whitestone Flood of 1938

THE ATLANTA CONSTITUTION

HOUSE SWEEPS ROOSEVELT LEADERS ASIDE, TURNING REORGANIZATION DOWN, 204 TO 196

13 in Home Swept to Death by Floodwaters

CHAMBER REFUSES VOTE OF CONFIDENCE IN CHIEF EXECUTIVE

How Votes Were Cast By States

The Whitestone Flood of 1938

On April 7, 1938, storms and torrential rains made their way across the southeast. Tornadoes and floods trapped hundreds of people and killed many from Texas all the way to Georgia. Local historian Robert Scott Davis, Jr. appropriately called the event "A Night of Terror."

The tiny unincorporated mining town of Whitestone, Georgia is situated along Talona Creek and crosses the boundaries of Pickens and Gilmer Counties. At the time, around 200 people lived in this valley–a valley which would be nearly wiped clean by the morning of April 8. Heavy rains caused Talona Creek to swell far beyond her bounds, filling the quaint valley quickly. Residents woke sleeping neighbors as everyone climbed toward higher ground. By the time the sleeping Connor family and two young girls who were houseguests were awakened, the water in their home was already knee-deep.

Forrest Conner, son James, and brother-in-law Carl Lindsey made it out of the house alive just as the rising waters picked up the family home from its stone foundation and carried it down Talona Creek. Understanding the fate of what was to happen to their family, the three men swam back to the house and climbed inside, prepared to go down with the ship.

The house floated for about a quarter of a mile before crashing into an embankment and collapsing, killing all 13 individuals inside. Bodies, dead and alive, were buried in mud and debris, but search efforts intensified when word was able to make it out to the surrounding areas. It took so long because every bridge, road, and telephone line in the area were destroyed.

After the story was covered by news outlets across the nation, 10,000 or more people made their way to the area. Bodies were prepared to lie in state in the auditorium of Jasper School by J.G. Chapman. The photo at the bottom shows the Connors' mass grave at Philadelphia Baptist Church that made its way into Life Magazine.

Four O'Clocks

Four o'clocks. No, not the time. The flower—an old-timey southern garden staple. I don't know how long these have been here at our house, but they come back each year more vigorously than the year before. You can't kill 'em. Four o'clocks grow from seed, but they really spread underground by rhizome. My great great Aunt Elaine called it a 'tater. She had four o'clocks in front of her little old house for as long as I can remember.

It was one of those houses that was split down the middle and you had to walk through one room to get to another. She raised four kids there and lost a husband before his prime—that was Nanny's brother, Sam. Living to just shy of 90, like my Nanny, that woman exuded a tenacious spirit right up until the very end.

People talk about strong southern women as "steel magnolias" because of the movie (a favorite of mine, don't get me wrong), but I think they're more like four o'clocks. Beautiful in an understated manner. Colorful. Dainty, but powerful. And unstoppable. Until they're ready to stop, on their own terms, and no one else's. The season was just about over for these girls, but I'll enjoy them when I see them again. Same to you, Aunt Elaine.

Mrs. Mary Lovings's Pimiento Cheese Recipe

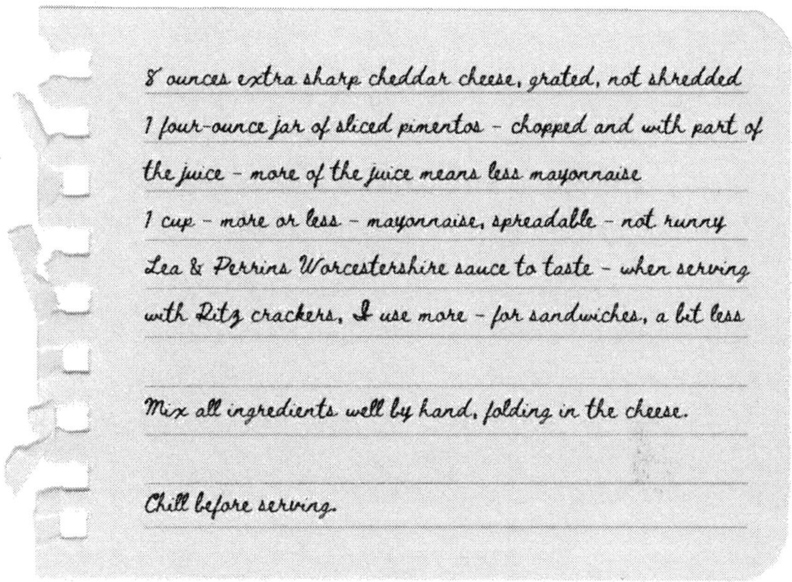

8 ounces extra sharp cheddar cheese, grated, not shredded
1 four-ounce jar of sliced pimentos - chopped and with part of
the juice - more of the juice means less mayonnaise
1 cup - more or less - mayonnaise, spreadable - not runny
Lea & Perrins Worcestershire sauce to taste - when serving
with Ritz crackers, I use more - for sandwiches, a bit less

Mix all ingredients well by hand, folding in the cheese.

Chill before serving.

I met Mary Gilbert Lovings through the Avondale Estates Garden Club where, at the time, she served as the chair of the Environmental and Sustainability Committee.

She taught for some time at the now defunct Avondale High School in our town. Mary was The Environmental Editor of the Garden Clubs of Georgia's publication Planting and Nurturing.

Mary and I are both Lifetime Members of the DeKalb Federation of Garden Clubs. She is the longest-serving member of Avondale Estates Garden Club.

Acknowledgments

I would like to extend a sincere thank you to the following people who made this story come to life from my brain to paper:

- **Alyssa Weaver Warfield, sister:** photography research
- **Andrew Kennedy, husband:** historical research, putting up with me and my eccentricities while I wrote this
- **Ann Dobson, former District Director for Congressman Ed Jenkins:** historical information regarding Ed Jenkins
- **Ashton Brasher, lesbian/best friend:** queer female intelligence, help with initial editing and making sense of my loquacious ramblings, marketing
- **Brina Jolin, Creative Director:** graphic design and artistry
- **Diana Collins, retired, Georgia Power Company:** electricity billing information
- **Dr. Teri Peitso-Holbrook, retired Associate Professor Emerita of Literacy and Language Arts, Georgia State University:** writing guidance and publishing process consultation
- **Isaac Holaway, Lieutenant, Pickens County Fire Rescue Services:** fire and arson consultation
- **Jody Weaver, Chief Marshal, Pickens County Marshal's Office:** law enforcement consultation
- **Leslie Chapman Miller, daughter of Charles Chapman and granddaughter of J.G. & Florence Rabun Chapman:** information about and the usage of her family's legacy in Chapman Funeral Home and her grandmother's likeness in this novel
- **Lindsay Killebrew, Loan Officer, Summit Funding:** mortgage procedure advice
- **Paula Heard:** final editing and all-around good person
- **Mark Godfrey, retired Coroner, Pickens County Office of the Coroner:** suicidal death and body transport consultation
- **Whitney Patterson & Delleene Worley, Agents, Alfa Insurance, Bill Lawrence Agency:** insurance information

Made in the USA
Columbia, SC
17 June 2025